THE SILENT CITY

The City was deserted. There was no one left. Oh, Gil and Marianne and the others were here, of course, but they were machines, Papa explained. There were only the machines and Papa and her.

One night Elisa had a dream. She was walking in the City through an endless succession of ramps, staircases, corridors, and crosswalks. After walking a long, long time, Elisa came to a part of the city that looked like the Outside. There were streets with tame trees, and all along the streets were houses, with cars parked close to the sidewalks, and lawns and flower beds. She was very much afraid of the houses and cars and neat trees. They were all going to die. They were already dead.

Elisa touched a handle on a door. Behind it lights of every color were sunk in the walls, with ranks of instrument panels, everything blinking, clicking, humming. In the middle of the room was a huge pinkish blob, red-veined and glistening, bubbling with a squelching noise. It was talking to Elisa. It was saying, "Come along. I'll tell you a story." It was Grandpa.

Elisa woke up screaming. Was she really awake? She felt herself dripping and dribbling on the bed, a soft pink blob. Closing eyes that were no longer there, she willed herself frantically to wake up, wake up. But when she saw the Papa-machine leaning over her, she screamed louder than ever. . . .

"A metamorphic journey into disturbing possibilities of gender, social order, and genetic science."—William Gibson

THE
SILENT
CITY

ELISABETH VONARBURG
TRANSLATED BY
JANE BRIERLEY

BANTAM BOOKS
NEW YORK • TORONTO • LONDON • SYDNEY • AUCKLAND

*This edition contains the complete text
of the original edition.
The author has made minor adjustments for the American edition.*

THE SILENT CITY

A Bantam Spectra Book / published by arrangement with Press Porcépic Limited

PRINTING HISTORY
Originally published in French as Le Silence de la Cité
*copyright © 1981 by Editions Denoel, Paris, France
Porcépic Books edition published 1988
Bantam edition / August 1992*

ISBN 0-553-29789-9

Published simultaneously in the United States and Canada

PRINTED IN THE UNITED STATES OF AMERICA

RAD   0 9 8 7 6 5 4 3 2 1

For Jean-Joel
who wanted something to read.

THE
SILENT
CITY

PART

1

SHE DIDN'T KNOW HE COULD DIE.

He had dark, weather-beaten skin, a mane of tangled white hair, and hazel eyes that were always smiling from a network of wrinkles. Perhaps it was the wrinkles that were always smiling. You couldn't tell just by looking at his mouth—his mustache was too thick. Grandpa. She used to call him Grandpa.

She didn't know he was a machine.

She almost never needed to use her communication bracelet. If she lost her doll or fell, if Gil and Marianne hurt her while playing, or if they fought, he'd be there before she'd even begun to cry. Sometimes he'd talk, sometimes he wouldn't say much, but he was there when she really needed him. She couldn't tell why, but when he smelled of tobacco or grass cuttings, when his mustache looked yellowish, he was more—*there*. Then she could tell quite clearly if he was in a good mood, or cross, or thinking of other things. And she could tell just how much he loved her. That was when he was really *Grandpa*.

She couldn't remember learning his name, any

more than she remembered learning her own. He was always Grandpa and nothing else, just as she was Elisa. Any names she'd learned belonged to other people: Papa, Serena, Sybil, Mario, Max, John, Christine, Gil, Marianne, Andreas, Peter, Sandra. At night before going to sleep, she used to recite the names of everyone she knew in the City. Sometimes voices answered, floating in the shadows around the big, vaguely luminous pillar in the middle of her room. She carried them into her sleep like a talisman.

This wasn't how she said good night to Grandpa, though. He was always the one to put her to bed.

With time—only later did she count by years and understand, "I was three . . . I was five"—some of these voices fell silent and their owners disappeared from the Cityscape. Mario, John, Christine.

"They've gone away," said Grandpa.

Elisa said nothing for a moment, then found the courage to ask, "Will they come back?"

Grandpa seemed sad that day. He appeared to hesitate. His eyes crinkled in a smile, but he wasn't smiling. "No, they won't come back."

He hadn't told her that he, too, would go.

⚡ **2** ⚡

THE SENTINEL DOESN'T EVEN TRY TO STOP the ommach. With a choking cry he hurls himself to one side, arms clasped around his head for protection. Metal reverberates as he crashes against the hulk of the hydraulic excavator where he's standing guard. The noise alerts the others. Voices stop. A hissing rush is heard as water vaporizes on contact with hot cinders, extinguishing the firelight. But the ommach's infrared vision is unimpaired. He can still see the shapes of men tensed for action, weapons raised, and the outlines of women and children silently running for cover.

Front searchlight. Full power. Now. The violent white light freezes all the silhouettes for an instant. In the foreground stands a short, stocky man, one arm raised in front of his eyes. The intense light dims. The men lower their weapons, still blinded by the glare. From behind, an elderly man comes forward and makes the sign of submission: a lance laid flat on two hands stretched forward, palms up.

Advance hand, place it on sleeve. The muscles of the old man's thin, outstretched arms quiver, his face contorts. *Easy, now. Although it's not a bad thing for ommachs to have a rather heavy hand.*

The ommach's eye sweeps around. The men, about a dozen of them, have retreated toward the group of women and children. The weapons have disappeared. A cloud of thick steam rises from the doused fire. *Laser.* The steam increases briefly, dissipates; the newly dry wood bursts into flame as the men and women huddle closer to one another.

"What does the ommach want?" The old chief tries to keep his voice from shaking.

"Get the children together."

The old man stares. For a moment he is absolutely still. *Increase front spotlight. A little red in the eyes below for good measure.* The old man lowers his head and turns to face the rest of the tribe.

"Bring the children here."

Some women come forward, their shoulders drooping, pushing and pulling the children who are hanging onto their tunics. Not a cry, not a wail. Only three babies, sleeping on their mothers' backs. *Eight children. No, eleven with the babies. Not bad. Only thirty-odd women. They must be doing away with the extra girls. A growing tendency it seems.*

The little group of silent women and children watch the ommach's approach with terrified eyes. The youngest child must be four, the eldest about ten.

"Undress them."

Like rag dolls, the children let their elders take off their clothes as they stare at the ommach. There is a sound of tearing cloth, a child's protesting voice, a slap. *Three boys. Apparently normal. These females of the North have a good yield. But how many girls have been eliminated? And how many abnormal births? The percentage is going up all the time. The effects of the virus aren't about to disappear. Stabilization point – hah! Desprats must be hallucinating. We haven't even got to the bottom of the curve yet.*

The first boy gives a yelp of pain and suprise when the ommach's fingernail slits open the skin of his forehead. His hand goes up to his face and comes away red. The wails rise to a higher pitch. A woman claps her hand over his mouth. The second child is a girl. She also cries out when the nail slashes her forehead. The last is the eldest boy. He lifts his head and looks steadily at the ommach. He doesn't lower his eyes as the sharp finger moves toward his forehead. Some of the children try to wipe off the blood that is beginning to stream into their eyes.

"No!" The impact of the ommach's voice makes them jump; their hands drop. After a minute most of the children stop bleeding. The blood of the youngest boy and three of the girls is already coagulating. *Excellent.*

"Water." A woman hastens to obey, returns with a wet piece of cloth, holds it out to the ommach, her eyes lowered. The foreheads of two of the girls show a clean incision that is again beginning to bleed a little. On the forehead of the remaining boy and girl, the wound has already closed. A rapid sweep of the scanner reveals that the cells are in the process of rebuilding themselves.

"Who are the mothers of these children?"

The women shrink back from one of the group, leaving her in the middle of a wide space. *Mother of both? Brother and sister. Too bad.*

"And the father?"

"Hanse!" calls the old chief. A man comes forward. He has white hair but he is young all the same, not much more than twenty-five. *The children are dark-haired. Degeneration in the father? We'll have to watch this trait.* The ommach turns to the two children huddled against one another, and hands them each a tracer capsule. "Swallow it." They do as they are told, eyes wide. The ommach registers the beep indicating that the capsule has attached itself to the stomach wall.

"Hanse and the woman will come with me." The woman is pushed forward by the others. The man hesitates, his lance half-raised. "It won't be for long."

The tribe remains motionless as the ommach moves off with the man and woman. One of the children begins to cry at the sight of her mother going away. No one tries to silence her. At the moddex the ommach fastens the man and woman into their seats, puts them to sleep, and lifts off.

Paul sets the system on automatic and throws himself back with a sigh as the screens dim. In an hour the specimens will be in the City.

For a moment Paul lies motionless under the network of wires covering his head and body. Then, one by one, he detaches the electrodes. The robot's eyes, nose, ears; the robot's voice, hands, legs. As usual he feels somewhat empty, a little weak, cut off from a body that is stronger than his ever could be, and equipped with senses he could never have. At times like these he can almost understand why some people in the City no longer live except through robots. He stands up and stretches. How many in the tribes really believe that the ommachs are supernatural beings? More and more, probably, as time passes, wiping out the memory of a dead civilization. Humanoid machines, humachs, ommachs. How many up there still know the meaning of the name given to the robots of the subterranean Cities by their more clear-sighted ancestors?

More clear-sighted. Really? Paul smiles at his wan reflection in the empty plasglass of the screens. "Machines." Reassuring mumbojumbo to keep the terror at bay. No, today's primitive tribes are more clear-sighted. Maybe they see the living nightmare of the Decline for what it is, see through the technological claptrap to the brute force, the greed for raw power raised to the level of a cult. *The primitive mind is unbeatable as far as things spiritual are concerned. It grasps the essential. Smells a symbol a mile off.*

"Well, Paul, so the gods have visited the mortals once again?"

He finishes unplugging the wires without turning around. He knows the question is rhetorical, anyway. Marquande has followed every moment of it on her own screens. She wouldn't be there otherwise, wouldn't come to needle him again. The voice moves closer.

"This makes how many since you found the first ones? Fourteen? Fifteen? So you're still looking for the perfect mutant?" Marquande lifts a thigh onto the console and leans over to smooth away a lock of hair on Paul's forehead. He makes an effort not to turn away. "Ah, youth! Youth! Such a fine scientific frenzy!"

Has she been drinking? No. She is near enough for him to smell her breath. It's sweet and heavy, but there isn't a trace of alcohol. Drugs? No. Her eyes are normal. As she strokes his hair, Paul stares at her, taking in the fine, aristocratic pallor of the skin drawn over the delicate bone structure. No ultraviolet rays for Marquande de Styx. She's proud of living in the City; she *is* the City. She sets the fashions, makes them passé, brings them back again. She has another, less important power that she still likes to wield from time to time. Politics. She rules the City, either by herself or through her lovers, and has done so since—since when?

"Since always," she replies with a laugh. She looks up and meets Paul's gaze. Her eyelids flutter, as though she's been caught out. Her hand drops and for a fraction of a second the mask dissolves. Paul watches as her eyes and mouth take on a creeping frailty that ought to move him. But he's merely disgusted. He knows, and she knows, that this perfect body is now only an envelope worn thin by too many rejuvenations, a layer of varnish ready to crack at the first blow. Underneath, the horrors of artificially delayed decrepitude lie in wait.

Some day I'll be like her. No. I'll kill myself first!

He smiles at his melodramatic thoughts. There's no need to kill himself. He should know that by now. He can simply refuse to undergo the rejuvenating treatments. Anyway, they're only half as effective once you're past forty. *You've still got ten years to decide, hypocrite.*

Marquande mistakes his smile for something else and kisses him on the cheek, near the mouth. Too near. "Hasn't my big boy got anything better to do at night than hunt wild muties?" So that's it. He wonders what has caused this sudden outbreak of motherly tenderness. The mutie woman and her children just now? Or something else Marquande saw, on another of the screens constantly spying on the City? She slips her arm around Paul's neck, reiterating the question, her voice throaty, suggestive. Paul reaches for her waist dutifully. With mingled irony and misgiving he asks himself whether he'll be up to it. But you don't turn down Marquande de Styx. Especially when you're her son.

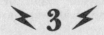

IT HAPPENED SHORTLY AFTER SERENA WENT away. Grandpa was telling Elisa a story. She was sitting on his lap, snuggling against him with her head burrowing into the crook of his neck, and she could feel his voice reverberating on her forehead. Her eyes were closed, and he rocked her gently as he talked. She knew the story by heart: it was about the little girl who lived in an enchanted castle where everyone was asleep. There were only machines in the castle, and even though they did everything the little girl wanted, they were still machines. One day the machines stopped. The little girl saw a big door open and she went Outside.

Usually, when they got to this part, Grandpa wasn't really telling a story anymore. He asked questions, and if Elisa couldn't answer he would press the controls, and screens would light up, showing pictures of Outside (he also called it the Exterior or the Surface). It was huge, all green and blue, black and white, or else a lot of red and brown—*spring, summer, winter,* or *fall.* There were animals everywhere, just like in the park, and there was water. But there were a lot more animals, and the water was rushing, leaping, foaming (and in winter enormous curtains of *ice* hung round the waterfalls). Sometimes there were *clouds* in the sky. And there were people too, although always far away. Then Grandpa stopped the picture and said, "But the little girl isn't big enough to go and see the people. When she's big enough she'll go." When he said this Elisa knew, not without a certain thrilling anxiety, that the little girl must be called Elisa and that the story wasn't really a story.

One day Grandpa would explain everything. She was sure he would. In fact Elisa liked that story best, because it was a secret that she and Grandpa shared. "This is our own story," he used to say. That's how it always started off, even before "Once upon a time." "You mustn't tell anyone," went the ritual. "Not even Papa?" And the ritual answer was, "Especially not Papa."

"Speshlynotpapa, speshlynotpapa," Elisa loved to chant when she was very little, and Grandpa would say it in her ear so as to tickle her with his mustache, which had a funny way of moving when he said the words. One day she asked, "Why not Papa?"

"Because it's a *surprise!*" he whispered, and Elisa was satisfied. It would be fun to surprise Papa for a change. Papa didn't come often; once a month he spent the whole day with her. Elisa learned to count the days so that she would know when to expect him, but he never came on the same day. It was always a surprise, although the day began with the same strange game. Papa would put a sort of wire hat on Elisa and then cut into the end of her finger. It hurt, but not for long. Anyway, the idea of the game was to stop it hurting and make it get better as quickly as possible. All you had to do was stop the blood and close the cut. He explained it to her, and said she could do it if she wanted to. And she did it. As time went on the cuts became deeper, right to the bone. Papa would now put Elisa's finger to sleep so it wouldn't hurt too much ("Anesthesia"—she'd given that name to the doll with the eyes that closed). But the game was still the same: close the cut as soon as possible. When it was over, Papa congratulated her and was very kind the rest of the day, taking her to the playground in the park and giving her rides on the merry-go-round. He told her stories about fairies and princesses that were like Grandpa's, but somehow different.

After all, it wouldn't have been much fun if the two people she loved most did the same thing all the time. There was Grandpa's world, and Papa's world. For her, Grandpa was everyday life with its familiar activities—washing, dressing, eating—the real world, functioning smoothly, safely. Papa was fantasy, the unexpected, the dream, in spite of the harsh, regulated brilliance of his laboratory where the first game of the day took place. Each day she waited for the surprise and greeted Papa with delighted excitement and gratitude when he appeared, even though he wasn't often *there* the way Grandpa was, even though she couldn't sense (as she could from the smell of Grandpa's tobacco or the warmth of his presence) Papa's pleasure in being with her, his love for her.

That day (yes, Serena had gone away three days before), there were no questions, no screens. Grandpa didn't even seem to want to tell the story. When he said "Speshlynotpapa" his voice sounded funny, as if he were very cross. Whatever it was, he wasn't really *there*. Elisa was drowsy and only half listened to him. The whole world slept, the machines stopped, and the little girl was going to the Outside. But the tone of Grandpa's voice was different. Angry. The castle-city was no longer an enchanted place. It was empty, immobile, silent. Frightening. And the people who slept there were never going to wake up. Never.

At that moment Grandpa made a strange sound,

as if he were strangling. His arms tightened around
Elisa, roughly pulling her against his chest. Then he
stopped moving, stopped talking. Elisa tried to look
up at his face, but one of Grandpa's hands was caught
in her hair, and she couldn't turn her head.

"Grandpa?"

No answer. Grandpa's chest was absolutely still.
Elisa laughed uneasily. What a strange game. It must
be a game, mustn't it? She twisted in an effort to get
out of Grandpa's arms, but he was squeezing her too
tight. It was almost impossible to breathe, and the
hand on her head kept pulling her hair each time she
tried to move.

"Grandpa, stop it!"

No answer. Elisa decided she definitely did not like
this game. "Grandpa, stop it!" she said again, in the
plaintive tone that usually heralded tears. But this
time the familiar signal didn't seem to work. Grandpa
remained perfectly silent, perfectly still.

Elisa panicked, thrashing about violently, vainly.
The rigid arms locked her against the hard chest. She
screamed.

After a long while Papa came to her. He touched
Grandpa's shoulder. "Richard?" he said. Then, without trying to free Elisa, he walked over to the nearest
communication pillar and touched some switches.
The screens began to shimmer with pictures that Elisa
couldn't see very clearly. Papa came back and she began to cry again. Papa really was *there*, but he was so
angry, so sad. And at the moment he didn't love her
very much either. He took hold of Grandpa's arms,
vainly trying to wrench them apart. Then he muttered
something under his breath and disappeared from
her field of vision. He came back with a kind of stick
in his hand, and made a cold, blue flame come out of
one end. He began slicing through Grandpa's right
arm.

Papa was doing this dreadful thing so calmly, and
the smell coming from Grandpa was so different, so
horrible, that Elisa stopped crying. It smelled like stuff
burning, not at all like Grandpa's tobacco. Papa sliced

through the whole arm, disentangled the hand
clenched in Elisa's hair, and took her in his arms. But
all she could see was the thing on the ground and
Grandpa's gaping shoulder stump, full of wires and
melted blobs.

Papa was very angry, or perhaps he was upset. As
Elisa passed by the pillar with its screens still lit up,
she saw a thin, brown old man, with white hair and a
yellow mustache. The screens showed him full face, in
profile, and from the back. He was motionless, tipped
back in a reclining chair, and on his head was a hat
with wires on it. His eyes were staring and his lips
drawn back on yellow teeth. She didn't recognize him
at first.

⚡ 4 ⚡

THE BABY DOESN'T CRY. ITS ARMS AND LEGS
wave slowly back and forth, as though still swimming
in the amniotic fluid behind the translucent wall of
the artificial womb. Its face contracts and relaxes in
rhythm with its tiny fists. Paul finishes wiping the pink
skin and begins his examination. He forces himself to
move slowly, calmly. First the reflexes. Normal. But
why wouldn't they be? Years spent rooting out undesirable genes, refining this masterpiece. EEG, normal. Of
course.

Suddenly the lines on the screen jump. The baby
begins to wriggle, its face red. Paul leans over murmuring senseless, reassuring noises, and the lines
smooth out. Now for the final test. He picks up the
scalpel. His hand hesitates a moment above the small,
plump body. He has done this test several times on the
embryo in vitro, but this isn't the same. The flesh is so
smooth, so firm. His other hand clasps the baby, holding it still. The clasp becomes a caress as his fingers
move over the chest, the slightly concave abdomen,
the small pubic mound with its tiny dimple at the end

of the narrow slit where the thighs meet. The baby squirms under his caress. Paul lifts one of the miniature hands, looks closely as it closes on his index finger, and gives a little tug. Such a strong grip for such tiny fingers. *You're not in a tree now, you're at the other end of evolution. Do you know that, you technogenetic miracle? No, of course you don't.*

Paul smiles. It's not really a test, just a symbolic gesture. The artist's signature. The scalpel lightly touches the abdomen above the navel. Thin as a hair, a red line appears. Paul turns on the chronometer. Five and six-one-hundredths of a second later, the line disappears. The baby hasn't even cried. Paul lifts it up in the air with an exuberant laugh. "That's the stuff, daughter mine!" The baby lets out a howl. Naturally. Paul holds her close, murmuring, "Sh-h, sh-h!" He wraps her up and fetches the bottle that is waiting in its thermostatic bath. Greedily, the baby begins to suck.

A multicoloured mandala undulates on one of the screens. Paul represses an irritated grimace. *Desprats. Forgot to plug in the scrambler again.*

"Unto us a child is born," a soft but slightly cracked voice sings. "Congratulations Paul. I admire your magnificent devotion to the job. Are you about to cut this one up, too?"

Paul shrugs. "No. I'll keep it."

"Of course, it's a girl," says the voice after a brief pause. "Interesting." A short laugh. "The joy and staff of our old age. Are you starting off any others?"

"Not right away. The first phase is done with. Now I have to study the development of the subject chronologically."

The mandala undulates in silence for a long moment and Paul thinks Desprats is going to cut the communication. But the old voice speaks again. "What are you going to call her?"

He hasn't thought about it. His eyes light upon the identifying mark engraved on the stand for the thermostatic bath: EL-I. Eli. Elise.

"Elisa."

"Are you going to christen her?" Desprats laughs. "I want to be the godfather. After all, I did help a bit. Know what? It would be a great occasion for getting everyone together. We'll bring presents. It's a respectable tradition. The gifts of the Magi. Cinderella's twelve good fairies. No, that's Snow White, isn't it? Twelve good and one bad, in any case. If you like, I'll take care of the invitations."

Paul is about to shrug, but stops himself. After all, why not? It would be a chance to see who's still alive in the City. And what condition they're in. To see Serena.

"All right."

Two screens light up immediately. "What a delightful idea! I'll look after the meal, Paul," exclaims the acid voice of Sybil Horner behind the whirlpool of violent colours she always uses as a symbol. And Alghieri's voice chimes in: "I'll need three weeks to organize everything."

But a fourth screen lights up, and Serena's face smiles at Paul. "It'll be the twenty-fifth of December in a month. Why not wait until then?"

Paul studies her with a pleasure that he doesn't try to hide. She's the only one who isn't afraid to show herself, and with good reason. She's doing all right. Perfect skin, shining green eyes, no wrinkles—she knows how to choose the right lighting. It's the first time she's spoken to him since their last argument. When was that? Six months ago? He can't really remember now. It's not very important, anyway; he doesn't count the days like he did in the beginning. But he's pleased to see her. She's chosen a good moment to bury the hatchet. (*Her* hatchet. I've got better things to do!) The twenty-fifth of December is his birthday; he'll be a hundred and fifteen.

Paul smiles at Serena and reflects inwardly that it marks another birthday: the Project.

Did he give it this name right away? To be honest, he must admit he didn't. It was more a pastime at first. Or a whim. Or a sort of joke. As he had watched the blood flow slowly from his slashed wrists on the day he turned twenty-six, he'd suddenly thought of this embryonic capacity for autoregeneration discovered by accident in the mutants of the Exterior, and had decided to create a new race out of them. What was that, if not a sign of humor?

As he'd watched the blood flow from his wrists. Perhaps it wasn't humor, after all. He hadn't been very humorous in those days. Looking back, the grotesque nature of the thing seems almost too ridiculous. Had he really tried to kill himself that way? Now he begins to understand Marquande's reaction when she came into his room and saw him bleeding.

In her place he'd have laughed too.

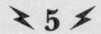

ELISA DIDN'T TAKE LONG TO GRASP WHAT HAD happened. Grandpa's stories had prepared her for it. Grandpa was a machine. And Gil, Marianne, Peter, Sandra, everybody was a machine. Even Papa was a machine.

It took Elisa a little longer to realize that there were real machines like Gil, Marianne, or the rest of her playmates, and *machine-men* such as Grandpa, Sybil, and Papa. A machine with someone inside. No, behind. Well, a machine connected to someone alive, a real person, somewhere in the City.

And Grandpa was *dead*. He'd never come back.

Did that mean the others were dead too? Mario, John, Serena?

"Yes," said Papa, shrugging his shoulders. He was truly there that day, and Elisa could feel that he didn't want to talk about these things. She knew how to tell the difference now, because she realized that there was a difference. When it was a machine, the person wasn't *there*: she felt nothing.

"And are you going to die too?" she murmured, on the brink of tears. He didn't look at her for a long time, too shaken to respond. At last he took Elisa in his arms and she began to cry because he was so sad and because he loved her so much at that moment. "I won't die for a long time, dearest. Not for a long, long time. And you won't either."

(Later she would see this scene and many, many others recorded by the City's omnipresent sensors. She would look at the young-old face of Paul, and remember the emotions that she thought she felt in him then—that despair, that love—and she would say to herself that she had understood nothing. And even later, much, much later, she would look at these scenes again and see them differently.)

⚡ 6 ⚡

THINGS MOVE SWIFTLY. THE COFFIN ADVANCES on the rolling carpet, pushes open the swinging doors, and teeters on the edge of the void. No flames. *I would have liked flames. The symbol. She would have liked them too. Hell.*

But the coffin and corpse of Marquande de Styx are now molecules that the City has stored, or already reorganized. *When will we eat you, Mother? How she detested that name.*

Paul turns to go.

At first he sees only her eyes. Green eyes, really green, the colour of grass. Synthetic grass, of course. Probably contact lenses, he says to himself. Or else it's a machine. But the sardonic reflex doesn't work. He's been taken by surprise and finds her beautiful. Why not just admit it? And she's no machine, not her. He casts about momentarily for something to say, then is afraid she may speak. It surely won't measure up, at least not to her beauty, to her youth, to the affirmation of that young body beneath the light fabric of her suit. *I'm alive. You're alive.*

She takes his arm and they walk across the City for

a long time without meeting anyone. He's not sure who is leading who, but it hardly matters. Indolent thoughts float through his mind. *Serena Desprats. The little girl has grown up. Serena. What a perfect name for her. The last little girl of the City, at the burial of the last female survivor of the Decline. Not "burial." Marquande would have hated that. Rotting. . . .* The word is like a rock against the flow of his thoughts, reverberating in his mind like some infernal Open Sesame, revealing a cavernous void.

Serena stops. They look at each other. Paul doesn't know whether he wants to hug or hit her. The green eyes contemplate him without blinking, and he feels a shock wave of naked terror, as though a huge precipice of white fire yawned inside him. Vertigo rocks him; he stretches out his hands, touches the skin, the flesh. They stay still a moment, holding onto each other. Thought returns, a mixture of stupefaction, anger, then shame. *What's come over me? I'm afraid. I'm afraid!*

He tries to escape the inner voice by losing himself in sensation: the body that fits so easily against his, the fragrance of the black hair against his mouth. The body moves away from his, the green eyes look fixedly at him. "You're afraid too?" says the clear young voice.

(Later, he will often say that at this moment he fell in love with Serena. And even later—very much later—when they are no longer in love or love each other differently, he will say that this tie binds them still. That moment. The memory of that moment. Or the illusion of that moment, of that very brief, intense moment when he felt himself truly naked before her and when he suddenly stopped being ashamed, because she was naked too. Stopped being afraid at the very moment of answering that yes, he too was afraid.)

But now he only hears himself saying, "Yes." He marvels, astonished. He kisses her. They look for somewhere to make love, not hard to find in that deserted part of the City. And when he realizes that for her it's the first time, he is already hopelessly, deliciously lost in love. Afterward he asks her, "Why did you come?" And she answers indirectly, "We're the last, aren't we?"

The last children. Yes. He's thirty-six, she's seventeen, but he gets the point.

"I was glad when Sernikov sabotaged the genetic bank two years ago," she says.

"So was I," says Paul. That's not quite true. It set his research back considerably. But it was true at the time, he remembers. He understands what she means.

After a moment of silence, she asks, "Did you still hate her?" He marvels at how the question hits home and is about to say, "Not really," when suddenly a surge of hate floods through him at the memory of Marquande, and he changes his answer to a disconsolate, "Not all the time."

She raises herself on one elbow and looks him squarely in the eye. "You have no father and I have no mother. They went to the bank on a whim and had a child made to order." She clasps him close again. "I'm glad Sernikov destroyed it all."

And he, he's glad Sernikov didn't destroy everything, not the incubators, not the genetic labs. But he isn't going to tell Serena that. Not now. A desperate tenderness overwhelms him at this first small betrayal. But he will tell her later, he'll talk about his research, his Project. She'll understand. A new race capable of surviving in a transformed world. Human beings who won't be afraid of wounds, illness, or radiation. Cellular regeneration, and in the final analysis, total mastery of the life process. Probably not immortality: the malevolent dream of the Cities will die with their last inhabitants. But a long and healthy life, a death without decrepitude—that is possible. Serena will comprehend the grandeur of the Project and the necessity of sacrifice. She has probably decided not to undergo the rejuvenating treatments, a decision he'd come to several years ago. But she'll understand that they need time. She'll grow up. All at once he's aware of thinking, *she's young.* And he wants to laugh and cry at the same time, to find himself succumbing to such a catch phrase. But it's true. And he's been through the growing-up process. He knows the stages of the road she will be taking. He'll help her.

NOW THE CITY WAS DESERTED, LIKE IN GRAND-pa's story. There was no one left. Oh, Gil and Marianne and the others were here, of course, but they were machines. Even the real Sybil and Max never came out. *They're too old,* Papa explained. And he explained a lot of other things too, things Grandpa had never told Elisa. Old age for the people of the City wasn't like ordinary old age; they were able to live for years and years, but at some point the body caught up with time lost, becoming old very quickly. Then they had to stay at home, with wires and tubes everywhere and machines to keep them alive. They could go on like this for a long time, sleeping mostly, while the machine that looked like them was living for them in the City.

And the City was deserted. Elisa had always thought there were people outside on the other levels, beyond the well-worn circle of her walks with Grandpa or Papa. Other little girls, other grandpas. She now realized that nobody had ever said so; it had been left to her imagination. But in fact there were only Papa, Sybil, Max, and herself. She really knew nothing about the last two, though, as it was now clear that she'd only ever seen their machine selves. The machines were young, like Papa. Sybil was blond and pink; Max, dark-haired and chunky. But what were they really like?

One night Elisa had a dream. She was walking in the City, on and on, through an endless succession of ramps, staircases, corridors, and crosswalks. From level to level she went. On one level there were big, dark rooms where gigantic machines talked softly to themselves in words she didn't understand, and on another

she found the park, but the animals were all gone.
The shadowless light and the silence were everywhere.
And after walking for a long, long time, Elisa came to
another part of the City, quite different from any she
knew. It looked like the Outside, the old Outside that
Grandpa sometimes used to show on the screens.
There were streets with tame trees enclosed in little
square plots covered with gratings. And all along the
streets were houses, with cars parked close to the sidewalks, and lawns as neat as the trees, with the grass all
the same length and little flowers in the beds.

She was very much afraid of the houses and the
cars and the neat trees. They were all going to die.
They were already dead. When she looked closely, she
noticed that everything was flat; it was only a picture,
and not a very good one, either. Elisa wanted to go
away, but in spite of herself she felt an urge to see the
other side of the picture. How? She touched a painted
handle on a painted door and made a twisting motion. The door opened. Behind it was a corridor with
a lot of doors. Elisa was more and more afraid, but she
had to go on. She came to the first door—a real door
with a real handle—and opened it, all the time desperately wanting not to open it.

Lights of every colour were sunk in the walls;
slanted tables held ranks of instrument panels, but-
tons, and levers, just like in Papa's laboratory, with everything blinking, clicking, humming. In the middle
of the room, surrounded by wires and tubes and lying
on a reclining seat was a huge pinkish blob, red-
veined and glistening, bubbling, slowly rising, falling,
rising, with a squelching noise. And it was talking. It
was saying to Elisa, *Come along, I'm going to tell you a
story*. It was Grandpa!

Elisa managed to turn and run. But once back in
the corridor she had to open the other doors. And in
each room were pink blobs that smiled and talked to
her, and the voices belonged to Mario, to Serena,
to—. The blobs had no eyes, no mouths, no faces, but
they were alive, alive. The last one had Papa's voice,
and Elisa couldn't stop herself from going toward it,

from going into it, her hands, her legs, her head, her whole body melting and mingling with the pink blob.

Elisa woke up screaming.

Was she really awake? She felt herself dripping and dribbling onto the bed, a soft, pink blob. Closing eyes that were no longer there, she willed herself frantically to wake up, wake up. But when she saw the Papa-machine leaning over her, she screamed louder than ever.

When the real Papa came at last, it took hours and hours for Elisa to tell him about her dream, and especially to explain how she knew the difference between machines and people. Papa seemed astonished, and she had the feeling that he didn't quite believe her, but after that night the Papa-machine disappeared and never came back. She had to wait longer for the real Papa to appear when she called, and often she had to make do with seeing him on the screens, but it was always, always better than the machine.

Elisa wanted all the machines to disappear, but she realized that Papa was used to them and would have missed them. And anyway, it set his mind at rest to know they were with her.

"But they aren't real people!" Elisa protested. "They think they are, but I know it isn't true!"

"And if I programmed them to know they were machines, would you like that better?"

After thinking about it a few times, Elisa decided that, yes, she would like it better.

THE MORNING OF THE PARTY, PAUL FINDS some pseudo-medieval clothing in the vestibule of his apartment. He puts it on, feeling both annoyed and amused. What have the old fools dreamed up now? Directions blink on and off the screens of his communication columns, his own and those spaced regularly along the halls. At the entrance to the appointed room he stops for a moment, taken aback by the noise, then enters, divided between laughter and a growing irritation. There's a crowd. Alghieri must have got all the robots in the City going again. The room has been transformed into a chateau interior, complete with pillars, tapestries, armour, a huge fireplace with a fake fire burning, and narrow stained-glass windows shedding a prismatic light. A large round table surrounded by carved, high-backed chairs stands in the middle of the room.

"Ah, Sir Lancelot!" a voice rasps behind Paul.

The crown and brocade costume are royal; the voice is Richard Desprats'. The face, framed in a short, reddish-blond beard, belongs to the Desprats of time past. A synthetic mask. But underneath? Man or machine? A gratified smile twinkles in the brown eyes. Paul watches the expressive play of the artificial flesh, quite unable to decide whether the real Desprats lies behind it. One is supposed to come to these gatherings in person. But the last was so long ago.

"Are the others here yet?"

"Most of them. The Lady Guinevere is waiting for you to pay your respects, Sir Lancelot."

Paul looks in the direction indicated. Serena, splendid in green and gold, stands in the middle of a group of men and women, each more magnificent than the next. He shakes his head. "Really, Richard."

"Arthur, not Richard." Desprats raises his forefinger in admonition and frowns haughtily. "Don't get your kings mixed."

The Knights of the Round Table. So Desprats has chosen the theme for the party. The adulterous trio: Arthur, Lancelot, and Guinevere. Paul nods his head, grudgingly appreciating the irony of the casting. Desprats was Marquande's favorite lover for a long time. He persists in calling Paul "son" occasionally, although he's about Paul's age, give or take ten years, and had nothing to do with Paul's begetting. The point of the joke is obviously Serena-Guinevere, the daughter-wife. It would have been no joke thirty years ago, before time had neutralized Desprats. But his incestuous desires have died down since then. Maybe he's too attached to his old sage image to let it slip in public. Or else he really has turned into an old sage. Paul wouldn't put it past him.

Serena moves regally to meet Paul, and he bows ceremoniously. She laughs, Sybil Horner's laugh. Paul straightens up, forcing his expression to remain impassive. So, an evening of head-swapping—is that it? And Paul is no doubt the only one wearing his own head. Desprats always liked devious jokes. Probably he's there behind his fake young face the whole time, chuckling to himself.

What the hell. Leave them to their silly games. After all, what else have they got? So everyone's wearing a mask. Big deal. They've all been wearing masks for ages. Masks behind masks behind masks. Lies to the nth degree. Not a bad idea for the party's theme. In fact, it's the truth. The Cities have always been disguised. At first they were called observation stations or temporary shelters, although the people who dreamed them up knew perfectly well there was nothing left to observe on the Surface, and that "temporary" meant permanent. Later, the stations and shelters were disguised as cities, with fake parks, fake sky, fake rain, fake democratic elections, and real servitude for hundreds of ordinary citizens who took refuge here at the very end, thanks to a sudden afterthought of the legal owners: the political, military, and scientific leaders, and the few millionaires who'd paid through the nose for their places. The cream of the jest was the lie about supposed immortality and the travesty of a "fair" lottery to choose who'd be immortal. In reality, the choice depended on the whim of those in power. Or, in the long run, on the whim of one's genes. They were the final arbiters, responsible for whether or not the rejuvenating treatments "took." But the laws of evolution had been fully respected: after nearly three hundred years, only the fittest have survived.

How many of these supermen are there, anyway?

Paul looks around, trying to find familiar faces but knowing that none of them is genuine. Today the dead walk and talk. There may even be humans disguised as machines, who knows? It would be quite in keeping.

He takes a goblet of champagne—an anachronism—from a tray. By the time he's drunk it down he feels like smiling again. It's funny that he can still get angry like this. Comforting, actually. Get angry? Get annoyed, nothing more. Desprats would be amused, is amused, deep in discussion with a tall man in black whose back is turned; he catches Paul's eye and winks. The man in black turns around to look. Alghieri. Just as Paul remembers him, with his carefully cultivated satanic look, complete with blue beard. Paul goes over and gives him a hearty slap on the back. (Yes, it's a machine. More solid than a human body. A thump like that didn't budge it.) "You've outdone yourself, Mario."

The ommach bows and bares its teeth in Alghieri's shark-toothed smile. Truly hallucinatory. Desprats and Alghieri have made great strides over the purely functional models that Paul's still using. They seem to have reached an astonishing degree of sophistication. He tells them so, then lets himself float from one group to another, recognizing as he goes several familiar faces from his youth or later, but not bothering much about what's behind them. No Serena, though. No Marquande, either. No doubt there are more surprises in store. Skilful jugglers, acrobats, and tumblers leap and roll to an accompaniment of admiring cries. There are even animal tricks. All phony, obviously.

The round table is laid with gold, silver gilt, crystal, and fine china. Alghieri seems to have abandoned any pretense of being medieval. Sybil had the last word, more likely. Eighteen places set. Are there really that many survivors left? It's possible that Desprats has arranged things to keep the number a secret.

Trumpets sound. Arthur and Bluebeard approach the table with the pseudo-Serena, and Paul does the same. Four serving men enter, bearing an enormous gilded cup on a shield. They put it on the table. Inside is the sleeping baby, resting on crimson padding. Surprised and angry, Paul gives a snort.

"You find the Holy Grail funny, Sir Lancelot?" queries Desprats.

"It wasn't Lancelot who found the Grail, Richard," answers Paul. "Sorry, I mean Your Majesty."

"You're right. It was his son." Alghieri smiles. "We do our best. In any case, we didn't say you'd found the Holy Grail."

Paul keeps his temper in check and says nothing. The trumpets blare. What, again? The whole thing's getting ridiculous.

A cloud of women in floating, sparkling robes, wand in hand, waft into the hall. Twelve of them. Fairies. They glide toward Paul, and he notices that they're all the same, except for the colour of their eyes and hair. Each one has the face of Annette Schwartz. It's just like Desprats to give Elisa twelve fairy godmothers modelled on the woman who tried to blow up the City a hundred and fifty years ago. The first fairy speaks, and Paul thinks disgustedly that perhaps it isn't Desprats' idea after all. He hears Serena's voice saying, "She shall reign over the ommachs of the City." When the second fairy touches the cup-cradle with her wand, again it's Serena's voice saying, "She shall be as beautiful as the night."

"As quiet as a hologram," chants the third fairy, taking up the refrain.

And so it goes, until the eleventh says, "She shall have no child, but they shall all be girls."

Lightning and thunder. A thin shape in a gold and black dress materializes suddenly beside the table. The baby doesn't wake up. The idiots must have drugged her, thinks Paul with annoyance. Unless it's also a fake. He looks at the hologram more closely. Marquande, of course.

"I see you forgot to invite me," says the familiar voice, slightly more grating than Paul remembers it. "I've a gift for the little princess, nevertheless. When she turns twenty, she'll prick her finger and live forever."

The shape disappears in another flash of lightning, while the fairies and the crowd of robot onlookers break into sorrowful wails. The last fairy (the dark-haired version of Annette Schwartz, with eyes as green as grass) has said nothing yet. She goes over to the table. "I cannot undo what my older sister has done, but I can soften the blow. When Elisa turns twenty, she will prick her finger, but she will only live for two hundred and eighty years, seven months, and three days."

Everyone claps and sits down to eat as the serving men remove the cup-cradle from the table and place it nearby. Paul, of course, finds himself next to the green-eyed fairy. "As I recall," he says to his neighbour, "everything in the castle stops with the princess. It's a comfort to know that the City won't have so long to live."

"I'd have made it shorter if I could," Serena's voice replies, "but I'm only a beginner fairy."

Paul looks at the green eyes. "Are you in your second childhood or what?" he says bluntly.

"Don't be such an old grouch, Paul! Poor scientist, obsessed with his research and incapable of sharing the simple human joys."

"Simple? Human?" Paul raises his eyebrows in exaggerated puzzlement.

"Well, aren't we the virtuous one!"

"Anyway, I think your prediction is wrong," he answers in a lighter tone, feeling the gaze of Desprats just opposite them. "There's never been any question of giving treatments to the baby."

"I didn't actually think my prediction would come true," murmurs Serena.

Paul eats, watching the other guests. Apart from Sybil and Desprats, the only ones eating are a man with the face of Jean Renaud, and the three Annettes.

"Who's Renaud?" asks Paul, trying to turn the conversation into less awkward channels.

"Christine. But you're supposed to guess."

Christine Hoembecke in the body of her one-time

lover. Yes, he should have guessed. "And the Annettes?"

"Guess, Paul."

"That's all there are left?"

"Don't spoil the fun, Paul. You won't try to guess?"

"Only eight survivors, and you find that funny?"

The green eyes harden. "Yes, inasmuch as both of
us are among them."

Ah! Still thinking about that childish suicide pact, is
she? But she hadn't bothered to remind him about it
when the date came round.

"You're right," he says, beginning to eat again. "It's
pretty funny."

"Are you going to make any more like her?" asks
Serena after a moment. Paul is annoyed, but gives no
sign of it. She's not going to start that again!

"I've got to gather the maximum data on the subject."

"Fifteen to twenty years of studies."

"At least. Alghieri is quite able to produce highly
realistic playmates for her, judging by his present machines. This little girl will probably have a far more
normal childhood than we did, Serena. And
anyway—."

"Anyway, that's not the problem at the moment.
This child is only a prototype."

"Exactly."

Paul jabs at the hors-d'oeuvres with unwonted energy. Always the same old argument. He isn't going to
let himself be drawn in this time, like he was six
months ago—or was it a year? A long time, anyhow.

"There's no reason why she shouldn't be happy
here, Serena. You must admit we haven't been all that
miserable. And you know very well I've no intention of
treating her like anything but a human being. I'm not
an ogre, after all."

"You could have fooled me, considering your present activities," whispers Serena fiercely. "Your first
mutants—. But that isn't the problem, is it? The problem is that you get used to being a god. You like it,
don't you?"

"That's a lie and you know it!" hisses Paul. He sees Desprats turn toward them and tries to calm down. "I want to improve what exists. There was a time when you went along with the idea."

"You've no intention of improving anything. You've simply found a good reason for staying alive, that's all."

"Life continues on the Surface, Serena, and we owe it something."

"Life doesn't have to continue here in the City!"

"Elisa's children and the others will leave the City."

"And you'll watch them go, of course!"

"If I can, yes!"

Desprats lifts an appeasing hand. "Lancelot, one mustn't argue with the fairies. It could have dire results. Tell us instead what you wish for your daughter."

"She's not my daughter, and my wish is that she be viable and functional."

Paul looks around the table, at the indiscernibly false faces, the attentive, mocking smiles. Suddenly he's had enough. He throws down his knife and fork, stands up, and picks the baby out of her ridiculous golden cradle. It really is the baby, her weight is right. He walks out of the room, but not fast enough to escape Desprats' Parthian shot.

"You're getting old, Paul!"

⚡ 9 ⚡

ELISA TURNS SEVEN, NINE, TEN. ELISA LEARNS to speak directly to the computer that Papa calls "the City." Elisa performs her first dissection: a mouse. Elisa learns to use teaching machines. Elisa works in the lab with Papa.

Elisa works in the lab with *Paul.* She is twelve, and he's just told her that he's not really her father, but that she's here because of him and he loves her just the same.

"You aren't the last child of the City, Elisa, you're the first of a new race. You have a unique faculty, one that will make the madness of the Cities unnecessary. You'll live a long time, dearest, and you won't need machines to do it. There'll be others like you, and one day you'll leave the City."

Elisa smiles. That's like Grandpa's story. She tells Paul the story, thinking he'll be pleased to find she already knows about it. But he looks cross, and she asks anxiously what she has said wrong.

"It isn't that, exactly," says Papa (*Paul*), "your grandfather, who wasn't your grandfather at all, any more than I'm your father, had some rather odd ideas about the City."

With relief, Elisa realizes that Paul isn't angry with her, but with Grandpa—no, he calls him Richard Desprats.

Paul drops on his haunches in front of her. He's so tall! "When I say 'you'll leave,' I don't mean you, dearest. Nor your children. You'll have children, you know, lots of them. I'm speaking of your race. In a way, you'll be part of them, because they'll be your descendants and they'll have the same faculty. Do you understand?"

She thinks she understands very well. She's already had her first genetics lessons from Paul. She doesn't really mind having to stay in the City, anyway; it'll mean she won't leave Papa—Paul. And she'd be afraid, Outside, all alone. It's too big. She understands very well: she and her race will repopulate the City, and when there are enough of them they'll leave.

No? That isn't quite it?

"You've seen what Outside is like, haven't you? Life there is very different. The people Outside are still savages. I explained why."

Grandpa, Desprats, also explained why. Often. Successive *nuclear accidents, pollution,* small *wars* everywhere, and too many people. Barely enough to eat, and Earth itself becoming angry. Earthquakes, awakening *volcanoes,* changing *climates,* famines, epidemics, and finally the great *tides* that changed the *continents.*

The words were already familiar. Papa had made their meaning clearer.

"I don't know if it was the Earth that got angry," smiles Papa. "That's what Desprats thought. But the result was the same. We have to wait until they're ready Outside. We in the Cities are the trustees of a treasure, Elisa. Knowledge. The sciences, the arts, the wisdom of the ages. We are the guardians. You and your descendants will be the guardians. You'll keep the people of the Exterior under surveillance and you'll continue my research. It's very important, Elisa. You've got to learn a lot, work a lot, dearest. Do you know why?"

"Because they make more girls than boys Outside," says Elisa, to show she'd remembered the lesson. Paul's satisfied beam is her reward.

"That's right. As long as they make more girls than boys, you can't go out. We're going to develop your faculty here in the City, and when we've solved the problem of too many girls, and the people Outside are closer to being ready, we'll give them the treasure of the Cities. You and I, Elisa." He laughs lightly. "We'll remake the world, all right?"

"All right!" She laughs. He's teasing her, but she can tell he means it too. And why not? He's omnipotent. He'll remake the world. And Elisa decides to work twice as hard to measure up to his expectations and deserve his confidence.

Elisa works. She is plunged into a sulfuric acid bath; into a liquid oxygen bath; into a vacuum container. Paul watches the instruments, gauging her reactions.

Elisa and Paul watch her little finger, which he has amputated, grow day after day.

Elisa and Paul watch her little finger, which he has amputated, grow hour after hour.

Elisa is fifteen and looking at all these past Elisas on the monitor. Today Paul has solemnly accorded her a personal access code to the City, enabling her to question the memory banks directly. Later she discovers she can't expect answers to everything. After thinking it over, she decides there's nothing unusual about this.

(The City, all-seeing all the time, has recorded other images, but Elisa won't call them up until much later: Elisa naked in front of a mirror, touching her small new breasts curiously. Elisa watching two naked bodies struggling on a bed. Elisa watching two naked bodies *making love* on a bed. Elisa discovering that she can get pleasure from touching herself there, and there, and *there*.)

Elisa naked in front of a mirror, caressing her sixteen-year-old's breasts and wondering whether Paul is looking at her.

⚡ 10 ⚡

PAUL IS ABOUT TO CALL HER, BUT WHEN THE picture comes up on his screens he cuts the switch. For some minutes he sits very still in front of the empty screen, looking at his own reflection, the familiar facial features, unchanged.

Unchanged. . . . If it were really a mirror, he'd be able to see the almost imperceptible sagging that less expert eyes would miss, the overall weakening of muscle tone that blurs the sharpness of his features. He's in great shape, all the same. The results of the most recent analyses showed less than one hundredth of a percent drop in relation to constant factors. His capacity for erection is as good as ever. He stands up, amused and annoyed with himself. His libido is well aware that he's merely toying with a familiar anxiety. He can't fool it. *Really, Paul Kramer, what are you thinking of!*

Of smooth skin, gleaming in the dusk, of small, erect breasts. . . .

He fiddles absent-mindedly with the controls, calling up various bits of the City on the monitor. Robot gardeners in the park, an escalator. Another corner of the park, near the waterfall. The genetics lab. A splendid view of the centrifuge. An incubator. *The baby has grown quickly. It's time to get the next generation going. She began to menstruate very late, at fifteen; have to work on this with the next. Would she have stopped the blood if she hadn't known it was normal, if she'd thought she was ill? Must see about that too, with the others. Her control is clearly getting more and more conscious.* He can't get Elisa out of his mind. He's thinking about her, and not as the subject of a lab experiment. *Mid-life crisis. Nonsense.*

The screens flicker with rapidly changing images of the City. He hardly sees them. The great hall on Level Three. An air vent, somewhere or other. A series of deactivated control panels. A section of blue wall, with a bit of bed and a torn book in the foreground. The park again. Max's bald, rosy skull underneath the network of tubes and wires, and lighted screens in front of him.

Lighted screens: white bodies stretched on the ground, the same body seen from several angles; the right arm comes and goes between the raised thighs, the head rolls from right to left, and the curly hair swings back and forth, alternately revealing and veiling the closed eyes, the half open, trembling mouth: "Paul, oh Paul!"

Paul freezes. Then his hand bangs the keyboard, and the screens go dark.

"Are you that much of a puritan, Paul?" It's the grating, sarcastic voice of Sybil Horner.

He presses the scrambler and drops into the chair, resting his head on his folded arms. Scrambler. He must install a scrambler in Elisa's rooms. He should have done it before. He listens to the irregular beating of his heart, almost terrified by the intensity of his anger. Those two *slugs*, watching her!

He must talk to her. He can't let her keep on. . . .

He lifts his head and his reflection moves in the screen in front of him. Keep on what? Masturbating?

She has a perfect right to, if she wants. To have fantasies? How can he stop her? There isn't anyone else. He should have thought of that. How could he *not* have thought of it? He should have got hold of some male when he knew she would be viable. Or even not just some male, but another actual mutant. Or given her neutralizers. He should have. But he didn't. So now what?

Talk to her. Get it out in the open, at any rate. And afterward? She's a woman now. Has he the right to deny her? Actually, he'd be doing her a favour. Also, it would be interesting to see just how far she could control her body under those conditions.

Also, you want to.

Well, yes, he wants to. So what? It means he's really alive. He puts his hand on his hardened penis and bursts out laughing. And she wants to. The oldest biological reaction, the primordial affirmation of eternity. Isn't this what he's devoted himself to—that life should go on? But first he has to install the scrambler in her rooms. Then prepare her, gently, for the transition from fantasy to reality. *I'll make it an unforgettable experience. You'll see, Elisa.*

He hasn't forgotten his first time either, but for other reasons. Marquande hadn't been particularly subtle about getting him into her bed.

⚡ 11 ⚡

IN THE PARK. A JAPANESE LANDSCAPE AT THE moment: pink cherries, ginkgo trees, dwarf evergreens, little bridges, white gravel. The morning's rain has not yet dried off and it shines under the light of the reflectors. Unseen birds trill their song, and robot gardeners are silhouetted beside the pond, busy with new beds.

"They ought to make the park bigger," says Elisa's voice off-camera. "Make everything a park."

She appears onscreen beside Paul. They walk slowly, side by side. Elisa is wearing a very short red and white dress; her brown, curly hair stands out in a halo around her head. Paul is all in white, shorts and a tennis shirt. They are carrying tennis racquets, and pass in front of the camera. There is a brief back shot and then the next camera picks them up full face again.

"It could be done," says Paul.

"Everything that we don't use—."

"Yes. It'd take time, but it could be done."

"Well, let's do it then, since it can be done."

"Does one have to do something just because it can be done?"

"Why not?" says Elisa defiantly. "That's how the human race has always functioned, hasn't it?"

Paul's smile alters. Then he says softly, "It can't be said the process did it much good. But we'll see."

Elisa gives him a sidelong glance in turn.

Elisa and Paul beside the pond. Elisa, wearing a white bikini, comes out of the water. Paul is lying on his stomach, his chin resting on his arms. She goes up to him and sprays him, shaking her hair above him. He rolls over in protest, grabs her by the knees and tumbles her into the grass, grabbing handfuls of it and rubbing her face with it. She tries to tickle him as she struggles. He pins her down, half lying on top of her, his face close to hers. They are no longer laughing. Elisa raises her head and presses her lips against Paul's. He lets go of her and straightens up. "Little girl—."

"No!" mutters Elisa furiously through her teeth, eyes closed.

He smiles slowly. "I know."

She opens her eyes and Paul's smile vanishes immediately. She looks steadily at him for a moment, then wraps her arms around his neck and speaks, her voice muffled.

"It's you and me. What else? You know it, too. You must."

He strokes her cheek, a distant, perhaps sad look in his eyes.

"And you," he murmurs, "what do you know?"

"That it's normal. That it's good." She speaks earnestly, her brows knitted.

He shakes his head. "You're a little girl, just the same."

She bites her lips. "So? You were little too, once."

"A long time ago."

"I don't care! I don't!"

He looks at her for a long moment, then the slow smile spreads over his features again. He bends over and brushes her lips with his mouth. "Neither do I, my beauty, neither do I."

He gets up, offering her a helping hand, and looks straight into the nearest camera with a wicked grin.

"But let's go home first."

⚡ 12 ⚡

ELISA AND PAUL COME OUT OF THE THEATER. Elisa's low-necked, clinging evening dress has the smooth gleam of liquid steel. Paul is wearing a suit of black and violet.

"I still don't see what Garfield's interpretation adds to the play, but he's certainly a great actor."

"But if Orestes was a homosexual, that changes everything! His relationship with Electra, the mother's murder—."

Paul shakes his head ruefully. "Really, the way they plod through all these reinterpretations of the classics!"

"But it's all in Euripides. You yourself said so. They have a perfect right to choose a particular approach."

"At the expense of all the other aspects?"

"As a demonstration."

"But life isn't a demonstration, Elisa. All values coexist. And nothing can be proved definitively. That's the aesthetic illusion. In reality, Orestes has three dozen equally valid reasons to love and hate his mother, his father, his sister, himself. And that's why in real life the Orestes types kill no one, and life goes on as usual."

"Crimes of passion don't exist, then?" exclaims Elisa, sounding shocked.

"Oh, yes. Committed by people who are afraid of the complexity of life. It's the typical act of simplification."

"The typical aesthetic act, then," says Elisa sagely.

Paul laughs. "There is more than one kind of aesthetics. The aesthetics of emptiness, and the aesthetics of fullness, for example. Personally, I prefer the latter, even if it is a bit of a jumble."

"Life?"

"Of course."

Elisa gives Paul a hard stare, but his gaze is elsewhere. He keeps on walking, a rueful smile on his face. She puts her arms around his waist and rests her head on his shoulder.

"You like things to be complicated."

"Elisa, things *are* complicated!" says Paul with a laugh, his arm around her shoulders. "I'd like it better if they were simple."

"Some things are simple."

"Some things look simple."

"Joy, pleasure, love!" protests Elisa. Paul shakes his head and laughs, and they walk on for a moment without saying anything.

"Joy, pleasure, love," repeats Paul finally. "Yes, it looks simple from one point of view. But there are so many kinds of joy, so many different ways of loving."

"I find love simple," says Elisa a little sulkily.

Paul gives her a hug. "Some days it is, my darling."

Max died this morning.

In the lab, Paul works absent-mindedly, preoccupied with his thoughts. Several times he replies gruffly to Elisa's questions. Then, as she works in her corner, anxious and unhappy, he goes over to her. "Max died this morning." They look at each other. He takes her in his arms—or she takes him; she isn't sure who makes the first move. She presses against him, feeling his distress and grief, remembering the day long ago when, as a very small girl, she sensed the same dismay in him. Now she understands it better: he's afraid. She strokes the blond, slightly fading curls, kisses his face where the tiny wrinkles won't go away. She loves him with all her being, desperately, helplessly. She isn't a little girl now: she knows he'll die, and that she will have to live on after him, without him.

She is twenty years old.

There is a knock at the door. Paul says, "Come in," and turns around. A woman enters. It isn't Elisa, but he can't tell who it is at first.

"Serena?"

A violent joy floods through him. He runs toward her, she holds out her arms, smiling. He touches her: yes, it's Serena. He draws her toward the bed and she goes willingly, lies down, looking at him with the old half-smile, eyes shining, right eyebrow a little raised. He bends over her, but she lays a finger on his lips and stops him.

"Not now, Paul."

His annoyance is as great as his joy. Not again!

She smiles a little sadly. "You can't, Paul. You have to be dead."

His first angry impulse suddenly fades. Why not try to please her? After all, she's come back. He lies down beside her on the bed, closing his eyes and breathing gently in an effort to keep his chest from heaving. I am dead, he thinks with all his might. The sound of her is close. A soft laugh, the slight swish of clothes being removed. His penis stiffens in spite of himself. He wasn't aware of his nakedness until now, when Serena lays her hand on his abdomen. The hand slides downward, and her chiding voice murmurs, "No, no, you've got to be dead." But she keeps stroking his penis. The pleasure is excruciating. Paul tries to think, I'm dead, but he can feel the excitement rising within him. He opens his eyes in terror to see Serena's face hovering over his. But it is distant, inaccessible. Time seems to have stopped, as he has stopped, on the brink of an orgasm. The tension becomes painful, spreading from his penis to his rib cage and coiling around his heart. "You've got to be dead, Paul," says Serena, smiling.

"No!"

Paul is awake, heart pounding, throat dry. He must be awake: there's the familiar room in the half light. He turns toward Elisa, wanting to hold her close, to lose himself in her warm flesh. . . . This isn't Elisa! He can see the woman's features clearly in the soft light of the communication column. Serena! He panics briefly, then tells himself that he's still dreaming. Closing his eyes, he lies back, determined that when he opens them again Elisa will be there. After a moment of this waking nightmare he looks again. Elisa. He turns over with relief. His dream is under control. He empties his mind and forces himself to sleep.

⚡ 13 ⚡

IT MUST HAVE BEEN THE LOBBY OF SOME bank, some great corporation. A high, wide space in the form of a hexagon. The counters have gone and windows have been cut into the walls—tall, narrow windows, with thick, barely transparent glass. The only light comes from oil lamps and tall candelabras. On the wall at the end of the lobby is a huge mosaic, its colours still fairly bright. A rustic scene, women harvesting. Fair, rosy-cheeked women in pastel tunics, gathering golden sheaves. Along a blue horizon stands a city's profile, a lacy cutout of skyscrapers, monuments, churches, and smokestacks. Above the harvest scene a banner floats in the sky, but its mosaic words—probably the name of a bank or some motto—have been carefully chipped away.

The lobby is now a throne room and audience hall, as shown by the respectful crowd standing in a half-circle in front of the mosaic wall. To be more exact, in front of the chair placed on a platform with five wide steps. The platform is made of concrete blocks, a harsh and incongruous contrast to the smooth black and white tiles of the floor. Someone must have realized this, as rugs and skins have been thrown over the concrete to disguise most of it.

The throne is also partly covered with furs. On it sits a man in his forties, wearing a pale, richly embroidered leather tunic and wide trousers tucked into gleaming black boots, laced to the knee. On his lap rests a short sabre in a sheath of precious metal—a ceremonial weapon, evidently, the handle encrusted with coloured gems. On either side of the throne and at several strategic spots around the hall stand guards, armed with guns and heavy cartridge belts slung crosswise over their chests. The crowd—all men—don't appear to be armed.

The scene is being observed from an angle to the left of the throne, about a dozen yards away. "Take it a little closer," murmurs Elisa. "I'd like a better view." The man on the throne gets bigger, and details become clearer: a square face with a full, blond beard; thick, rather tangled hair; a squat nose; and blue almond eyes beneath frowning brows. A leonine mask.

"He doesn't look very friendly, this Kurtess."

"That's because he's beginning to realize that holding power is no sinecure. Once the excitement of the *coup* has subsided and the purges are done with, he's got to get on with business as usual. Pretty damned boring, in fact. They're usually starting a war somewhere or other just to keep themselves from falling asleep. But Kurtess is a little different from the other warlords. He's had some education, and in his way he's very intelligent."

The man on screen has finished speaking, something about tribute in horses and the Northeast regions. The language is hard to understand, a bastard mixture of German and Russian. He turns for the next item of business to the counsellor standing at the foot of the steps with the crowd. As his head turns, his eyes cross the camera's lens and there is a shadow of a smile.

"He looked at you!"

"Of course. I'm one of his old cronies, a faithful right arm. That ommach was sent in by me over five years ago."

"Paul! Look at that red-headed man in front, near the guard!"

The camera pans past faces young and not so young, most of them bearded, some bored, some interested. Close-up of a young man with curly red hair, face sharp as a knife blade, watchful and intense, lips compressed. He looks at the throne while his right arm moves, as though feeling for something in his garments.

The screen blurs. The pan is too quick. Brief shot of the chieftain rising from his throne. Close-up of his astounded face, then a hand and arm across the screen, knocking him down. Shouts and explosions.

"Paul!"

Elisa rushes to Paul as he collapses into the chair, eyes staring. She rips off the wires that connect him to the ommach. He moves slightly, murmurs weakly, "Wait, it's all right . . . wait."

She scrutinizes him anxiously. He's as white as a sheet, almost blue, his nostrils pinched, mouth open, gasping for breath.

"It's all right, I tell you . . . try . . . to restore the circuits."

Elisa hesitates, then turns to the control panel. Nothing but snow on the screen, but there is a crackle of sound, the murmur of a crowd, brusque orders. "Everyone out! Out!" Above the confusion comes the voice of Kurtess: "Garnier? Garnier?" Another voice, farther away: "He's not bleeding."

Paul pushes Elisa away from the control panel. He seems recovered, his skin no longer has that horrible blue tinge.

"Are you sure you're all right?"

He shakes his head impatiently, busy with the controls, gauging the extent of the damage. "Yes, dammit! Irretrievable. Shot in head and chest. I should have made it stronger."

A distant voice shouts, "Where the hell is that doctor!"

Kurtess's voice intervenes with a cutting edge. "I don't think he'll be needing one."

"Can't blow it up, in any case," mutters Paul between clenched teeth. "Everyone within a hundred metre radius would go too. Dammit! What got into me? I just had to let him be killed, and the problem would have been solved."

Another voice, very close, mutters, "He sure is heavy."

Suddenly the sound goes dead and the snow blanks to grey. Paul abandons the controls and sinks back into the chair. "Kaput."

Elisa sits down in the nearest chair, not daring to ask yet again if he's all right. Lately, he gets annoyed when she fusses about his health, even if he's tired. In order not to lose contact, she starts to talk.

"They're going to examine it."

"Obviously!"

"But do you think they can understand—?"

"Metal and plastic? They aren't utter cavemen! And some will make the connection with the old fables. Kurtess will."

"But can he deduce our existence from that, do you think?"

"Why do you suppose the City pointed him out to me? Why do you suppose I took the trouble to plant an ommach in his entourage? This Kurtess is dangerous. He's already had contact with one City, or at least with documents that mention Cities."

Elisa is worried by Paul's agitation. It must be the shock. He took the brunt of those bullets for an instant.

She waits until he's calmed down a little, then asks gently, "What can he do to us?"

"Do to us? Not much, I imagine."

"Well, why worry about it?"

Paul takes several deep breaths, then turns to her, apparently himself again. "You're right," he says, smiling. "But I'd rather it hadn't happened." He rises shakily and grasps the back of the chair. Elisa grabs his arm in alarm, but he shakes her off. "We'll have to send in another ommach," he grumbles. "One that can bleed."

"Perhaps you should rest a bit," Elisa can't help saying. She can see his jaw muscles tighten, but he makes an effort to relax.

"I'm perfectly all right, I tell you."

It's too much for Elisa. She holds him tight, her face buried in his chest. "I was afraid, that's all," she says in a very small voice. She feels Paul's arms close around her, feels his mouth in her hair, on her forehead. But she also feels that he is somewhat irritated, somewhat distant, and she moves out of his embrace before he can gently push her away.

Elisa watches the results printing out on the screen. Another dead end. What a bore. Three months of work, hundreds of calculations, and an entire program—a total waste. They'll have to start from scratch. Again. Paul won't like that.

She ought to get going right away on a new tack. Instead, she throws herself back in the chair and sighs. She's not good for anything right now. She needs time, time to think about this new failure, time to let it sink in. Time to get a clearer idea of causes and consequences, to see where future research should be focused. In fact, she needs a change of scene.

Should she call Paul? No, he's working. And anyway, the idea of disturbing him just to say she's failed again—. She wonders once more whether she shouldn't have insisted on having a baby last year, despite the problems. No. She rejects the idea immediately. It's not her right. Paul's arguments are completely understandable. She shouldn't waste her genes having a child by him that can't regenerate itself. It's a recessive trait. And the idea of having a child Outside is—well, she remembers Paul's disheartened expression as he said, "Elisa, I have to confess that I've already tried the experiment." Then the diagrams and graphs on the screen, interpreted by Paul: take the genes of mutants whose embryos had her special faculties, cross them with her genes, and you could get children capable of partial regeneration. "But their life span was reduced by two thirds, Elisa." On the Outside, for some reason or other, the regenerative polygene was found to be linked to a gene that caused accelerated aging. "I eliminated the embryos, Elisa, as soon as I realized what was happening."

Of course she hadn't the right to inflict such a thing on an innocent child. For a year now she'd been working on this problem, without success. Every attempt to wipe out the undesirable genes had ended in failure. Sometimes it seemed that she hadn't all the necessary data, that she'd overlooked something. But Paul simply shrugged when she mentioned it. "You know all you need to know. I haven't trained you all these years for nothing, I hope?" And he cut off communication.

Elisa sighs again, letting her hands wander over the keys. Without thinking, she types a code. The screens light up, and a now familiar scene appears. A small village somewhere in the south, far from the City, by the lakes beyond the mountains. She happened on the scene quite by accident, unsure at first whether it was something in the past, recorded and preserved by the City, or something picked up by sensors that were still operative. Now she knows that it's the present, that she's plugged into a very old surveillance program for this Outside region, a program set up by Richard Desprats and never discontinued.

"Elisa!"

She gives a start. Paul's angry face appears on the screen, obliterating the village.

"Haven't you got something better to do?"

"No. Not at the moment," she snaps. Her face reddens as resentment rises. Can't she amuse herself for five minutes without feeling guilty? She tells him that the experiment has failed and transmits the results.

He studies them, frowning. "Got any explanations?"

"Not yet."

"Well, what are you waiting for? I want them tomorrow."

He switches off. Elisa is left in front of the empty screen, cheeks burning, throat constricted. She swallows. I'm not going to cry, she tells herself. I'm not.

"The honeymoon sure is over," says a voice, a little sad yet amused. It takes a moment for Elisa to recognize the coloured swirl on one of the screens. Sybil Horner? It's been such a long time.

"He's tired," says Elisa, more for her own benefit than for the invisible Sybil. "And this research is very important."

"I'm afraid it may be more than just fatigue," says Sybil. "And as for this research . . . What does he tell you about *his* experiments?"

Elisa is about to say that Paul is not accountable to her, when Paul's voice comes through again, although no screen lights up.

"Leave Elisa alone, Sybil. She's got work to do." Sybil's swirl disappears. "She won't disturb you again," says the invisible Paul. "Remember, I want that report tomorrow."

Elisa would like to ask whether they're dining together this evening, but he's already cut the communication.

⚡ 14 ⚡

THE NEXT MORNING, AFTER A VIRTUALLY sleepless night, Elisa crosses the park on her way to the laboratory. She stops for a moment beside the pond. It's only eight o'clock, after all. The robot gardeners have moved the little island, but the blue-green ducks are still circling it unconcernedly, their invisible

webbed feet propelling them round and round. Elisa
has always been fascinated by their static mobility. This
morning it seems to typify the City, moving change-
lessly through time. She can't recall the dreams of her
fitful sleep, but yesterday's failure weighs heavily on
her still, even though she now knows the reasons for
it.

Just as she begins to move on, Elisa sees a figure
coming toward her. She stops, surprised. It isn't Paul,
but a woman in white slacks and a multicoloured tunic. She has unruly blond hair and a face like a cat's.
Sybil, of course. The Sybil-machine. What's going on?
Sybil hasn't come out for years, at least not around
Elisa or Paul.

The machine stops beside Elisa and smiles but says
nothing. Elisa watches, her curiosity piqued. She
hasn't seen an ommach close up for some time. She'd
forgotten how real they look. The robot gardeners are
clearly just that: their false human faces have been removed long ago, at Elisa's request. But Sybil's machine
is incredibly like the real thing. (Like the *real* Sybil,
but a past Sybil, maybe even someone completely different. After all, she's never seen the real Sybil.) And
that expression: Half amused, half embarrassed. Embarrassed? Why would Sybil be embarrassed?

"Got your report finished?" says the machine, finally. The voice is perfect too. Why wouldn't it be?
Somewhere there is a chest, lungs, a larynx to create
it. All the machine does is turn it into a pleasant
young voice.

"Yes," answers Elisa, and begins to walk away from
the pond. The machine moves with her.

"I hope you didn't fight over me. Paul must be *very*
angry. He's completely cut me off from your lab." The
machine laughs. "Very rude of him. In the old days
that sort of thing just wasn't done. This research must
be pretty important for him to be so impolite."

Elisa can't decide whether she should answer, or
what to say if she does. She's lost the habit of talking
to anyone but Paul, or the City. The machine doesn't

seem to mind. In any case, Sybil must be perfectly aware of what they're working on.

"You look a bit peaked," says the machine—says *Sybil*—after a moment. "Why don't you get some rest? You should take some exercise and stop working at this crazy pace. And nibbling on sandwiches isn't exactly the best thing for someone who's still growing."

Elisa looks at the Sybil-machine with astonishment.

"That's right," says Sybil. "You're barely twenty-two, even though you think you're so grown up."

Elisa bursts out laughing. "Sybil, is that really you? You're like someone out of an old soap opera. An anxious mother hen."

The Sybil-machine smiles. "I could well be your mother—your grandmother and great grandmother, too, if you like." The smile disappears. "And I really am anxious. Do you realize how thin you're getting? You used to have such nice curves. You look like a teenager again, all angles. I know Paul is, well, preoccupied at the moment, even frankly ascetic, but—"

Elisa isn't really shocked. She knows that nothing can be kept private in the City. When she and Paul first became lovers, she was glad that their respective apartments were protected by the scrambler. Now she doesn't care, and anyway, there isn't much to hide at the moment.

"You're not going to go on like this for years, are you?" says Sybil. "How long is it since you've actually seen Paul?"

"Three weeks. But as long as the problem he's having with his research isn't solved, well, you ought to know that Paul can hardly think of anything else. You know him better than I do, don't you?"

Elisa only realizes what she's saying once the words are out. It's true that Sybil knows Paul better than she does. Not better, but for longer. But she's known him *like that*, too. Elisa is sure of it, but not jealous. After all, Sybil was out of the running before Elisa was even born.

Sybil's thoughts appear to have been along the same lines.

"Longer than you, anyway," she says with a little smile. They walk side by side, saying nothing. Then the Sybil-machine takes Elisa's arm. The synthetic skin is warm and soft. Elisa gives a small, inward shudder at the thought that no one has touched her for three weeks. And no one but Paul has touched her for years. Why does it seem so strange, all of a sudden?

"Elisa, I'm going to speak to you frankly. I'm worried about you." Sybil's voice is hoarse, and the machine smiles awkwardly. "Yes, I know. I haven't shown myself much. But that doesn't stop me from being there, from tuning in every now and then. And from thinking." Her quiet laugh has a sad sound. "I haven't much else to do, you know."

Elisa thinks of the immobile body directing the machine from afar. She feels uncomfortable, yet full of pity.

"What are you going to do with your life, Elisa?" says Sybil after a moment.

Elisa shrugs. "Keep on working. Keep on learning. Bring up the next generation when we've solved the problem of longevity. Keep up Paul's research on the *T* virus."

"Without Paul."

Elisa doesn't answer right away. She feels irritated by Sybil's remark. She knows it's because the subject is an awkward one. She takes care to avoid thinking about it, but it's always there, suppressed but there. Particularly in the last few weeks with Paul so distant, so worried, his face increasingly lined when it appears on the screens. Elisa feels vaguely guilty, as she always does about this subject.

"Not for a long time."

"Elisa, do you know how old Paul is?"

"No. So what?" Elisa is defensive, bothered by the realization that she doesn't know.

"It's time you asked, don't you think?" says the Sybil-machine, holding Elisa's arm firmly. The voice is distressed but determined. "I'm a hundred and fifty-three, my girl. Paul and I are contemporaries, give or take a few years. He's a hundred and thirty-seven years old, Elisa."

A hundred and thirty-seven. Elisa echoes it silently. It doesn't mean a thing. She thinks only of Paul's body, Paul's smile, with a sudden, violent desire that astounds her. That body is thirty, thirty-five at most. A hundred and thirty-seven is meaningless. What does time mean in the City?

"He was a hundred and fifteen at the time of your birth. The City had already existed for three hundred and thirty-five years, and had been sealed off from the Outside three hundred and twenty years before you were born. The first longevity treatments had just begun. Our grandparents saw the last of the great tides, Elisa, the final Decline. On the Outside, over ten generations have lived and died. Over ten generations, Elisa, from primitive tribes to warlords."

"So what!" Elisa breaks in. She doesn't want to hear any more, doesn't want the years to begin unfolding into a span of real time, into something other than mere numbers.

The Sybil-machine stops walking and looks at her for a moment. The face is full of compassion. "So Paul is *old*, Elisa. Pretty soon the treatments won't work."

Elisa jerks away, but the persuasive voice follows her. "You've got to face up to reality, Elisa. There was a time when that was Paul's favourite maxim. I was forced to, well, retire about thirty years ago. Paul is holding his own remarkably well, I grant you. It runs in the family. His mother held on for a very long time, too. But. . . ."

"But what?"

The machine starts walking again, and Elisa follows after a brief hesitation.

"With most people, the body gives out first. The cells appear to have a limited capacity for regeneration. But with some it's the mind that goes."

Elisa shrugs, but Sybil continues. "Yes. The brain is part of the body, of course. I see that Paul has converted you to his obdurate pragmatism. Has he made you study the aging process and how the treatments work?"

"Of course."

"Then you know that their major impact is on the nerve cells, particularly the brain cells. When our bodies give out, and even when we die," (does the precise voice falter for a second?) "our brains are still good for a few years. In fact, brain transplants were the big hope when the Cities first came into operation. Or rather, grafting another body onto the brain. An artificial body, or a natural one. But it didn't work." Sybil shakes her head sadly. "A lot of things didn't work. We hoped for great results from cloning, but—."

"Too many variables," murmurs Elisa.

"And not enough motivation, mainly. We'd found a way to live longer—the treatments—and we concentrated our whole research effort on that. The other possibilities were abandoned as soon as we ran up against apparently insurmountable obstacles. In any case, the trend was not toward basic research. Science was a diversion. Paul has always been a deviant from that point of view."

"Because he believes in life?"

"Because he's always behaved as though he would never die. In a way, he's always been crazier than the rest of us."

"Paul isn't crazy!"

"That's not what I mean, my girl. He has great and noble projects for the future of humanity. I don't necessarily agree with everything he does, but I recognize his devotion and I respect it. What I mean is that, in order to reach his objective, he's always suppressed his fear of death. There's no doubt that man sometimes achieves great things because he can ignore death. But I don't think it's very healthy to blot it out completely, especially when time is running out." The machine stops again and gives Elisa a hazel-eyed stare. "Paul is *old*, Elisa. With some, it's the body that goes; with others, the mind. Marquande de Styx went mad long before her body stopped responding to the treatments. Did he tell you that?"

"No," whispers Elisa. She clears her throat and says more distinctly, "No."

"Evidently he didn't tell you how she died, either.

There's a lot you don't know, Elisa," says the gentle voice of the machine that is Sybil. "About the City, about yourself, about Paul. Have you ever asked him why he hasn't given you your own *total* access code to the City's memory bank?"

"Spying doesn't interest me," replies Elisa drily.

"Tut, tut. Don't fly off the handle. There aren't many real distractions in the City. When you've seen the same play or film for the umpteenth time like I have well ... The life around us is the only reality here. It always has been. It's the only thing that's always changing, that can even provide a few surprises, sometimes."

"There's the Outside."

"Ah, yes. The Outside. It's amusing, from time to time—even interesting. But they're too different from us. It's hard to really care. Come on, haven't you ever had the urge to find out about Paul's life before you were born? To know him better, love him better?"

"If I do, I ask him. Anyway, I've got work to do, Sybil."

"I know, I know." Sybil keeps walking beside her. "But does he always answer? And does he tell you everything? He tells you what he wants you to know."

"Well, what of it?"

"You seem to think he always knows what's best for you! Elisa, you're not ten years old! Paul isn't God the Father. He's a human being, with weaknesses and illusions, someone who *makes mistakes*! He doesn't always know what's good for you, or for him. If things develop in the way I'm afraid they might. . . ."

The machine grips Elisa's arm, forcing her to stop and turn. "You love him, don't you? Well, if things go wrong, he'll need you. He'll need you to know who he is, everything he is. Think about it, Elisa."

They begin walking again, not speaking. Elisa glances sideways at the machine, at the preoccupied face, the eyes lost in the distance. It would be easy to think that this is the real Sybil, here, except for this kind of silence, this impression of inertia, this emptiness that Elisa feels where a real person would radiate a vague luminosity, a warmth, a vibration.

"But what can I do?" murmurs Elisa at last, totally lost.

The Sybil-machine fumbles in her pocket and brings out a paper folded in two. She hands it to Elisa.

"You can always ask Paul for total access to the City. But in case he refuses, you can use mine."

In her mind, Elisa rehearses several indirect ways of asking Paul for the T.A. code, then checks herself suddenly. What's going on? Is she beginning to believe Sybil? Elisa feels ashamed and calls Paul. She is straightforward. "Paul, I want my own total access code to the City."

Paul frowns. "What for, for God's sake? Have you finished your report?"

"Yes."

"Transmit it."

"I thought—I thought I'd take it to you myself this afternoon. Or could we eat together? It's three weeks since we really saw each other, Paul. A little holiday, perhaps?" Her voice becomes caressing, she is trying to coax him and is somewhat disgusted with herself. *Oh Paul, what's happening to us?*

For a moment he says nothing, still frowning. Then he seems to relax a little, says yes, and cuts the communication. Elisa fingers Sybil's bit of paper for a while. No. No. First she must talk to Paul. But what if Sybil is right? What if Paul needs her—or if her ignorance prevents her from helping him?

Only one. She'll ask only one thing. She types Sybil's code and asks for data on the death of Marquande de Styx.

When the screen goes blank, she sits motionless. The minutes tick by. Finally, she calls Sybil. No answer. Then she remembers that Paul had cut off the line between the lab and Sybil's place. What should she do? The machine! She asks the City to establish contact through the machine, and the pink and white face comes up on the screen. At first the expression is totally blank, then it becomes animated as Sybil takes possession of the machine. "Not like this," she says, before Elisa can say a word. "At your place, in ten minutes."

When Elisa reaches her apartment the machine is already there. Elisa goes to press the scrambler key for her screen, but it's already down. She looks at the Sybil-machine. The head nods silently.

Elisa sinks down into a chair.

"Do you think he's going to let himself be tested?" says Sybil evenly.

Elisa looks at her hands. "I don't know," she whispers finally, feeling like a traitor.

"He didn't give you the code, did he?"

"I didn't really ask for it." Elisa tries to protest, but her voice breaks on the last word. The Sybil-machine draws up a chair, sits down, and leans over to clasp one of Elisa's hands.

"I know it's hard, my dear."

"But what can I do, Sybil?"

"Learn as much as you can about him. When you really understand him, you'll be in a much better position to convince him to undergo tests. In any case, there's nothing to say he'll go the same way as his mother. At the moment, his symptoms—well, he's tired, been working too hard, concerned about your research. And he's alone, Elisa." Elisa starts to protest, but the machine puts a finger on her lips. "Think about it, Elisa. Since Max's death I'm the only one left who knows who he really is. The only one who can share his memories. He's always wanted to be strong and wise for you. He loves you and he's always wanted to spare you anxiety. But it's a terrible burden to bear, Elisa, this flawless image that he's tried to project for you. Especially now, with your research getting bogged down. When he's feeling his age, his fatigue, and all the accumulated fears that keep coming back, perhaps. . . ."

Elisa shakes her head, overwhelmed by it all. She

sees Paul's face again—Paul, so old, so distant in time, but barely younger than the Paul she knew—looking at his mother's coffin rolling slowly toward oblivion. She sees his eyes, the expression of pure panic just before the young Paul took the young Serena in his arms, and how his fear subsided when Serena asked, "You're afraid, too?"

Yes, he needs *her*, Elisa. He needs to share his burden of fear, the weight of too many memories.

≽ 15 ≼

ELISA WATCHES PAUL'S LAB. PAUL SITS IN front of the computer bank. The wall screens show the incubator room from various angles. The screens right in front of Paul project a close-up of an artificial womb and its contents, seen by thermograph, scanner, computer reconstruction—all different ways of penetrating the transparent membrane. The embryo is human and several months old.

Richard Desprats stands beside Paul, leaning over to look at the screens. The Desprats-machine? It can't be; this Desprats is much younger than the machine Elisa knew. His hair is just going gray and his moustache isn't the white brush that Elisa remembers as a child. The two men are watching the embryo on the screens. The images change, some imperceptibly, others, like the thermograph, with spectacular effect. On other screens columns of figures scroll by, then restabilize with occasional fluctuations.

"The reaction to outside stimuli is highly satisfactory, you see," says Paul. "Development is completely normal so far, and the phylogenetic recapitulation has gone off without a hitch!"

"But now the organism considers sexual differentiation as pathological," concludes Desprats. "Interesting. A hormone treatment?"

"It's considered an attack, and quickly 'cured.' "

Desprats sits down in the chair next to Paul, takes out a pipe, and begins filling it carefully, ignoring Paul's irritated expression.

"And you think it's a *Trickster* virus mutation."

"Well, it's logical, isn't it? The *T* disrupts the random distribution of the sexes, producing more females than males. The polygene that I isolated in my mutants prevents androgenization and feminization."

"I see. By restoring the situation as it was prior to differentiation. What do you call your polygene? It's typically negentropic. Makes one wonder how carriers could be born. In fact, it's purpose is to maintain the organism in perfect stasis."

"We have to suppose that the subjects from whom I took the genetic material were themselves the result of polygenetic mutation. Call it *N* if you like."

Desprats smiles through the pipe smoke. "I begin to understand your difficulties, and why it took so long to get this far. Either the carrier develops normally, but the autoregenerative factor is almost totally suppressed, or else you get autoregeneration, but the individual doesn't develop. It's a good philosophical argument for justifying entropy; an old argument, at any rate. To grow is to die a little, but with no death, there's no life."

"I've no intention of creating immortals, Richard. Just people who live a long time, and without technological crutches."

"But how do you carry out this research without the City's resources, my dear Paul? The very thing you want to do away with is what may give you the means to succeed. Quite a paradox."

Paul shrugs again. "That's nothing new either."

"There's nothing new under our subterranean suns," murmurs Desprats. "But what are you going to do with embryos that won't differentiate sexually?"

"Keep on searching, of course, until I've solved this problem, just like the others."

"Aren't you running a little short of material?"

"Yes. It's time for a little expedition to the Outside."

Desprats sucks on his pipe for a moment as he stares at the screens.

"The mutation isn't evolving out there?"

"Apparently not—fortunately. Just as well not to have to keep on correcting or eliminating other undesirable variations. There's already a gap of several generations between my *N* and those on the Outside. I've quite enough calculations to run through as it is. But that's routine."

Elisa switches the screen off. *Routine.* A conversation that took place fifty, maybe sixty years ago, and as a result a man and a woman were marked from childhood like cattle, then seized, drugged, taken to the City, and returned to the Outside once Paul had removed a sample of the ovaries and sperm. They hadn't the slightest recollection of what had happened. The woman was now sterile and so became a slave, or possibly was killed if she belonged to a really primitive tribe. If she lived in the more civilized regions, she'd be an object of shame, an outcast.

Routine. As it was—is now?—routine to make selected lab subjects procreate as soon as possible before removing the woman's ovaries, and to tag their children, so that the genes would perpetuate themselves on the Outside, thereby providing a future stock of material. Routine. By now Elisa feels only a dull pain. No more horror, no more despair, just a sense of overwhelming despondency. In a way, she even understands that Paul could hardly do otherwise.

What? Hundreds of embryos sacrificed, dozens of women destined to drag out their existence in sterility, their inexplicable disappearance and reappearance sometimes bringing death?

But she can't blame Paul if savages are savages. Anyway, the embryos weren't human beings.

Weren't they? One of them became Elisa. But most significant of all was the fact that Paul could have brought others to maturity if he'd wanted to. He could have repopulated the City ages ago. He had lied to her, lied. How could he? How can she not have sensed it? But he knows about her capacity for empathy; he must have found some way of controlling the physiological changes caused by emotion, changes that she has learned to sense. It isn't surprising that he so often makes contact on screen instead of in person. That way, it is easy to lie.

He lied. He lied about the experiment that crossed her genes with genes from the Outside. He'd crossed them with the genes of mutants from the Badlands. The Badlands, of all places! He didn't try it with mutants from the strains he'd so carefully cultivated over the years. No accelerated aging gene there, so it would have been quite possible to cross them with Elisa's line to produce children with her special faculties. Why had he done it? Why? To be sure of failing? To have a good reason for putting off his project for dispersing Elisa's genes on the Outside? To be able to *keep on living?*

Elisa slumps in her chair, overwhelmed by it all. Lies, lies, lies. About himself, about others. About her. She doesn't come from the City's banks. She isn't a mutation discovered by chance in the last little girl born in the City. Does it matter? Does it matter whether she's the result of years of experimentation and research? He *had* wanted her, after all.

Why? Because she's the subject of an ongoing experiment.

Subject. Of an experiment.

But he can't have lied the whole time! He *didn't* lie all the time. When they were together, when they made love, she could feel that he truly loved her. She really could. She couldn't have been wrong about that!

There are so many ways of loving, Paul had said. She remembers. What does she know of love? She remembers Grandpa's love. But love between a man and a woman—what does she know about it, apart from films, books, the documents of the City? She only knows Paul's love, the emotion she sensed in him and always interpreted as love, the same love she feels for him.

But it isn't necessarily the same. Maybe he loves her like she loved her doll when she was small, or the various little animals that were given to her. Or like she *loves* her work in the lab when she feels it's going well.

She doesn't want to think. It's too painful. She turns the screens on again and plunges once more into Paul's memories, Paul's secrets, Paul's lies.

Paul at fifteen in Marquande's arms; then, when she's gone, Paul frantically washing himself again and again, sobbing with rage. Paul pacing up and down his bedroom, just before his first anti-senescence treatment, after insisting for years that he'd never go through with it. Paul and Serena weeping in each other's arms, swearing to kill themselves together. Paul and the body of Serena, dead by her own hand after a terrible quarrel. Paul, Paul's memories, secrets, lies, mistakes, betrayals, and even his sufferings—everything that over the years has made up this unknown man: Paul.

Paul watches Elisa watching Paul. He's not so furious as he was. She's going to know everything? So what? So much the better. He should have given her a T.A. code before. All that energy wasted in lying! He'll explain things, they'll talk about it, she'll understand. He'll make her understand. She's his, he made her, she will understand. No, he won't punish her. She has a right to know it all. He was going to tell her soon, anyway. Yes, he would have told her. But Sybil—it must have been Sybil who gave her a code. Sybil. A red wave of fury envelops him, presses in on him. His head is throbbing, his throat constricted, his hands clenched. Sybil.

⚡ 16 ⚡

THE SCREENS GLIMMER BLINDLY. ELISA HAS fallen asleep without switching them off. Paul flicks a finger and they go blank. He bends over Elisa and strokes her hair and forehead, kissing her gently. Poor little girl.

"Elisa? Wake up, my darling."

She gives a start and opens her eyes. When she sees him, a fleeting anxiety shows in her face. He smiles and waits. There, she's felt his calm, and she's calm too.

"I was going to give you your T.A. code, you know," he says softly, putting a finger on her lips. "No, don't say anything. I should have told you before. It's a good thing you know the truth, the whole truth."

She stares at him, dazed, then throws herself into his arms. He holds her close, rocking her and smiling.

"You understand, don't you?" he murmurs against her hair. "This life is so long. Perhaps I wanted to forget a little, to be with you as though I were as new as you. Not to overwhelm you with all those memories, not to hurt you. I wanted to give you the code, but something always came up and I'd say, 'Tomorrow, tomorrow.' You're not angry, are you? You understand?"

She sobs bitterly as she leans against him, the little girl she once was. How afraid she's been! She was afraid he didn't love her. But he does love her, how he loves her at this moment! "I love you," he says, laughing with her.

When she's calmed down somewhat, he takes her back to his place. Everything is just as he ordered it: the table set, soft lighting, music, flowers. Elisa takes it all in with a certain surprise. Paul laughs.

"You must be famished. You've spent all day and half the night glued to the screens, haven't you? Sit down. I've ordered all your favourite dishes. But first," and he takes two goblets just filled by the robot waiter, "champagne! We should celebrate. No more secrets, right? Elisa, I can't tell you what a relief it is to have this weight off my mind. But now we're together, aren't we? Really together." He lifts his glass. "To truth. And to love, Elisa. To the long years we've got left to live together. To our success."

She looks at him, still lost, her glass half raised. He smiles. "To you, Elisa," and he drinks, keeping his eyes on her. She drinks with him.

They sit down and Paul begins sampling the hors d'oeuvres. Elisa takes a few, but doesn't eat.

"How did you know?" she says at last. "The scrambler in my room—?"

"Come on, Elisa, that's for the others, not for me. We won't need it now, anyway. But sh-h-h; let's not talk about it. It's over and done with."

She looks hesitantly at him, then lowers her head and starts to eat gingerly. He can see she's still in a state of shock, and he touches her cheek tenderly.

"We'll talk about it later. Not now, Elisa." He watches as she responds to his caressing tone. She relaxes and smiles at him timidly. He knew she'd understand, that nothing and no one would come between them! "Let's think of the future, instead. Of your children, Elisa. *Our* children. How many would you like? As many as you want. Dozens. Hundreds! The whole city full of children, Elisa. Can you picture it?"

He fills the empty glasses. Elisa stops eating and stares. He leans toward her and pats her hand. "We'll get there, my love, don't worry. We've succeeded so far, haven't we? And we have the time."

She downs her champagne in one gulp and holds out her glass for a refill. Paul obliges with a laugh of pure exultation. He hasn't felt this good in months. The question of lying had been bothering him more than he realized. Poor Elisa. He'd given her a rough time. But he'll make it up to her. That is a promise.

She lifts her head and their eyes meet. He smiles tenderly.

"Paul."

"Yes, my darling."

"You'll be able to take it easy now. You've been neglecting yourself lately."

"Of course we'll take it easy. Together. Like we used to in the beginning, remember? Just the two of us. We'll do something completely different. Remember Kurtess? Well, we're going to take care of him. Make him forget the Cities for good. We'll take a look at all those little kingdoms popping up in the Southwest. After all, we've got to keep an eye on developments, and see which of them deserves our help."

He'll have to give her a change of scene, poor kid. Their glasses are empty. He refills them.

She enters. He recognizes her clearly in the morning light: the half smile, the black hair cascading over bare shoulders. He holds out his arms, smiling, love flooding through him. She moves to the bed. He knows what to do now, and lies down, closing his eyes and listening to the sounds of her undressing, aware that she'll come to him. There, a finger strokes his penis; it quivers like a startled animal though he had expected her touch. Then the hand closes, gently insistent. He's used to it now, knows it's a game. He pretends to be dead, and she caresses him, chiding, until the pleasure of love rises to a climax. But today he's not afraid. He knows it's a dream. And he feels strong, calm, sure that he can control the dream.

To test his power, he puts a hand on hers and stops the caress. He opens his eyes to meet her green gaze and smiles. "Your turn to be dead, Serena. You are dead, aren't you? You have to be dead."

She smiles slowly and lies down, closing her eyes and breathing very, very softly as he strokes her.

So soft, so smooth, so firm. Ah, what a dream! It's never been so good.

He lets his left hand glide the length of her still body, concentrating on his sensations, marvelling at their vividness. What an amazing machine the brain is. But he mustn't think too much or the dream will dissolve. He bends over and kisses the closed eyes, the cheek, the warm lips, while his hand stops on the curl-covered mound of Venus. He knows how to give her pleasure. How well he remembers. She can't stay dead for long.

There, she's moving in spite of herself, sighing, opening her eyes, and murmuring, "Paul?" He closes her mouth with a kiss and lies on top of her, letting the familiar rhythms carry them both into rapture. Oh, how good, how *good* it is!

He's a little afraid of waking at the climax, but no. He can hear her moaning beneath him in the last throb of pleasure. Lifting a long black lock off her forehead, he kisses her. She opens her eyes and smiles, turning her head a little so that he can kiss her throat just where there's a warm little valley. She stiffens. He lifts his head. She's looking at the ceiling with an expression of—is it stupefaction? Now he looks, too, and sees only the two of them in the mirror, their bodies intertwined. And Serena's face.

She's changing. He looks down at the face beneath him. She's *changing*, changed, no longer Serena. A mop of curly hair, brown eyes, a shorter nose; and the mouth, the cheekbones—. He jerks backward. The dream is out of control. This isn't Serena, it's Elisa. With dull resentment he closes his eyes and lies back, determined to wake up.

A hand shakes him. "Paul!" It's Elisa's voice; he opens his eyes to see her terrified face. He must be awake now. What's wrong with her, anyway? Shaking him like this, and gasping, "Paul, what happened? It wasn't me." The voice rises shrilly: *"It wasn't me!"*

"Sh-h-h, it was only a dream," he says, trying to take her in his arms. But she's as stiff as a poker, muscles rigid, body trembling.

"It wasn't me, it wasn't!"

"No, it was Serena," he says soothingly. "But it was a dream, a dream."

She doesn't seem to be listening. "We made love," she whispers. "I wasn't dreaming. We made love and—."

He grabs her by the shoulders and gives her a little shake. "I was dreaming of Serena, that's all. It's over now."

She stares at him. "You were dreaming that you made love to Serena?"

"Yes, a dream. You know what dreams are like." He shrugs.

"But you weren't asleep, Paul. I felt you caressing

me. That's what woke me up. You weren't asleep. I saw you. Your eyes were open." She's panting now. "And that wasn't me in the mirror. But it *was* me, all the same! You were making love with *me!*"

He shakes his head, annoyed but feeling a momentary doubt. It felt so real. . . . But of course it would! It was Serena, after all!

"It was a dream," he insists.

Elisa looks at him steadily, not moving. Finally she says, in an odd voice, "Oh, Paul."

"Well, what? Do you think I'm a sleepwalker?"

She sits down, not looking at him, pressing her knees together. And yes, she smells of love and the sheets are all rumpled. But it doesn't mean a thing: they made love before going to sleep. "I don't know," she murmurs. "I don't know." She turns toward him. "But Paul, if it was a dream, or even if you had a fit of—."

"It was a dream!"

"Then why did I see what I did? *I* wasn't dreaming. I was awake, and I saw—. It wasn't me, it was Serena. I recognized her. I was awake. I'm not crazy."

He becomes exasperated. It's too much. He loses patience, grabs her arm, and starts to shake her. "So I'm the one who's crazy, is that it? But you don't understand! It was a dream, I tell you, a DREAM."

He stops shaking her—it makes his head ring. Little idiot! Why is he bothering with a stupid kid like this! She thinks he's mad. Him, mad! Obviously she believes everything that bitch Sybil told her. Little idiot. And to think of the time he's wasted on her. Ungrateful wretch. He pushes her away roughly when she tries to put her arms around him. He's got better things to do than put up with a snivelling, hysterical kid. There's work waiting for him in the lab.

⚡ 17 ⚡

ELISA GETS DRESSED SLOWLY. PART OF HER
doesn't want to think. What's happened? He loved
her. She felt it, she couldn't be wrong. And he *is* mad.
She felt that too, a confusion behind everything he
said, like a light just dim enough to make it hard to
see, a sort of hum. Last night (was it just last night?)
during the meal, it wasn't so clear, wasn't there all the
time. It went away altogether sometimes, and Paul was
with her, the Paul she knew and who loved her. But at
other moments there was that confusion, that impression of a—of something shifting very slowly, somewhere inside him. Very slowly, but threatening, like an
iceberg that begins to tip.

What's happened? He had a dream, and somehow
or other she got caught up in it? But she was awake.
She saw Serena in the mirror. And he wasn't asleep.
Do sleepwalkers have their eyes open? And it doesn't
go on for so long. Not like this.

What to do, what to *do?*

She'd have to take care of him. Help him. But how?
By force? Send robots to—. She must talk to Sybil.
Sybil will tell her what's best. Sybil will know what to
do. Elisa goes to the communication column and
types Sybil's code. Nothing. Has Paul cut the circuits
there, too? She calls up the City and asks for a line
through the Sybil-machine.

"Machine out of commission," replies the City.

"Out of commission? Since when?"

"Ceased functions at 21:04."

Elisa's brain is numb, unable to react.

"And Sybil Horner?"

"Sybil Horner ceased functions at 21:04."

Elisa's legs go limp as she wobbles to the bed, care-
less of whether the screen is on or not. Alone. She's

alone. Alone with Paul. She alone must decide what to do. She must do *something*.

She returns to the column and types Paul's code. For a moment she sees him scrutinizing the screens. Then he sees her too, and impatiently flicks off the contact.

She can't get through to the City again. Paul's orders.

For a long moment Elisa remains quite still, her head spinning. She feels incredibly heavy, her chest like a lump of lead. Just breathing takes every bit of strength. She hasn't enough energy left to think. Somewhere in her brain an idea struggles to take shape, fades, forms, and fades again. She catches at it. Paul . . . the City. He knows it better than she does. Knows the computers better, can use them more skillfully . . . she must . . . she can't do anything until she's got more . . . he'll get the better of her every time.

She goes back to the column. "Has someone—?" How can she phrase it? "Has someone looked after Sybil Horner?"

"No."

"Where is she, exactly?"

Level Four, in the depths of the City. Elisa leaves Paul's rooms. The false daylight is shining, the sky is blue. In the park, robot gardeners are going about their work as usual, and the birds are singing. Elisa moves mechanically down escalators, along conveyor belts, through halls and passages, barely conscious of what she sees. She's left her communication bracelet at Paul's and every now and then stops beside a column to ask the way.

She's almost there when a motionless silhouette looms up in the passage. She goes up to it, her heart constricted. It's the Sybil-machine, halted in a strange posture, half-turned as though toward someone, arms raised in front of the face. And the expression—the eyes protruding, the features contorted in a terrified grimace. Elisa backs away, giving the machine-statue a wide berth as she hurries on, almost running.

• • •

Sybil's bucket-chair is partly turned away from the door. An open hand lies on the left armrest, motionless, the palm facing upward: the hand of an old woman. Walls and control panels glisten wetly. Under the blood, electronic snow fills the screens.

Elisa flees, running in earnest this time.

⚡ 18 ⚡

WHEN SHE STOPS RUNNING AND LOOKS around her, she has the eerie feeling that comes in dreams—the feeling of being in a strange place, but a place that one *recognizes*.

The next instant she hears the voice. Is *she* going mad? But the voice calls again, "Elisa!" The voice of Richard Desprats. Elisa looks around. Now she knows where she is. This is where she grew up: Level One of the City. Nothing has changed: the small garden remains immaculate, the aviary is there with its birds. The funny wooden house with the verandas still stands at the end of the garden. And there, at the garden gate, is the communication column disguised as a tree, and a voice coming from it, saying for the third time, "Elisa!"

She goes forward, feeling this must be a dream, but not an unpleasant dream. A screen is lit, and the face of Richard Desprats watches Elisa with concern. The dead are alive, the living are dead. Logical. At the same time, another part of her reasons that she must have triggered an alarm by coming into the garden. This face is an electronic simulation, a computer program that has suddenly been reactivated. As in a dream, she feels very lucid, calm, detached. Nothing can harm her. "Hello, Grandpa. Paul is mad," she says, and waits. The electronic ghost nods his head.

"I know. He killed Sybil. That's what woke me up."

Elisa sits down on the little bench circling the tree

and leans her head against the synthetic bark, feeling her energy ebb. "Woke you up?"

"I predicted something like this. I placed special sensors on everyone. If there was a violent death, the City was to wake me."

"But you're dead, Grandpa," says Elisa sensibly.

"Of course." The phantom smiles. "But my computer simulation is still active and has been storing data in various programs since my death. Including programs about you."

"About me?" Elisa has a sudden urge to laugh. "There are programs about me? A good fairy sleeping all these years in the labyrinths of electronic circuits, and waking up just when she's needed? What a nice story."

"You're very tired," says the phantom. Elisa realizes, with a start, that a small faceless robot is standing in front of her. The play of light on the smooth, polished surface seems to give it the merest hint of humanity. The robot offers her a small round tray with a large glass full of white liquid.

"Drink your milk; time to go to sleep."

Elisa recognizes the childhood phrase and the affectionate but firm tone. She does what Grandpa tells her, and takes the glass, drinks, and follows the robot into the house. After a few steps she yawns, and by the time she's stretched out in the familiar little bedroom (how everything has shrunk!) she's already asleep.

"I've got some pictures to show you, Elisa," says the quiet voice of Desprats. It's the next day, the next morning. She acquiesces silently. A dozen immobile faces light up all at once on as many screens: Serena, Marquande de Styx, Desprats, and others—men and women whom Elisa isn't sure she recognizes. There are figures in the corner of each picture, giving the date and hour.

"It was always at night," remarked the voice, "and you were always with Paul." The images began to shift slowly until they became Elisa, asleep. "You'll notice the particular luminosity at the moment of metamorphosis." Other infrared images appear. "Evidently, the metabolism must speed up considerably. There's an enormous expenditure of energy, just as there is when your cells regenerate. Even the speed is similar. The process seems to be linked to Paul, however."

Somewhere in the murky depths where Elisa is floating, something quivers.

"I've got something else to show you, Elisa," says the simulated voice. All the screens but one go blank. A pink blob appears—a gently undulating, simmering, bubbling blob that becomes a small girl silently howling. Silently, because there is no sound with the screen image.

Now there is sound: Elisa is screaming, her hands gripping the arms of her chair. Something pricks her; she feels it from a great distance. Everything turns grey, white, fades into nothing.

The movement accelerates, the sighs become groans, cries, then subside. Paul raises himself on his elbows, and a head of black hair appears beneath him. The eyes open: very green. Long black tresses fan out on the sheet. Smile. The head turns slightly to the left and the green eyes look straight into the camera. The smile remains for a moment, then fades. Slow motion: the eyes stare, the eyebrows rise, the mouth gapes.

The stupefied expression is masked for a moment by Paul's questioning face turning toward the camera. It reappears in slower motion, frame by frame. At first there is the slightest blurring of features, as though they were a reflection in water, rippled by a faint breath of wind. Then details sharpen: the eyes change shape and colour as the skin alters in texture; the contours of the nose, cheekbones and chin seem to melt; the black tresses lighten to ash brown, and the hair itself moves on the sheet, shrinking and curling as though it had a life of its own.

Elisa stops the picture and looks at herself on the screen. Then she reverses it to the face with the green eyes and stops it again to contemplate Serena. She sweeps her hand across the keyboard to erase it all.

Nevertheless she can't get away from the actual *fact*: the City doesn't record hallucinations or dreams.

"You had the nightmare dozens of times when you were little, after my death." Desprats' simulated voice, calm, warm, and attentive, is a remarkable feat of programming. "Each time you metamorphosed back very quickly as you woke. Paul wasn't there when you woke up; he used to get there afterward."

When Elisa can speak without shaking, she says, "Yes, in the dream. He was in the dream. The thing— the pink thing. You were all like that. And I went up to him, and he—absorbed me."

"Ah," said the voice, "but *you* weren't dreaming about Serena and the others; it must have been him. There is a constant factor, however: the dream."

"I'd completely forgotten . . ." she quavers, unable to control her voice.

"Totally suppressed it, Elisa?"

She frowns and folds her arms. "All right, so it was a dream. But why? How? And why didn't Paul realize what was happening?"

"In the first place, he never thought such a thing possible. You didn't either, did you? I think that's why you never metamorphosed when you were awake. Your unconscious knows you can do it, but your conscious self doesn't."

"But now I do!" She sticks her hand out. "Change! See, nothing happens."

The indulgent little laugh is really well simulated. "You *know* it, but you don't *believe* it, not in your heart of hearts. As a matter of fact, when you regenerate some part of your anatomy, it's your body that does the work. You don't consciously tell it how to treat this or that deviation from the norm. Your body knows what the norm is and re-establishes it automatically. All you consciously do is accelerate the process. That's not the case here. It isn't a question of your health. It's a complete metamorphosis of your body's basic material. I'm convinced it's not just skin deep, not even muscle deep. You must be able to change completely, if the result of your dream is anything to judge by. From skin right down to—to blood type. Why should there be a limit, apart from body mass, and even that—."

Elisa looks at her hands, the texture of her skin, the lines on her palms, her fingertips. Unique. Totally personal. But the lines on your hands change with time. Something to do with the body's development, aging, and physical trauma. And with other things, according to the palmists. Life spelled out in the lines of your hand: past, present, and future! The past, all right. But the future? Why not? The short term physical future, at any rate. The body is always sending signals about its condition, warnings about what's in store. That's how good doctors always made their diagnoses, after all.

But to metamorphose totally?

"You've thought about it a lot, haven't you?" says Elisa. She's aware of speaking to the simulated Desprats as though he were real, but what else can she do? It's a real person in the sense that a human being stores data, sets up correlations, draws conclusions, and responds to stimuli.

"Yes," says the voice calmly.

"But why wasn't Paul aware of any of this?"

"I told you. He never thought such a thing possible. He's very limited in his way, you know, and inflexibly pragmatic. A regenerative faculty like yours is nothing but a normal bodily function infinitely multiplied. He has no problem accepting that. He's always been a little uncomfortable with the idea that you have some control over the speed of regeneration. He never made a point of speed, has he? But the idea that your mind can change the form and composition of your body—well, he simply never *thought* of it."

"But the pictures on the screen!"

"He didn't see them."

"But it's impossible that he never happened to—." Elisa frowns. "What you mean is, you arranged things so he'd never see them."

"My prime directive is to protect you," replies the simulated Desprats, ignoring her last remark.

"But why do you think. . . ." Elisa falls silent, remembering Paul's experiments on the first mutants, discovered by chance.

It's not the same thing! Anyway, he didn't make them suffer. He just—he just killed them.

But not her! He wouldn't harm her!

She rises and strides up and down the room, hugging herself miserably. She can metamorphose when she's dreaming. Big deal. Or when Paul is dreaming beside her. But she has no recollection of sharing his dreams. Is her sense of empathy ten times stronger when she's asleep? Almost telepathic?

She sits down again. It's better to ask the program questions than to stay trapped in this circle of pain. "Why did I see these particular images? And why didn't it happen every time I slept?"

"There must be some particular emotional stimulus that triggers the process," says the tranquil voice. "Some point in common between the recurring dream about the pink blob and Paul's dreams. The pink blob was a nightmare for you, wasn't it?"

"Oh, yes," murmurs Elisa. Then she sees what the program is getting at: Paul's dreams were nightmares, too. Serena, Marquande—Marquande who died mad, Serena who killed herself. Yes, she can see that they might be nightmares. But what about the others, people she didn't even know?

Ah, they died, too.

Death.

But Paul dreamt about *making love* with Serena!

A terrible anxiety grips Elisa. Death. Love. The pink blob that smiled at her, mouthless, the thing that drew her toward it, armless. Death? Was that what triggered the metamorphosis? The idea of death? Or the fear of death? To change. To become—to become death, the dead one. But then the dead one is alive. Death is alive.

She doesn't want to die. She doesn't!

"Elisa?" queries the program in a distant voice. Elisa opens her eyes. The little robot is beside her, holding a pressure hypodermic. She wants to scream, but instead finds herself floating away, far away from her body. Everything goes black.

Elisa's naked body is stretched on a high, narrow table. Small, colored patches mark the attached electrodes. The surrounding walls are filled with screens, some showing the body from different angles while others give analyses or computer simulations, based on a variety of sensor data. Still others show graphs of vital functions. The body appears to be completely relaxed, breathing deeply. The brain scan shows deep-trance theta waves. A voice, the voice of Richard Desprats, is slowly counting: "eight ... nine ... ten."

Screens go wild as the body on the table gradually changes. Skin darkens, muscles and flesh ripple, move, and melt to form a lithe, slender frame: the body of an adolescent. Facial features alter, taking on strong negroid traits, and the hair is now short, black, and frizzy.

The screens settle down.

"I'm going to count backwards, now," says the voice. "When I get to zero, you will resume your original form. Ten ... nine ... eight ... seven...."

At zero the screens go wild again, while the body slowly reverts to its original form.

⟡ 19 ⟡

"YOU MUST LEAVE, ELISA."

"I know." Elisa stares at the garden from the bench around the communication-tree. This is the tenth time the program has said it, the tenth time she's answered the same thing. She feels paralysed. Leave the City.

"He'll find you in the end, Elisa. He's almost as good as I am at manipulating computers. We can't run the risk."

"And what if he does find me? Is he going to chop

me into little pieces?" she snaps, in a feeble attempt at sarcasm.

"He's mad, Elisa, irreversibly—and you know it. You saw Marquande. His symptoms are the same."

"We could have tried to do something for him," she muttters doggedly.

"To gain him a few months of misery? Elisa, you've got to leave him be. He's a threat to us. We don't even know exactly what he's up to right now, except by inference. You've got to leave."

"I'm not ready," she protests, without conviction.

"You're as ready as you'll ever be. Anyway, I'll be with you."

"But what if they don't trust you?"

"They've forgotten about ommachs. They've forgotten about the Cities ages ago."

Then why is he so determined to stop the Cities? He's explained it thoroughly, this project of stopping Cities that are still operative, with or generally without humans, on the land mass that once was Europe. All over the world, too. Even Cities where access is now underwater, or buried beneath glaciers or tons of earth. Stop them all, one after another, and then return to stop *this* City, the last City. By that time Paul will be dead. The City will be empty, totally empty, as in the old story. And the little girl will halt the City before leaving it forever.

"The Cities are a relic of the past." The program has said it over and over. "A buried past, Elisa, a disastrous past. The humans now living don't need them. They have the right to live their own lives, to decide their own fate. Some legacies can be crushing."

How convinced the simulated voice sounds! This is Richard Desprats' spiritual testament, carefully constructed to bridge the intervening span of time. He made sure of that, just as he made sure Elisa would be there to receive it. He foresaw it all. She can see how he went about it. She was a pawn in his game. Just as she was a pawn in Sybil's complex game with (or against?) Paul. Just as in Paul's strategy against what?

Phantoms? Himself? A pawn, anyway. She had been a pawn.

But how can she be sure? Desprats loved her. So did Sybil, perhaps, in her curious way. So did Paul. How can she unravel intricate relationships woven long before she was born, threads of love, jealousy, hate, vengeance—twisted so long ago by beings mostly unknown to her? Oh, she's seen them on the screens. The city recorded their images, all right, but what about the life behind the images, the *motives* for their actions? She begins to understand what Paul meant when he said there were many different motives for each human action. Does one understand one's own motives? How can one understand those of others when they're only seen from the outside? That's what she'd seen: the reflection of reflections. How naive she was to think it would be simple. All she can do at the moment is imagine what their relationships might have been, build a series of possible stories, all beginning with, "What if . . . ?"

She must keep in mind that all the motives coexisted, that Desprats had loved and was or is using her, just as Sybil and Paul used and loved her, perhaps? But she'd let herself be used, she'd been more than willing to participate in the experiments with Paul on her regenerative capacities. And hadn't she considered manipulating Paul *for his own good*? Because she loved him? Is it still manipulation when it's mutual, conscious, and willing? Love. . . .

But she knows nothing of love! Not much, at any rate. She's a child who has barely lived. Twenty-two years, but in a contrived universe. And what would she learn on the Outside? To lie.

She looks at her hands, the texture of the skin, the lines marking the palm, the fingertips. *Unique. Absolutely personal.* She's still not accustomed to seeing the solid wrists and long, bony fingers. She touches the cheekbones, the unfamiliar line of nose and jaw. She'll have to shave again. Disbelief threatens once more. How can she keep this male body when she knows, really *knows*, that she's a woman? That she's—*herself,* dammit! But post-hypnotic suggestion has taken control of part of her mind, ordering millions of chemical reactions, millions of exchanges among millions of cells, without her being aware. Her beard grows, her voice deepens, and her testicles manufacture sperm.

Hesitantly, she touches her penis. When will she get used to this strange lump between her thighs? When, if ever, will her brain make the adjustment? When will that hypothetical and diffuse image of self that is the ego take it all in? Who knows: perhaps she'll get so accustomed to it that her penis will actually work. She considers the idea, amused yet repelled. Make love again? Make love with women? She can't imagine it right now. Later. When she's used to her maleness. She's got to get used to it.

She won't though, if she doesn't leave the City. The program has said so repeatedly. Perhaps it's true. She must go Outside. People who meet her on the Outside will see a young man called Hanse. What better body, what better name than that of the unknown man who disappeared so long ago, and who is her forebear? She has even imitated his strangely white hair.

"There's continual interaction, even when you're awake," the program has said. "Remember how your body changed during the three weeks you were away from Paul? He always liked voluptuous women, and when the two of you were together that's how you were. But when you were apart, you resumed your own somatotype: slender and rather bony. Among people who think of you as a man and know nothing about you, the post-hypnotic suggestion will certainly be reinforced. You'll be perfectly safe."

They'll see a man and I'll be a man. The image of a man. But I won't be a man!

I can be anyone. I am everyone, no one.

A shudder of rebellion runs through her. Why not remain Elisa? Why agree to this lie? Then she shrugs. She'd soon regret such honesty, Outside. There are too many women Outside; they don't count for much where men rule, the rare men, the precious agents of reproduction. At best, women are harem slaves; at worst, kitchen skivies or slave-labourers in fields and mines. Outside, even with a man to accompany her, a woman wouldn't get far. Even if that man were in fact a powerful machine, able to defend her against all comers. In any case, it would give away everything, and the existence of the Cities must remain a secret—until there is no secret because there are no Cities.

And afterward? But afterward is too far away. Elisa won't, can't envisage it.

"You must go." The ommach is standing in front of her. He doesn't look like Richard Desprats. They didn't want to risk Paul recognizing him on the screens if, by chance, he was doing a routine check of the Outside. But it's Desprats' voice that speaks. For all practical purposes, this *is* Desprats. He doesn't force her decision. He just keeps saying the same thing, waiting for her to make up her mind.

When she rises to follow him, she hardly knows why. But she is leaving. Now.

PART

2

⚡ 1 ⚡

THE RUINS HAD ONCE BEEN A LARGE TOWN, or section of a city. Toward the northeast the street grid is discernible, with the occasional building still standing. But to the south and west, the city gives way to fields reclaimed from the rubble—rubble used for endless rebuilding.

In the centre of a cleared zone an imposing mass rises: three identical towers, thirty storeys high and apparently intact, arranged in a triangle to form what must have been a residential or commercial complex. The upper windows are missing, but there is a hint of humanity in the faint glimmer of light on the ground and first floors of one of the buildings.

Curious. It's summer, after all. People ought to be outside, taking advantage of the first cool twilight air. Instead, they're all inside—humans and animals. There isn't a single lookout around, not even a dog.

Just like the other community, says Elisa, automatically subvocalizing. Ostrer doesn't answer right away. He's probing the thickening night, all sensors alert.

No ommachs here, at any rate, he says, *and no spy sensors.*

Very odd, that concentration of ommachs that alerted them some fifty kilometers to the west, in the other community: Malverde. And since then, nothing. Just a few hamlets with houses shut tight. And now this Vietelli community: a large one, although unfortified, and not a single ommach.

In the dim light, the space between the buildings looks as though it had been a plaza and occasionally their feet hit paving stones. Now, it's a storage area. The ommach, guided by infrared vision, threads his way through the labyrinth of haystacks, woodpiles, machinery and other material. Elisa follows. At last they reach the inhabited buildings and skirt the walls in search of an entrance. The enormous plate-glass expanses of an earlier era have been reduced to the occasional high, narrow window, fitted with an opaque glazing that reveals nothing. Even this is masked by heavy curtains that filter the interior light to a vague wash of colour.

Finally they hit upon an entry. The glass doors have long since been replaced by metal panels reinforced with planks, inset with a small but massive wooden door that echoes dully beneath Ostrer's knock.

No answer. Elisa goes to the nearest window and bangs on the glass. The faint light goes out instantly. "We're travellers," Elisa calls out, pressing close to the glass. "Just two of us!" She has an idea. "You're not going to leave us outside in the dark!" she pleads in a frightened voice.

After a moment a noise is heard behind the door, and a small peephole opens, letting out a stream of light. "Come over here," says a male voice. Elisa obeys, blinking as she moves into the light. The fear behind the door is so strong she can sense it, despite the barrier of heavy wood. The man peering through the peep-hole sees a tall young man with white hair. Will he turn them away as possible mutants? It's happened before, mostly in the Northeast. And this is the last community before the Badlands. *Before the City.*

"Pass your hand through the wicket," says the voice. Elisa does, then yanks it back with a sharp cry. The forefinger has a cut in it.

Ah, says Ostrer, *I told you this would come in handy some day.* He sticks his hand through the wicket when ordered, yanks it back and shows the synthetic blood to the watchers behind the door.

Much confabulation. Finally locks turn, bars slide back, and the door opens a few inches. Elisa and Ostrer slip through, and the heavy panel immediately shuts behind them with a dull thud.

You do the talking as usual, says Ostrer, *I'll see to the sensors.*

Elisa looks around. The air is hot and stifling, the atmosphere of fear palpable. A dozen men armed with guns, axes, and long knives are ranged in a half circle around the door. Farther back are other men, about twenty of them, also bristling with weapons and equally terrified.

This is the lobby of what must have been a spacious mall. Behind the men Elisa can see a raised square surrounded by concrete benches studded with blue mosaics: an old fountain, now empty except for sand and children's toys, old bits of wood and discoloured plastic, balls, and cans.

A squat, redheaded man with a surly expression steps forward. The movement focuses Elisa's attention. "Who are you and where do you come from?" It's the man who opened the wicket.

"I am Hanse," answers Elisa, deliberately sucking her forefinger. "He's Ostrer. We're travellers from the south. We'd like a place to sleep and something to eat, and perhaps some provisions. We're strong, we'll work in exchange."

The man studies them, his suspicions not quite allayed, but says at last, awkwardly, "I'm Carlo Vietelli. Welcome."

The men look relieved and lower their weapons.

"Some are not so welcome," says Elisa significantly. The man nods. "Forgive this reception. The Vietelli

clan is known for its hospitality and we usually live up
to our reputation."

He says no more, but signals them to follow. Most
of the men are already spread out, guarding the entrances to the large corridors leading into the lobby.
About a dozen remain, and these fall into step with
the travellers.

After consuming the food and drink brought by a
young blond girl, eyes wide with curiosity, Elisa wipes
her mouth with the back of her hand and takes stock
of her surroundings. There are a good fifty people
crowded into the big, windowless room. It must be a
kind of common room for the clan. No doubt there
are just as many people outside, getting a minute by
minute description from those who can see what's going on. She notices the usual mass of female faces—
young and old, toddlers included—behind the dozen
men who must be the actual Vietelli family. The other
men must belong to families who have declared their
allegiance to the Vietellis. There seem to be quite a
few of them. The Vietellis are worthy of their trust: a
brave if naive family. Their door is thick, but it
wouldn't stand up to a determined ommach for long.

"Have you come from very far south?" asks Carlo
Vietelli. As a matter of course he speaks to Ostrer, the
elder of the two travellers.

"My friend doesn't talk," says Elisa in that special
tone that is generally understood, although reactions
vary. Here, Ostrer's apparent affliction is regarded
sympathetically. People aren't thrown into agonies of
exorcism like they are farther to the north or east.
There is the usual pause, long enough for Vietelli to
readjust his ideas about who is the dominant figure of
the pair. He turns to Hanse. "We don't often have
travellers here."

"We've come from the coast. We'd heard about
Captain Malverde and wanted to visit him. He's a
great leader. They say even the Emperor Kurtess is
afraid of him."

The hall buzzes with reaction, most of it negative, a mixture of hate and fear.

"He is a great leader," agrees Vietelli, looking away.

"He's managed to get a lot of men together in his army," says Elisa at a venture. The crowd greets this in silence, confirming her initial impression: hate, terror, revulsion. "You must be blessed by the Lord in this region," she goes on, attentive now. "You have so many boys."

Vietelli looks around the room, and Elisa does the same. Women, teenagers, little girls—they must have woken up the children. There are more of them now, but not many males. Same as everywhere else.

"We bless the Lord for the lives he has given us," replies Vietelli. The crowd responds with a murmured, "Amen."

Not very talkative. Should I be more direct?

Let them get used to us. You don't want to put them off.

"Maybe we can talk about it tomorrow," says Elisa. "We've had a long journey."

The same blond girl who served their meal takes them to a room. It's empty except for two mattresses. She shows them the washroom and bids them goodnight.

Hey, Ostrer, they've got a sink and toilet that work!

How nice for you, Elisa.

Elisa has trouble falling asleep. The pervasive tension in the community keeps her on edge. Most people are still awake. After an hour she gives up trying.

There's a guard posted outside our door, Ostrer warns her, *and none of the men are asleep.*

Have you placed the sensors already? I didn't even see you doing it this time. He must have been quick. The conversation with Vietelli after supper didn't last long.

I'm getting better all the time.

Elisa grins and goes out, surprising the guard. He gives her an embarrassed smile.

"It's too hot," she says. "Do you always keep the windows closed in summer?"

The man wipes his forehead with his arm. He's hot, too; the curly hair is damp with sweat. He's fairly young, barely thirty—a taller version of Carlo Vietelli, almost as tall as Elisa, in fact. Humans on the Outside have shrunk in stature. If Elisa were a woman he'd be disconcerted by her height; but she's Hanse, a man of about the same age. After a brief pause he relaxes.

"No."

Elisa shows him her index finger. She's been careful not to heal the cut. "It's something to do with this, I suppose," she says conspiratorially. With any luck he'll think she knows more than she really does. He nods, shaken by violent emotions—hate and despair.

"They kidnapped two women yesterday."

"Malverde's men?"

"*Men!* Malverde's demons!" He spits on the ground.

"Couldn't you stop them?" This should be an insult, but it passes unnoticed.

"We never see them do it."

"How do you know it's Malverde, then?"

"Everyone knows he's made a pact with the devil!" *Do you hear that, Ostrer?*

"He gives them our women in exchange for demons to man his army."

Ostrer, are you sure there's no City near here that we don't know about?

There's only one, Elisa.

But Paul must be dead!

Ask him what the Devil does with the women.

Elisa tries to keep her nerves from getting the better of her. After a short silence she inquires, "The women—do they ever come back?"

The young man doesn't answer immediately. He swallows. "We find—bodies," he says hoarsely. "Some of them are completely—." His voice breaks and he lowers his head.

An icy terror grips Elisa. She stares at the young Vietelli, heedless of Ostrer's disembodied voice in the implant behind her ear. After more than four years? Paul, alive?

"Can't you do something?" she asks when she can finally speak.

The young man shrugs and wipes his brow again.

"By the time we knew what was happening, it was too late. Malverde had too many men in his army. Those who tried to attack—well, we soon realized it was hopeless."

"How long has this been going on?"

"About three years. A bit more."

Yes, says Ostrer, *that fits in with Malverde's rise to power. Somebody is messing with the political and military set-up in the Southeast.*

But it doesn't mean it's Paul!

Elisa, we've stopped all the Cities but one.

Maybe there are some you don't know about!

Ostrer doesn't bother to answer.

"Have you spoken to Malverde?"

"Those who tried got straight denials and had their taxes raised. In the end, people became resigned to it. We've got order in the region now, and the Badlands tribes don't dare attack. Trade is good. Some people would prefer to have demons do the fighting. If it costs a few women, well—."

Yes, obviously. What are a few women among so many? But the young man rubs the breech of his gun, his eyes distant, his teeth clenched.

"You don't seem to agree," says Elisa, watching him. His evident grief confirms her impression.

"They took one of my wives," he mutters.

A wife he loved, maybe. Relations between men and women are sometimes still harmonious in this region. Not like in the North and East.

"We care for our women," he says defiantly.

"I understand," says Elisa, moved by his sorrow.

There is a pause. He looks at her curiously, his grief apparently forgotten. "Do you have a home some-place?"

Ah yes. No women. Men without women. Of course. It would be a scandal, even a crime in some places. Here, it's peculiar, at least.

"Yes," Elisa lies. But after all it's not really a lie.

"And have you left your wives?"

There it is. Elisa assumes a suitably mournful expression and is silent for a moment. Then, not looking at the young man, she says, "Neither I nor my friend can produce children. We were born too near the Badlands." Even that's got a grain of truth in it; the City lies beneath a region where the mutation rate is still high.

"Oh!" says the young man, drawing back a little. After a moment he shakes his head and mutters, "Cursed be the Abominations." He is full of sympathy.

Elisa completes the familiar litany: "Cursed be the Abominations that have brought desolation upon humanity." He seems to recognize it. These people apparently share the myths of the southerners. *The Devil hath spread his empire beneath the Earth, and one day Hell did burst forth. The Abominations walked upon the Earth and led men into temptation, and in his wrath God made the Earth rise up against the Devil and his idolaters, burying Hell once more beneath the lava of the volcanoes and the waters of the sea, and striking men from generation unto generation.* . . . And why not? It's an interpretation that rather mixes up responsibilities and gets the facts backwards: the Abominations were for the most part created by humans, with the Cities beneath the earth being the final manifestation—but why not? At least it gives some meaning to this awful mess, and puts humanity once more under the eye of a God who knows what He's doing.

And Paul is the Devil.

To get away from this thought, Elisa asks, "And what are the priests doing about it?"

"They pray, and so do we," replies the young man. Perhaps he feels his tone is less than respectful since he quickly adds, "The Lord will help us in the end. The Devil can't win."

Tell him that the Lord is going to help them sooner than he thinks, Elisa.

She frowns, then puts a hand on the young man's shoulder. "The Lord is going to help you, and sooner than you think." He stares at her in wonder. She looks him in the eye, unsmiling, then turns and starts to walk away.

"Hey, wait!" She turns around. He looks perplexed.

"My—my name is Manilo, Manilo Vietelli," he says finally. That certainly isn't what he wanted to say. Elisa nods and goes back to the bedroom.

Was it really necessary to do the messenger of God act again?

These people are deeply religious, Elisa. They will help us more willingly, should the need arise, if they think we have friends in high places.

Why don't we just tell them the truth?

Because they haven't got the conceptual framework to comprehend it. It would take far too long to explain. We've got to act quickly, don't you think?

But to feed their superstitions—.

Wouldn't you rather have them superstitious but alive?

She can't counter that. She takes off her short tunic and lies down on her back, her head supported by her arms. Her nostrils dilate involuntary at her male smell. She sweated profusely in the common room to be like everyone else and not attract attention. She wipes a finger across her chest: the hair is sticky. A good bath, tomorrow! She rests her hands on the mattress, well away from her body, and tries to relax, controlling her skin temperature once more.

We'll have to make a reconnaissance flight to the City tomorrow, says Ostrer.

With the moddex? He'll spot us.

Perhaps he's already spotted us.

When they flew over Malverde's fortress the other night—but perhaps there weren't any sensors aimed at the sky. He's met with no resistance for over three years, so why would he suspect anything? Maybe he's even forgotten they exist. Still, they'll have to assume the worst: he hasn't forgotten them. He's watching for them to reappear. He knows they've stopped the other Cities, and he's spotted them. And he's mad. Totally, irreversibly mad. (Raving mad. No need for guesswork in this regard. "The bodies are found totally—." Manilo hadn't finished his sentence, but his meaning was clear.)

Elisa sits up and rests her chin on her knees, watching Ostrer as he sits in the gloom, communicating with the moddex. His body sheds a faint light. Paul, still alive. But in what state? She had hoped that the return to the City would be sad but peaceful. After more than four years she had finally come to think of Paul with a sort of calm—by imagining him dead; he *was* dead. And now he was alive, living a life more dreadful than any death. Alive and murderous. They had to stop him, not just the City, but—.

Kill him? Elisa's whole body shrinks from the idea, but she forces herself to consider the facts. *He certainly won't be stopped without a struggle. He'll defend himself, try to kill us. If he's spotted us, he'll try to get rid of us as quickly as possible.*

"Ostrer—."

Don't talk, says Ostrer. For a moment she's confused. Is Ostrer telepathic? Then she realizes that she has subvocalized her thoughts, and that the implant in her throat transmitted her fears to Ostrer.

It'll be interesting to see what he does if he has spotted us, the ommach continues. *If he doesn't do anything that doesn't mean he hasn't seen us. We've got to know how far he's prepared to go, and what stage he's at, exactly. According to the moddex's computations he should be almost in the terminal phase. He appears to have survived for a remarkably long time. Even now he only has passing fits of homicidal mania. The rest of the time his paranoia must be pretty well under control, since he's able to function well enough to carry out complex operations, as with Malverde.*

The voice transmitted by the sensor behind Elisa's ear is almost atonal, and Elisa listens with a kind of horror to Ostrer's detached remarks. Actually, she isn't sure he'd express any emotion, even if he were speaking aloud. The simulation programmed by Desprats seems inhuman to her each time she comes into contact with real humans.

Why should he burden himself with emotions, anyway? He's programmed not to show any unless it's necessary. And it isn't necessary now. Collecting data, evaluating it, drawing conclusions, and acting: that's what's necessary.

You'll go alone, tomorrow, says Ostrer. *No use putting all our eggs in one basket.*

He makes no further comment, but stretches out on his mattress to wait. The faint light that he emits dims a little, becoming almost subliminal. Elisa thinks, absently, that he's like a real person sleeping. But inside she has no real sense of him.

Tomorrow she'll make a reconnaissance flight. That's sensible. In the moddex she'll be able to defend herself if the City attacks (if *Paul* attacks). And Ostrer can defend himself, and possibly the Vietellis, if an attack is launched against the community. It wouldn't work the other way round. She's the one who'll go to see whether the City has been programmed to fend off undesirable visitors.

She lies down, but the tight knot of anxiety holds her sleepless. She knows she can control her body, eradicate this emotion, but it would be a lie. No, she must accept the anxiety, study the reason for it, admit she's human. She's done it hundreds of times in the last four years.

2

ON HER RETURN FROM THE CITY, ELISA LEAVES the moddex in the waters of the small lake to the west of the community and goes back to Vietelli on foot. As she gets near she frowns in puzzlement: a large number of people are gathered on the plaza. The closer she gets, the stronger she senses their collective grief, enveloping them like a dense fog shot through with flashes of terror.

Ostrer?

But she's still out of range for subvocal contact. She hurries on. There must be a hundred people there— the whole community. Stifled sobs reach her, but no words. She'd been in touch with Ostrer via moddex during her reconnaissance trip to the City environs.

Everything had been fine. The walk from the lake had taken a little less than an hour. What had happened in that time?

Ostrer.

They found the women. You saw nothing in your walk back from the lake?

No. Dead?

Very.

She races toward the assembled people. Heads turn. The crowd parts silently to let her through. On the ground is a large, dark patch, a blanket covering two formless shapes. She lifts the blanket and looks at two red things. For a moment she feels nothing: they don't look like anything she can relate to. Then a violent wave of nausea shakes her. Instinctively she tries to control it. She's back in the blood-splattered little room, looking at the thing in the chair—and on the floor, over the computer banks, the screens, everywhere. "Sybil," she says aloud.

Elisa, get a grip on yourself! says Ostrer, touching her shoulder.

This time she controls her body, cutting the adrenalin, slowing the heartbeat, and secreting calming substances. Then she drops the blanket back over the mutilated bodies and stands up. She lets her voice retain its icy tone. "When? Who brought them back?"

Half an hour ago, Ostrer begins, but Carlo Vietelli's voice is heard, muffled and dejected.

"Half an hour ago. Nearly everyone was working in the fields. There were only a dozen women around. They say one minute there was nothing, and the next—*this.*"

Drugged, very likely, says Ostrer. *I was in the fields too, but the sensors stopped working for at least twenty minutes. I urged Vietelli to go back, but we lost time arguing and we were over fifteeen minutes from the community. They were killed and mutilated on the spot. It took less than twenty minutes.*

Elisa looks at the onlookers' stricken faces and sees Manilo in the front. His eyes are closed, and his mouth contorts silently. There are two women kneeling beside him and a third standing, the young one who looked after Elisa and Ostrer the night before. She's staring at the blood-soaked blanket. Her face is very pale, but she feels neither terror nor horror. An intense fury, almost maniacal, possesses her. She lifts her eyes as though she can feel Elisa watching her.

It's Elisa who looks away, feeling the same fury now, having tasted it in this girl.

He knows we're here, doesn't he?

The timing and the nature of the act show it. It's a message. I think it's time to perform a miracle, Elisa.

She doesn't argue, but instantly begins changing her skin density to reflect the light radiating from Ostrer. Someone notices, gives a stifled cry, and points. All eyes are fixed on Elisa and Ostrer as they begin to shine.

"This is the last evil deed. These are the last sacrificial lambs. God has heard your prayers and has sent us to you." She can sense the hope in the people around them, can feel their response to her utter conviction. The fact that this is a hoax doesn't matter.

The moddex is here, says Ostrer. It hovers above the plaza, glowing silently, a second sun whose light is not blinding.

"The Lord has stretched forth his hand over you," says Elisa, pointing to the sky. The crowd gasps as they raise their eyes and drop to their knees before the spreading pool of blood.

But one does not look heavenward. Elisa meets her intense gaze. The rage is still there, mingled with a fierce adoration that is almost as terrifying.

The baptism of blood, says Ostrer's disembodied voice. *They'll need it. We'll have to create a diversion with Malverde while we take care of the City.*

It takes several hours to explain what they expect of the Vietellis without destroying the credibility of their supernatural persona: the Vietellis must go into battle against Malverde. Finally, as night falls, couriers are sent to neighbouring villages with instructions to deliver their messages well away from the spy-sensors.

Ostrer gives them little boxes that will light up if sensors are close by. "Invisible demons," Elisa calls them. The messengers take them readily: The boxes are sacred amulets; no further explanation is necessary.

Paul knows we're here in any event, Elisa says to herself. He knows we're up to something, and probably has a pretty good idea what it is: to stop the City. But he doesn't know when or how. The false clues that the messengers have been told to let fall around the sensors may give him the idea that we're planning a massive attack on the City with suicide troops. Maybe he's just mad enough to think that we'd do such a senseless thing.

But Paul's degree of madness and his periods of lucidity are unknown factors in the equation. The moddex computer considers the Malverde diversion as the strategy most likely to succeed. Speed is of the essence. Malverde's ommachs are controlled from the City. It's crucial that Elisa and Ostrer stop the City soon enough to prevent a total massacre.

Elisa turns over on her mattress. Half these people are headed for certain death. They know it as well as she does, but their faith supports them, and their desire for vengeance. She has nothing to support her, nothing but the truth: God and the Devil, who are to do battle on the morrow, are men. Not even that. God is the electronic memory of a man, implanted in a machine.

And what about her—Elisa? At least she's human, even if she isn't really a man or a woman. But she has no illusions. Her role is a very minor one. Ostrer-Desprats would have carried out his objective without her. Anyway, stopping the Cities wasn't her idea, even though it's become her mission, even though now, for the last City, she has to agree with Desprats.

The same question keeps recurring as they near their final goal: *what about afterward?* Will she live on the Outside? That would mean perpetuating a lie: there's no question of being a woman Outside. The way they are treated has filled her with horror, disgust and rage these last four years. But what could she do?

She cannot be a woman outside. And she's really not at ease in her man's body.

We've got visitors, says Ostrer.

A few seconds later there is a knock at the door. It's the intense young woman, Judith, Manilo's youngest wife. Her blond hair swings loose; she wears a light tunic and carries a bottle and three wine glasses.

Elisa watches her, perplexed, registering the young woman's confused emotions. She finds them difficult to identify: there is the strong undercurrent of anger that seems to be Judith's keynote, but the rest. . . . Elisa knows she can't really capture the more subtle shades of feeling, only raw emotions common to all: pleasure, pain, desire, fear, love, and hate. But the fine tuning, the things that show the real and personal nature of such emotions, these are beyond her. Judith seems especially on edge, at any rate, despite her calm manner.

"What's wrong, Judith?" asks Elisa gently.

Without answering, the young woman sets the glasses on the floor and begins to fill them.

"Your heart is troubled," Elisa insists.

Judith gives a start and looks at Elisa. The flickering candlelight makes her pupils huge, her eyes dark in the small, delicately pointed face with its high forehead and full lips. The expression is what ages her. She says nothing, but holds out a glass to Elisa, who takes it mechanically. She hands another to Ostrer, who also takes it after a slight hesitation. "To those who are about to die." Judith raises her glass and drinks it in one gulp, then fixes her eyes on Elisa. "A lot of people will die tomorrow, won't they?" Is it a reproach?

"It's the fate of men," mutters Elisa unwillingly.

"Not only *men*!" Judith sits on her heels, her hands clenched. "We can die, too!" Her voice is low and ardent. "And we can kill. Tell them to let us fight tomorrow—those of us who want to. If we're strong enough to haul stones and work in the fields, we're strong enough to fight!"

It's an idea, says Ostrer. *The more there are, the better.*

Axes and knives against sophisticated killing machines!

You've no problem about men fighting. They're worth a lot more to the community than women. And if women are willing—well, why not?

Elisa stares at Ostrer, speechless. She downs her drink, her cheeks burning. What's the matter with her? Ostrer is absolutely right. It's the size of the attacking force that will make tomorrow's diversion look authentic. But to send *women* into the fray . . . Well, what's so extraordinary about that? Judith is right, too. They can certainly fight with as much energy as the men, if not as skillfully. They can be massacred just as easily as men!

Is that why she's so shocked by the idea? But she finds it quite all right for men. What's the matter? Is she so used to her male body that she's beginning to *think* like men on the Outside? The Vietellis never thought of sending women; it goes against all their traditions. Caught up in their attitudes and group prejudices, it never occurred to her either. And yet their reasoning is false. Ostrer is the one who's right. Women are expendable. Not men.

But perhaps the men of the Outside aren't motivated purely by chivalry. One doesn't arm slaves: it might give them ideas. After all, women are inferior here, despite being better treated than in the North or the West where they're blamed for the Decline, for consorting with Satan. God has not punished men, but women, women and their progeny. When the time of the Abominations came, says the New Bible, they wanted to take advantage of it, to change their bodies, to be like men. God rightly punished them by condemning them to produce an abundance of daughters—slaves as they themselves became slaves. The anti-feminist reaction was especially violent in the North and West, where the first wholesale killings took place as Europe fell into social and economic decay.

When Elisa compares the present myth with its distant origin, she finds both irrelevant. In front of her is a real person, a person who experiences their actual consequences every day. Granted, it's a little different here in the South. But, although conditions are less harsh, women here live the same as women in the North. They are slaves. "I said to my *handmaid*, 'Come,' and she came, 'Go.' and she went," says the New Bible. There are no menservants in this newest Scripture. The very word has vanished. Women are objects to be manipulated at will.

Elisa hears herself say, "That's a good idea."

Send more people to be killed? Yes, if that's what they want. Let them choose their fate at least once, those who can! Who knows? Perhaps this shared baptism of blood may change things between men and women.

Judith straightens up, her eyes shining. "You'll tell them?"

"Tomorrow morning. And we'll send a message to the other communities."

Yes. It will be an incontrovertible command of the Lord.

The girl remains motionless for a moment, then takes the bottle and fills the empty glasses again.

"Do you want to die, Judith?" asks Elisa softly after they drink. This time there's no toast.

"No." The girl looks at her empty glass. "But if we don't attack Malverde and his demons, I'll die anyway. I'd rather go down fighting, not—not like Carla or Sentina." She shudders, no longer keyed up, looking very young, very vulnerable.

Elisa touches her shoulder, and the contact produces a strange sensation, strange but not unpleasant.

"You won't die, Judith."

How does she know? Suddenly she's passionate about protecting this girl's life. She won't let her fight against Malverde. She'll take Judith in the moddex. Elisa caresses the girl's shoulder, overcome by a searing pity that brings tears to her eyes. So young, so beautiful. She *is* beautiful, with her hair falling smoothly, her throat and shoulders bared by the loose-fitting tunic.

Ostrer gets up.

"Where are you going, Ostrer?"

I'm leaving you alone, he says.

What's the matter with him? Nothing. He's a machine with a machine's brain. Judith is very real, very human. Elisa feels her hand on Judith's shoulder and withdraws it, trying to get control of herself. Her throat is dry, her muscles taut. What's the matter with her?

An erection.

She bursts out laughing, completely caught off guard. Now. An erection now. Accustomed to a man's world, eh? Oh, yes! She's furious, and turns away brusquely.

Judith stares at her. "Manilo says it's all right," she murmurs. "It's the custom with travellers."

Of course. And it broadens the genetic base.

"Manilo didn't tell you I couldn't have children?" Elisa laughs again. "Anyway, both of you have forgotten that I'm not a man." It's too funny. For the first time she's telling the absolute truth and Judith is going to understand something totally different.

"Oh yes, you are men," says Judith with a stubborn little smile.

"We have the shape of men," Elisa begins, assuming a more solemn tone and feeling somewhat relieved to slip back into her role as divine messenger.

"No. There's no God," says Judith defiantly, but she doesn't look as confident as she sounds. Elisa studies her but says nothing, vaguely amused and at the same time disquieted by Judith's physical presence. Her erection hasn't diminished, despite her efforts. She ought to be worried: her body is almost out of control. But she can't think of anything but Judith.

"See? If there was a God I'd be struck by lightning right now," says Judith, but she sounds a little relieved. Elisa can't help laughing. How old is this kid? Eighteen? Twenty? Not even that. She wants to fight the Devil and doesn't believe in God. The girl's got nerve.

The girl is very attractive.

Judith smiles and raises her hand to touch Elisa's cheek. "There is no God," she murmurs again. "And you're no messenger. You're both men, and Malverde's demons are men, too, of course, but they have powers and weapons we don't understand, that's all. You must have, too, if you think you can destroy the source of Evil, as you say you can. But you're men, all of you." Her face hardens again. "Men—some of them are beasts," she says through clenched teeth. "Not all. They're better here. Manilo is. But where I come from they're beasts. I'm from the North. Beasts. You're going to the North tomorrow, aren't you? The source of Evil is in the North. I was sure of it."

As Judith talks she strokes Elisa's face, neck, and shoulders beneath the loosely laced tunic. Elisa takes her hands, trying at the same time to control her erection.

"You've had too much to drink, Judith." She tries to speak softly, but her voice is uncontrollably hoarse.

"No. I want it. Manilo approves, but even if he didn't, I'd have come to you anyway." She continues stroking Elisa with one hand while the other finishes unlacing the tunic. "I want it, just once with someone I've chosen myself. You, Hanse. Because you're good, because you're brave. Because you're handsome. And because I'm not *obliged* to."

Elisa takes Judith by the shoulders. Her head is spinning and she's still vaguely concerned about her lack of control. But what matters is Judith, her nearness, her passion.

"You're sure you want this?"

"Yes."

"I'm—I'm not sterile, Judith." Is that what she meant to say? Elisa doesn't know any more.

"So much the better. Maybe I'll have a child that I want as well."

Elisa touches the ardent face held up to her. This is what she wants herself: to be the mistress of her fate. She can't refuse Judith the same thing. And she wants it—she wants it. She wants to make love. Now, after all this time? But she's ready for it, it's normal. After all, it's herself, Elisa underneath; what does it matter which sex expresses her desire? She doesn't want to control that desire, perhaps *can't*. Dreamily, she registers a thrill of fear and excitement. So strange—or is it simply that this is the first time in four years that she's wanted a lover?

Is this how a man's body reacts to desire? It isn't so very different, though she can't quite remember what it was like before. Perhaps she doesn't want to remember. Her hand slides down Judith's neck and shoulder, resting briefly on a breast. So this is what it's like to touch a woman's body, another woman's body. Judith puts her arm around Elisa's neck and kisses her. Slightly shocked, Elisa doesn't respond at first, then, as an intense, almost painful urge rises from her groin to her throat, she clasps Judith in her arms.

Her breathing becomes laboured and she feels like crying. This woman's body is so strange yet so familiar, so warm against hers, so *alive*, and we're the same, you and I—I understand you so well and I love you and it doesn't matter if my body isn't really my body, what does it mean isn't my body, it's *me* it's me Elisa Hanse no matter what body I am myself and pleasure is pleasure that's all love is love oh you're so soft and smooth and firm and your mouth your breath your tongue moving alive your body alive and against you on you I'm moving alive alive in you hot hot soft and open mouth oh yes devour me come take me come cover me come come *Oh Paul!*

⚡ 3 ⚡

IN HER DREAM SHE WAKES BUT CANNOT MOVE. Her body is paralyzed, her lids refuse to open. Someone's there, a presence, close by. She tells herself she's awake, that no one's there, that she's going to move now, now; but now recedes indefinitely and she can't make herself move, she's too afraid. She listens, hoping her ears will assure her no one's there. But that infinitely subtle change in the sibilant silence, isn't that a faint noise, a breath, a SOMEONE?

She wakes. And there *is* someone.

Judith?

Someone else. A familiar presence, and yet one that she doesn't quite recognize. But she knows what her body feels, though her brain doesn't understand: she's afraid.

"Wake up, Elisa."

Paul.

Paul, leaning against the wall beside the closed door, dressed like one of the men in the community. He hasn't changed. Blond hair, smooth face, grey-blue eyes still intense, and the smile, the head slightly tilted, slightly turned so that his eyes look sideways. He's holding something in his hands, kneading it absent-mindedly as he watches Elisa.

Ostrer! Ostrer?

"Hello, Elisa," says Paul. His voice relaxed, agreeable, almost mischievous, as though he's just played a good joke on her. And he's speaking Litali, the language of the community.

Elisa sits up slowly, casting a look at Judith. The girl is seated on the mattress, her back against the wall, hands on thighs and eyes staring.

"Don't worry about her. She can see and hear, but she won't move until I allow her to."

Drugged? Hypnotized? Elisa sits against the wall too, feeling the cold, rough surface on her back. She looks at Paul. The room is so small that she can see him clearly in the light from the window, even though he's leaning against the opposite wall. Was he always that tall? He's a little thinner. Unchanged and even younger! How is it possible? And calm. He's so calm. There's no immediate danger. Ostrer. *Ostrer?* Nothing. What's Paul done to him, and how?

"Elisa, Elisa. What a crazy thing to go off like that. There's so much work. I need you, you know."

Should she keep him talking, waiting for someone to—.

"I thought you weren't planning to help the Outside so soon." Good, his voice is calm and measured. "And not in this way."

"Only madmen never change their minds, as you well know," he continues, winking at her. "The sooner they're unified, the sooner they'll evolve. Kurtess in the Northeast, Malverde in the South, and soon there'll be a single leader in the West and Southwest as well. Then the strongest will take over. Did you know that social engineering is as fascinating as genetic manipulation? Desprats should have kept it up." He drops the bantering tone. "But that's not what I need you for, Elisa, as I'm sure you're aware. To begin with, I need *you*, period." He smiles tenderly, with a genuine tenderness that she can feel. "And then, Elisa, you have such a wonderful faculty! Total metamorphosis! There are extraordinary things to be done. Do you realize that this is the answer to our insoluble problem? The ratio of the sexes? The problem has vanished, Elisa. Your very existence has annihilated it. Woman, man—there's no problem now. People will become what they want. Amazing!"

He can't control his enthusiasm. She watches him, her throat constricted.

"No," he says, "all those little adventures with barbarians were in fact nothing more than a pastime. I was waiting for you to come back, Elisa. You're the important one from every angle."

It's true. She can feel that's what he thinks. She can't be wrong: it's too clear. Is he lucid right now, or is he more mad than ever? He's talking as though nothing has happened, as though they were going to walk out of here arm in arm. Elisa tries to control her desperate terror.

"What have you done with Ostrer?" she asks once she can speak evenly.

"Desprats? Oh, nothing. I've got portable scramblers, now. You'd be amazed at all the gadgets I've had to develop to work on these barbarians." He tips his chin at Judith. "Instant hypnosis, for example. A little cocktail of light hallucinogens."

"And the others?"

"Sleeping the sleep of the righteous. Doubly so, actually, as they're about to fight the Holy War." He laughs. "The Lord's messengers! I had a good laugh over that, Elisa. I haven't found anything so funny for a long time. You know, things have been a little too easy in the last four years. But the past three days, with you around—well, you two make adversaries worthy of me!"

"This isn't a game, Paul!" Elisa hears herself protesting weakly.

He stops kneading the thing in his hands and eyes her maliciously, his head still cocked. "Is that so? Come now, Elisa, you don't really want to send these people to get themselves killed at Malverde? That's carrying it a bit far, isn't it? In any case, it's Desprats' idea. He doesn't give a damn about people's well-being; he's got only one idea, and sticks to it. You know very well they don't stand a chance against ommachs. It would be a needless slaughter."

A needless slaughter. *He's* saying *that?* Elisa swallows the retort that springs to her lips; she tucks her knees against her chest and measures the distance between her and Paul. Would she have time to overpower him? He's really very tall, but he's unarmed. Unless that thing he's holding—she must keep calm. Chat him up. Keep talking, and while they're conversing get up naturally and walk over to him.

"What are you holding?" she asks as innocently as possible. Paul is taken a little aback by this change of subject. He looks at his hands, smiles, and holds up the object for Elisa to see. It's a mask of synthetic flesh, complete with curly red hair and brown eyes. At first Elisa doesn't recognize the contorted and empty face. Then the resemblance strikes her: Manilo.

"When?" she asks after a pause, controlling her nausea.

Paul laughs, obviously pleased. "Being in contact with Desprats has certainly made you laconic, Elisa. No superfluous phrases, no beating about the bush: you get right to the point. When. Yesterday afternoon as he came back from the great council of war."

He watches her attentively, smiling, letting her draw the obvious conclusions. After killing the two young women, he'd hidden. He knows their entire plan of attack. And Manilo—.

"Actually, I'd only thought of coming to get you during the night. But when this girl came in hot for her male, I couldn't resist. I sent her to you with a little aphrodisiac. It was too funny. Interesting as well." His eyes travel over Elisa's body. "Really fascinating. A man's body in perfect working order. I never saw you function in quite that way. Impressive. Fascinating."

Are there sensors here? Ostrer didn't spot them! She clenches her teeth, blushing furiously.

Paul, unaware of her anger, goes on. "You'll have a lot to tell me. You know both, shall we say, 'sides of the coin'? I'm sure you understand me much better now. Ah, Elisa, we're going to do great things together! But there's lots of time to talk about that in the City."

He moves away from the wall and she gets up. Now? But he looks at her hard, frowning. "You're not cross because I've put a spoke in your little wheel, are you? You agree with me that this attack on Malverde is an absurd idea?" He seems genuinely concerned. Suddenly his face clears. "What a fool I am! You wanted to see how women would fight! It would be interesting, I admit. I always thought women were more bloody-minded than men. Nearly two centuries of slavery, but it hasn't made much difference, not even in these women, if this one's eloquence of last night is anything to go by." He begins pensively kneading the resilient flesh of the mask again, frowning slightly. "Of course, in one sense it might be useful. Teach them a lesson. The dissidents would be subdued for a long time to come. And there'd be fewer women."

Elisa listens incredulously, feeling desperate. In the last few seconds, something troubled has slipped into Paul's benevolent calm.

"Fewer women," he repeats, twisting the mask. "That's their problem on the Outside. Too many women. They don't eliminate enough at birth. And here in the South, they're too well treated. They survive too long. The longer they live, the more girls they bear; it's a vicious circle. They should be eliminated before they have children. Not all, obviously, but on a regular basis. Like weeds."

He seems taller, more massive, and the heavy cloud of emotion that surrounds him is thicker than ever. Elisa has forgotten her plan of jumping him, and stares at him with mingled horror and disbelief. Is that his madness: misogyny? And he kills women on the pretext of solving the problem of female overpopulation? Perhaps he doesn't even know *how* he kills them.

All at once she understands what Ostrer meant when he said repeatedly, "Paul is dead, Elisa." Yes, Paul, the Paul she loved, is dead—if he ever existed. And when she discovered what he really was, she wanted to believe that he was merely a more complex Paul, more *real* than the one she'd known before. But even that unknown whom she believed herself ready to love and help, even *he* has vanished. There are traces, flotsam after a shipwreck. Filled with heart-breaking pity, Elisa murmurs, "Oh Paul. . . ."

He looks at her, takes a deep breath, and manages a little smile of excuse. "Yes, it's a considerable problem, considerable. But with you it will soon be resolved, won't it? Come on, we've got to get out of here before these people wake up. But you're right, we'll let them fight. I'll program the ommachs so that the toll isn't too disastrous, all the same. We'll reprogram your Ostrer, and he'll lead the attack. With women. He'll be carrying out God's orders, right? Come on."

She doesn't budge. The indecision is agony. What should she do? Try to reason with him? No, it wouldn't work. Follow him and wait for a suitable moment to attack him?

He looks at her, frowning. "Well, what is it?"

"I'd like to understand how you managed it," she says, aware how feeble this sounds.

"Later!" Paul snaps. He takes her by the arm, and she can't help recoiling. He stares at her, incredulous at first, and then suspicious. "You don't want to come?" he says through clenched teeth. "So I've been wrong about you? Have you understood nothing? Are you still the same sentimental little idiot you were four years ago? I'd hoped that after all this time you'd have grown up! I let you go, I delayed my research for you, and that's how you thank me"

Elisa shrinks before his rage, terrified. Her back is to the wall. Paul's emotions are like a searing whirlwind, an immense but silent storm.

"Maybe it's that body of yours that's giving you ideas. But it doesn't mean a thing, Elisa. Not a thing. You can't even metamorphose when you want to. You've got to have a whole circus: trance, post-hypnotic suggestion. You're not in control, Elisa, not at all. You've got to come with me and learn to really control this faculty, just as I taught you to control regeneration. That's it, isn't it? You think you're a man, a master?" His rage becomes more apparent. "Hanse, eh? You've got a cock, you fuck women, and you think you're a big shot! Well, it means nothing, Elisa, nothing. You aren't in control. But what you can't do by yourself, I can make you do, like *that!*"

He snaps his fingers.

Elisa's body gives a jolt, like a dreamer falling. She feels a prickling, a crawling—no, a violent heat and the impression of—of dribbling. The sensation is so strong, so intense, that she looks at her thighs, horrified, thinking she must have lost control of her bladder.

Her penis is slowly shrinking. The hair on her chest is disappearing, and breasts are thrusting forward. Throughout her body, muscles and flesh are reorganizing their tissue—arms, back, thighs, belly. . . .

With stupified horror, she tries to stop the process, to control this body that is changing despite her will, but she can't, she can't! It won't obey her! There must be some explanation, there must! She touches her altered body; she recognizes it, but it's impossible! Paul snapped his fingers and she changed. It's impossible.

"Yes, it's you, Elisa," says the genial voice of Paul. "That's what you really are; you know it and I know it. Who knows it better than I do? I made you, Elisa, and I made you a woman. You are mine. You can only be mine, be with me. You see: I turn up, and right away you're yourself again."

She touches herself again, looks at her body, the full breasts, the rounded thighs. *This isn't me.* This is the other Elisa, Paul's Elisa; *but it isn't me.*

Her panic subsides. There must be some explanation. How long has he been here? How long was she asleep? That sensation of paralysis when she woke up . . . Drugged. He must have drugged her, must have found her data hidden by Desprats. And he must have conditioned her, as Desprats did, to respond to *his* signal. Her mind, while sleeping, sought the image Paul had always made of her: the voluptuous body, hyper-feminine, almost maternal. Yes, that's it. But it isn't her. It never was. And he's not talking to her, but to a phantom Elisa that is dead. A loving Elisa, naive, ever ready to be manipulated by Paul, an Elisa that would clearly have been cowed by this demonstration of his power over her. He doesn't know she no longer exists.

"I hoped it wouldn't come to this," he says with an expression of real regret. "I'm disappointed, very disappointed, Elisa. You don't really believe I'd let that old fool Desprats destroy my City and thwart my plans, do you? Destroy the other Cities, yes; it suited my book. But did you think I'd let you play around on the Outside indefinitely? It's time to grow up, Elisa. You are my project—an important part of my project, at least. I've spent years and years perfecting you. And now, just when you're revealing marvellous possibilities, do you think I'm going to let you go? I thought you had a more developed sense of responsibility."

He seems more pained than genuinely angry, and shakes his head reproachfully. "Elisa, Elisa! What were you thinking of? Living among these savages in your male form? Do you really think there's a place for you there? You'd be bored to tears in a few weeks. You're not made for that kind of life. Your tastes are more—more refined, you know it perfectly well. Do you think you could hide your physical capabilities from them indefinitely? Your ability to regenerate? And you can't control your ability to metamorphose; sooner or later, perhaps in your sleep, you'll give yourself away. Then what? They'll think you're an Abomination, Elisa, and they'll kill you. You don't want to die, do you? But if you stay with these people, you surely will die."

Elisa shivers as she folds her arms across her naked breasts. She wants to believe that it's because he's touched a nerve: her obsession with *afterward*. But no, it's not that. It's because he's talking about death, Elisa—dying. And you don't want to die, do you?

Closing her eyes, she slumps against the wall. She hears Paul come closer, but has no strength to move, drained by the metamorphosis. He takes her arm gently and draws her upward. Her willpower has evaporated and she is so very tired. If she could only lie down and sleep, sleep. . . . She hears Paul's voice again, harsher this time, commanding, "Come, Judith."

Judith? She opens her eyes and sees that Judith has risen. Why Judith? Feebly, she resists the arm pulling her, mouthing faintly, "Why Judith?"

"Because you may have impregnated her," says Paul with a shrug, "and I want to see the result."

Judith? Turned into a laboratory animal? Anger swells in Elisa's chest. Revolt flares up, dispersing her confused exhaustion.

"Wait." She says. Then louder, "Wait!"

He gives her an irritated look. "What is it?"

Elisa listens to the forces rumbling within her. "I—I want to get dressed."

"Well, hurry up about it!"

She feels for her tunic, and her hand touches something cold—the empty bottle.

With one quick motion she smashes it, rising and turning as she leaps at Paul's throat. Something hot spurts onto her face and she recoils. Paul is staring at her, eyes bulging. "Elisa?" he gurgles, and crumples forward, falling on top of her. Instinctively she stretches out her arms to catch him, and the weight of his body brings her to her knees. Blood is gushing out of the open artery, and air whistles through the gaping trachea. Elisa's eyes are fixed on Paul's face: she has never seen an expression of such utter disbelief in her life.

After a moment she looks up. Judith is standing motionless, frozen where she was when Paul fell. There is blood on her face and breast. Elisa touches her own face and feels the sticky liquid. *Baptism of blood,* she thinks, and the thought reverberates: *baptism of blood, baptism of blood.* Something moves in her mind, forming itself into words and thoughts: *baptism, blood, battle, Malverde, battle, Ostrer, tomorrow, today, battle.*

She sloughs off the torpor, rises, and goes over to Judith. Only the staring eyes give any sign of life in the cataleptic face. What do they express? Terror, horror, rage? Judith has seen everything, heard everything. Paul spoke Litali expressly for Judith's benefit, just to twist the knife in the wound. And she is still Paul's prisoner, even though Paul is dead.

"Judith. It's me, Hanse. My body has changed, but it's me. He's dead, Judith; you're free."

No. It must be Paul's voice, Paul's command.

She goes over to the cadaver and forces herself to search the sodden clothing. Nothing. Wait: a little silver-coloured box with two lights. Is this the scrambler he was talking about? She finds a button and presses it. *Ostrer?*

What? Awake already?

Ostrer, come quickly!

She takes a blanket and tries to wipe the blood off Judith and herself. Ostrer enters just as she is about to cover Paul's body. He kneels beside it, touching the face lightly with his fingertips. He grabs hold of something and pulls, then stands up, holding Paul's face in his hands.

A mask.

Elisa is petrified with shock for a moment, then bends over the corpse. The face is ghastly pale, deeply wrinkled. The skull is nearly bald. She steps back and closes her eyes.

"When did you metamorphose?" It's Ostrer's voice, very gentle, very calm.

"He drugged me during the night. Suggestion—he snapped his fingers." She finds it difficult to speak, but Ostrer is satisfied. When she opens her eyes he is drawing the blanket over Paul. No, he's rolling Paul in the blanket. Slowly, haltingly, she begins to collect her thoughts. The others—they mustn't find Paul here.

She remembers why she called Ostrer. Judith. They've got to free Judith.

"He drugged Judith, too. She can't move. She's been conditioned. Can you imitate Paul's voice?"

Ostrer stands up and goes over to examine Judith. "No problem. All we have to do is tell her to forget everything she's seen and heard."

Judith saw everything, heard everything, but can she understand it all? It's better that she forget, better for her.

"Wait, Ostrer."

The ommach turns toward her. "Not for too long. Everybody will be awake soon."

What will happen if Judith remembers? What will she do? What will she think, now? What has she understood? Elisa approaches the girl, studying her carefully for any signs of captive emotion. Fear. Anger.

"What's the matter, Elisa? You can't mean to take this girl with us?"

Obviously he doesn't understand.

"Don't tell her to forget, Ostrer."

"She'll tell the others everything."

Elisa pauses, then speaks in Litali. "Tell her—tell her not to be afraid, even if she doesn't understand everything she saw. And tell her not to speak about it to the others unless she thinks they'll understand, too."

Judith is still staring at her. She hasn't moved. What do the eyes express? Astonishment? Joy? Elisa can't tell. But it's all she can do, all she'll agree to do to Judith.

The ommach remains quiet for a moment. What will she do if he refuses? She can't force him. Talk it over, perhaps. She waits, aware that she is depending on the programming of a machine by a man who's been dead for twenty years.

The ommach turns toward Judith. "Don't be afraid, even if you don't understand everything you've seen and heard," he says, using Paul's voice. "Only tell the others what they can understand. You are free."

Judith topples as Elisa jumps forward to catch her and lay her on the mattress.

"She's only fainted," says Ostrer. "We've got to decide what to do."

Elisa looks at him with some surprise. Hasn't he already decided?

"We've got to get to the City right away. Either we deprogram the Malverde ommachs without saying anything to the Vietelli people, and they go into battle as planned, or we come back and tell them that it is no longer necessary to fight. What do you want?"

Elisa gets up slowly. The ommach studies her attentively. She has to remind herself that this is a machine. Does he mean what she thinks he means? Is it possible that he's understood . . . that his program includes . . . ? Could Desprats have anticipated this eventuality? The machine is offering her a choice. A real choice? How can they explain to the Vietellis that there's no need to attack? Will they have to tell more lies? But if they let the Vietellis fight, that'll be another lie. They'll find ommachs that can't fight, and Malverde's troops in a state of terrified disarray, unlikely to put up an effective resistance. What will they think in that case? That God struck down the demons for them, as a reward for their faith and courage? Or will they realize the truth when they examine an ommach closely?

What truth? What will they understand?

What they can. What they want to. If they're fooled, they're fooling themselves.

Elisa considers Judith anxiously. Is this all she can do, all she can expect? A choice between two lies, and uncertainty whichever choice she makes? She looks at Ostrer again.

"Is it up to me to decide?"

He nods silently.

"I thought—I thought that you didn't want them to know we existed."

"Insofar as it's possible."

She studies his familiar, expressive features for a moment. It's ridiculous to think of him as a human being, but she can't help it. Just how much of Desprats has survived in the simulation? *Insofar as it's possible.* So there was a limit to how far he could program into the future? But it's certainly possible to lie to the Vietelli. It's possible to program all the Malverde ommachs to return to the City, for example. It was possible to tell Judith to forget everything, and he didn't do it. Of course, she noticed the change he made: *Only tell the others what they can understand.* It doesn't matter; he's left Judith's memory intact, left her the freedom to do with it what she will.

"Decide, Elisa. They're going to wake up soon."

"We'll deprogram the ommachs and say nothing. We won't come back."

The ommach nods, then seizes the corpse wrapped in its blanket and throws it over his shoulder. He goes out. Elisa looks at Judith one last time, then follows him.

$$\approx 4 \approx$$

ELISA WATCHES THE PLAINS AND HILLS SLIP by on the moddex screens, and great stretches of forest where ancient ruins are barely visible. A wave of dizziness washes over her; she waits a moment before checking her body. What if she could no longer control it? As she examines herself, her confidence returns along with the thousands of sensations and images that she's learned to associate with her inner workings. She's in control again, and the vertigo subsides. It doesn't disappear however. Of course, she's starving. It's the metamorphosis that's done it. She gets out the emergency rations.

When she feels better she tries to turn herself into Hanse again, but without much conviction. Useless, as she expected. Paul destroyed the post-hypnotic command that maintained her male appearance.

She tries not to remember her feeling of total helplessness, the horrible sense of being dispossessed of her body. Instead, she concentrates on the technical details. The transformation took place so easily, so quickly. And yet the first time she became Hanse it took half a day—more, in fact—and she had Desprats to help her, to keep her continually informed about the progress of the metamorphosis. Once she'd become accustomed to the male body and knew it from the inside out, she had less trouble conforming to the desired end product. But changing was never instantaneous. Paul was right. She isn't really in control. Not at all.

To distract her thoughts, she watches the screens. Here are the mountains already; in ten minutes they'll be at the City. Other images appear: the Vietelli community waking up. Ostrer is reconnoitering the sensors he left there, but Elisa sweeps the back of her hand across the controls. "Leave them alone."

Ostrer says nothing, and Elisa wonders what computations the machine is processing, what will be the final reaction of the Desprats simulation. She's never thought much about the machine, really. It's merely been the repository of Desprats' will. Desprats executioner of the Cities. Desprats had not only given Ostrer his voice, but a good many of his familiar mannerisms. She supposed that it was to set her at ease, to make her function more efficiently. She accepted it. But now she isn't so sure.

"Don't you want to know what's going on?" asks Ostrer at last.

Elisa shrugs. "It isn't difficult to imagine. They're waking up to find Manilo dead, they're coming to look for us and they'll find Judith."

And then? What will Judith say? Elisa can't really

imagine. Isn't this exactly why she wanted Judith to re-member the events she'd witnessed? Elisa will be con-tent not to know, satisfied that this is what gives Judith and the Vietellis comparative freedom.

What were you thinking, Judith, as Paul raved on? What were you *really* thinking? That it was a struggle among demons? Among humans? And that Ostrer and I went off in league with your enemies? Or did you think that this unknown man had robbed you of your one free act? Maybe he didn't rob you entirely, Judith. He sent you to make love with me, but perhaps that's what you really wanted. Paul could never have invented those reasons you gave me. You thought them up on your own, and they were as convincing as the aphrodisiac. I'd like to think so, anyway. And your desire to do battle, that was you, and you alone. Paul never ordered you to say those things. In any event, Judith, you've won. Paul is dead.

A child. Is it possible that I've given you a child? How hard it will be, how hard not to want to know! But that's how it's got to be. No more screens—ever. You and your people will be on your own. You'll all be free.

The moddex slows down. They're at the City al-ready. Ostrer is searching the central computer to de-activate the defense mechanisms set by Paul. Paul. They'll have to take care of him. He would have liked to be cremated. That's what he said to Serena, anyway. And after that? Stop the City.

And after that?

The moddex loses altitude as the camouflage on the landing pad peels away. Contact. The platform sinks slowly into the access bay. Decompression and decontamination systems activate as soon as they touch bottom. When the City is satisfied that they of-fer no threat, the airlock door opens.

Elisa goes first. Without looking back, she says to Ostrer, "Can we wait until tomorrow to—to do what there is to do?"

"Certainly," replies the ommach.

·   ·   ·

When Elisa wakes the next morning, she finds break-fast waiting for her in the little garden beside the communication-tree. The little robot is nowhere to be seen, but when she sits down the main screen lights up and Desprats' face appears. Of course he hasn't changed, but it gives Elisa an absurd thrill of pleasure to see him the same as ever. Then it occurs to her that she'll probably never see Ostrer again. It's foolish to feel sad, but unaccountably she does. She tries to turn her thoughts to other things by listening to Desprats' inconsequential patter: has she slept well, did she like the breakfast? Yes, she says, thinking all the while that this is very unlike Desprats. It comes as no surprise, and in fact is rather amusing, when he finally says, "Would you like me to take care of Paul?"

There is a long pause. "No," she replies. She pushes the synthetic jam around on her plate. "Is there some way to arrange for a cremation? It's what Paul always said he wanted, when he was young and talked about death with Serena."

"I'll see to it. Level Three. When you've finished there, come to the genetic lab."

She is on the point of asking, "Why there?" but stops herself. Why not there? It's perfectly adequate. After all, she started from there.

Elisa can't think of any words as Paul's coffin advances slowly toward the door of the cremation oven. She doesn't know whether one is supposed to say any-thing. She feels numb, her mind filled with disjointed images, fragments of memory, Paul's face, a smile, an expression of tenderness or anger, his forehead, a glimpsed profile. But she can't bring it all together, can't see him whole; already she's losing him. And yet all those images of him lie sleeping, intact, in the City's memory. They too will disappear when the City stops.

The City. Desprats is going to stop the City. Why does she think of him as *killing* it? That's absurd. She's tired, that's all. But the anguish won't go away; it has nothing to do with the corpse that topples into the

flames, blazes up, and vanishes. Elisa leaves the impro-
vised crematorium, walking slowly through the silent
City. Escalators and moving sidewalks start up as she
approaches, and stop once she's passed by. Corridors,
passages, halls, galleries—it all looks the same, as
though she had never left. Every chord of memory
cries out that she is at home, that she has *come home.*
With growing dismay, she tries to think of the landscape Outside, the placid rivers, the sunsets, the sea—.
No. Beautiful, but strange, foreign. Here she's truly at
home. Must she leave, never to return?

She presses on angrily. Has the City got her so conditioned that the very idea of leaving it forever fills
her with dread? Yet she must leave. And the City must
stop. The City is a potential danger for humans on the
Outside.

Is it really a threat, now that Paul has gone? *She* certainly won't use it against anyone! And as for
Desprats. . . . Well, in any case, it's all been decided, so
why worry? He's going to stop the City. And stop himself? Has he programmed another ommach, or the
same one, but with his own features, to accompany
her into the great world? What's the good of all these
idle questions, anyway? He's waiting for her in the genetic lab. She'll find out what he's decided when she
gets there.

At the last moment, just before she enters the lab, a
fear assails her: will there be embryos in the incubators? There aren't, but maybe Desprats has already dis-
posed of them. She'd rather not ask.

The lab looks the same as ever. When she enters,
Desprats' face appears on the main screen. He says
nothing. Neither does she. What is there to say? She
sits down in an armchair and examines her body without much interest. It's tired, but she decides to leave
things as they are. Whether physical or mental, this
lassitude is her true reaction. Why not let her body
speak to her?

After a while Desprats' voice speaks. "My work is
finished, Elisa."

She looks at him, not comprehending what she hears. The City is still functioning. Is he speaking about what still has to be done? She tries to shake off her torpor. "Where are we going afterward?"

"I don't know, Elisa. I stop here."

Is he going to leave her alone then? She has no trouble identifying her reaction to this news: fear. It would be better if it were something else—satisfaction, resignation, or nothing at all, mere indifference to a neutral fact. But why should she lie to herself? She's afraid. To be alone. Outside? But surely he's provided for her in some way?

"Where should I go?"

"I don't know, Elisa. It's up to you to decide. You can leave, or you can stay in the City."

"You aren't stopping the City?"

"I myself stop here. My work is finished. The rest is up to you."

Elisa is struck dumb for a moment, looking at the face that watches her from the screen. She manages to speak, finally.

"Why?"

"Because now you can decide."

The image vanishes and the screens go blank. Elisa sits forward in her chair after a moment, says, "But—." Then she calls, "Desprats?" Then, "Grandpa?" Nothing. She draws her chair close to the keyboard and types Desprats' code. Two words appear on the screen: PROGRAM DISCONTINUED. At the end of half an hour, after she's tried every possible code she can think of, she's forced to give up. There's not a trace of the program or programs that made up the pseudo-personality of Desprats in the City's memory banks.

Elisa throws herself back in her chair and runs her hands through her short, brown curls. The first shock is over. Now she's got to think. It's useless to keep looking at the main computer. All that does is put off the inevitable moment when she must face up to the last words of the vanished voice: *because now you can decide.* Now. She can decide. Because she has enough data to work with?

Stop the City or not. Well, wasn't she just regretting the fact that she had no say about it? But what is she supposed to decide? *Now you can decide.* He meant to say, "Now you know how to choose," didn't he? He must have arranged everything so that she'd decide in a certain way. He must have intended something. But what?

He didn't need her to stop the Cities. He got her out because she couldn't stay in the City with Paul. But would it have been so difficult for him to dispose of Paul? She doesn't think so, now. Maybe he didn't want to. *We've got to leave him alone,* he'd said when she suggested looking after Paul against his will.

Leave him alone. Like she is now left alone. Did Desprats engineer her liberation? Was everything that happened over the last four years an apprenticeship? She'd been put to the test and had emerged victorious from her confrontation with Paul.

She'd killed Paul.

Is *that* what Desprats' program was waiting for, before terminating? How did he really make use of her? But did he make use of her? He set up a program to watch over her. He helped her when she needed it, and he made her leave the City. When she discovered its existence after Sybil's death, with the unending horror of learning the truth about Paul, Sybil, and herself, she automatically thought that the computerized spirit of Desprats was also using her as a pawn in some battle—some game—of incomprehensible origin with Paul, or against Paul. Now she's no longer sure. If she has been Desprats' pawn, she has absolutely no idea what was at stake, or what her move should be at this point.

She left the City. She lived on the Outside. She killed Paul.

What if she hadn't killed Paul? If he'd defended himself and killed *her*? But she remembers the dumbfounded expression that Paul carried into death. While she lay sleeping, he could have conditioned her *not* to attack him, to follow him without question while he was at it. He didn't, though. It never occurred to him that she'd attack him. He thought she might resist, and that's why he gave her a demonstration of his power: metamorphosis on demand. But could Desprats foresee Paul's mental processes twenty years into the future? No, Desprats must have envisaged this situation first of all, as well as other possible scenarios. Paul would kill her after killing Sybil. Or before killing Sybil. Or Paul would take her back to the City by force. Or Paul would be the victor in the final confrontation. And what had Desprats meant to do in each case? She hasn't the slightest idea.

But that would mean that all the while she thought she was following the ommach, Desprats was following her. She thought she was being led. Was she in fact *free*? Watched but free? The program was following her evolution. Maybe it gave her a little nudge now and then, so she'd be ready when she met Paul once more.

Maybe. But maybe not. She'd never know.

Suddenly Elisa rises, illumined by a novel idea: *and when Desprats perfected this program, he didn't know exactly how she would evolve.* Just like her own ambivalence with Judith, yesterday. Is that it? Is that what brought the program to an end? Her reluctance to manipulate pawns on a chessboard?

Is it a fiction, this belief that when things go right it's because you've done what was necessary, this belief that if people react the way you want them to it's because you've engineered it? Like images on a screen that can be arranged as stories, but whose real, hidden life is forever inaccessible and can only be guessed? Like Paul, who easily manipulated an Elisa that no longer existed except in his mind; a Paul who was killed by an Elisa he'd never seen. A completely logical Paul, completely consistent in his machinations. Completely mad.

A fiction.

And yet you have to act, don't you? Choosing to act or not to act is immaterial: either way you're still doing *something*. She'd realized that yesterday, when she decided to let the Vietellis and their allies fight against Malverde without telling them the battle was no longer necessary. One can't escape action, and one can't escape the wish to exercise foresight. Foresee that it will snow, and build a shelter; foresee that the river may flood, and build a dike.

So there are other fictions: the belief that one can manipulate everything, and the belief that one can avoid manipulating others.

But to act, react, prepare for the future—to be human—*and to know that one can be wrong, that the best laid plans* . . . then it's no longer a fiction. Then it's a wager.

Desprats—why does she want to call him Grandpa again?—what wager did he make? And so far in advance? And with no chance of ever knowing the outcome? Was it supreme folly, this great generosity?

And what wager will *she* make?

PART

3

⚡ 1 ⚡

THE BABY DOESN'T CRY. ARMS AND LEGS MOVE in the water as though still floating in the amniotic fluid behind the transparent skin of the artificial womb. The baby is quiet. Every now and then its tiny fists contract and relax, and the baby smiles. Elisa finishes bathing it, wiping the rosy skin dry and laying the infant on the work table to examine its reflexes. Normal. EEG—fine.

She looks at the small plump body. The Project's first baby. Shouldn't there be a speech, some words of historic significance? "I baptize thee. . . ." No, not Adam. And anyway, it's a girl for the moment. "Abra." Elisa smiles, but realizes that she's moved.

The baby starts to wiggle. Elisa leans over with soothing noises, takes off her blouse, and holds the infant close. Before long it finds the breast and begins to suck. A thrill of pleasure shoots through Elisa. (So it's true?) She sits down while Halter deactivates the empty incubator and takes the bath away. She'll take the other two out of the incubators in a little while. All is well, all will be well. In six months, the other three.

She smiles wryly at the sucking infant. *Make the most of it, baby; you'll be the only one.*

Baby: the word is masculine in Franglei. Very inadequate in the circumstances, since they'll all be girls. At least until the first metamorphosis, six or seven years from now. There'll be thirty-six children at that point. What a brood! It's a good thing she's got ommachs to help her. Shouldn't they be called femmachs? No: she couldn't bring herself to use such a name for ommachs with female bodies, even though it would be the logical thing to do. But a more primitive logic insists that whatever they look like, robots are essentially male. *Conditioning, Elisa, conditioning.*

Absent-mindedly, she caresses the smooth, firm little body, aware her thoughts are wandering. She lets herself go, basking in the deep contentment radiating from the baby.

⚡ 2 ⚡

THE FIRE CRACKLES IN THE HUGE STOVE. OUTside it's snowing. Andra and Aria are in a corner arguing in their strange baby-talk. Nani and Halter haven't returned from the City yet. Elisa realizes she's worried but tries to shrug it off. What could happen to robots in a totally deserted area, no matter how bad the storm? The trouble is she's beginning to think of them as real people, in spite of herself. In her heart of hearts, she's not surprised. She programmed them to be like real people, after all; it was necessary for the children.

Elisa continues reading, but can't concentrate. Upstairs she can hear a child crying and the quiet voice of Lussi trying to calm it. Probably a nightmare. So young. Three years old and already they're having nightmares. (But without any metamorphoses, thank God.) The crying gets louder. She'll have to go up. The capacity for empathy that she shares with the children has its uses, but with eighteen toddlers it's no longer practical. She can't be with all of them all the time! Too bad the ommachs haven't got the same faculty.

And why not? It would only be a matter of fine-tuning. There must be a way of perfecting the ommachs' sensors so as to detect chemical changes linked to emotions, at least on contact to begin with, and later in close proximity.

She stares blindly at her book, frowning, as premises and theories surge through her brain. She'd have to go into the City herself again, use the learning machines. Those migraines. . . . But the knowledge of Desprats and Alghieri is still in the data banks, as is everything else.

Lussi's call draws her from her cogitations. The cries have become yells. Other babies have wakened and set up a contagious howling. With a sigh Elisa puts her book down and goes to calm the yelling baby. Probably Abra, as usual, and when she's quieted down she'll ask Elisa to tell her a story. Anything to get attention. And yet the others of her generation are generally placid, as placid as any toddler who is learning to walk. Abra, who learned to talk sooner, walk sooner, is also the most demanding.

Elisa smiles with slight irony as she climbs the stairs. Is it because she nursed Abra? Because there's a closer bond between them? A greater possessiveness on the part of the child? A good thing she didn't nurse the others! But she'd wanted to see what it was like; she hadn't thought about the possible consequences.

Feeling guilty, Elisa hurries up the stairs.

3

"ELISA! ELISA!"

The excited voice of Abra and the sound of running feet. Elisa wipes her flour-caked hands on her apron and turns toward the kitchen door just in time to see a red-faced Abra, hair all disheveled, burst in shouting, "Andra has fallen down. She's fallen!"

"Where, Abra?"

"Over by the cowds!"

"Cows," says Elisa automatically. "Did she hurt herself much?"

"Come and see, come and see," says Abra, tugging at her hand.

Elisa strides across the yard, Abra trotting by her side blurting out her version of what had happened. Once Elisa makes sense of it all, she realizes there isn't anything to be alarmed about and slows down. Andra had climbed up on the fence around the cow pasture and fallen, gashing her knee.

Near the fence, three small figures stand around Andra, who is still seated on the ground and whimpering as she holds her knee. When she sees Elisa her face contorts and she starts howling again. Elisa crouches down beside the child to check the wound. Underneath the coagulating blood only a scar remains, and already it's fading. "Why are you crying?" Elisa asks the child. "It isn't hurting any more."

The little girl suddenly stops crying, her big black eyes widening with a scandalized look. "I *fell*!"

"But your knee's all right, isn't it?"

The child looks at her knee, her expression puzzled and sulky. Elisa suppresses a smile.

"Andra's a baby," says Abra scornfully. Andra's mouth begins to quiver, and Elisa strokes the cheek still wet with tears.

"Andra is four, just like you, and she got a fright because she had a big fall. Why did you climb on the fence, Andra?"

"I didn't want to. Abra told me to!"

Elisa turns toward the culprit, but Abra is quick to protest in turn.

"We never get hurt anyhow; we get better right away!"

Elisa hits Abra's bare shoulder with her fist, and the

child sits down hard on her rump, so taken aback that she forgets to cry. "Doesn't that hurt? And when you fall down stairs or cut yourself like you did the other day, doesn't that hurt, too?"

Abra rubs her shoulder automatically, but Elisa knows there won't be a bruise.

"Just because you heal quickly doesn't mean you should do stupid things on purpose," Elisa continues severely. "This is the last time I'm going to say it, Abra, all right?"

The little girl hangs her head and murmurs, "All right."

FOR ONCE THE CHILDREN SEEM COMPLETELY subdued. They clutch the handrail on the moving sidewalk and stare. Only Abra is showing off, but she keeps a tight hold on Elisa's hand.

In the lab, Elisa lets the children explore their new environment, and when she feels they're accustomed to it she claps her hands. "All right everybody, listen!" The little girls sense her seriousness and quietly cluster around her. Elisa considers the six faces with shining eyes looking up at her. Brown eyes, blue, black. Hair dark brown or chestnut. Arella is smaller, Alana more dumpy; Abra has an oval face and high cheekbones, Andra frizzy hair and a pointed chin; Aria's mouth is big and full-lipped, her cheeks round, while Anicia is pale and thin, almost transparent in her fragility. Yes, they are certainly different from one another, these first-generation girls; and so are the ones that followed, as a matter of fact. Personalities are developing differently, too. Abra is more forward, Arella sunny-natured, Andra likes music, Anicia has a precocious head for figures. So why should she wonder about their individuality?

No doubt because she knows that she made them

out of the same basic material, and that the genetic combinations may be numerous, but not limitless. Or perhaps it's because her capacity for empathy underscores the children's similar emotions: curiosity, excitement, anxiety.

"You know why I've brought you here."

"To change us," chimes in Abra immediately.

"That's right. When we cut ourselves, we can stop the bleeding, and when we're sick, we can cure ourselves," she begins.

As she talks, she congratulates herself once again that no spontaneous metamorphosis has ever occurred; probably a sign that none of them has ever been traumatized the way she was. But it also means that metamorphosis is just one of the stories Elisa tells them to get them to sleep. She'll have to make it real for them.

"It's the same thing with changing," she says at the end of her explanation.

"But it takes much longer, and it's difficult," says Abra, who knows the stories well.

"Yes. As I told you, you can't change yourself whenever you want, the way you can take care of an injury. It's a lot more complicated. You've got to concentrate very, very hard. Later on you'll learn to do it without machines, but for the first time, the machines will help you."

Elisa fervently hopes that she won't have to make use of the City like this too often. There didn't seem to be any other way of doing it quickly and effectively the first time, but it was hard to resign herself to the necessity, just as it was hard to reconcile herself to what she must do now.

"But first of all I'm going to show you. I'm going to concentrate very hard, with the help of the machines, and when I've finished I'll be a man."

"Like Halter?" asks Aria.

"Halter isn't a man," retorts Abra loftily, "he's an ommach."

"But his body is a man's," interrupts Elisa, and Abra looks at the floor. "Go and sit in the chairs now, and watch carefully. You mustn't make any noise. All right?"

The little girls murmur obediently and sit down. Halter dims the lights. Elisa gets undressed and stretches out on the work table, puts on the head-phones, and begins the relaxation exercises. She feels the trance taking over: time slows, then stops. The change command reverberates in the middle of a sus-pended universe, and time begins to move forward once more. Elisa feels her body again, the strange-ness—and yet the familiarity—of Hanse's body after all this time, and the mixed feelings of the children: surprise, excitement, fear.

Who is afraid? She sits up. Abra? Abra's afraid?

Abra is the first to get up from her chair and plant herself in front of Elisa, scowling. Typical. Abra's the one who deliberately walks around in the dark be-cause she's afraid of it and because she's annoyed at being afraid. Elisa smiles with tender amusement. "You can touch. It's me, Abra."

The child lifts a hesitant hand and touches Elisa's chest. The other children advance rather timidly. Abra takes courage and fingers Elisa's penis. "Like Halter," she says. But she's still uncomfortable about it. "You're not going to stay like that?" she asks finally, and Elisa can clearly sense her protest.

"Oh no! It was just to show you," Elisa replies with a smile.

"Are we going to be like you?" queries Aria, puz-zled.

"No, you're too young. We can change our bodies, but there are limits." She takes the piece of wet clay that she brought for precisely this part of the demon-stration. "You can get bigger and fatter, but you can only use what you start with." As she talks, she models a body-shape, then makes it thinner and longer. "If you wanted to be as big as me, you'd get so thin, so-o-o thin," she goes on, stretching the thread-like figure until the clay falls apart, "that you'd break. I'm a grown-up, an adult woman, and therefore I can change into a man. You're little girls, so you can change into . . ." she lets her voice trail off, and of course it's Abra who finishes the sentence.

"Little boys!"

"But how are we going to do it?" demands Aria.

"You're going to sit down in the chairs, first of all. Then I'll give you something to make you sleep, except you won't really be asleep, you'll be able to see the screens and watch how your body changes, inside and outside. That'll help you change properly."

She explains the principle of biofeedback again. The children go back to their chairs and obediently swallow the pill she hands out. Only Abra looks at the pill in her open hand and makes a face.

"But you're going to stay here?"

"All the time, Abra. I'm the one who's going to tell you how to change."

The brown eyes stare at her as though looking for Elisa behind the mask of Hanse. "Do you like little boys better than little girls?"

Elisa smiles. "Little boy or little girl, it will always be *you*, Abra, just as the others will always be Arella, Andra, and Aria. You're *you*, no matter what body you're in."

Abra sniffs and swallows the pill.

Now the lab is very quiet; the control screens show the children's brain waves approaching deep trance. Elisa bends forward to the microphone that will transmit her voice to each of the children through the headphones in the chairs. "You are going to open your eyes and look at the screens, in front of you. . . ."

⚡ 5 ⚡

OUTSIDE, THE DISPUTE IS TURNING INTO A quarrel. "We're the ones who decide, anyhow!" shouts Ari's angry voice. "Why you?" retorts Brunie. "Because we're boys!" states Abram.

WHAT?

Elisa is outside in a bound and the children turn toward her in unison. There are about a dozen girls—the five and six year-olds—and three boys. Anders is there too. They all feel her anger and remain silent. Elisa looks at each in turn. This has got to stop right away!

"What's going on here?"

"Abram always wants to boss everything with Ari!" protests one of the littlest (is it Carla? Yes). Elisa turns toward the accused.

"And why would they settle everything by themselves?"

Several voices clamour in reply. "He says it's because they're boys!"

"Boy or girl, that doesn't change anything," says Elisa distinctly, frowning. She lets the silence stretch out so that all the children get a clear message: she's very cross. "You're all going to be boys when you're seven, anyway."

Abram stares, incredulous. "They're going to be boys too? Everybody?"

She should have told them earlier. Now she understands. They thought it a special favour, or Abram persuaded them that it was. In a way, it's not as serious as she imagined. Abram doesn't think he's better than the others because he's a boy, but because Elisa must consider the first-generation children superior. Why would she have enabled them to change, otherwise?

"Yes, everybody," Elisa says less severely, and on an impulse adds, "And everybody will change back into girls, too."

That wasn't her original plan, but in view of developments it might be a good idea. They won't get too attached to their male bodies. Alternating would be better. Every, say, two years. Until the final metamorphosis. Then, when they become boys for good, they won't forget their female experience. She should have thought of it before. They'll be better equipped to change things somewhat on the Outside; they'll find it easier to empathize with women.

Abram looks dissatisfied. *You'll have to get used to it,*

my boy. Still, beneath the sulking she can feel how hurt he is. She ruffles his hair and smiles. "You know, Abram, you're a very pretty girl, too." Then she becomes serious again. "Girl or boy, it's the same thing. If the others don't want to do something, leave them be. You don't like it when people make you do things against your will, do you Abram?"

Mm-m. Taking a bit of a risk there. But Abram is too disconcerted to think of applying this remark to orders given by Elisa or the ommachs. He sniffs and rubs his nose. "No-o-o."

"But why do we have to change?" asks Carla a little plaintively.

Elisa squats down and places her hands on the child's shoulders. "I've already explained, Carla. When you're grown up you'll go Outside."

"There aren't enough boys Outside," interrupts Abram copying Elisa's patient tone, eager to regain approval. "That's why we'll all be boys when we leave."

"But why do we have to go?" Carla persists.

"So that people on the Outside will become like us," replies Abram peremptorily, then condescends to explain. "So that they won't bleed any more and can cure themselves when they're sick, and change when they want to."

Elisa watches the childrens' reactions. At first they were a little hesitant, but Abram's version, and especially his authoritative tone, seems to have won them over better than more technical explanations.

"But what's the Outside like?" persists Carla. Elisa senses that the questions are becoming an unconscious game, and she leaves it to the boys to tell the little girls what they've understood—or made up—on the basis of the books she's given them. Later on, when the girls have read the books for themselves, they'll sort out the truth from fantasy. Come to think of it, why couldn't the City produce picture books about the Outside? She could give them to the children when they are two or three years old. She must tell Halter to see about it.

When she feels the game has gone on long enough,

she claps her hands and calls, "Get ready for supper, children!"

The group breaks up, grumbling a little. The youngest go back to the waiting ommachs, and the seven and eight-year-olds follow Elisa home. She watches them file by as they go to wash their hands in the kitchen. This is the root of the problem: she's kept the first two generations with her. She knows them better individually than all the others. Now that there are—how many? forty-eight?—yes, forty-eight, and the community is turning into a village, she can't possibly know them all as well as the older children. There'll have to be alternating there, too, to avoid creating an elite group that always lives with her. All the children need to be in contact with her. Ommachs can't replace a human being completely, even with their artificial empathy. They're able to receive, but not to give. Of course, the children have their peer group as well as their older siblings, but they need regular adult contact.

"Elisa, Elisa," whines Bertie, "Bella put soap in my eye on purpose!"

Elisa listens to Lussi's voice trying to pacify the rising strife, but as is often the case, the ommach can't manage to restore peace. She heaves a sigh and goes into the kitchen. Ommachs are adults, but she, Elisa, is the only human being, and well the children know it, even if they treat the ommachs like real people. The children need a *mother*, or someone who behaves like a mother even if she isn't called by that name.

As she walks into the kitchen amid the noise and splashing, she imagines with horrified amusement what it would be like if all this brood called her "Mama."

Come to think of it, they could just as well call her "Papa."

⚡ 6 ⚡

"WHY DON'T WE USE THE CITY'S SCREENS?"

Around the table there is suddenly silence. No one looks at Abra, and Elisa realizes that no one is looking at her, either. She takes a deep breath. The question was bound to come up sooner or later. And of course it was Abra who asked it.

"Because it isn't necessary," says Elisa calmly. "You have the books in the library. They were made by the City from its documents." (This was the only time she'd departed from her policy toward the City, since the time she'd gone in to train the children in their first metamorphosis. Would she live to regret it?)

Abra looks around the table at the other members of the children's council. She appears to gain silent encouragement from them, because she goes on. "But they show the Outside the way it was over twenty years ago. We don't know what it's like now."

"Anyway," remarks Bertram, "you generation-A kids aren't going Outside for another six years."

Andra leaps to Abra's defence. "But we'll have to know what it's like in seven years from now, obviously."

"You'll know," says Elisa, and everyone looks at her, even the representatives of the youngest, who don't understand what it's about but have felt the dissension in the air. "The only way to find out will be to get first-hand information. Not through you, of course."

"Through the ommachs!" exclaims Carla.

Elisa smiles at her. "That's it: through the ommachs."

"That's going to take time," says Bruno, "what with the trips, gathering data—."

"Ommachs can get around pretty fast when no one's looking," says Elisa. "And you'll only be going Outside on this continent. You won't need to know what's happening in the rest of the world. A year will be enough, in my opinion."

"One year," says Bruno meditatively in the ensuing silence. "But then we'll still have to digest all the information."

"Nothing to it," says Elisa. "As the ommachs gather information they'll transmit it directly to the City, and it will be printed out for you as it comes in."

"But in that case the books will have to be continually updated once we've begun to leave," says Carla in her treble voice. "The E generation will leave five years after the A, and a lot of things could happen Outside in that time."

"And what's more," says Andra, taking the argument a step further, "quite apart from major events we'll need to know about the changing details of everyday life, perhaps more than anything else."

Leaning back in her chair, Elisa listens to them, satisfied. The discussion is following the lines she hoped it would. But when a brief silence occurs, Abra raises her voice again.

"I don't understand why we'd waste all that time when we could start right now: we could look at the screens for a while each day to find out what's happening *as* it happens, and consult the City so we'd have the necessary background then and there."

Elisa leans forward to get a better view of the adolescent Abra, sitting on her left at the very end of the table. Abra doesn't look at her.

"I've already explained why you mustn't use the screens or the City," Elisa says, forcing her voice to stay calm. "You won't be able to make use of them once you're Outside. It's a dangerous tool. You understood this so well that you agreed among yourselves to forget the City's existence through post-hypnotic suggestion after your final change, before leaving for the Outside."

"But we've already used it for changing and for books," remarks Andra.

"That's the difference. You mustn't use it to spy on people Outside. I thought we'd agreed on that."

There is a brief silence. Elisa sees the heads nod in

accord, even the representatives of the youngest, who recognize a familiar subject.

"But it wouldn't be spying," insists Abra after a moment.

Elisa represses a grimace of annoyance. "It amounts to the same thing," she replies, putting her hands flat on the table. "The City must not be used in this way. Only for metamorphosis training and producing books, and that's it."

"And the new children," says Abra. "Every year."

"And the new children needed for the Project for another six years," admits Elisa, keeping her voice steady.

"And the ommachs," says Abra.

This time Elisa lets herself smile. "Abra clearly wants to prove something," she says to no one in particular.

"Why not use the screens for the Project, too?" asks the intrepid Abra. "It's no different from using the City for incubators or ommachs."

Elisa watches the reactions of the others closely. Most of them are perplexed, even embarrassed. A few—the older ones—appear determined to support Abra despite their apparent neutrality.

Elisa gives a rather obvious sigh. "It's very different. I thought you'd understood this long ago, Abra."

Abra blinks but doesn't lower her eyes. "It would be an awful lot more practical," she says, trying to plead her case again.

"Exactly," says Elisa firmly. "You mustn't get used to making a game out of watching people without their knowing it, the very people among whom you'll be living. They're not strange beasts. It's dishonest to see without being seen, and to see things you wouldn't see even if you were with them. The ommachs can go and gather all the information needed. That isn't exactly honest, either, but it seems like an acceptable compromise to me. The meeting today concerns information needed by those who'll leave for the Outside first, and how we can obtain it. Ommachs are a good means, and I move we vote on it."

The result doesn't surprise her: the council has voted unanimously in favour of the motion. The meeting is over and the children move off in chattering groups toward the kitchen where Lussi is waiting with milk and cookies.

Elisa goes over to add some wood to the dwindling fire. Soon, she senses a presence behind her. Abra, probably. It must be. Curious, how different she is from the others. Boy or girl, it doesn't matter. *Or am I the one who sees her differently? Because she's the first, despite everything?* No; on that basis, Andra or Aria could just as well be considered the first. But Abra is the first child that Elisa brought out of the incubators, the first she named. And the only one she nursed at her breast. *And that's why she's more my daughter? Ridiculous.*

But it's entirely possible that Abra considers Elisa more her mother. There is a special tie, and that's a fact. *Abra exasperates me more than the others.* Elisa smiles. But Abra seems to be someone special. The others feel the same. Elisa has been careful to treat her just like everyone else, and yet since the council was set up three years ago there's no doubt about it: Abra, with the tacit consent of the others, is clearly the voice of opposition.

The voice of opposition. Elisa smiles again as she pokes the fire energetically. A pretty slim opposition, and always reasonable. More the devil's advocate, really, the voice of contradiction dutifully pointing out objections. Very healthy, actually.

She turns around. Abra is waiting, looking embarrassed.

"You're not mad?" asks the teenager somewhat gruffly.

Elisa strokes her cheek. "Not a bit," she says, surprised.

"But you looked mad."

"Absolutely not. We had a good discussion."

Abra stares at the fire, apparently still ill at ease. The flickering light plays over her features: the high cheekbones, the beautiful, rather full lips. Elisa observes the girl with pleasure. At her last change, Abra altered her female body a little. Now she's somewhat taller, more slender, with curly blond hair and grey eyes. It's very becoming.

"What is it, Abra?" asks Elisa gently.

"I still don't understand why you don't want to use the City more."

Elisa stiffens. Not that again.

"It's not as though we *had* to keep using it," persists Abra. "It would be just for a bit, until we were all settled Outside."

Elisa puts the fire-tongs on the rack beside the bellows.

"We'd *forget* it," Abra goes on. "No one on the Outside would ever know, since we ourselves would have forgotten the City."

Elisa straightens up. "No, Abra. I've explained it to you several times. If you still don't understand, all I can say is, 'No.' You'll understand later."

She looks at the dejected girl, and forces herself to smile and add, as she used to when Abra was little, "All right?"

There is a pause, then Abra hangs her head and murmurs, "All right."

⚡ **7** ⚡

THE BIG WHITE CAT STANDS MOTIONLESS IN the middle of the yard, its head turned toward Elisa, frozen in the stance it held when she surprised it by opening the door of her house. Bigger than a wildcat, as big as a leopard, although its head and ears suggest a lynx. If Elisa's sense of empathy with animals is reliable, this one doesn't seem afraid. It's the first time she's ever met one, although the ommachs have mentioned noticing them in the forest. But she has in fact seen these animals, long ago, on the City's screens, when she was little. It was an experiment. Mario— what was his name? Mario Alghieri. He settled them in the Southwest, if she remembers rightly. Could they have come this far north? Was the Southwest too hot?

The big cat gives a wide yawn that reveals a pink and black palate, and continues nonchalantly on its way.

Elisa smiles. What graceful arrogance! She'd better tell the children, all the same. This one doesn't look vicious, but you never know.

She looks at the sky and the trees, drinking in the calm, slightly cool air, and feels contentment rising within her. A fine autumn day. The list of daily chores runs through her head with comfortable familiarity. Breakfast. Milk the cows. Work with the twelve and thirteen-year-olds. Finish harvesting potatoes with the eight and nine-year-olds. Oversee jam-making with the oldest. They'll be changing tonight. Bake cakes. Better not make too much of this metamorphosis, though. As time goes by it takes on the air of a ceremony, a festival—metamorphosis with a capital *M*. Should she talk it over with them? In private or in council? After all, they'll never change again. Once they're twenty, they'll remain boys.

The village certainly looks its best in the fall. The warm sheen of the wooden houses harmonizes with the russet and yellow leaves, a bright streak against the blue sky, a last burst of colour before the winter snows. Seven houses, weathering to silver-grey with the passing years. Her smile is only half amused as she looks around the semicircle. She'd made such an effort to differentiate the village from the City that the result looks more like something out of those old films she used to watch with Desprats as a little girl. What did he call them? *Westerns*. Square logs, the chinks carefully filled, a raised foundation, and a veranda all around. Inside it's the same thing: polished wood floors, a huge fireplace of stone and brick, skins and furs as rugs, the rustic furniture ungainly but solid. Almost no community on the Outside lives in houses like this. There, most villages are built on the edge of ruined cities, using whatever materials come to hand: concrete, ironwork, plastic. It doesn't matter, really. Here the children are accustomed to the frugal life—

almost Spartan, in fact—and that's what counts. They'll know how to cope when they go Outside.

Outside. That word again: "Outside." The children adopted the term without a second thought. It doesn't mean the same thing to them, obviously. *Outside. You are Outside, Elisa.* But this recurrent mental slip merely emphasizes the fact that all she's been able to do is set up a sheltered enclave.

A little saddened, she stares at the long, low houses, sturdy on their stone foundations. Beyond are the yellowing trees of the orchard, the big garden, the cowshed and the barnyard, and further still is the forest, somewhat tamed in the last fifteen years. A familiar scene. Why does it suddenly seem changed? It's as though the white cat had altered everything, brusquely telescoping a span of over thirty years.

Elisa pushes away a lock of hair that has fallen over her forehead. *Over thirty years.* The figure is meaningless. But she was certainly five when Mario finished his cat experiment. Or was it Max? Yes; Alghieri was already dead by that time. She well remembers being given a few "dud" cats that would've been put down, otherwise. That was the year Desprats died.

I'm thirty-six years old.

Funny how figures seem to multiply of their own accord. The Project has been under way for fifteen years. In five years, the first children will leave. The moment of truth is drawing near. And in twenty years, the Project will be finished. Twenty years. A long time, twenty years. Where was she twenty years ago?

Watching the City screens and dreaming about Paul.

And twenty years from now, where and what will she be? Will she have changed? She can't imagine it, of course, despite trying. Her body won't have altered much, in any case, though her faculty for regeneration seems to have lessened in the past few years. But it's been a steady process; it doesn't seem to have speeded up at all. At this rate it will be decades before she can no longer regenerate, before she begins to grow old normally.

When he was little, Abram—Abra—asked her about the faculty of regeneration. The little girl had just become aware of it. Elisa did her best to explain it; Abra was barely four after all! She told the child that her body maintained itself automatically according to its ideal model. Abra had thought for a long while, and then said, "Why do we get bigger, then?"

Elisa had burst out laughing, struck simultaneously by the intelligence that lay behind the question and the innocent feeling that had prompted it. Abra didn't want to grow up. She wanted to remain Elisa's baby. And Elisa had to explain that growing up wasn't a sickness, that the body found it normal.

Grow, grow old. Die. Was it Andra that asked the question? Elisa hadn't been able to answer, except to say that no human being was immortal. Now she knows that the ability to regenerate diminishes with age. She also knows how fast it diminishes, and has a pretty good idea of exactly how long she has left to live. No self-regeneration after sixty-five or seventy, if the decline doesn't speed up before that time. She'll look thirty at that point. After that, it's anybody's guess: normal aging, if she takes certain precautions; in other words, about sixty useful years? Or rapid decline and collapse within the space of a few years? Well, she'll find out, that much is certain. Anyway, it's her life, her death. She'll decide for herself. And the Project will have been completed long ago.

And afterward? She smiles a little, recognizing the familiar question. After the Project, what will you do, Elisa? Ah, but the Project won't be finished when the last boy has left. She'll have to visit the various communities where they've settled or which they've founded. Follow up the results of cross-breeding with Outside genes. That sounds like a lot of travelling. Would using a moddex be a serious infringement of the rules she's set herself? Perhaps not, she thinks with a smile. But she'll have plenty of time; why should she want to go faster?

And if she gets tired of travelling, there's always that unresolved problem of the *Trickster* virus that causes the human race to produce more females than males. Oh, she'll have lots to occupy her.

And afterward? The question doesn't want to go away. She goes back inside.

There is a noise in the kitchen. Who's on breakfast duty this week? Don and Daniel? Are they up already? But there's only one person in the kitchen, and Elisa frowns a little as she recognizes Abram. He must have come in by the back door while she was outside. He keeps on cutting bread, not turning around as she comes in. He's tense and anxious, but determined. To do what? What's going on? Thinking ruefully of her peaceful early morning mood, Elisa goes to get a couple of bowls, puts the milk on the stove, and takes the jam and cheese out of the cupboard. Abram sits down across from her, eyes lowered. It's two weeks since she's seen him. He's been off cutting wood with the ommachs. She doesn't see much of him these days except at council meetings or when they happen to pass each other in the garden or elsewhere. He's grown: the shoulders are broader beneath his linen shirt, the arms more muscled. He has the thin face of an adolescent, however, with the skin tanned but still smooth. Elisa pats the arm resting on the table, touched by his palpable distress. He shudders.

"Tell me, Abram."

The grey eyes rest on hers. "I don't want to change any more." He speaks in a somewhat muffled voice.

Is that all? Elisa's first reaction is one of surprise and relief. To give herself time to think, she goes over to the stove to watch the milk. It matters to him. He's afraid of making her angry, probably. Change every two years: that's the rule, and everyone submits to it without argument. She's not surprised that Abram is the first to object. And on the brink of puberty, to boot. Like her, they have been late maturing. But Outside people have the same tendency, and the fertility period in women is decreasing as well: menopause at thirty-five or forty. The men don't seem to be affected. Maybe it's because they don't live long enough to show it. Their average life span is fifty-five.

Should she insist that they live through puberty in their girls' bodies? Does it really matter?

She goes to get the sugar from the sideboard, and lingers a moment before sitting down again. She can sense his embarrassment. Of course she thought about the problem, but only in theory. Puberty. She'd never given much consideration to this aspect of the children's relationships. Over the years there had been erotic relationships that came and went, and the inevitable questions had been asked, either of her or the ommachs. Apparently there'd never been any major difficulty, at least none that the peer group or the older ones hadn't been able to settle without consulting the grownups.

But soon they'll be sexually functional. Fertile. Let them have children among themselves? She thought of it at one point. But the answer was no, definitely not. The risk of some defective gene becoming active was hardly greater for their children than for them (after all, it was the same genetic material, carefully refined by Paul). But it would be a waste of time. The children would become progressively closer to being identical. Anyway, producing children would create emotional ties that would complicate their departure for the Outside considerably.

Nevertheless, the experience of giving birth for these future males. . . . No. They'd *all* have to have children to make it fair. Some wouldn't want to. There are limits to what she's willing to subject them to, and this is clearly beyond such limits! No; the thing to do is simply call together all those concerned and remind them that procreation is a part of their physical functions that they can consciously control.

She sits down again and pours the milk into the bowls. Her long silence has increased Abram's anxiety still further.

"You want to remain a boy, Abram? Why?"

He keeps his eyes lowered. "Because I—I like it better."

"Hardly a very detailed explanation, Abram. Try again."

He stirs his milk, frowning. "Anyhow, we're supposed to be boys when we leave, aren't we? We're changing into girls so that we won't forget what it's like once we're Outside. There's no chance of my forgetting: I was a girl for ten years out of fifteen."

"But in ten years you'll only have been a girl for ten out of twenty-five. That's no reason, Abram. You'll have to come up with something better than that."

He raises his head, sensing that she's amused, and relaxes a little.

"I really prefer being a boy, Elisa. I feel better, that's all. I can't tell you why."

He seems genuinely upset at his inability to explain himself more adequately, and lowers his head again. Elisa looks at the thick blond curls falling over the smooth forehead. Strange. Is it a premature identification with the role he'll have to fill on the Outside in five years? A whim? No, he seems sincere. She'll have to think about it in tranquility. If others come to her with the same request, she'll need to have worked something out. She can't force him to change, obviously.

"Fine. Stay a boy as long as you want, and if you feel like changing again, let me know, that's all. All right?"

Why not make it the rule? Free choice of sex after fifteen? It's an idea. She'll call the council together in a little while.

"You're not angry?"

She supresses a slight irritation. Can't he sense that she isn't angry? "Of course not. Boy or girl, I've already told you, it doesn't matter as far as I'm concerned. Not before you leave, in any case."

He doesn't seem satisfied, all the same. Does he want her to say she prefers him as a boy? It wouldn't be false, just an exaggeration on her part. She would have liked to let them choose the sex they preferred for going Outside, but they'd had to admit there wasn't really any choice. They'd agreed that they didn't genuinely want to be girls on the Outside. "We couldn't do anything except have babies until we were worn out, and what's more we'd have to work like slaves," Andra had said, expressing the general feeling. "If we want to change something Outside we have to be men."

And if they were men their genes would spread a lot quicker. But none of them seemed to have thought of that, and Elisa didn't remind them.

ELISA LOOKS ANXIOUSLY OUT OF THE WINdow. It began snowing again this morning, and since early afternoon a wind has sprung up, raising swirling gusts that lash and hiss against the windowpanes. It's getting dark. The children shouldn't have gone hunting yesterday. But yesterday the weather was fine.

She pulls herself together. They're practically adults now. In two years they'll begin to leave. And Halter is with them. Nothing can happen. She goes back to her seat by the fire, picking up her book. They have to learn how to cope, in any event, no matter what the weather. The very presence of an ommach is already a breach of the principle of independence voted on by the council, as Abram had pointed out. But they'd taken some of the younger children with them, and she preferred not to run any risks. In eighteen years she hasn't lost a single child, and she isn't going to begin now.

She starts reading again, but can't help listening to the wind. Francie, Florie, and Gil sit on the staircase arguing about who's a bad sport. Francie and Florie against Gil, of course. They're always in cahoots, no matter what sex they are at the moment. She observes them with amusement. After all, character has nothing to do with sex: they're insufferable when they're girls and equally so as boys. Well, not insufferable. Young, full of mischief, bubbling over with life.

No sign of the hunters. Did they go farther than

planned? They should have turned back as soon as the wind sprang up. They should be home by now.

She senses that one of the youngsters sitting on the woodbox has risen and is coming over to her. She pretends to read, but the child isn't fooled: he knows she's worried. He sits on the arm of the chair. It's Kara—Kari this year, but she can't tell the difference merely by empathy. He hasn't been a boy for long enough. It usually takes nearly a year for new males to gravitate toward the oldest boys. A significant difference that can be observed through empathy takes several years to emerge. Odd, it wasn't the case with the first children. But it's normal, in fact. The younger children have models: Abram, Ari, and Anders, the ones who haven't changed since puberty. Kari climbs onto her lap when she acknowledges his presence. She snuggles him close, breathing in the warm odour of a small human animal and stroking his soft cheek. The children of that particular year all have green eyes. She'd tried to make them as different as possible, as with each new generation, but there simply aren't enough somatypes, just as there are limited possibilities with the available material. All of them had eyes in shades of green that season. A statistical fluctuation. And they kept their green eyes when they metamorphosed, of course; it's only with the third or fourth change that they begin experimenting with their bodies. Early on, they need stable identities.

She's past the *P* generation now. Patric, Pierre, Pavel—hm-m-m, isn't that Paul in Russian? Why not Paul? Hasn't she in fact followed part of his dream, just as she's followed Desprats' dream? Paul. It would be strange to have a Paul. *After all this time, Elisa?* But she's compromised: Pavel is called Paula whenever he's a girl.

Whenever he's a girl. Suddenly the bizarre nature of the phrase strikes Elisa. It's funny, she always gives them boys' names to begin with. And yet, until the first change at the age of seven, they're girls. She ought to think of the last generation as Patricias, Petras, and Paulas. What a stupid custom, anyway. Why have different names for boys and girls? But that's how it is Outside. *And admit it, Elisa, you think of them more as boys than girls. You think of them as the finished product: Outside they'll be boys.*

Elisa feels dissatisfied with herself. But she might as well face it: the longer she's involved in the Project, the harder it is to think of the children as distinct individuals. The first have established their personalities firmly in her mind—Abram, Ari, Anders. Even in the first three generations, she's intimate with the children's characters, those she kept an eye on continually, the ones she ran into problems with and who helped her correct her initial mistakes. Later, well, she's able to identify several individuals in each generation, the ones who for some reason or other have attracted her attention. Francis and Florent, for example, because they're always together. Karel, because he draws so well. Louis, who was lost for a day in the forest. It can't be otherwise with over a hundred children in the village.

Kari is still snuggled against Elisa, his eyes closed. She smiles and rocks him, basking in the contented peacefulness of the child. She, too, closes her eyes, aware of the child's breathing, the warmth of the flames, the now subdued voices of the others. It feels good. She can't have been completely wrong to create all this.

A wave of excitement, the sound of feet and voices comes from the porch. The hunters. Lussi is already at the door as Abram enters, still dressed in his outdoor clothes. He is holding a body in his arms. Elisa leaps up in alarm. But it's a tiny stranger in furs and ill-sewn skins. Halter comes in carrying two other bodies, followed by the rest of the hunters, boys and girls, also carrying bodies. A cold draught sweeps through the room and the wind howls past the open doors. "Close the doors, for God's sake!" someone shouts.

"Hot water and blankets," says Elisa. "Put some more wood on the fire." She begins to undress the stranger, and the others do the same with the twenty or so bodies stretched out on the floor.

It's a man, small, dark-skinned, and very thin. At first Elisa thinks it's an adolescent: he is beardless and the rest of his body is almost entirely hairless. Then she takes his icy hands in hers, and understands: six fingers, nearly all the same length, with an unusually long thumb. Mutants.

"We found them at the base of the mountain," says Abram, rubbing another body beside Elisa. "We were on our way home—we started back as soon as the blizzard hit—and we came across the one you have there, half dead on the village road. When we realized that there were several of them, we retraced his tracks and found the rest."

Elisa continues massaging the icy body, and the little man shudders. There is some frostbite, but the trouble is mostly hunger and exhaustion. Halter has already injected the necessary revitalizing substances, and later the little man will get a full meal.

Elisa examines the others. Ten women, three men, and six children, two very young. Thin, but in fairly good condition. All of them have twelve fingers and toes, but almost no body hair except for eyebrows, eyelashes, and hair on their heads.

"Abram, alert the others and bring beds."

Elisa returns to the little man. His eyes are open and he is looking around with—no, not with astonishment. It's more like grateful wonderment. He murmurs something, making a sign toward his neck. He wears a collar with an amulet in the shape of a disk, a bit of polished bone. Elisa takes a minute to catch what he's saying. "I knew I'd find it." He's speaking a mixture of German and Russian, the language of the East. She hasn't heard it for ages. He tries to get up. She helps him into a sitting position and gives him a few mouthfuls of soup. After he's swallowed it he collapses against her arm. She lies him down again. His eyes are still open and he's looking at her with —fervor?

"My name is Elisa. What's yours?"

The answer sounds like "Meo."

"Are these people part of your family, your clan?"

"My clan," says the little man. "We are the Sestis, Goddess." He touches his amulet again and closes his eyes, smiling.

Abram comes in with the others, bringing beds. Elisa watches until they're settled. They should be left alone to recover their strength. There'll be time for discussing theology when they're all back on their feet.

⚡ 9 ⚡

WHEN ELISA COMES DOWN FROM HER BED-room next morning, she finds Meo deep in conversation with Abram, who stayed the night in the house. The little man is up and seems in fairly good shape. In fact, the speed of his recovery is astonishing. He looks like an adolescent beside Abram, who towers head and shoulders above him. When the mutant sees Elisa coming down the stairs, he bows to her, touching his amulet.

"You shouldn't be up, Meo," she says, speaking his language.

He bows his head penitently. "I wanted to see my wives."

"One of them is pregnant," says Abram in Franglei. "The foetus is doing well. These people have a lot of stamina. They've apparently come over three hundred and fifty kilometers with practically no food. They come from the eastern heartland."

"Have you had anything to eat this morning, Meo?" asks Elisa.

"No, Goddess."

"My name is Elisa. I'm not a goddess. Come and eat with me. Abram, have you had breakfast?"

"I was about to when I heard him."

The little man follows them. Elisa indicates a chair, and he bows reverently as he sits down opposite her.

She pours out some milk, butters a piece of bread, and helps herself to the cheese. Meo watches her.

"Help yourself, Meo," she says, continuing to eat as she watches him. He copies her movements exactly, and his face lights up as he tastes the buttered bread. She lets him eat, and when he's finished she asks, "Why did you come here, Meo?"

"Because the gods are here," he replies. "We were hungry, we were cold. The tribe didn't want us because there were too many of us and we were hunting on their territory. There wasn't much game left, anyway. We were all going to die."

"And what made you think there were gods here?"

Meo touches his amulet. "My great-grandfather saw them. He was hunting and he saw the ship of the gods pass by. He saw it land, far away, on the Mountain of Three Teeth. The gods visited the women of the tribe, and it was after this that the Sestis were born."

Elisa's eyes meet Abram's. He raises his eyebrows. The Mountain of Three Teeth. Underneath is the City. True, it can be seen from far away, looking from the east. They must have seen a moddex. She looks at the thin face, brown and hairless. Difficult to tell his age.

"How many seasons ago was that?"

"Ninety-two," replies Meo without hesitation

Ninety-two *seasons*? His *great* grandfather? How long do they live, then? Elisa bites her lip and has to make an effort to steady her voice before asking, "Are you old, Meo?"

He looks a little taken aback, then replies, "Yes, I'm twenty-eight seasons old."

"How many seasons did your father live?"

"Twenty-three. He died when the tribe drove us out." Halter has just come in and seated himself at the other end of the table. Elisa turns toward him, but she already knows what he's going to say. "He carries a gene similar to the children's."

The dates fit. Paul's experiment. Crossing her genes with mutants from the Outside. She looks at his long, bony hands with their strange thumbs, hands that overlap as they hug the bowl. She feels numb. Paul had lied to her about this, too. He had allowed the results of the experiment to live.

Her children.

"And your clan," she forces herself to say, "is that all that's left of the Sestis?"

"The tribe killed a great many. The others wanted to stay in the plain. My family followed me. They knew I'd find the gods."

"We aren't gods, Meo," Elisa repeats mechanically. She has a vague feeling that she'll be saying this a lot. She cuts herself some bread. He can watch her eating and still think she's divine! But the Badlands tribes had really sunk to a very primitive level. She gets up.

"Keep on eating, Meo. If you need anything, ask Halter here."

She goes into the common room and glances at the sleeping Sestis. One of the children is sucking his thumb, and his overly long fingers have a strange, feral way of wrapping themselves around his face. Elisa moves to the window. The snow stopped during the night, and the morning promises to become one of those glorious winter days that she loves, blue and white beneath the sun. She feels someone standing behind her, but rests her forehead against the glass instead of turning around. Whoever it is comes up beside her and leans against the window frame. Abram of course. She sighs and turns around.

He makes an effort to smile. "Pretty queer hunting. What are we going to do with them?"

"What do you expect? We'll keep them here for the rest of the winter, and then we'll see what they want to do."

"According to what Meo told me, they're looking for new territory to settle. He brought his family here to live close to the gods."

She folds her arms, exasperated. "They'll find out that we're not gods simply by living with us!"

Abram sits on the window sill. "But if they stay, won't it interfere with the Project?"

"I don't see why."

"Anyhow, if they see us change they'll have a hard time believing we aren't supernatural beings."

"They won't see us," begins Elisa. Then she frowns. "But they'll see that there are changes. They're not stupid, judging by Meo." She thinks for a moment, bothered by the idea. "In any case, there's no change planned until the spring. And if they really want to stay here, we'll help them settle by the lake. Thirty kilometers away should be enough."

But during the two remaining months of winter, they'll be there. They don't speak Franglei, but they'll learn it through their contact with the children. Why hide the truth? Will they believe that the children are supernatural? But after living with them for a while, they'll realize that this isn't the case. Will they tell others? Who would they tell? The nearest human settlements are over three hundred kilometers to the south as the crow flies. The other Badlands tribes? There isn't a single one within a radius of a hundred kilometers. Anyway, they aren't going to be troubled by one legend more. Let these Sestis stay here. That way they'll remain within easy reach—they and what they know about the children.

She'll have to call a meeting of the children's council and outline the problem. She'll explain as little as possible: there's no point giving them precise details about the origin of the Sestis. Most of the children will be delighted to have something new in the village. Primitive as they are, the Sestis will give the children a real, human experience, direct and beneficial.

Elisa smiles. "You know, Abram, when all's said and done I think you had good hunting."

He looks at her out of the corner of his eye. "I thought you were displeased."

"Me? No, not really. It's just that—." She hesitates. How can she explain it?

"That they're experiments, too," concludes Abram in a curiously tense voice.

She realizes with astonishment that she is hugging her chest fiercely. She forces herself to relax. The boy has obviously deduced it from what Meo said. Gods visiting the tribe: it was pretty explicit. And Halter said that their genes were similar to the children's. Quite normal for Abram to react this way. Almost normal.

"Experiments *too*, Abram? You are *not* experiments."

He blinks his eyes at her hurt tone of voice, and says hastily, "I know, but it's because they're also—also your children."

Elisa makes herself breathe calmly. Abram must have meant to say something else. It's crazy. He couldn't have said what she thought he said. Of course. The children know precisely where they came from, and—less precisely, since it wasn't necessary— where Elisa came from. Curiously enough, only the first two or three generations persisted in asking the question. The subsequent generations appeared to find the existence of their older siblings sufficient justification for their own existence, or even Elisa's existence. The past that she's invented to explain the mutation's origin included very little about the City.

"Genes that are fairly similiar," she says with studied carelessness. "The mutation—or comparable mutations—has existed on the Outside in a, well, a wild state for a long time."

"No," says Abram.

Suddenly she is aware of his emotion. Is it anguish? She frowns at him. "What do you mean, no?"

He forces himself to look her in the eye. "They're our half brothers and sisters, so to speak, four generations removed." He blurts it out, but his voice falters toward the end.

Elisa turns back to the window, feeling like a block of revolving stone. She stares blindly at the frost patterns on the pane until she can manage to speak clearly, then says just one word: "When?"

Abram's distress increases, but she senses it as though from a great distance. "A few years ago," he mutters. His tone becomes imploring. "I wanted—," He hesitates. "I wanted to know you."

She turns abruptly and he steps back, hitting his head against the window frame. "By spying on me!"

"No! I just wanted to know what had happened in the City before us. I came upon the pictures by accident. Later on I searched a bit more methodically, but—"

What pictures?

"—that's how I learned about the Sestis. I didn't know their name, though. I thought he'd eliminated them."

Elisa's whole body begins to tremble involuntarily. Nerves. She fights to control it, almost more enraged at this physical betrayal than at Abram's disobedience. Ruthlessly she forces her body to become quiet, although the effort leaves her feeling limp. She sits on the window sill to keep her legs from buckling.

"What pictures, Abram?"

There is a long pause, during which she glares at him. Is he going to try to lie, now? Finally he speaks, almost under his breath. "You and Paul."

"Was it interesting?" she hisses between clenched teeth.

Abram blushes and stammers, looking at the floor, "No, at the end, at Vietelli."

Ah, *those* pictures! Suddenly Elisa is surprised to find herself laughing. Her effort to re-establish body control has produced a sort of serenity.

"He discovers with horror that his mother is a murderess," she says, her voice heavy with sarcasm.

"Not you! It was self-defense! Justice! *He* was the murderer."

For a moment Elisa contemplates the young, ardent face, while exploring her own body, now satifactorily under control. She sees the situation more clearly. It's not such a catastrophe.

"How did you manage, Abram?"

He seizes her meaning immediately. "Halter helped me."

Halter. Of course. She has never explicitly forbidden the ommachs—. In fact, they're programmed to cooperate with the children, although Elisa has curtailed the extent of this cooperation. There are questions that they can't answer truthfully. But she never thought of putting the City itself off limits, to bar physical access. Very well. She'll see to it. She hadn't reckoned with Abram's curiosity. What about the other children?

"Did any of the others do it?"

"No! I never told a soul."

She relaxes. His denial is sincere, almost horrified, in fact. The damage is contained. All she needs to know is how much Abram saw.

"Did you do it often?"

"Only once. In fact, I don't know very much, Elisa."

Is he trying to reassure her? She gives him a small, wry smile and watches him shrink into the window alcove.

"You never for a moment considered that if I hadn't ever talked about it, it was because I didn't want to, because it was nobody's business but mine, and that you had no need to know?"

"I do," murmurs Abram, "I need to know."

Elisa represses the rising bubble of anger, and merely stares wordlessly at the boy. But although he shrinks into himself yet further, a stubborn core of resistance remains.

"I wanted to know *you*, Elisa. You created us, we live with you, and for most of us you are ... simply *there*, like the sky or the forest. You just *are*." He straightens a little. "But you're also a human being, aren't you? You didn't begin life the day we first children were born. I wanted to know something about you, about where you came from, who you were before us."

"What I told you wasn't enough."

"To start with, yes. But not later on. And then ..." he hesitates, then with characteristic impulsiveness blurts out what he's afraid to say. "You were so dead set against our using the screens."

Elisa turns to the window again, resting a hand on the pane and feeling the frost melt beneath her palm. Of course. Of course. The astonishing thing is that only Abram did it. She ought to be congratulating herself on how well the children had behaved.

"I only did it once," Abram continues. "I couldn't

help myself. But after that I never asked why you didn't want us to use the screens, do you remember?"

She glances at him, sees the hesitant, pleading smile, and finds it within herself to respond. She'd asked herself, too, why he'd suddenly stopped pestering her about it.

"And now I'm telling you." He says it with renewed assurance, and she looks him in the eye.

"Is it something to be proud of, Abram?"

He looks down, but she grabs his chin. "No. You do wrong to boast about it, but it's true that you could have kept it to yourself forever."

He blinks, bewildered at feeling her anger subside.

Elisa smiles. "You picked a pretty awkward moment, though."

"I wanted to—." He sniffs, looks at her for a moment, and then bursts out laughing, wanting her to share the joke, the joke on him: "I wanted to give you something else to think about."

She is momentarily dumbfounded, then breaks into laughter, too.

"You looked so sad, all alone with your memories."

"You wanted to let me know that I wasn't so alone. How nice of you." But there's no real bitterness in her voice.

The boy's smile widens, although still a little tentative. "You ought to rely on us more, you know."

"I do rely on you, Abram. But not to take charge of my past. I'm quite capable of looking after it myself."

He feels the rebuff and loses his smile, but persists. "You said to us one day that—that one can't avoid a commitment to others. You've committed yourself to us. We . . . love you."

She looks at him for a moment, saying nothing. We have rights over you, is that what he means? It's the truth.

There is a noise behind them. The Sestis are waking up. One of the youngsters begins crying softly. Elisa ruffles Abram's hair in the old, familiar way.

"Come on; we've got to see to your relatives."

⚡ 10 ⚡

IN THE YARD, THE SNOWMEN ARE MELTING and the earth is emerging in dark, spongy patches. The weather is mild. Francie and Florie have dragged the benches outside and are peeling the vegetables in the sun with two of the younger Sestis. Elisa and Meo are seated on a bench nearby. Some of the other children are scraping the packed snow from the door-steps to the houses. A gaggle of the youngest, with the Sestis in the lead, comes tearing by on the heels of two older boys waving short sticks, whooping wildly as they pass Elisa and Meo and disappear in the direction of the orchard.

"They seem to get on well together," remarks Elisa, giving Meo a sidelong glance. The little man nods thoughtfully.

The change is going to take place in three days, and as usual it will be something of a gala occasion. Meo has never questioned Elisa during the two months he and his wives have spent with her. The children's faculty for self-regeneration, which it was impossible not to notice, didn't surprise the Sestis. They possess it themselves to a lesser degree. The gene responsible for their premature aging partially inhibits the regenerative gene. But this approaching *change*, on the other hand, which the children must have been chattering to the newcomers about for days. . . .

"The gods have blessed you with many boys," says Meo finally. Elisa suppresses a smile and replies, "Yes," satisfied at this further proof that she's no longer a goddess, although Meo doesn't seem quite sure what status he ought to assign her. She's undeniably head of the community, but she's a woman. And yet, if she really is a woman, how can so young a person be the mother of over a hundred children? She doesn't live with any of the men. The Sestis have no inkling of the real nature of the ommachs at this point: the children have been so accustomed to treating them like human beings that apparently it hasn't occurred to them to tell their new playfellows the truth.

Meo watches Francie and Florie as they peel the vegetables and prattle in low voices with the two Sestis. He's embarrassed, probably because he doesn't know how to continue the conversation. Elisa is amused, and decides to help him out a little. "After the party we'll have six new little girls, and new boys, too."

"Six new babies; yes, Abram told me." As he says it, Meo can't help glancing at Elisa's flat abdomen. "My wife Shiga will also have a baby soon." Sesti babies are born after three months' gestation—a normal period, if one considers that the adults have an average life span of barely thirty seasons. Elisa has resumed the research she abandoned nearly twenty years ago. Now that she has all the data, it hasn't taken long to find the answer. The next Sesti generation should live a normal life, although they'll still have six fingers on each hand. But not the child about to be born.

"The village women don't make children like the Sesti women," says Meo, still pursuing his idea.

"You're right. I don't conceive children in my belly, but outside my body, in a sort of . . . belly box."

Meo takes this information in his stride, as well as the sudden swing from small talk to serious conversation. "And the other women?" he asks after a moment.

"They aren't really women. They're—." The Sestis can't comprehend the concept of such complex machines. The children's simple double-barreled shotguns fill them with awe and admiration. Elisa changes her explanation, saying, "They can't have any children because their bodies are made of metal, not flesh."

That's a pretty rough description of an ommach, but it will have to do. Meo seems to take it fairly calmly, in any case, and stubbornly returns to his subject. "Then you are the mother of many children."

"With the belly box, it's easy. I can make several at once."

There is a considerable pause at this, and Elisa, both perplexed and amused, steals a glance at the little man. What must he think? He doesn't seem frightened by the idea, anyhow. That's good.

"The new children will be girls," he says.

"Yes. They'll only become boys at fourteen," says Elisa composedly. The little man stiffens a little, but she goes on. "After that, they'll change regularly so as to get to know both kinds of body well. In the end they choose." *While waiting to leave.*

Meo thinks this over for a moment. "Can you change, too?" he asks at last. Elisa is pleased with him; he still isn't afraid.

"Yes, but I only do it to give life to the children." *And the number of children you can make with a few cubic centimetres of sperm in a controlled environment is amazing.*

"You are the children's mother and father," says Meo slowly. He looks at her with astonishment and respect, but no fear. His reaction is pretty similar to that of the children when they learned how they were made and what Elisa was to them. At last he touches the amulet and murmurs, "The gods are great."

Elisa is a little disappointed at this, reflects that one can't expect too much all at once. The Sestis have a perfectly logical approach to help them adjust to all things unknown and threatening. Isn't it better this way? They will evolve gradually.

The children have finished their work. They take the bowls full of peeled vegetables and go back to the kitchen. Out they come again, this time headed for the barnyard with their peelings. Florie keeps up an animated discussion, giving Seio, the youngest Sesti boy, a dig in the ribs while Francie slips her arm around Barro's neck. Despite their smaller stature, the Sestis' mental development is just about equal to that of the two teenagers.

"Yes, they get along well," murmurs Meo. Elisa looks at him in surprise. Why is he worried?

⚡ 11 ⚡

AS WITH EVERY PERIOD OF METAMORPHOSIS, accommodation throughout the village has been shuffled according to the children's preferences and available space. The morning after the party, Francie, who has become Francis again, doesn't come down to breakfast, and Florie, who hasn't changed, leaps out of her chair when Elisa says laughingly that she's going to drag him out of bed.

"Don't bother, I'll go!"

Elisa frowns. The flash of anxiety hasn't escaped her. Since she's closer to the staircase than Florie, she reaches Francis' door first. She knocks, sensing an awakening on the other side of the door. Ah, Francis isn't alone. Is that all? She's a little surprised at Florie's reaction, but sings out, "Breakfast, Francis." She turns to go, absent-mindedly trying to identify his companion, but it must be a girl she doesn't know well. Then she frowns again. Does she sense anxiety on the other side of the door? Or is it fear? What's going on? She glances at Florie, who has followed her upstairs and is standing on the last step, hesitating. Elisa knocks again. "May I come in, Francis?"

There is a long pause. Are those muffled whispers she hears? Then Francis' voice, not very enthusiastic. "Yes."

Somewhat comforted, Elisa opens the door.

Barro and Francis, naked, seated on the very rumpled bed. Barro tries to get up, moved by fear and guilt, but Francis defiantly holds him back. There is a kind of despair about him that he doesn't attempt to control.

Elisa makes sure she's calm. Why wouldn't she be? Francis' very fear and distress would induce her to be calm if she weren't already perfectly in control. It isn't very serious, in any case. She knows that these homosexual infatuations have occurred several times between various children, but she had thought Francis had satisfied this sort of curiosity or perhaps just wasn't interested. Obviously the Sestis are quite a novelty. It won't be the last time. Under the circumstances, it hardly matters that it's between boys.

"Go and have breakfast, Barro," she says to the young Sesti with a reassuring smile.

"Stay here!" Francis grabs the boy's arm with a new ferocity that astounds Elisa. Can't he feel that she's not angry?

"What's the matter, Francis?" she asks as kindly as possible.

"He can hear what you've got to say."

Elisa raises her eyebrows. "But I've nothing particular to say." Out of the corner of her eye she can see Florie standing by the door, absorbed and tense. Of course she knew about it. Does this have something to do with her not changing this time? Seio? Things are getting a bit involved. "Come in, Florie."

Florie sits down on the bed beside the others. Elisa considers them briefly, saying nothing. There is a hostility about them. It comes through very clearly from Francis, whereas with Florie it's a sort of resistance. It bothers her, and she has to control her irritation. What's wrong with these kids, anyhow? They're just dramatizing a few little sexual games.

But if Seio is involved as well, there'll be problems. They're clearly interfertile. She takes a chance, and says, "Florie, go and get Seio, will you?"

Touché! She's caught the start of surprise and fear, quickly suppressed but unmistakable.

"No," says Florie, lowering her head.

How long has this been going on? She should have been more alert to the possibility. Is that why Meo is worried? Elisa draws a chair up to the bed and sits down, forcing herself to project a feeling of calm and understanding, even amusement. Get their feet back on the ground. That's the thing to do. God knows what they've been imagining.

"Don't you think he'll be interested by what I have to say?"

Florie and Francis exchange glances. "We've never done anything!" exclaims Florie. It's a sincere protest, and just possibly a reproach to Francis. Are the inseparable friends at odds about this?

"But you didn't change this time," remarks Elisa.

Florie doesn't answer, and Elisa is touched by her obvious chagrin. "It isn't a reproach, Florie."

"There's no point, anyway!" says Francis roughly.

"No point to what?"

Francis waves a hand in exasperation and doesn't reply. His emotions are too strong for words, and it's these emotions that surprise and worry Elisa: frustration, anger, rebellion.

"Whether we change or not, it doesn't make a bit of difference," says Florie, speaking for Francis. "And not for them either."

Elisa looks directly at each in turn, feeling both amused and exasperated. "Well, maybe it's crystal clear to you, but I'm confused. Would you mind enlightening me?"

Florie and Francis look at each other, but neither can speak. Finally Barro speaks up in his slow, quiet voice. "As far as love goes, it doesn't change anything," he says, searching for the Franglei words. "But with life, it does." Then he hangs his head, as though frightened by his temerity, and stares at his long, interlaced fingers.

"Barro is eighteen seasons old," says Florie. "In five seasons he might be dead." She falls silent, as though she couldn't bear to go on.

"In five seasons he might be dead!" rages Francis. His voice breaks on the last word, and he reiterates, "Dead!" glaring accusingly at Elisa. "And Seio, too. And we'll—." He makes another despairing gesture, leaving his sentence hanging, as though mere words couldn't express his feeling. Elisa feels her heart sink.

"Francis, I'm doing everything I can. You know it."

"I know!" says Francis between clenched teeth, disconsolate and overwhelmed by the magnitude of his distress. Barro touches his arm lightly but says nothing; he looks a lot like Meo—Barro is the first son—and as she contemplates him Elisa realizes that his size has misled her again. Barro isn't an adolescent: he's past the middle of his life. Biologically speaking he's a man. He should have had a wife and children by now. Psychologically, of course, the Sestis have never adapted. They have never really built a culture or a society that relates to their brief existence. They've been in almost constant contact with the "normal" members of the tribe, who live longer and who have always considered them more or less as youngsters. Three months spent in the village haven't changed that background. In any case, they may develop faster on the physical level, but they haven't had time to build up the kind of human experience that would enable them to go beyond the adolescent stage, psychologically speaking. By their standards, Meo is practically an old man, and yet his mental age is about equivalent to Abram's.

The children must have become aware of all this in a rather muddled way. With the generosity of youth, they feel a desperate sympathy for the Sestis' fate. Heartsore and a little ashamed at having underestimated the problem, Elisa repeats, "I did what I could, Francis."

Instinctively Francis takes Barro's hand in his. Now he touches the long, slender fingers one by one. Too many. "What right had anyone to do this?" he murmurs, as though he hadn't heard. "What right?"

Then he bursts out roughly, "What did you think you were, down there in the City? What do you think you *are?*"

"Francis!" cries Florie, trying to stop him.

Francis turns on her in hopeless anger. "Don't you see what she's like? *Her* plans, *her* projects, *her* experiments, that's all that matters. She doesn't give a shit for the rest of us, just like the other one!"

What's he talking about?

They turn toward her, panic-stricken. She tries to

contain her anger. "You know it isn't true, Francis. You know it isn't!"

All three of them jump, and she realizes that her voice has risen to a shout. She makes a tremendous effort to control herself. "You know you're being unjust, Francis. You're sorry for Barro and the others, and it makes you unjust. I don't know what Abram's been telling you, but he knows, and *you* know very well why I brought you into the world and what you mean to me. I've never forced you to act against your will."

"And if we refuse to leave, what then?" Francis looks defiant.

She leans against the back of the chair and folds her arms. Is this what it's come to? And she didn't see it coming? Who's this *we* he's talking about, anyway? Only Florie and himself? Or others? But it isn't serious. He's caught up emotionally in the Sestis' predicament and is trying to hurt her as a kind of consolation. He's a child, after all. They're all children, dramatizing everything, living for the moment without really thinking of the future.

"Who doesn't want to go?" She asks, finding she's able to remain calm without too much difficulty.

Florie answers without looking at her. "Francis and me."

Elisa nods her head, feeling relieved. She was right: it's just an escapade, a rebellious outburst motivated by the Sestis' problem. Nothing serious.

"You won't be leaving for five years, in any case. There's time to think about it," she says indulgently.

An exasperated Francis turns to Florie. "See? I told you so!"

"We've been thinking about it for a long time," says Florie hesitantly. "We don't want to go Outside. We want to stay together, Francis and me."

"And Seio? And Barro?" Elisa can't help being a little sarcastic.

Florie rests a hand on Barro's knee. "It's not the same," she stammers, embarrassed. "They can't—change."

And they'll be dead in five years or so, says Elisa to herself. Is that what Florie is thinking, too, but doesn't want to say? Perhaps, though surely not with the same cynicism. But it isn't being cynical, it's just being realistic.

"They understand, anyhow," persists Florie, "and that doesn't change anything about our love. Barro said so, and it's true. It doesn't change anything between Francis and me, girl or boy. And it doesn't change anything between us and them. We simply—." She gives Francis an imploring glance, but he shakes his head, frowning. "Francis and I simply don't want to be separated," she says brokenly. "It doesn't matter whether either of us is a boy or girl: we don't care. But we want to stay together. We love each other." Her voice is almost inaudible.

Elisa feels a wild desire to laugh. They love each other! What do they know about love? What sort of love can there be between them? They're nothing but children, they haven't the faintest idea, they haven't thought it out. They'll get over it when they really become aware of what they are. But for the moment there's no point hurting their feelings. This business with the Sestis has upset them. That's understandable.

She gets up. "We'll talk about all this again," she says calmly. "You've got plenty of time to think about it. And for the Sestis, Francis, I've done everything I can. Contrary to what you seem to think, I don't consider myself a god. I know my limitations, believe me. I regret them, but I have to accept them. One day you'll understand that. As for your relationships with Barro and Seio, it's really none of my business. But think about them: Seio can have children, Florie, even if the problem doesn't arise with Barro—unless you're planning to change again, Francis. Think about what you're doing. I can't think for you. Let me know what you decide."

She goes out of the room, but just after the door is closed she hears Francis exclaim bitterly, "I told you it was no use!"

Elisa hesitates, but her hand is no longer on the doorknob, and she goes downstairs trying to dampen her anger for the benefit of the children in the common room. Abram. Where is Abram? She finds him in the shed milking the cows. He turns his head as she approaches, surprised at first, then worried. He stops pulling on the cow's teats, and the animal lets out a protesting moo.

"Abram," says Elisa calmly, "what have you been telling Francis and Florent?"

Abram is utterly still for a second. Then, "Florie," he says, resuming his milking.

"What did you tell them?"

"You found them with Barro and Seio," he says coolly.

Elisa quells an exasperated exclamation. Abram has the most irritating way recently of always controlling his emotions, putting up a smooth, bland facade!

"That's not the problem. You told them about Paul!"

The milk splashes rhythmically into the pail, making a small pattering noise against the sides.

"They questioned me about the Sestis. They'd already figured out the basics. I didn't have to tell them much."

Elisa keeps her temper. After all, what's the point of overindulging these uncontrolled emotions? But her anger, however disembodied, is still there.

"If you knew about Seio and Barro, why didn't you tell me?" She regrets the words as soon as they're out of her mouth. She's laid herself wide open for a stinging comeback. Why would he tell her anything? But Abram continues milking in silence. She senses his emotions indistinctly; his control may be a little shaky, but he's managed to blur his feelings. All the same, he's not as cool and collected as he'd like her to think.

Elisa's compensatory instinct restores her composure. She smiles wryly to herself: what's got into her, jumping down Abram's throat as though he were responsible for the other children? It isn't very wise to imply that he has an important, special role, when he's all too ready to assume it on his own.

"Have they had this idea about not leaving for long? About staying together?"

"It was in the air. I think their relationships with Seio and Barro have made them grow up faster than they wanted to."

This kid is talking about growing up?

"They're just children. Why, they're not even fifteen years old."

Abram keeps up his methodical milking. "How old were you when you made love with Paul for the first time?" he says smoothly.

For a moment, Elisa is speechless, her head buzzing with furious retorts. Then she regains control, giving herself time as she strokes the cow's plump flank. "I was older than they were. And yet I was still a kid; I wasn't really sure what I was doing."

"You *thought* you were sure, though, didn't you? What would you have said to someone who called you a kid?"

Elisa shrugs. "That has no bearing on the present situation."

"Really?"

She tries to answer the question honestly. Is there a similarity? No, none! Paul was—. She feels an icy silence within her. *A real person.* She was thinking "a real person"! But the children are real people!

What's wrong, when all's said and done? Francis and Florent, Florie, want to stay together. They think they love each other. They're no longer prepared to leave when the time comes. What's so shocking about that? Two children less for the Project, out of over a hundred: what does it matter? She'd never considered forcing anyone to leave.

The trouble is you never thought anyone would refuse. The children have been indoctrinated from birth.

No, not indoctrinated! She's explained to them about the Project, they've talked it over, and they've taken part in the final planning.

Yes, the first three or four generations. But those that came later simply had to accept what had already been settled before their time.

But they accepted it, just the same! Anyway, that's not what's bothering her. She isn't upset by the fact that Francis and Florie are refusing to leave. What, then? The fact that they love each other? The reason they gave for refusing to leave? Their desire to stay together?

Real people. Why should this absurd phrase keep ringing in her head? She turns to Abram, who is watching her but hastily looks away. The milk begins squirting into the pail again. Still that constrained calm, covering emotions that she's increasingly unable to identify. Is there something wrong with him, too?

"What did they say to you?" she asks, attempting to resume the conversation.

"That they would like to keep on being able to change. That going Outside doesn't interest them if it means being separated."

"Do any of the others think the same way?"

Why didn't someone tell me? Elisa continues to stroke the cow, vaguely aware of the comforting warmth of the animal and the sound of the other cows chewing their cud or moving in their stalls. She alters the question for Abram. "Why didn't you tell me," she says, and watches his reaction.

He takes it in his stride. "You have other things to do. It's not that important. Nothing serious. It's a sort of mental game, mostly. As they get older they see that the Project is a good thing, and also they want to leave because they're curious to see what it's like Outside. We talk these things over among ourselves."

We talk these things over among ourselves. What of it? She knew about it, she's always known that a good part of the children's lives and problems are worked out away from her and the ommachs. But now she sees that while she'd registered the fact intellectually, she'd never really imagined what they could have to talk about. Or that they might discuss things they wouldn't tell her.

She leans against the shed wall, feeling perplexed. What's going on? Two kids have juvenile ideas, and for some reason she's completely undone. Nothing serious, Abram said. Just a passing phase.

And what if it isn't just a passing phase?

Why, come to that, is she so upset at the idea of Francis and Florie staying together?

"Do you think they're more serious about it than the others?" she asks Abram, aware that she is definitely turning to him for help. But how can he help her?

He can't, apparently. "I don't know," he replies. "For the moment they're serious. I haven't any idea how they'll feel about it later on. They're always together."

Together. She listens to the word echoing within her. Yes, that's what's bothering her. That the children think they're in love, when—when what? When it's just a question of proximity? When genetically they're even closer than brother and sister?

Not real people. Is that it? She can't take them seriously, not because they're too young, but because in her heart of hearts she doesn't think of them as really *two*.

Her sense of shocked consternation almost makes her want to laugh. Does she still have the illusion, the fantasy, after all these years, that the children aren't distinct individuals? As if they were a single being in several bodies? Does that explain why she's never attached much importance to their sexual games? It didn't mean anything, *because they were playing with themselves*. But in that case she should be more worried about Francis's and Florie's relations with the two Sestis.

Come on, Elisa. You're shocked, good and proper. Admit it. Not shocked. Worried. Because this is a real relationship, with others that are truly *other*, and the consequences for them—. Yes, shocked. Because Francis chose to be male with Barro. Repetition. The mirror image. But does being the same sex wipe out your individuality? Just because they both have penises doesn't make Francis and Barro the same *person*. Anyway, it's all nonsense. What is Francis's sex? He hasn't any! Or else it's whatever he wants.

Elisa doesn't know whether she's horrified or

amused. She takes a deep breath and tries to regain her composure. She can't possibly think these things, not after years of telling the children that, boy or girl, they are themselves and it's all that matters!

She can feel Abram's eyes on her, and she turns her head to look at him. This time he doesn't lower his eyes, but he's still controlling his emotions. A feeling of dizziness overtakes her; it's as though she were facing a total stranger. The sensation passes off, but why is it easier to think of him as another person, rather than Francis and Florie? Because he was the firstborn? Because he knows more about her?

"And you, Abram, what do you think? About Francis and Florie, about leaving?"

"Francis and Florie? I told you, I don't know. They're always together, they've always loved each other like this."

"And you think it's serious. You don't think it's an illusion, that it's just because they've always been together?

"In that case we should all share the same illusion. But it's not the case. Each of us is different; that's what you've always told us. For some reason or other, they have a special bond. I don't know if it's serious, as you say, but it's certainly real. You mustn't force them."

"Of course not."

Abram gets up. The pail is full, and he takes it over to the large vat by the door to empty it. Elisa watches him, silhouetted against the open doorway: tall, lean, yet muscular. He comes back, grabs the stool, and sets it in front of another cow. The rhythmic squirting begins again.

"To make a long story short, you don't think there's anything to worry about. All we have to do is wait. Francis seemed particularly aggressive to me, however."

"That's because he's unhappy about Barro. And he must have been afraid of your reaction if you found them together."

"Afraid? I've never been a dragon about that sort of thing. You've always been perfectly free on that score."

"They're no doubt feeling guilty about not wanting to leave," says Abram after a moment's silence.

No doubt. She flicks a fly away from her face. She hesitates, but she's got to know, to set her mind at rest. "And you, Abram?"

The squirting stops, then starts again. "Well, I'd like to know something about the Outside as it is now."

Elisa raises her eyebrows. "You won't be leaving for two years! And the ommachs will report directly to the City, which will produce documentation for you as you need it. A year will be ample time to bring you up to date."

Abram straightens up and wipes his forehead with an arm, pushing away the tumbling hair. The light from the doorway falls briefly on him and Elisa blinks. But Abram doesn't give her time to question her fleeting sense of *déja-vu*. "And what about you, Elisa?"

"Me?"

"You don't want to go Outside with us?"

She laughs. "I've got other things to do besides being a tourist, Abram. The Sestis to save, for one thing, remember?"

There is a pause, and then he repeats, rather obdurately, "Well, I'd like to know what's happening Outside right now." The cow moves restlessly. Abram soothes her and begins milking again. "Why not send ommachs out right away, Elisa?"

She frowns at his childish stubbornness. "Because it isn't necessary. And because the council has decided to send them out only a year before the first departures. You voted for the motion, didn't you?"

Abram continues milking and says nothing.

Elisa considers the incident closed. "When are you going to begin building for the Sestis?" she asks.

Abram lifts his head and looks at her for a moment. His face is in the shadow, and his emotions are strangely clouded as well.

"When the ground has thawed."

⚡ 12 ⚡

ELISA STOPS THE HORSES ON TOP OF THE promontory overlooking the site chosen by the Sestis for their future village. Work is pretty far advanced. A fairly large clearing has been made beside the lake, with tree trunks and stones piled nearby. Nearly half the stumps have been cleared and dumped beside the trunks.

Most of the Sestis are there, both men and women. Only the babies have remained in the village. A cart returns from emptying its load of stone. A small girl is perched on one of the horses, which jogs peacefully along despite the bare little feet hammering its sides. The youngster sees Elisa and gives a big wave, to which she replies while setting her wagon in motion.

Elisa asks for Abram, and finds him busy stacking tree trunks. She would have spotted his red shirt anyway, without asking. When he sees Elisa he jumps down and strides over to her. She is about to give him a hug, but he stops in front of her, eyes squinting in the reflected glare of the sun on the lake.

"You came all by yourself?"

Elisa raises her eyebrows. "I don't often get the chance, with all that brood you left in the village. I needed a change of scene. You don't need an army to bring provisions, as far as I know."

"There are a lot of white cats about."

Elisa bursts out laughing. "I still know how to use a gun, you know. Anyway, they're not dangerous. Help me unload the food. We've made cakes for you."

"Gerri!" yells Abram. A deeply tanned teenager clambers down the woodpile and jumps into the wagon. Together they guide the horses toward the cabins and tents that make up the camp.

"How's it going?" asks Elisa as she passes a sack of

flour to Abram, while Gerri gravely marks down the list of provisions in a notebook.

"It's coming along fine. We'll have finished clearing earlier than planned. We'll be able to start work on the foundations next week. Here, let me do that. It's too heavy for you. You must be tired. Wouldn't you like to rest?"

Elisa puts the small barrel down at his feet. "What solicitude, Abram! I didn't think I was that decrepit."

To her astonishment he blushes. "It's not that. You must be tired, that's all."

"Of course not," she says, laughing and pulling a big package from the bottom of the wagon. "Take care, these are the cakes."

All the same, she's sweating by the time they've finished. The beating summer sun is beginning to take its toll, as is the five-hour drive over the bumpy trail cut through the forest by the children. She checks her body and balances her metabolism, although feeling a little guilty about doing so. The children know they're supposed to live like normal human beings Outside, and that they shouldn't use their regenerative faculties except in emergencies. She smiles, amused by her twinge of conscience. They decided in council to use it as little as possible, even in the village. It's not the first time the children have taken her proposals a step further.

"I think I'll have a dip in the lake. Coming, Abram?"

He hesitates, then follows her. They get towels and walk along the shore to the bathing cove. The noise of the site fades in the distance, cut off by the thick forest. Elisa slips out of her clothes and dives in. The first shock of cold water brings her blowing to the surface. Abram is still on the shore. She waves, and he undresses and dives in. She tries to catch him, but he eludes her, and swim as she may, she can't overtake him. She gives up and floats on her back, watching him swim back to shore with a powerful crawl and get out. "Okay, okay, showoff, I know you swim better than I do!" she shouts, laughing.

Still laughing, she emerges from the water and towels herself down vigourously. Abram is already pulling on his pants.

"Leaving so soon? Work, work, eh?"

He smiles hesitantly. "I can stay a little, if you like."

Elisa spreads her towel on the sandy grass and stretches out with a sigh of ease. "I wouldn't want to keep you from your duties!" she jokes. Abram takes his role as foreman so very seriously.

He sits down, clasping his knees. "The day is almost over, anyway."

Elisa closes her eyes, listening to her gratified body, naked in the sun. She should come to the site more often. How calm it is, after the village full of children under fourteen! Then she becomes aware of a growing awkwardness, a tension that takes a little while to penetrate. She opens her eyes to see Abram turn away. Mystified, she studies his profile, clear-cut against the blue sky.

"Something wrong, Abram?"

He stiffens, and she feels him struggling to control his uneasiness. It fades, but doesn't disappear. "No. Why?"

She sits up, about to say indulgently that he ought to know he can't keep anything from her for very long. Suddenly they both turn their heads: from the forest comes the sound of growling and snarling, and twigs snapping. Then a laugh, followed by a female voice choking, "Stop it!"

Abram is on his feet; Elisa hasn't time to register surprise at his violent emotions bordering on panic. A naked girl appears on the edge of the forest, a towel thrown over one shoulder. Beside her, leaping about like a puppy, is a white feline. The girl is Florie. She freezes at the sight of Elisa and Abram. So does the cat.

For a moment Elisa is dumbfounded. Then she gives Abram a dig in the ribs and laughs. "Are those your fierce beasts?" Turning toward the new arrivals, she says, "Beauty and the beast," admiring the young girl's slim grace. "I had an idea they might be tamed. Hello, Florie."

Florie smiles timidly in return. "When did you arrive?"

Elisa frowns. What's eating Florie? Why is she so flustered, although that's an understatement, to say the least! "Just now. Have you had that cat tamed for long?" Elisa adds, pointing to the immobile animal at Florie's side. It's a big one. The head is almost level with Florie's hip.

There is the slightest hesitation before Florie answers, "Since we got here."

Elisa can sense Abram's relief. She folds her arms; let's see what happens. "What's going on here?"

"Nothing," says Florie too hastily, glancing at Abram. Is there a plea in that glance? "I trained him, that's all."

The cat suddenly moves, going over to Elisa with slow, deliberate steps. It stops in front of her, sits up on its hind legs, and changes.

As though caught in a shimmer of heat, a slow-moving mirage, the white fur melts, the tiger-like muzzle and the big paws. . . . In front of Elisa stands a naked adolescent, eyes flashing.

Francis.

Pain brings Elisa to her senses: she's clenching her fists so hard that the nails are biting into the skin. Her head swims as she unfolds her fingers one by one. Her teeth are clenched, too, she realizes, and her whole body is one big knot. She struggles desperately to regain control. Slowly she takes in her surroundings, the people standing around her, staring at her. Florie, Abram, and Francis. Terrified.

"How—?" A mere croak. Hearing it shocks her so much that she can't go on.

Francis raises his chin defiantly, despite his fear. "It's easy. You just have to want to do it." A short white fuzz spreads over his body, then disappears. "Easy. Any one of us can do it. Why wouldn't we?"

"That's enough, Francis," says Abram brusquely, advancing toward Elisa and the boy. "Get back to camp."

Francis doesn't budge. "Why do you want to lie to her? She made us, didn't she? She ought to know it's possible."

"It's not possible," Elisa hears herself murmur in a choking voice, "not without machines, without the trance, not just like that!"

"Of course it's possible," exclaims Francis. "You may be too afraid to do it, but we're not!"

"Francis," growls Abram, his hand raised.

The boy stands his ground. "Go ahead, boss, hit me!" he shouts, his voice rising to a shriek. "Keep on shielding her, your precious Elisa!"

The blow sends Francis rolling on the ground. Florie jumps on Abram, but he throws her off with the back of his hand.

"Stop!" screams Elisa.

Suddenly everyone is still. She looks at each of them in turn: Francis on the ground, Florie half up, Abram. . . . She feels she ought to explode, but strangely enough she's filled with a sort of monstrous calm. "Francis and Florie, go back to camp. I'll deal with you later."

Francis rises, helping Florie up, and they both go, shoulders adroop.

Elisa's calm, like the eye of the storm, appears to vanish with them. She sits down abruptly, feeling her legs go weak. A shadow falls across her. It's Abram; he hands her clothes to her. She stands up and puts them on, forcing herself to think, to find the words to fill the echoing emptiness that seems to surround her. *You just have to want to do it.* Change. Whenever they want. They can—. No need for machines, for trances. Of course. She'd always thought—. Paul. For her it was linked to Paul. She'd never been able to transform herself completely otherwise. Without him. But not the children. Of course not the children.

At last she manages a coherent thought: it's not surprising the children voted for post-hypnotic prohibition of metamorphosis, once they were Outside; they'd betray themselves all too easily otherwise.

Elisa feels herself become calm quite suddenly, and other thoughts crowd in. They did vote for it. They want the Project to succeed, to be carried through. Whatever faculties they may possess, they're behind the Project. *They're behind me.* Francis and Florie—are Francis and Florie. They have a special problem, but it isn't typical of the rest. Probably.

She turns to Abram, who is looking at the ground, his arms folded. "Does everybody do it, Abram, change into just anything?"

"No. Francis is a case. The young ones do it to begin with, but they soon get over the novelty." He looks up and adds, explicitly, "We make them get over it. After the age of ten or twelve, it's finished. There was a relapse when the Sestis appeared on the scene, but that's over now."

Elisa shakes her head reproachfully. "And that's one of the things you don't tell the grownups."

Abram looks at her with surprising intensity. "Would you have wanted to know?"

"Of course! It's important to know that you haven't the same limitations as I have. For the Project, it's very important."

"The Project," says Abram, dropping his head again. He picks up the towels. "We don't really exist outside of the Project, do we?"

She quells her sense of surprise and anger. "Don't talk nonsense, Abram," she begins. He puts the towels over his arm and looks up at her. He's no longer trying to hide his emotions. Perhaps he can't. He is very unhappy.

"Abram," says Elisa brokenly, "you don't really believe that?"

He stares at her, lost. "I don't know."

"Abram, you've all built up the Project as much as I have, more if anything. We've always discussed it."

Abram shakes his head, still staring at her. No. *No?*

"You don't realize.... You've never realized...." He seems to be choking.

"What, Abram?"

"That it's always you who decides!" he says, throwing the towels down on the ground. "You make proposals, you guide the discussion—."

"What!" She hears herself shouting and recovers herself. "That's not true and you know it. You all make proposals that I've never even thought of: post-hypnotic conditioning to forget the City, metamorphosis, you were the ones who—."

"We, we! But do you think we don't know what you want, even if you don't say it, even if you don't know yourself? Don't you think we can *feel* it? Do you think we can resist you? We love you, Elisa, you created us!"

Don't you think we can feel it? Francis's words echo in her ear, an ironic counterpoint: *You may be afraid to do it.* And something else: *Shield her, your precious Elisa.* Did they always anticipate her wishes? Had the council been a game, something they went along with all this time? Was the Project something they just went along with, too? No, not the Project! They wouldn't have lied to her to that extent, they couldn't have. Empathy is a two-way street. They're basically behind the Project. They're prepared to go Outside.

Abram goes over and touches her arm. "Come on; the sun is setting and it's getting cool."

She shakes him off. "You, Abram, you're behind the Project, aren't you? You know that it's a good thing, that we ought to carry it through?"

The silence is too long. Abram's expression is one of anguish.

"I—yes, of course. We have rare faculties, and we have no right to let them be lost."

"But?"

"Elisa," he says gruffly, "why—?" He stops, then says more quietly, "What gave you the idea of the Project?"

She moves a few steps along the shore, feeling exasperated. "You just said it yourself, for heaven's sake, and I must have told you myself a hundred times: I had rare faculties, and I hadn't the right to let them be lost, to wait for the slim possibility that some chance mutation might develop similar faculties on the Outside."

She turns around, sensing that Abram has followed. The sun is sinking and it throws off less heat, but its light has become gold and softly luminous. A part of her mind admires the clean lines of Abram's torso, the splendid, smooth shoulders, and the curls, darkened by the water, sculptured against his brow. His clear, grey eyes are more limpid than usual in this light. How odd that he decided on this somatotype, so different from his original physique. Where did he find the model? During his escapade in the City, probably, when he consulted the screens. Something stirs in her at the thought, possibly a remnant of anger. She has no time to analyze the sensation.

"Why didn't you simply stay Outside?" asks Abram, his voice muffled.

"Because it wouldn't have been effective, Abram. I've already told you that as well!"

"You could have remained a man," he says quietly.

Elisa stiffens. "What's this all about, Abram? You're no longer prepared to leave?"

He doesn't answer immediately. Instead, he looks at her intently, although he seems to be looking right through her. Finally he mutters, "I don't know any more."

With carefully controlled voice, Elisa asks, "Why, Abram?"

His emotions are hard to discern. He's trying to hide them again, with some success. But his control breaks down when he says, "Because I want to stay with you."

She laughs, a fraction of a second later than she would have liked, "Ah, that's not possible, Abram. Big boys must leave their mamas."

But she can feel that her body isn't laughing; her body is afraid. Her throat is dry, her muscles tensed for flight.

"You aren't my *mama*," says Abram indistinctly.

"No, much worse," she says lightly. Something has

slipped into Abram's expression, something she can't quite grasp, something—.

Someone.

"Well, I'm going back to camp. We've got to see about dinner. Let's talk about it some other time, all right?"

She waits for a second, and as he says nothing, she leaves.

You're running away, Elisa.

Absolutely, she says to herself with an effort at sarcasm. But the other Elisa isn't taken in by it. *You shouldn't have let it pass without saying something.*

What about? Abram's oedipal fixation? No, that's just it, I had to avoid giving it more importance than it deserved.

You were afraid.

Afraid to get involved in useless argument, yes! It was neither the time nor the place for it. The kid felt it himself, anyway. He didn't persist.

The kid is a man, Elisa. The kid resembles someone you know, Elisa.

She kicks a pebble and starts walking faster. Ridiculous. No, she was a little surprised, that's all. That he had chosen such an unsuitable moment. She was thinking of something completely different.

Really, Elisa?

For God's sake, she's got better things to do than think about Abram's hormones!

What about yours, Elisa?

What an idea! What's that got to do with anything, anyway? In the first place, she has no hormones. That is to say, she's got them perfectly under control. In any case, sexuality hasn't much to do with hormones. It's all in your head; she ought to know. She's managed to get along without it for twenty years, because she had more important things to do.

She hurries toward the cabins. The fires are lit and supper is being prepared. The sun is sinking fast, and the air is cooling off quickly. She automatically hugs her light jacket close for warmth, then, with conscious defiance, she deliberately controls her body temperature. Hormones, really! It would do Abram good to go away. Perhaps he ought to leave sooner than planned.

⚡ 13 ⚡

FRANCIS AND FLORIE DON'T TURN UP FOR DINner. Neither does Abram. Elisa notes their absence with annoyance, wondering what the other children must think. No one appears to be very concerned. Elisa tries to forget this afternoon's scene, but she can't get rid of the thought that behind their smiles and affectionate gestures the children are watching her. As soon as she can, she heads for bed.

She isn't really surprised to find herself in front of the tent that Abram shares with Anders and Ari. The tent is dark and silent. She lifts the flap. "Abram?" No answer. The tent is empty. In the slice of light falling through the opening, Elisa sees that Abram's things are gone. She hurries over to the corral where the horses are grazing, peering through the moonlit dusk for the unmistakable silhouette of Abram's white mare.

She isn't there.

The little idiot has gone back to the village. With Francis and Florie? Perhaps. They've taken a wagon, in that case. She certainly isn't going to check it out! Furious, Elisa goes to bed.

The next morning the other children begin asking about the three absentees. Elisa can't tell whether they believe her, but she says Abram has gone to the village, and Francis and Florie have probably decided to take a holiday. Her holidays are over and they must all get back to work.

Elisa reaches the village early in the afternoon, her horse in a lather. She left the wagon at the lake. She can't decide which emotion is uppermost: anger or anxiety.

Francis and Florie are there. They look at her accusingly, but that is all. Abram? No one has seen Abram. His room is tidy. Only a few familiar little objects and some of his clothes are missing. On the night table is a piece of paper, folded in four, with Elisa's name written on it.

And nothing written inside.

And suddenly, as she carefully refolds the white paper, Elisa knows whom Abram looks like, whom Abram chose to look like. Impossible to ignore it, now. It's not a shock, though, not a blinding flash; it's a quiet flooding of knowledge, an inescapable flow that fills her mind and body, leaving her no place to hide, no place that she cannot know whom Abram resembles.

PART

4

⚡ 1 ⚡

THE VIETELLI REGION HAS CHANGED. THE ruins of the town surrounding the three highrises have been virtually cannibalized. Traces of the city grid emerge: crumbled walls, a few streets that are now roads or paths between field and wood. Barns and silos dot the plain, but not many dwellings. Most of the population must live in the three highrises. Possibly, they're easier to defend. Vietelli looks more like a fortress than it once did, ringed by triangular fortifications and huge earthworks topped by wooden palisades and square towers. A single gate on the southwest side faces away from the Badlands.

A blue and yellow flag waves above one highrise that shows the marks of fire. The tops of the two other buildings glitter in the sun. "Glass panes," says Halter in response to Elisa's question. Greenhouses, probably. Why not? There was a town here, and abundant documentation. These people haven't started from scratch. Elisa shrugs. Abram has taken a lot of trouble to leave an obvious trail. Did he lead her here because he thought she'd be amazed? Childish of him. Heaven knows what fixation he's got about the Outside because of the screens. What's he been imagining on the basis of such fragmented, misleading data? He should have talked to her about it. She would have explained once again that all the stories he's fabricated are simply that: stories. He can't know, he can't really understand what happened a long time ago. She herself is uncertain about her memories. Imagine having made his face look like Paul's! But she didn't even love Paul, not really, not like she believed at the time. Poor Abram, fabricating Paul's face.

But you didn't realize it, Elisa. Not until he went away.

She sets her horse in motion with a sudden pressure of the knee. "Halter, remember not to appear too curious, and say as little as possible about us."

Halter doesn't answer. There's no need to remind him: ommachs never forget.

They're well into spring here, and the trees are a cloud of green and copper. In the ditches the winter-brown grasses have thrust up new shoots. Small, horn-less brown cows graze in the pastures beside long-legged sheep and stunted, shaggy white horses. The domestic aminals on the Outside aren't like those in her village, with genes preserved intact by the City's computer banks. Elisa frowns: that's something she hadn't thought of. She'd left too quickly; there hadn't been time. Their own great roans will certainly be noticed. Already they've drawn curious stares from the occupants of a passing cart.

"About the horses, Halter. Say we've come from a great distance and that we've revived an old breed."

One improvisation after another. Really, Elisa, Abram would be only too happy to see how much he's rattled you. You took off without a second thought, all for a crazy kid. Too late now. She should have turned back when she saw he wasn't going to let himself be caught, when she saw he wanted her to follow his trail—to Vietelli. Why? What does the little idiot think? That she doesn't want to leave the village because she was traumatized Outside? What cheap psychology! That was twenty years ago, Abram, and I'd do it all over if I had to!

Except change yourself.

She hadn't had time. A needless risk, anyway, since there might be people in Vietelli who remember Hanse.

There might be Judith at Vietelli.

All the more reason. Judith didn't see much of Elisa and won't remember her so well. Maybe Judith isn't even there. Twenty years. Anyhow, that's not the point. The point is to find Abram, reason with him, take him back to the village.

You won't even try to find out what's happened to Judith?

There'll probably be no need to even ask.

The plaza is crowded. A market or a festival, or both. Brightly-coloured booths, canvas awnings, butcher stalls, chickens cackling, vendors arguing, laughter and shouting, snatches of music from a guitar or mandolin, and the clear, rhythmic ring of hammer on anvil. Soldiers patrol through the crowd in pairs, distinguishable by their blue and yellow jackets, navy shirts, and black trousers. And their guns. Rifles, guns, definitely not homemade. A good many of the things for sale look like factory products, as a matter of fact. Elisa picks up a hunting knife and examines it: stainless steel. On the blade near the handle is the trademark: Wardenberg. There was a town of that name in the north, near one of the last Cities stopped by Desprats. Elisa puts down the knife, noting that the fat old saleswoman swathed in voluminous black is looking at her with hostile curiosity. Not hostile, maybe, but suspicious.

She isn't the only one. Elisa feels other stares, and sighs. Of course, a woman in men's clothing. Halter's company isn't enough to absolve her of this transgression. She murmurs to the ommach, "Find out what's going on, Halter. I'll be with the horses."

A man is there, one knee propped on a hay bale, stroking the muzzle of Elisa's horse. A slim, deeply-tanned man in tight-fitting, tawny leather garments, black hair tinged with grey, a hawk-like profile that becomes an angular face as it turns toward her. Striking blue eyes in a thirtyish face, smiling, friendly. Watchful.

"Fine animals you've got there."

Elisa gives a noncommittal grunt and pretends to look for something in a saddlebag.

"We don't see many of these around here," he continues, undaunted.

Out of the corner of her eye Elisa sees Halter striding toward her. Already? The ommach stops beside her but says nothing.

"You wouldn't sell animals like this," says the man easily to Halter, as though the ommach had been there the whole time.

"No," replies Halter.

"It would be worth your while if you wanted to. There must be others where you come from. The Northwest, eh?"

The voice is just right, the facial expression as well: that of a man genuinely interested. But Elisa can sense the suspicion, the hidden tension. While his eyes are on Halter, she takes the opportunity of giving the ommach an imperceptible nod in response to his questioning glance.

"Yes," says Halter, "from the Northwest."

"It's your accent," smiles the man. "We don't get many travellers from the Northwest, although we had one yesterday. He had a fine horse, too."

"Is he still here?" asks Halter with just the right note of indifference.

"He left almost immediately. Heading for Libera, the city of women. Much good may it do him."

The blue eyes observe them each attentively. The man smiles at Halter, revealing even, white teeth. "My name is Corrio. Are you just passing through or looking for work? We could use a hefty fellow like you around here. And if your horses are stallions, maybe we could arrange something. How about it?"

"Just passing through," says Halter. "Where's Libera?"

Elisa controls her impulse to interfere. No use expecting much subtlety from an ommach; he wasn't programmed for it. And a woman would certainly not be expected to take the conversational initiative, even if she *is* dressed like a man.

"Don't you know? East of here. I thought Libera was better known than that. That guy yesterday knew where it was. Even if it wasn't much good to him."

"Why not?" asks Halter at Elisa's prompting.

"Come on! It's a city of *women*! No man can get in." He jerks his chin in Elisa's direction. "If you're thinking of going in with her, forget it."

The man starts petting the horse again. Elisa bites her lip. A city of women. All right, she might as well ask.

"Is Libera far?" She senses the man's satisfaction as he turns toward her, but she doesn't care.

"Two days' journey, if nothing happens to delay you. But you can leave with Judith tomorrow."

"Who's Judith?"

"Well!" says the man, smiling broadly. He is surprised and curious, just the same, although he conceals it. "She's—I guess you'd call her the chief of the free women. Haven't you ever heard of her? She'd be annoyed to learn that not everyone in the Northwest knows who she is."

Elisa shouldn't insist, but she's got to find out. "Judith, the one who used to be Manilo Vietelli's third wife?"

The man nods, smiling from ear to ear but even more surprised. His face has hardened slightly, despite the smile. "That's it. Today's a great day. The official reconciliation between Vietelli and the free women. Between Manilo and Judith."

Manilo? But Manilo is dead. Elisa sits down abruptly on a hay bale. *Strange that this should be the straw that breaks the camel's back. My poor Paul.* "No needless violence," he'd said, and she'd felt a scream rise in her throat. How could he say that when he was butchering women? No needless violence? And it was true, he hadn't killed Manilo.

She lifts her head. Blue and yellow soldiers have materialized around them. Halter stiffens, but she puts a hand on his arm.

"Come," says the man with smiling ferocity. "I'll introduce you. You must have some interesting things to tell us." He pauses. "About the Northwest. Your young friend didn't stay long enough, yesterday."

⚡ 2 ⚡

CURIOUS AND GENERALLY HOSTILE STARES follow them as they are led off to the west tower, the one Elisa remembers from her first visit to Vietelli. The old ornamental fountain is still there, still a children's sandbox; there are about twenty playing in it, voices echoing in the huge hall. Girls, a few boys maybe. It's hard to tell. They're between two and five years old, and all of them have cropped hair. Three old women sit watching them, sewing or husking vegetables. Elisa can feel an anxious look following her as she walks by the sandbox. She turns her head and one of the old women immediately drops her head to look at her work. Her face is disfigured by a great scar where a sword cut has broken her nose and slashed the left side, from forehead to jaw.

So they did fight against Malverde? Or else a women's revolt. . . .

The soldiers halt before a studded wooden portal. Corrio opens it. The door swings back easily, despite its thickness, to reveal the sound of voices. He turns to Elisa, finger on lips, and whispers sarcastically, "Quiet please; you're witnessing history in the making."

Twenty years earlier this was the Vietellis' common room. Now, large windows open onto the outside; tapestries cover the walls, and tiles have been laid on the floor. A massive wooden table stands in the centre of the room, surrounded by a dozen high-backed chairs, all occupied. Some twenty people are standing at a little distance from the table in two distinct groups: one on the right, clad in blue and yellow uniforms, and another on the left, wearing padded jackets, tunics, and full brown or black trousers in various styles. The dark-trousered ones are women, fairly young, with cropped hair and noncommittal expressions. No one is armed.

A guard stands with his back to the door. He turns around, sensing it open. Corrio signals him to be silent and pushes Halter and Elisa to his left, against the wall. "Stay there." He walks over to the table.

"Don't do anything until I give you a sign," Elisa murmurs to Halter in Franglei. She gives herself a rapid internal inspection and calms her body. Only then does she look over the shoulders of the others to see the table. Corrio is bending over the man at the right end. Manilo, fiftyish, his red hair just tinged with grey, now looks exactly like Carlo Vietelli. Elisa glances at his neighbors, those facing the door. A fairly old man in uniform, another in a green and brown jacket, another. . . . At the centre of the table is the first woman: thin, blond, black eyes beneath a broad, flat forehead. No. The one next to her is too young, and the one after that has the flat nose, jet black hair, and almond eyes of an Asiatic.

"Well," says a clear voice at the other end of the table, "since Corrio has done us the honour of rejoining us, perhaps we can get on with business? Unless he cares to do us the further honour of explaining his sudden departure."

Elisa can't see the woman speaking; she tries to shift her position but the guard restrains her. "He said to stay here."

"We've got distinguished visitors," replies Corrio smoothly. "That is to say, a male and a female visitor. From the Northwest. And with horses as fine as yours, my dear Judith. Friends of yours, perhaps?" Over the heads of the observers, he catches Elisa's eye. "Come here, you two."

Elisa moves forward before the soldier can actually push her. People turn and make way. Curiosity, surprise—alarm. But she has no time to discern the source of the alarm. "Over here!" signals Corrio, and she stops between him and Manilo.

At the other end of the table, both hands resting on the edge as though she were about to rise, is Judith. Oh yes, it's Judith. The clear grey eyes, the rounded forehead, the full lips. Elisa recognizes her all too well, despite the cap of short white hair. *(White?)* Judith relaxes. As she leans back in her chair again the slanting light picks out the signs of age Elisa is looking for, the lines around the eyes, between the eyebrows, the deeper fold at the corners of the mouth.

Astonishment, then joy, flash behind the grey eyes resting on Elisa. Joy. And now Judith's impassive face conceals jubilation.

"Yes," notes Corrio, "a friend of yours." He turns to Manilo. "Quite a coincidence, isn't it? Three people out of the Northwest in two days, all with the same big horses and all so strangely ignorant. But on the other hand, so curiously knowledgeable. This one doesn't know where Libera is, but she's aware that Judith was your third wife. Odd."

"Has all this got something to do with today's meeting?" asks Judith dryly. "We're discussing serious business, Sin'ri Malverde."

Malverde? A Malverde with Manilo in Vietelli?

"Where's the man? Let him come forward, too," says Corrio. Halter pushes his way through the bystanders, who step aside before his tall bulk. "What about him, is he also a friend of yours?"

Judith gives Halter a quick once-over and looks away indifferently. "My friendships are nobody's business but my own," she says curtly.

Manilo looks puzzled and vexed. "Who are these people?"

"Really, does it matter? Let's get back to work, shall we?"

The group of men begin to mutter, while the women gather closer together. Manilo slaps the flat of his hand on the table and turns to stare at Elisa.

"Your name?"

Elisa senses a nebulous anxiety. She hesitates, glancing toward Judith, who quickly turns her eyes away. The anxiety recedes. "I'm called Kramer," she says uneasily.

"No first name?"

"Elisa," Judith says wearily, with studied sarcasm. "She's an old friend. I wasn't aware we were going to discuss our private lives, Manilo. If so, do you really want all these people around?"

Manilo doesn't react. No one reacts. Elisa is amazed. Manilo at least must recognize the name. Judith must have told him about it, must have told them all about Paul, the metamorphosis, the murder, and Paul's death.

"Good idea," says Corrio facetiously. "We're a bit crowded here for family reunions. What do you say we keep it intimate, Manilo?"

"Enough, Corrio," says Manilo. He doesn't raise his voice, but Corrio's sneer disappears. "Judith, who are these people?"

Judith folds her arms. "It has nothing to do with today's meeting."

Manilo sighs and turns once more to Elisa. "Why are you here? Where do you come from?"

"From the Northwest," Elisa lies. Then, to give the lie credibility, she adds the truth. "We're looking for the boy who passed through here yesterday."

"And who left for Libera," remarks Corrio.

Someone in the group of women sniggers. "We don't take *buggeri* either, Corrio; you ought to know."

Manilo lays a hand on Corrio's arm. The latter drops his head and clenches his fists. "As a matter of fact there are too many people here," says Manilo with apparent calm. "Judith, I'd like a word in private."

Judith hesitates, consults her women with a look, then shrugs. "So be it."

For a minute no one moves, then the men leave the room in a group. The women saunter out in their wake. Only the people seated at the table are left.

"They go, too," says Judith, with a smile for Manilo.

"But Kerri stays with me, since you're no doubt going to keep Corrio."

The woman who remains had been seated at Judith's left, her back to Elisa. Now she stands behind Judith's chair, a tall, heavy woman with an impassive expression that is somehow strange. But Elisa has no time to study it.

Manilo has risen. "Now Judith, I want to know what's going on. I've invited you here in good faith, and I'd like to think you came in the same spirit. Who is this woman, this man, and that boy yesterday, and why are they here?"

"I have no idea," replies Judith, her expression one of perfect sincerity.

She's lying. About what? She can't *know what brings me to Vietelli! Then she must think she knows.*

Suddenly Elisa has had enough. She yanks out one of the chairs and sits down. "Yes, just what is happening here?" They all turn to look at her. She studies them one by one: Corrio alert and tense beneath his sardonic air; Manilo perplexed and—unhappy? The big woman, Kerri—nothing, not a single emotion. No one there. No one? *An ommach!*

"I believe you haven't seen Judith for quite some time," Corrio says suavely.

Elisa recovers her self-control with a violent effort. "What's going on here?" she repeats, rising and turning toward Judith, who looks at her with fleeting astonishment.

"The free women are reconciling their differences with Vietelli, that's all," she says calmly.

"And *that* is a free woman?" says Elisa, pointing at the female ommach.

"That is Kerrí, my right hand," replies Judith. This time her astonishment is barely concealed. *What* is so surprising?

Elisa loses control, banging on the table as she shouts, "Enough! Who gave you this ommach? What are you up to, and what's going on here?"

Things happen fast. "Take Corrio, Kerri!" snaps Judith. The female ommach leaps at Corrio, throws an arm around his neck, and whips out a hidden knife, holding the blade against his throat.

"Don't make a move, Manilo," says Judith rising. "Not a word."

Manilo freezes halfway between sitting and standing, white beneath his freckles.

"I don't know what your game is, Elisa," adds Judith in the same quiet, cutting voice, "but don't you move either, and keep your man over there. Are you with me or against me?"

"Neither," says Elisa, completely bewildered. "I simply want to know what's going on!"

Judith looks at her closely. A hint of misgiving crosses her face, and she walks over to Elisa.

"Let her be Halter," says Elisa.

The ommach becomes immobile. Judith gives him a curious look. "Halter. The other one was called Ostrer, wasn't he? But this is one of them, too." She stands in front of Elisa, her expression diffident. "You really are Hanse, aren't you?"

Manilo collapses into his chair while Corrio struggles to free himself. But Kerri's hold on his throat tightens.

"I am Elisa," says Elisa, trying vainly to keep her voice from shaking. "I *was* Hanse. You didn't tell them, Judith. You didn't tell them anything."

An incredulous lift of the eyebrows, almost scandalized. "They wouldn't have believed me."

Elisa sits down again, her legs trembling. Her body is beyond her control. She would like to question Judith some more, but her voice has deserted her. She looks at Manilo, at Corrio half smothered by Kerri's arm, at Halter, still as a statue. The light filtering through the tall windows gleams on the polished surface of the table. Elisa feels blinded, in a dream. She's dreaming. As in a dream, she asks in a toneless voice, because she must ask, "What did you say, Judith, what did you do? Who gave you this ommach?" She expects no answer, and when Judith's voice sounds in her ear, she jumps.

"Then *you* didn't give it to me? It wasn't you?"

Judith is leaning over Elisa, looking at her. Elisa returns the scrutiny, watching fury replace disbelief in the painfully familiar face. "It wasn't you. It never was you!" Judith hisses. "In that case, what are you doing here?"

Elisa flinches. Such violence, such—suffering. Judith is wounded, terribly wounded. But Elisa doesn't understand. Why should she have to justify herself, and about what?

All she can say, finally, is, "I was following Abram."

But Judith has straightened up, once more in control of herself.

"Judith," says Manilo, shakily, rising, "Judith, please. We've both worked for this meeting. Too many things are at stake here. Vietelli has nothing to do with these people being here, I assure you. You know Corrio. He never knows when to stop being suspicious. He was thinking of the good of Vietelli. Whoever these people are, if you say they have nothing to do with today's meeting, I'm ready to believe you. I'm ready to hear your explanation. Stay, Judith. Too much hangs in the balance."

Corrio gives a stifled grunt. Judith scowls, then signs to her ommach. Corrio crumples to his knees, gasping for air. Manilo sits down again slowly without looking at Corrio. Judith returns to her seat at the end of the table.

"Tell your Corrio to keep out of it. I've come here to parley with you, not him."

"Never mind," croaks Corrio. "I get the point." He gets up and drops into the chair on Manilo's right, clutching his throat. He tries to catch his chief's eye but fails. Manilo forces himself not to look, staring instead at his hands, clenched in front of him.

"The door, Kerri," says Judith. The ommach stations herself stolidly at the entrance. *She'll fold her arms next*, thinks Elisa, hysterical laughter welling up. Not only does the ommach fold her arms, she plants her feet well apart and raises her chin. *Who programmed her, for God's sake?*

Manilo wipes his face. "Now, Judith, explain who this woman is and why you spoke about Hanse."

Judith doesn't answer right away. Elisa, dazed though she still is, can sense Judith's underlying tension. Is she getting ready to lie?

"This is Hanse," says Judith. Manilo doesn't react. "Those weren't Gods twenty years ago, Hanse and the other one, Ostrer," she continues. "You knew that already. They came from a City. But they wanted to stop it. There was one other man in their City, a madman who murdered our women and had armed Malverde. After killing Carla and Sentina, he stayed in the city and drugged you. He had a mask of your face. Remember the mask? He hypnotized me. I went to see Hanse, to make love with Hanse. Next morning the madman and Hanse got into an argument, but he kept calling her Elisa. He snapped his fingers and Hanse became a woman. Elisa. She has the power to change her body. After that she killed him and went back to the City with the other, Ostrer. They took the body with them."

There it is. The truth. How strange it is to hear Judith sum it up so neatly! But that's how it was. Why is she so tense, then? Elisa straightens in her chair.

"And afterward, Judith?" Elisa persists.

A sidelong glance. Yes, calculating. Judith makes a face. "You must have stopped Malverde's machines. When we attacked, they were out of commission."

"But what did you say, Judith?"

Judith grimaces. "That I'd killed the madman, the demon. That you'd gone away, saying we had no further need of you, since I had killed the one who was helping Malverde, but that you would help us from afar."

"And you convinced them to let women go into battle?"

"I backed her up," says Manilo wearily. "I agreed. I had agreed for a long time, Judith. Why didn't you tell me the whole truth?"

A brief flame lights up the grey eyes. "Would you have believed me?"

Manilo is suddenly still. He looks at Elisa and blinks, but says nothing.

"You don't even believe me now!" says Judith bitterly.

But it isn't really bitterness, just that hidden tension, something calculating.

Manilo raises a hand. "I'm ready to—."

"Let her change, then," breaks in Corrio.

"No!"

Elisa realizes she is standing, although she can't remember getting up. Who shouted like that? It must have been her; they're all staring. She forces herself to sit down, tries to control her jerky movements, to explain that she can't change at will, that it was Paul, it depended on Paul. Beneath it all she can feel a burning core of refusal. She's lying, she knows it, she could change but she won't, *she won't* change! She sees and feels Judith's disbelief, her anger, Manilo's tired bafflement, hears Corrio's snigger, but she can't say a word, she's suffocating.

"In any case, it's not really relevant to our business today." Manilo speaks quietly, but without conviction.

"And the ommach." Corrio's voice is biting. "She said that Kerri was an ommach. The Cities, Manilo. Judith's made an alliance with the Cities."

Judith stands up and smashes her fist on the table. "Take him, Kerri!"

Before Corrio can rise, the female ommach has him in a stranglehold, with the knife again at his throat.

"Enough of this!" Judith's fury masks an inner calm. "I told him not to interfere. You didn't tell him to keep his mouth shut, Manilo. As usual, he's the one you listen to. You were talking about confidence? I no longer believe you. If that's your overture, forget it. The free women will stay in Libera, and if we're attacked we'll defend ourselves. We're leaving now. And we'll take your precious Corrio with us, in case you'd like to stop us. He wanted to know what's going on in Libera? Well now he'll know. Nothing. We're not preparing for anything. I'll send him back to you once we're there, because I came in good faith, Manilo. Come, Elisa, your place is not here."

⚡ 3 ⚡

THIRTY KILOMETERS TO THE EAST OF VIETELLI, the rolling hills gradually flatten out into a grassy plain where the crumbling traces of old roads become more frequent. Stretches of vegetation, too thick and too green, and the occasional wet glitter mark areas of swampland. Far to the east a mist is rising, an opaque mass, its edge tinged red by the setting sun. In contrast to the luminous sky above, the mist seems almost tangible, resting over the unseen lake.

Elisa turns to the woman with Asiatic features who is riding at her side. "Magritta, how far till Libera?"

The woman has an odd hesitation. "A day's ride if all goes well. But we'll be stopping for the night soon."

Elisa stares at the woman, surprised by her shyness. Magritta looks away.

"Have you been with Judith long, Magritta?"

The tension lowers appreciably. "Since the beginning. Fifteen years."

"What was it like in the beginning?"

The woman hesitates again. "Difficult. They wanted to disarm us at Vietelli. The chieftains didn't want any more women soldiers. We left."

"They let you go?"

Magritta bares her large yellow teeth in a sarcastic smile. "Hardly."

"Magritta!" calls Judith from up front. Visibly relieved, the woman urges her horse forward. Elisa looks after her as the woman brings her horse into step with Judith's black horse, a great beast with a coat like satin, as are all the women's horses. Unmistakably a horse of the City, even if Judith has persistently refused to admit any connection. Elisa glances at Judith's back, straight as a ramrod. On her right is Halter's impassive profile. She gives an inward sigh: no use expecting much enlightenment from that quarter either. All he could tell her is what she already knows: Judith's ommach comes from the City, but refuses all contact with Halter.

Who? Who in the now deserted City has supplied this ommach? The children, Abram? No, it couldn't be! Abram might look at the screens, but he wouldn't do this! Her leaden brain refuses to work, but she forces it to consider the other possibility. Desprats. He lied to her. He hadn't terminated his program. For reasons that she doesn't even try to guess, he has continued to observe her, to manipulate her.

Perhaps it's only the Outside, he's kept on observing the Outside. There's no proof that he's interfered with her own or the children's lives. He might have merely observed and done nothing. But as long as she's ignorant of the facts it's as though.... To be free, to imagine that—.

What's all this contorted logic for, Elisa? This is exactly why you've never wanted to look at the screens to see what's happening Outside!

"Not much for small talk, these free women," says the sardonic voice of Corrio behind her. Now she finds that she's stopped her horse and is in the middle of the column. She waits for Corrio to catch up, then urges her horse forward. Corrio smiles sociably at her, as though his arms weren't tied behind his back and his horse's reins looped over the female guard's saddle.

"If I understand correctly, you don't know much? I thought City people were better informed."

She looks at him for a moment. *Don't know much is right!*

"I don't live in a City."

Corrio seems unperturbed by her short laugh. He studies her, eyes half closed. His obdurate hostility comes through beneath the affected sarcasm.

"Tell me the men's version, then," says Elisa wearily. "What happened after Malverde?"

Corrio's smile contracts a fraction, and he hesitates.

Elisa sighs. Corrio must be trying to see what advantage he can gain from his story, trying to figure out how to manipulate her.

"We created women's contingents at Vietelli. After Malverde fell and the so-called emperor Kurtess marched into the region hoping to profit from the confusion, the other chieftains also armed their women. Kurtess had to retreat and the women were disarmed. Not in Vietelli. Within five years Vietelli had become the strongest community. Judith—Judith is a remarkable woman."

Elisa contemplates Corrio's closed face, the hard eyes, the .jaws clenched in hate. Manilo, Judith, Corrio—beings who hadn't existed for her other than as faint memories. Here they are, twenty years later, having lived a life of which she knows nothing, about which she can only guess, appalled, at the web of loves, hates, unforgiven quarrels, a whole lifetime. A lifetime. *And what am I doing here? What did I do?* She chose to leave them to their own devices. Was she wrong? She let Judith choose, Vietelli choose. Judith chose to lie, and Vietelli replaced Malverde, *but it has nothing to do with me!*

She senses Corrio's stare and raises her eyes to see him turn away, again masking his inner feeling beneath a sardonic smile.

"A remarkable woman, Judith. The other chieftains finally had enough, however, and gave Vietelli an ultimatum. If the women weren't disarmed, it would mean war with all the communities. Manilo tried to reason with Judith. She departed in a welter of blood and thunder to set up a women's community on the shores of the lake, among the ruins of a city that they christened Libera. A city where there must have been quite a number of interesting things, because they stayed there, despite the fever. They have fine horses, don't you think?"

"Go on, Corrio," says Elisa.

Corrio's smile widens at her impassivity. "Well, that's all. It happened fifteen years ago. They stayed in the marsh and managed to survive. There were a few attempts to dislodge them, but the terrain was hardly propitious. Other women gradually began to make their way there from various communities in the region, and later from further afield, the north and east, mostly. Since they weren't up to anything they were finally left alone. And two months ago Manilo thought it was time to try to reconcile everyone, since it all happened so long ago. That's what you expected, isn't it?"

"I expected nothing." She hasn't the strength or the will to match his agressiveness. "I knew nothing, Corrio." She listens to her words, unable to discern her feelings. *I knew nothing.* It's a fact, that's all.

"Come on," says Corrio. "The Cities have always known very well what's happening."

The tone is still nonchalant, but the underlying emotions have changed. Elisa looks at Corrio, astounded by the flare of violence.

"How old are you, Corrio?"

She's caught him unawares. He takes a fraction too long to reply.

"Thirty-four."

He was fourteen at the time, then.

"You are the son of Stacio Malverde."

She expects a sarcastic smile, a look of understanding, with Corrio grasping her intent perfectly well. But now something heavy and dark unfolds within him. He says simply, "Yes."

"And what is the son of Stacio Malverde doing with the man who destroyed his father's fiefdom?"

Aha, she's touched a nerve. Corrio gives a start, trying to hide his involuntary reaction by shrugging his shoulders. Nevertheless, she can sense his continuing turmoil of spirit: anger, suffering, and fear.

"I didn't agree with my father," he says somewhat stiffly. "Some of us didn't like the demons, the ommachs, and their ways, even though we didn't know at the time that they were machines. Anyway," he adds with a logic that escapes Elisa, "I was the younger."

His inner pain intensifies at the word. Elisa lets the silence stretch out, bewildered by his emotion. One can fill in the gaps, of course. Older brothers, perhaps just one, and that one the father's favorite. The younger brother's love rejected. Maybe Malverde was a peaceable man before Paul tempted him with the vision of power. The young Corrio's despair at seeing his father turn into a cruel despot. Love changing to hate. Then the Vietelli's attack, the father's death, the brother's too, probably. Guilt piercing his adolescent soul once more, then collapse. Manilo taking him under his wing, probably motivated by a mixture of politics and true compassion. Transfer of filial love to Manilo and the inevitable confrontations with Judith.

Yes, it's easy to imagine a story. But that's all it is: a story. *Stories, Elisa, that's all you're capable of knowing. Even your memories have become stories, as much for the others as for yourself. Whose version is right? Where is the reality?*

A small noise draws her out of her bewildered state. Corrio gives a snort. "What can the Cities possibly want with us now? You're getting bored again, I suppose, in need of a little diversion?"

Elisa sees him blink and cower in the saddle. She lets her hand drop back on the pommel of her own saddle as she calms her enraged body. At last she says, in a voice carefully controlled, "Listen to me well, Corrio. I left the City, the last City, twenty years ago. I've had nothing to do with the Outside. I wanted you to live your own lives, and for that I killed, Corrio, I killed the man who caused Malverde's downfall, and it was no game. I have no idea what has happened in the last twenty years, *no idea!*"

Her horse shies, and she strokes it until it calms down.

"And just by chance you came to Vietelli today of all days," says Corrio after a slight pause. There is no defiance in his voice, only utter disbelief.

By chance. No, certainly not by chance. But that would take too long to explain. *That would be yet another story, wouldn't it, Elisa? Another story that you could make up to explain Abram's behavior?*

"I was looking for the boy who passed through Vietelli yesterday, that's all."

"And who is this boy?"

My son. Say it, Elisa. He's your son, isn't he? You're running after him, aren't you? Of course, he's not a real child, right?"

"My son."

Corrio no longer laughs scornfully, doesn't smile, doesn't say anything. After a moment he asks a genuine question. "Are you really what Judith said?"

Elisa nods. She has no strength left to be surprised or glad at Corrio's apparent about-face. They ride along in silence as the dusk thickens. The road twists and turns in the swamp, no doubt in response to the vagaries of solid ground. The racket of the toads and frogs ceases momentarily as the troop files past. The fading light catches the steely surface of the still water, broken only by clumps of sedge and the contorted arms of countless dead trees. As far as the eye can see are islands of greenery where the light spring foliage has not yet covered traces of crumbling walls. Here and there buildings rise, seemingly still intact, their rows of black, gaping windows opening onto the labyrinth of canals that were once streets. Clouds of insects fly up as the horses pass, and Elisa instinctively alters her skin secretions for protection.

"It's a girl," says Corrio suddenly.

Elisa looks at him uncomprehendingly. He returns her stare, his mouth smiling but humourless, his spirit shaken by confused emotions.

"She tried to make Manilo believe that it was his child, but in the end she told him who the father was. Twenty years ago. Judith had a daughter."

NIGHT HAS FALLEN BY THE TIME THE CAVAL-cade halts. Elisa slides off her horse, her boots squelching as she hits the spongy ground. Every now and then the moon shines through the heavy cloud cover, lighting up the gloom. Now that her vision has adapted, she can see a spit of land, one of the marsh islands covered with stunted willows. Beyond loom dark hulks silhouetted by the glint of water. More ruins.

She unsaddles her horse, stretches the blanket on the ground, and sits down, relaxing her quivering muscles, eliminating toxins, methodically working through the familiar maintenance check in a comforting ritual. Around her is the sound of women moving, a few words, laughter, the chink of iron, the hiss of damp wood burning. A puff of wind blows smoke in her face and she begins to cough. Halter hands her a gourd and she drinks. She's floating in a timeless limbo, in a dream. She mustn't let her mind wander, escape. This is no dream. *It's reality, Elisa. But which reality?*

Movement, an approaching shadow that stops beside her. Her hope is short-lived: it's not Judith, but a tall, slender girl whose auburn hair glows darkly in the dim light. There is something timid about the way she hands Elisa a bit of bread and cheese. Elisa studies her in the leaping flames of the campfire: a heart-shaped young face, large, firm mouth, and an expression of anxious solicitude. She shakes her head in refusal. "I'm not hungry. Go ahead and eat. What is your name?"

The girl stiffens, muttering something like, "Gavra," and strides off. What is she afraid of? What has Judith told the women? Elisa should get up, go find Judith, ask her. But she doesn't move, refusing to ask herself why, refusing to think. Judith has said, "Wait: you'll see," and so she'll wait. Somewhere, sometime, somehow, Judith will explain.

More stories, Elisa?

In an effort to stifle the inner voice, she gazes at the flicker of the campfire on faces, hair, and the slim, silvery leaves of the willows, letting the marsh sounds fill her consciousness with croaking, gurgling, the swish of grasses and the buzz of insects, something yelping twice, and the beat of invisible wings flapping somewhere above the trees.

Come.

"Come!"

Elisa jumps, and the dream voice (what dream? it's gone) blends with the voice of Judith, shaking her shoulder and whispering once more, "Come!"

Instinctively adjusting her night vision, Elisa gets to her feet. Halter is already up. A few shapes are stretched on the ground in blanket rolls and the women keeping watch crouch around the faint red coals of campfires. But the others have disappeared along with their horses.

"Come," Judith repeats impatiently. "Kerri is looking after your horses."

She shoves them toward the other side of the spit of land, where ruined masonry rises behind the willows. "Watch out for the steps." The warning is unnecessary, although Judith doesn't know it. Both Elisa and Halter see the opening between the walls, the moss and grass-covered steps, and the ceramic tiling, cracked and broken by vegetation.

At the foot of the steps is an arch, almost intact, leading into a large, low room. Just how large is difficult to tell in the gloom, but beyond is a black hole pierced by a tiny, moving light. Enough light to reveal to Elisa's eyes a large, vaulted corridor, its sweating walls full of cracks and loose bricks. Moss-filled puddles in the broken pavement show the marks of recent passage: horseshoes, judging by the muddy tracks. There is a dank smell mingled with horse dung and a whiff of skunk. The light moves, a dim lantern held at the end of a tunnel that must be a hundred metres long. Everything drips, visibly or invisibly, making a persistent rain that forms a continuo to their echoing footsteps.

The point of light draws closer and becomes Magritta, who begins walking as soon as Judith and Elisa reach her.

"Where are we going?" Elisa asks at length.

"To join the others."

"To Libera, by underground passages?"

"To Vietelli, by underground passages," corrects Judith with a fierce smile.

After a half hour walk through the flooded subway, the darkness begins to recede and Elisa has to adapt her vision again. Small electric lamps appear at a fork in the tunnel, lining the walls at regular intervals. There is no time to ask about the source of this power. Elisa is told to get back on her horse, and they trot the rest of the way, the deafening ring of the horses' hoofs effectively stopping all conversation.

An hour later, they ride out into an immense cavern. Tunnels open into it from all sides, although only one is illuminated. It must have been a maintenance shop for the subway cars that now lie in one corner, a heap of rusting skeletons. At the moment the cavern is a camp. Beneath white arc lamps stand a dozen or so large tents. Campfires are burning. The horses are corralled behind ropes in one corner, and numerous women rise as the riders appear. As she swings down from her horse, still dizzy from the noise, Elisa notices the guns stacked in sheaves before each tent.

Judith leads the way, not bothering to check whether she is being followed, dives into one of the tents, and strides past canvas partitions opening onto a central corridor. Elisa glimpses rows of camp beds, sleepy faces, and naked torsos sitting up as the visitors pass by. The corridor ends in a room of modest proportions containing a large table strewn with papers, a blue plastic thermos, an open case of ammunition holding down one corner of a map, and two walkie-talkies.

A woman in her forties, hair severely brushed back, rises as Judith enters. She wears mottled blue fatigues, tied at the waist with a twisted sash ending in gold-flecked pompons that contrast oddly with the rest of her outfit. They embrace briefly.

"Any problems shaking them off?" asks the woman,

handing the thermos to Judith, who takes it and collapses into a camp chair.

"No," she replies between mouthfuls, "I think we pretty well lost them in the swamp. We left a few girls there to preserve the illusion until morning. Have you found suitable replacements?"

"Leaving right away. They'll finish the job of losing the Vietellis tomorrow."

Judith offers the thermos to Elisa, who shakes her head. Judith shrugs and takes another swig.

"We'll attack as planned, then?" the woman asks.

"Not quite as planned, obviously." Judith puts down the thermos and points to something on the map. "How long would it take Doris to get through this way with all the rest?"

The woman frowns. "Empty Libera?"

"Judith," says Elisa, taking a step forward.

"We need diversion, since we can't count on the soporifics. It takes time to get over four hundred women through these passages, and later, when in the air ducts, it means moving in single file. I want to have a good number around the palisade, to prevent them from paying attention to what may be happening in the towers."

"Judith!" repeats Elisa.

This time Judith stops talking and looks at Elisa with a odd expression.

"You must be tired, it's true. Fedra will show you where you can sleep and wash, if you like. Don't you remember Fedra? She was the youngest of Carlo Vietelli's wives. Fedra, this is Elisa."

Elisa looks, not at Fedra, but at Judith. The years have dropped away from her face because of the soft light in the tent, and Elisa remembers another Judith, low-voiced and passionate: "We can die too, and we can kill!" There is another memory: an ardent, flame-like Judith; rage, despair, and faith burned in that flame, but it was a clear, pure flame. It is still there, flickering, smoking, distorted. How strangely familiar, and how uneasy Elisa feels at this familiarity.

"Go," says Judith gently, almost tenderly, "you must

be tired. I'll come and see you in a little while. Now I have work to do."

Elisa allows Fedra to lead her down the canvas corridor and show her the toilets and showers, probably renovated equipment that served the maintenance crews in days gone by. She notes vaguely the respectful, almost fearful looks of the women she passes. At one moment a sharp emotion penetrates her senses, cutting through the fog of Elisa's perceptions like a flash of steel. Anxiety and pain. She looks around, momentarily roused from her torpor, but sees only a few familiar faces nearby: Kerri, Magritta, the girl who offered her the water and then strode off. But she can't establish who is afraid, who feels pain. The effort is too great; she gives it up, gives herself up to Fedra and does what's expected of her, undressing, washing, toweling herself dry, and going into a little tent beside the larger one where she left Judith. When Fedra leaves, Elisa is seated on a camp bed, her willpower gone, arms resting on her knees and hands dangling free. Halter comes in and sits in a corner. She asks him nothing and he says nothing.

After a moment she tells herself she's going to close her eyes, just for a few minutes.

5

COME, ELISA, COME.

She sits up, her heart in her throat, sweating from every pore. Why is she so terrified? There seems to be no reason. A dream. What dream? Already it has faded. An impression remains—a color? Just a dream. Nothing to worry about. She must control the cramp in her diaphragm, her pounding heart. Halter's shape hasn't moved since a moment ago (when was that?). They must have lowered the arc lamps for the remainder of the night. It's very dark in the tent.

"Halter, what's the time?"

"Five twenty-six," says the ommach's calm, precise voice. Elisa feels a burst of affection at the comforting sound.

Real human beings are so unpredictable, aren't they?

"Has Judith come, Halter?"

"No."

She lies down and closes her eyes.

⚡ 6 ⚡

AT SIX O'CLOCK A HIGH-PITCHED WHINE echoes somewhere in the cave, followed by sounds of people rising, coming out of their tents. Footsteps, rustlings, low-voiced conversations carried by the still air, and the smell of food.

Footsteps approach Elisa's tent and stop in front of it. A hand thrusts aside the canvas flap. Elisa sits up, then rises. At first she can see nothing but a silhouette, strangely familiar against the backlight. But she can sense something that freezes her to the marrow. Fear. Violent fear turned aggressive.

At the same moment the arc lights beam brighter, illuminating the tent interior. Stupefaction now, from within and without, as though Elisa's own emotion were thrown back at her, as though she found herself face to face with a mirror image that was more than physical. The girl's hair is short and straight, but it's the same colour as Elisa's. The face is the same shape, the mobile mouth, the wide brown eyes, and the bony figure.

She looks like me! Elisa's mind yawns like a great cavern, where the words echo again and again, expanding, mocking. *Well, if she's your daughter, why wouldn't she look like you?*

The girl takes two quick steps forward, grabs Elisa's left hand. A quick movement, a burning pain in her palm. The ommach grabs the girl roughly.

"Leave her alone, Halter!"

The ommach stops short, supporting the girl to keep her from falling, then drops his hands. The girl still holds the knife. She stares at Elisa's hand. The blood has barely had time to well up before the wound begins to close.

The girl spins on her heel and flees.

⚡ 7 ⚡

OUTSIDE, JUDITH'S ANGRY, ASTOUNDED VOICE shouts, "Lia! Where are you going, Lia?" Hurried footsteps approach the tent, the flap is thrown back, and Judith bursts in. At the sight of Elisa she stands still.

"What has she done to you?"

Elisa looks at her outstretched hand. Not a mark. She lets her arm drop.

"She attacked you, is that it?"

Elisa blinks, feeling almost choked by Judith's fury. It explodes empathically within her as though the tent walls were confining and concentrating the emotion.

"Did you show her? Did she see? She never believed me, never!" As she speaks, Judith slaps one hand against a fist, switching hands as though tossing a ball back and forth. "She's like you. You saw the resemblance. She never wanted to believe me. Did she attack you, strike you? Did you show her?"

Elisa sinks back onto the bed, trying to put some space between herself and Judith, to get away from the incandescent rage and the suffering beneath it. But her empathic sensitivity won't let her.

"She only wanted to check," she says tonelessly, but Judith doesn't hear.

"She's never been able to change. That's why she wouldn't believe me. And yet how like you she is! But you can't tell her a thing. She has to see it for herself. You'll show her, you've got to show her. If you change, she can't avoid seeing it."

Suddenly she stops talking and turns toward Elisa.

Her rage subsides, surmounted by an equally strong
emotion, a sort of fierce adoration that is no less suffocating for Elisa. "I waited for this, Elisa. I waited so
long for you to come. When you sent me the ommach
after we set up Libera, I watched for you each day for
months. I thought you would come."

Has she forgotten what happened at Vietelli? "I
didn't send you the ommach, Judith!"

Judith halts the rush of jubilation, her mouth open.
She seems to deflate, to shrink.

"You didn't say it for Manilo's benefit, yesterday?
You weren't just play-acting?" The question gradually
becomes a statement. "It wasn't you who helped me, it
really wasn't you."

Involuntarily, Elisa glances at Halter. He is looking
intently at the two of them. Judith's emotions are a
thundercloud, dark and heavy, shot through with flickers of angry light, discernible even when she breathes
deeply, seems to calm herself, and sits down beside
Elisa.

"Who, then, if it wasn't you? The other, Ostrer?"
she says reasonably. She laughs abruptly, but a flash of
horror passes behind the grey eyes. "Or did you resus-
citate the other, the madman?"

"No!"

They stare at each other for a moment. Elisa is the
first to break the silence, wanly, with a low, "No."

"The other, then. Ostrer."

Elisa shakes her head, overcome. How can she explain Desprats to Judith? A dead man who survives in
a cluster of programs. She has no idea why one of
these programs should decide to help Judith—or how,
come to think of it.

"Were there others? In other Cities?"

"No. No, Ostrer and I, we stopped all the other
Cities. Ostrer was a machine, an ommach. But different. The City has the technology. When someone dies,
if his experiences, his memories have been saved, his
way of behaving or reacting, we can reconstitute his
personality, or simulate it, at least. For those who see
the ommach it's certainly as though. . . . "

Judith listens, not disbelieving, merely attentive. But how the inner storm cloud swells!

"Ostrer was that kind of ommach," Elisa concludes, feeling rather desperate. She can't keep silent, but what good will her words do? "He bore the personality of the man who looked after me when I was little. *(Who loved me?)* When we went back to the City, after Vietelli, he stopped. Made me believe he'd stopped. It wasn't true. I don't know why he lied."

"A machine that lies," murmurs Judith.

"He was much more than a machine," Elisa begins, then stops in discouragement. She isn't going to explain an electronic psychosimulation to Judith. Anyway, she herself was never able to rid herself entirely of the idea that Desprats' simulation was somehow alive.

"A machine," says Judith again, and Elisa goes up to her in alarm. "It was a machine that helped me." She drops her head to stare at her hands, her fingers slowly folding and unfolding. "And you, what were you doing?" she asks Elisa quietly. "You knew nothing, did nothing."

"I left the City."

"Where were you," repeats Judith more loudly, turning toward Elisa. "I needed you!"

"I wanted to let you live your own life," says Elisa. But the word sounds suddenly hollow in the face of Judith's reproach, her sorrowful indignation. Elisa tries to remember the moment of choice, the moment when she thought she was making a choice. Did she choose? That impetus which she took for certainty, was it merely compulsion, allowing others to choose and abrogating all responsibility herself?

"Our life," spits Judith, "you saw what our life was like, you knew it had to change!"

Elisa struggles to control herself and keep the discussion rational. "It *did* change, Judith, because of you. You didn't need me: you managed very well on your own."

Not on her own, not quite.

Taking advantage of Judith's silence, Elisa asks gently, "The ommach, Judith, what do you use it for?"

"A bodyguard," Judith answers in a colourless voice. "She's there to protect me. That's what she said."

What about the rest? The electrical power, the walkie-talkies, and probably a lot of similar things? Found in the ruins of the city christened "Libera"? Reconstituted with luck, tireless labour, and ingenuity. Surely they must have had help. If the ommach was programmed to protect Judith, it was easy to extend that protection. Over the years, Judith must have discerned this and made use of it.

Suddenly Elisa feels better, more in control of the situation. Reflect, reason—facts, that's what she needs. Everything is beginning to fall into place.

A likely story, Elisa? Well, yes, a likely story, a hypothesis. She can't go on indefinitely groping around in the dark and wringing her hands, can she? Elisa breathes deeply, satisfied and relieved to feel that she has crossed a threshold and tapped a secret reserve of energy. The facts. What are the facts? She has been thrust into a situation about which she knows little.

Abram thrust you into it. She rejects this reminder, this objection. Deal with Abram later. Abram is en route for Libera. He's out of it for the time being.

So she knows little, but things are getting critical. Judith, Manilo, the free women, the imminent attack on Vietelli. Everything is about to topple again. How could Judith lie like that! How could she have accepted Manilo's offer of peace for the sole purpose of betraying him? And he was acting in good faith. Elisa's empathy can't be wrong about his feelings.

No, Elisa, forget about your stories, your hypotheses. Stick to the facts. The free women are about to attack Vietelli. Those are the facts.

"When are you going to attack, Judith?"

"Tonight, as soon as Doris is in sight of Vietelli, we'll start going up through the conduits."

"And afterward? Do you think that the other communities are going to leave you alone?"

"The other communities." Judith's lips draw back

in a slow smile. "The other communities have fine rifles made in Wardenberg. They need ammunition for their rifles, and we can cut off their supply like *that.*" She makes a sudden fist. "We're the ones who organized the distribution network about six years ago. Without their knowledge, of course. The order has already gone out: not a single case of ammunition will enter the south as of today. Except for ourselves, naturally. We have plenty stockpiled here, anyway."

"But you could have . . . you could have. . . . " Elisa struggles to get the words out. "You could have won without firing a single shot if only you'd waited a little. Why—?"

"Because Manilo offered to meet us. We couldn't have hoped for a better chance," replies Judith impatiently. "Between Vietelli and Libera we can control the entire region. Once Vietelli is in our hands, the word will get around and women will come from everywhere to join us. And the chieftains will have to think about the women in their communities. What will happen back home while they're busy attacking us?"

Logical. Likely. Two fronts. And victory is contagious. There's no doubt it could work. Elisa contemplates Judith with horror.

No doubt? No flaw?

Manilo.

"Manilo is offering you peace, Judith."

"Manilo?" Judith laughs disdainfully. "Manilo's in no position to offer anything. None of the chieftains is. Fifty women are born for every man, even if at the moment there are ten men for every free woman. Manilo is afraid, that's all. He senses how the wind is blowing, and is trying to soften us up while getting ready to crush us. That's what I'd do in his place."

"But he's acting in good faith, Judith! I know it!"

"In good faith? I hope he's not stupid enough to believe in that!" Judith sneers, her face hardening. "It's them or us. Peaceful coexistence is impossible. They'll never willingly give up the power that should be ours through sheer force of numbers."

Elisa listens to Judith's oration, flabbergasted. Such old, worn-out arguments! Doesn't she realize what she's saying? Doesn't she see that she's a walking cliché, the Amazon, the Woman with the Whip, the Devourer of Men?

No, she doesn't. She's ready—and hundreds of women are ready—to die for her cliché. They see it as their truth.

And what do you know about their lives, Elisa? People aren't clichés for themselves. It's you—you see it because you are outside of the situation. And here, on the Outside, you're the only one who sees it. But perhaps they're the ones who are right.

She realizes that Judith has stopped talking and is looking at her with strong distrust.

"Why did you come?" she demands. "Why now? Are you going to stop us?"

Elisa lowers her head, unable to speak.

"Are you with us?" Judith persists, her voice increasingly trenchant.

And if I'm not with you, I'm against you? A flare of revolt shoots through Elisa. "Did you try to come to terms with Manilo? Did you even once envisage the possibility of an entente, of doing something about the present situation, of working toward a gradual sharing of power, of progressing? You can't change people's outlook by waving a magic wand, Judith. It takes work, patience, and education."

"Patience? Time? You talk like Manilo! We're here, alive now, and we've wasted enough time. There are women in slavery now, beaten, tortured, raped, and massacred *now*!"

"But not here, not in the South," protests Elisa feebly. "Here you can still try to come to terms."

Judith rises, disappointment and rancor blazing. "Is this why you've come out of your hole? To preach about patience, negotiations, and resignation? You needn't have bothered. Since you hadn't troubled yourself on our account for twenty years, you might have just as well kept to yourself!"

Elisa grabs Judith's arm and shakes it in despair. "I wanted you all to be free, Judith, free!"

They stare at each other, and suddenly Judith's rage is unaccountably swept away. She sits down again and takes Elisa by the shoulders. "Then be with us, stay with us," she murmurs passionately. "We need you. I need you. Lia—. You've got to show her that it's true, show them all. I told them you would change. I promised. Do you remember what the madman said? Neither man nor woman, but whatever you want. You are the example, the proof. One day we'll all be like you. Stay, Elisa, stay!" She touches Elisa's cheeks, hair, and lips. "I waited so long. I knew you'd come back. Stay."

At Judith's touch Elisa turns to stone. Her impulse is to either shrink back or push Judith away, but her body is beyond control, a hollow, inert shell, echoing with Judith's words. *Yes, stay Elisa,* urges an inner voice, while another whispers in horror, *No, no!*

As in a dream she hears Judith say, "I've got to go now. Come for breakfast. I'll be in my tent." She watches Judith rise and go out, staring at the tent flap gently moving long after it has dropped back into place. When it finally stops, she stretches out on the bed again and closes her eyes.

"What should I do, Halter?" she murmurs after a moment.

"It depends on what you *can* do, on what you want to do," replies the ommach easily. Of course. She programmed him to give this sort of answer to the children.

What you can do, Elisa. Try to get Judith to change her mind, to at least put off the attack and parley with Manilo. Try somehow to sabotage things—warn Manilo, kidnap Judith, let everybody spill each other's guts while she returns to her village. . . .

And what do you want to do, Elisa. Stay or go? She doesn't know. She just doesn't know.

⚡ 8 ⚡

THERE IS SOMEONE ELSE OUTSIDE, STANDING in front of the tent flap. "Elisa?"

Well why not. Another free woman, any one of them, wanting to see for themselves the walking miracle, the Promise: Elisa, the male-woman.

She shrugs and sits down again, running her fingers through her hair. "Come in."

It's the girl who said her name was Gavra last night. Fear and pain emanate from her. (Was she the one in the crowd, earlier?) The girl stands still for a moment, looking at Elisa, then collapses on the bed beside her.

"What do we do now, Elisa?"

Auburn hair, heart-shaped face, brown eyes. But behind the features hovers an all-embracing presence, intangible but unmistakable, Elisa senses the ineffable touch of this being, complex yet familiar.

Abram-Gavra lifts her head as she senses Elisa's reaction. "Didn't you recognize me?" She gives an embarrassed little grin. "I didn't think I was so good."

"To tell the truth, I thought you were on your way to Libera. And I had a few other things on my mind."

Her ability to come up with an easy retort amazes Elisa. Amused, even if a little bitter, she notes that once again she's surprised by people and events. But why would Abram have gone to Libera, knowing Judith was going to Vietelli? She didn't think, that's all.

You didn't think he might transform himself into someone other than Abra in order to fool you.

Elisa studies him. Studies *her*. Studies Abram, Abra, Gavra, someone whose distress, uncertainty, and fear are evident. And love. Uncertainty and fear for Elisa, distress and remorse at having brought her here. The stranger's voice contorts, the full lips begin to tremble. Suddenly she flings her arms around Elisa, pressing her head against Elisa's neck and gasping, "Oh, Elisa!"

Stroking the curly hair, so different to the touch from Abram-Abra's, Elisa gently rocks the body that is shaken by silent sobs. "I did it for you! You had to know, to come out. I thought—I didn't do it on purpose, but after what happened at the lake with Francis and Florie, we got to talking. All at once I couldn't stay any longer. I said to myself, she'll follow me. I wanted to show you. I knew she'd be there. Judith."

Elisa draws back a little and lifts the tear-stained face. "What about Judith?"

Abram-Gavra sniffles and wipes away the tears. "I wanted to talk to you about it at the lake. About what was happening on the Outside. For us too, for the children. But it didn't quite work out as I planned."

"But *what* about Judith?"

"Well. . . ." How well Elisa knows this typical sequence of emotions: hesitation, tension, and sudden relief as Abram plunges into doing or saying what scares him. She can't help smiling at its familiarity. A hesitant smile responds to hers. "I knew she'd borne a child by you. By Hanse. And that she believed in you, was waiting for you. For her, to change was a good thing, whereas for you it seemed to be bad."

Elisa is about to ask if the City has sensors in Libera, when she realizes that she would simply be avoiding Abram-Gavra's last words. Of course the City has sensors in Libera. The City has an *ommach* in Libera!

"I never said it was bad."

Abram-Gavra bites her lip. "But remember how you reacted when Francis changed in front of you?"

Elisa sits up. *Even better, Abram, I remember my reaction in Vietelli, when Corrio suggested I change.*

"I let you change . . . " she begins, but falls silent. She let them change sex, yes, as she herself had done. Each new generation, when they reached a suitable age. A regular change, preordained by her, reassuring. But Francis and Florie—the idea that the children could change without her knowledge into just anything. . . . She feels an inner revulsion. But she is looking at the tear-stained face and anxious expression of Abram in the eyes of Gavra.

Bad. To change. Into just anything. She waits, vaguely aware that there should be some illumination, some revelation at the shock of these words. But there is nothing, nothing at all.

"And you wanted to show me that changing is good?"

"I'm not sure anymore. I wanted to get you out of the village, that's certain. You know, I was—." The eyelids flutter and the brown eyes look away. "I was kind of beside myself."

Elisa lets the silence lengthen. She doesn't know what to say. In the end it's Abram-Gavra who says, with an embarrassed little laugh, "But we've got other problems now."

For a moment they remain in each other's arms, then move apart a little awkwardly. Abram-Gavra sniffs and passes a hand though her hair. At last she says, "We've got to stop them from attacking and make them enter into honest discussions with Manilo, at least."

Elisa is about to trample on what's left of her self-respect and ask what more the screens have shown Abram-Gavra, when Fedra's voice is heard outside the tent. "Breakfast is ready."

The young woman waits until Fedra's footsteps recede, then gets up. "I'll see what I can do. Can I have Halter? I'll send him back to you, and he can be our go-between. Try to talk to Judith."

There is a moment of hesitation, then Abram-Gavra leans over, kisses Elisa lightly on the cheek, turns, and rushes out. After a slight pause Elisa speaks.

"Go with him, Halter."

⚡ 9 ⚡

THE WORK TABLE IN JUDITH'S OFFICE HAS been cleared to make way for a motley assortment of bright plastic dishes. Folding chairs have been drawn up, and on the table sits a pot of steaming coffee, two baskets of sliced brown bread, cheese, honey, and, rather oddly, a bouquet of fresh flowers: pink and white daisies, mauve lupins, and tall blue flowers unknown to Elisa.

Ten or so women are standing around the table talking in low voices. With Elisa's arrival they stop. Only two look familiar: Magritta and Fedra, apart from the ommach Kerri. Judith is seated, and turns around as Elisa approaches. The whiteness of her fine and glossy hair beneath the overhead lamp strikes Elisa forcibly. Judith smiles and points to a chair on her right. Everyone sits down. Judith is tense beneath her smile. The others are very respectful, a little awkward, and expectant.

"Elisa, these are my lieutenants. You know Fedra and Magritta. Gertrudi and Masha are from Wardenberg. Miriam is from Collodi, a community in the Far South. Bardien is from the Northwest ... " and she goes round the table until she reaches a woman on Elisa's left, a greying, stocky black woman who, like two-thirds of those present, is from the South. "You know Elisa," she concludes. Heads nod. They smile a little timidly, eyes shining. Silence. Not a soul moves.

Judith takes a piece of bread and starts spreading it with honey. There is a general sense of relief as everyone helps themselves and passes round the honey and cheese. She serves Elisa coffee in a psychedelic orange cup. "We leave in two hours."

Elisa stares at the swirl of black liquid rising in the cup, well aware of the underlying query. But Judith hasn't asked the question point blank. Not yet.

"We'll be at Vietelli by the end of the afternoon, perhaps sooner." Judith smiles. "Underneath Vietelli, that is. Doris should get through the northeast tunnels around eleven o'clock or midnight. Allowing for a margin of safety, it should take two hours to get into position around the fortifications. Anyway, if the cloud cover holds, they won't see anything."

This is for Elisa's benefit, although she pretends to be talking to the others. Elisa says nothing but looks around the table. Most of the women are busy eating, but Fedra and Magritta are staring at her. What are they hoping for, what has Judith told them? That Elisa would help them? That her arrival would be a sign of magical intervention by the City to destroy Vietelli? No. Judith couldn't have told them that, couldn't believe such a thing.

They're simply looking at her because she's Elisa, the one Judith has told them about, the living proof that Judith told the truth.

A fetish, Elisa, to reinforce Judith's prestige and authority?

Elisa looks again at the women around her, suddenly aware of what's been bothering her. "Where is Lia?"

The atmosphere changes right away to one of embarrassed uneasiness, with a flash of anger from Judith, dissimulated beneath a smile. "Lia has a different timetable. She's working on the infirmary night shift. We've been here for a week, and there are always little accidents, things to be looked after."

Elisa stirs her coffee, studying the glutinous drops left by the honey. She senses the awkwardness and anger subside.

No. Keep them on edge.

"What have you done with Corrio?"

"He's under heavy guard in the main tunnel," replies Judith, trying not to scowl.

Silence again. Vaguely anxious this time.

"And once Vietelli is in your hands, what happens to the men?"

Surprise. They hadn't expected this. Judith responds quickly with a smile. "They're going to work."

Approbation all round.

"You're switching slaves, then?"

Surprise becomes apprehension, verging on distrust in Judith's case.

"It's time they realized what it's like."

"And once they have, then what?"

For all her quick intelligence, Judith is strangely incredulous, unwilling to believe that Elisa could be openly disapproving. Perhaps this isn't the wisest tactic, after all, what with Judith's violent nature always ready to explode. Elisa keeps any underlying defiance out of her voice and asks a genuine question.

"Won't they revolt? You'll have to watch them day and night. You'll never rest easy, and the more victorious you are, the greater the problem."

Judith and the women exchange glances. What is that common flash of emotion among them, quickly stifled but brutal? Heavier, darker than mere fear. Guilt?

Elisa frowns at each in turn. "You've got something in mind, haven't you?"

The eyes look away, except for Judith's, furious and hurt. But she isn't going to quarrel with her fetish in front of the others; she can't afford it.

Elisa swallows hard, with an inexplicable shudder of sorrow. *Oh, Judith! What am I doing?*

You're manipulating her, just as she's trying to manipulate you.

Elisa lowers her gaze to her cup and then, because she must, asks tonelessly, "What have you in mind?"

She can sense the range and priority of Judith's emotions, and above them all, fed by her chagrin and anger, is a calculating, disquieting calm.

"We have drugs in Libera," says Judith simply.

When Elisa raises her head she encounters a steady stare, defiant and, yes, serene. "Would you have preferred us to castrate them? We thought of it. But they're still necessary for reproduction. Drugs are the most humane solution, at least for the older ones. The children can probably be recuperated, and subsequent generations will be brought up differently. You mentioned education, I believe. We've thought of that too, you see. More coffee?"

Elisa shakes her head, appalled not so much by the horror of Judith's plans as her evident sincerity. "The most humane solution." She really believes it. Perfectly sincere, perfectly convinced. Perfectly convincing: the others nod their heads in agreement. The power of this wave of approval leaves Elisa dizzy and groping for her balance in the face of their utter certainty that what they're doing is right, their all too evident good faith. Nothing Elisa can say will breach this wall. She lowers her head, overwhelmed by the flash of triumph in Judith's eyes.

As though she had just dealt with a mere point of routine, Judith turns to the others and starts discussing details of the Vietelli operation. Elisa hardly listens, struggling miserably in the mire of confusion within her. She'd said nothing! She'd found nothing to say!

She's not even sure Judith is wrong!

It's too much. Elisa gets up, ignoring the stares, and hurries down the corridor, but not fast enough to avoid seeing Judith lay a restraining hand on Fedra. Burning with rage, shame, and despair, hardly knowing which is uppermost, she passes through the tent and out into the blinding, false light of the arc lamps. Everyone must be at breakfast. There's almost no one about. She looks at the tents, horses, cases, sheaves of rifles, the reality. *The proof, Elisa, the proof that you're wrong and they're right.* But that's not true, it's not possible!

The earth moves beneath her as a growl and then a dull roar fill the cavern. Stunned, she thinks for a moment it's her disbelief, her overpowering sense of revulsion that is shaking the cavern floor and walls. Then, in terror—an earthquake! The horses whinny and rear. Screams issue from the tents and women run out, some of them half-naked, as a tower of cases topples with a crash. After a moment Elisa becomes aware of a recognizable rhythm in the rumble of successive shock waves. Explosions.

A more violent, closer shock sends one of the arc lamps smashing to the ground with a sharp explosion. Elisa looks up to see a cloud of dust spilling from the ceiling as a whole section seems to ripple like water and collapse on top of a tent.

There is a second of silence as the ground stops shaking. Earth and stones rain down on the crumpled tent. Suddenly, everyone is running wildly in all directions, some heading for the tent. Judith's voice rings out behind Elisa: "Fedra, see to the exit. Magritta, the horses. Trudi, quiet the women down and get them working, and Kerri, find out what the damage is to the tunnel."

The women hurry away and Judith grabs Elisa's arm, pulling her toward the flattened tent with its nascent moans.

Kerri appears in no time, covered in mud and supporting a dark-haired girl whose face streams with blood. Elisa straightens up, tossing away the lump of rock she has just lifted from a crushed leg, and wipes her forehead.

"The tunnel to Vietelli?" asks Judith, her voice hoarse with dust.

"Blocked," says Kerri.

"He blew up everything," falters the girl. "He escaped and blew up everything. Malverde. He killed Galice. Gavra, the new one, found me knocked out. She was with the other,"—the girl makes a gesture toward Elisa that causes her to grimace with pain—"the man who was with her. Gavra and the man went after Malverde and I came to warn you. Everything blew up, everything."

≵ 10 ≵

LATER (BUT HOW MUCH LATER IT'S IMPOSSI-
ble to tell beneath the unchanging arc lamps), when
the last of the wounded has been carried off on a
stretcher, Elisa takes off her mask and gloves and follows Lia out of the infirmary tent. Nothing can surprise her now. The highly developed equipment, Lia's
skill, the general efficiency startled her at first. But of
course it's the City, Kerri, Desprats. She's reached the
limits of surprise, strength, everything. Following Lia
into the canteen, she sees mud-spattered women eating, hears tired voices asking about the wounded. Lia
responds in an exhausted tone.

Elisa moves mechanically to a seat opposite Lia as a
voice floats toward her. "I hope that bastard got killed,
too." She takes a mouthful of soup, but suddenly her
throat closes. *Abram.* She chokes on the soup and
starts coughing convulsively. Tears stream from her
eyes even after the coughing stops, but she keeps on
swallowing soup like an automaton.

Lia stretches out a hand and stops the soup-spoon
halfway between Elisa's mouth and the bowl. Elisa lets
it fall, pushes the bowl away, and drops her head on
her arms. The sound of her heartbroken sobs reaches
her from a great distance.

(Someone is watching her. Elisa searches all about,
but sees nothing, hears nothing, senses nothing except the impression of an eye resting on her, immense, enormous, filling all the space around her.
She is *in* the eye! She tries to call out, but not a sound
comes forth. An aura of catastrophe fills the eye, and
suddenly there are flames in the dark, a terrifying
noise, many voices screaming together, and someone,
someone she's got to find. She runs, telling herself
she can't run, not in an eye, but through the awful

groaning that surrounds her as she runs toward a shape that stands out blackly against a blazing background, she runs, filled with love and terror. *Mama! Mama!* There are too many people, gigantic beings all around her, and waves of hate, sorrow, and pain. She nears the black shape. If only she can reach it all will be well, she'll be safe. But the shape is no longer black now, it's red, and it burns, burns, and Elisa screams, her voice filling the eye, smashing against the invisible walls that splinter and fall on her, and the pain is terrible, vast, unending. . . .)

She opens her eyes on her own image. Terror grips her. She's still dreaming; the nightmare goes on. Then the face becomes Lia, ashen, muttering, "Wake up, wake up!"

Elisa sits up abruptly, holding her knees and shaking her head. "What's the time?"

"Three, four o'clock in the afternoon."

"Did I wake you up? Did I scream?"

Lia gets up, less emotional now. "It was nothing."

"I was dreaming about you," Elisa says, lifting her face to the other. "With you."

The young girl raises an eyebrow, apparently indifferent. She's terrified, in fact.

"You saw Judith wounded or burned at Vietelli, when you were little."

Lia stops cold, then shrugs nonchalantly. "Oh, she told you that, did she?"

"I dreamed it just now. You dreamed it just now, didn't you?"

Lia turns away, pretending to arrange the blankets. "I've got to see to the wounded," she says at last.

11

TWO OF THE WOUNDED WON'T MAKE IT through the day. The others are in fairly satisfactory condition. While they are examining them, Magritta comes into the tent.

"Judith wants to see you two."

Lia keeps on changing a bandage. "I'll come later."

In the cavern, some women are seated on the ground or on cases while others stand about, arms dangling aimlessly. Elisa can sense the stares following her, the uncertainty, the tentative hope they place in her. She follows Magritta without looking at them, afraid that someone might get up and take her arm, ask a question. What answer would she give?

Here is Judith's tent, the canvas corridor, the table, once more cleared for work, the dozen familiar faces, to some of which Elisa can't put a name.

"Where is Lia?" asks Judith curtly.

"Finishing up with the wounded."

Judith points to the chair on her right. Elisa hesitates. No one else is seated.

"I can stand."

Judith frowns slightly, but goes on with apparent unconcern. "Then let's recap the situation. Several hundred metres of tunnel leading to Vietelli have collapsed. It's impossible to clear it all away. Kerri says there's no one alive beneath the rubble. Knowing Corrio, I imagine he timed the explosives to allow him to get clear. As for the two others, Halter and Gavra, according to Lillian, the surviving guard, they'd gone off through the tunnel in pursuit of Corrio a good ten minutes before the explosions began. They may be alive, in that case. Possibly they've even captured Corrio."

Judith stops and looks around the table *Oh, you've got them eating out of your hand, Judith.*

"Let's take the most pessimistic view, however. Corrio gets away and reaches Vietelli, either through the tunnels leading to the towers or away to the north, through the Vieccia tunnel."

"Either way, he's going to warn Manilo," says the big, putty-faced blond called Gertrudi.

Magritta sinks into a chair. "In any case," she concludes, "the operation is kaput."

"*That* operation," says Judith calmly. Hope springs into the eyes staring at her. "Corrio is on foot. He won't get to Vietelli before tomorrow, let's say tomorrow at noon if he runs all the way. That's taking the least optimistic view. Anyway, he could do it. Now what's Manilo going to do? He doesn't know what our losses are, and he'll send messages to the other chieftains in order to get as many men together as possible. Then he'll ride here, hell bent for leather, to try and corner us in the cavern or take us in the open, while we're waiting for the others."

She unrolls a frayed, plastic-coated map. "But we'll be in Vietelli." She looks around at the circle of faces, triumphant this time. "Doris is on her way by the northeast underground network. We have plenty of time to cover the northeast terrain and skirt the hills to avoid being seen, thus making contact with Doris at Vietelli."

"That Manilo and his men will have left!" cries the black woman jubilantly.

"And that will fall without a shot being fired," adds Fedra, clapping her hands.

"And afterward?" comes a biting voice from behind.

Lia is standing there, clutching the canvas flap of Judith's headquarters and looking very pale.

"Krista has just died," she continues. "Pierrette won't get through the night, and Malka the same, probably." Her voice shakes. "How many more deaths? There'll still be a few men left in Vietelli; there's bound to be some fighting. And once we're installed, what then? The other chieftains will join forces against us once more."

"We'll hold Vietelli in hostage," remarks Judith coldly. "And soon they'll have no ammunition."

"They have other weapons! Anyhow, even if they do give in and agree to parley, what will it be worth?"

"We'll watch them closely." Judith's hard-shelled calm begins to crack and her voice becomes harsher. "There are fewer of them than us. It's up to us to see that their numbers shrink even further. We're the ones who have the children. You don't need too many men for that."

Lia stares steadily at Judith, her eyes wide. "A massacre, is that what you want?"

"Did they think twice about massacring us when we wanted to leave Vietelli fifteen years ago? Do they think twice about killing us with hard labor in the mines and quarries? And when we are born, do they think twice about eliminating us?"

Elisa listens, paralyzed. Suddenly she has recognized that faintly flickering light, that constant, jarring note underlying Judith's words: she is mad. Like Paul. And like Paul, she seems perfectly logical, consistent, sure of herself. Elisa distinctly senses how the others follow her reasoning and agree with it, even Fedra with her mitigating, "It won't come to that, Lia; they'll bow to the facts."

But if it does come to that, too bad, eh, Fedra?

Lia leans over the table toward Elisa. "Say something! Haven't you something to suggest, you, woman of the Cities?"

Everyone turns. Elisa crosses her arms over her breast in a defensive gesture. She won't. She's no oracle!

"I'm not here as a woman of the City. The City will not help you." What more can she say? Use the authority attributed to her by Judith as a means of persuading them to change their minds? But Judith will not tolerate further contradiction. In a strangled voice, Elisa states, "I am against violence."

Lia's amazed disappointment and scorn are palpable, as is the sober satisfaction of Judith, who says, "We weren't the ones who began the violence. The men imposed it on us. The sooner we hold power, the sooner violence will stop."

The other women turn toward Judith, toward her convinced, ardent will. Lia gives a shout of rage and runs out.

⚡ 12 ⚡

WITH A SIGH OF RELIEF, ELISA SLIDES OFF HER horse. Around her the others are dismounting as well. Above the snorting of horses and the soft tread of boots and hoofs comes the sound of tired voices through the fine, steady rain. Elisa helps Lia and Fedra set up a tent, then goes inside with Judith and the other two to share a cold meal. There will be no fires this night.

Once they have eaten, Judith sends Kerri to check on the sentinels. Elisa studies the black sky through the tent opening. Judith ordered a bivouac after skirting the hills, overlooking the plain toward Vietelli. She stretches out, feeling the damp cold of the earth through the tent floor, and listens to the sounds of the others getting ready for the night. Kerri comes in with a whispered report and settles down near the entrance. Although Elisa isn't cold, a shiver runs downs her spine. She wanted to tell Judith that she wouldn't come with them, that she was going home; but she couldn't do it. Judith is like a whirlwind that catches up everything in its wake. Go home, join the children? Unthinkable. The children, the village, the Project, the twenty years that have passed—they seem completely unreal. Reality is this darkness, these invisible presences beside her in the night, and the patter of the rain. Judith's dreams seem infinitely real. Because they imply the deaths of hundreds of men and women? *Death: is that the only reality, Elisa?*

She no longer knows. The darkness, the rain, the intermittent snuffling of the horses, this tiny slice of life that is the here and now, this is real. All the rest escapes her. She closes her eyes and regulates her breathing, forcing her body to carry her with it into sleep.

• • •

In the nebulous light of daybreak, Elisa pushes back the covers and goes to look for her horse, nibbling a piece of cheese as she walks although she's not hungry. She leads her horse back to the tent which Lia and Fedra are busy dismantling. Lia's emotions come through as an impenetrable wall of dejection. There are purple rings beneath her eyes. "Eat something before you leave," says the gruff voice of Fedra, full of tenderness. Lia says nothing, but takes a slice of bread and some cheese and goes to find her horse. When she returns, she asks Fedra whether she can go with the outriders to the south. Fedra continues to roll up the tent. "Go," she says, after a brief hesitation. Lia avoids Elisa and jumps on her horse, moving off at a quick trot.

Nearly two hours later, the women are on the road once more. The southern outriders return to report: nothing special.

"Where is Lia?" asks Elisa when the scouts pass by her.

"She's not back yet? She shouldn't be long." But an hour later Lia still hasn't come back. Elisa glances obliquely at Fedra's face, with its lines of anxiety deepening from one minute to the next. Finally Fedra urges her horse forward to the head of the cavalcade where Judith is riding. Elisa follows her.

"Judith, Lia hasn't come back."

Judith slows her horse to a walk and signals the group to go on without her. The two women look at each other. All at once Judith's face sags. "She wouldn't do that."

Elisa is amazed. Judith is incredulous, unwilling to believe that her daughter has betrayed her, and her first reaction is one of—wounded love? Then anger rises, a dull rage, deep, contained, terrifying in its intensity. She gives the order to close ranks and increase speed, and turns without another word to the head of the first group of riders.

It is when the sun begins to rise behind the cloud cover that a horse gallops up. "The Vietelli troops!"

shouts the rider. "Ten kilometres to the south, heading this way. Doris sent me. We saw them leaving for the northeast last night and she decided to follow them."

Judith has stopped her horse. The group stops with her. "Impossible!" The word runs from one rider to the next.

"They're there. I saw them myself!"

Judith bites her lips violently, livid with rage. She doesn't understand. Corrio hasn't had time to get through to Vietelli; it's barely seven in the morning. And even if Lia rode her horse into the ground and got there, Manilo's troops would still be mustering in preparation for leaving Vietelli.

No, Corrio is still in the tunnel. Elisa feels a brief moment of joy: that means Abram must be there too, safe and sound. Halter must have gone to warn Manilo, Halter who can run as fast as a fast-trotting horse, Halter for whom the darkness of the tunnel would pose no problem.

Elisa looks at Judith. Is she thinking the same thing?

But Judith is no longer interested in past details. Instead she scans the rolling plain. "Two companies behind the small wood," Elisa hears her mutter. "That drop to the north, yes, it's feasible." She turns to the girl. "Go back to Doris. Tell her where we are and bring her back. She'll take the Vietelli from the rear. We'll try to gain time. Fedra, call a staff meeting in five minutes, and see that ammunition is handed out to everyone. We'll allow them to come to us. Let them ride their horses to exhaustion! We'll choose our ground."

Elisa studies her, fascinated. Judith is so small, so slim, and yet she's like a blade—hard, brilliant, deadly. She listens while Judith explains the battle tactics to the various company commanders, notes their confidence in her, their love for her. These women are all ready to be cut to pieces for Judith, for the dream that she incarnates.

All at once, as she looks at the resolute faces, panic

grips Elisa. What is she doing here? Is she going to fight? She controls her terrified body. *Isn't that what you wanted? To stay with them. To the bitter end. Well, you stayed.*

To the point of killing? A shape at the end of her rifle, a pressure on the trigger, and the shape falls. But it's grotesque! Monstrous! She isn't going to do it, she can't, she *won't!*

Reality, Elisa. You wanted reality. Why do you think you followed Abram to Vietelli? You wanted to go Outside, to find reality.

In Vietelli? The reality that stopped in Vietelli with the death of Paul?

In Judith's loins?

Lia, the fruit of reality?

A woman comes up to Elisa and hands her a small but heavy sack. "Use them sparingly," she says, and moves off. Elisa plunges her hand into the sack and stands still, rolling the bullets between her fingers for a long moment. *The seeds of reality, Elisa?*

⚡ 13 ⚡

IT IS FULL DAYLIGHT NOW, A GREY, MILKY light filtering through a veil of clouds. It might clear later on. Judith has taken up her position on a slight rise facing the small wood where Fedra and two companies lie in wait—about a hundred and fifty women. On Judith's right two other companies under Magritta are half hidden by a dip in a hollow. Here, weather-beaten ruins thrust up from the soil like the old bones of some gigantic, inconceivable skeleton. One company remains with Judith, turned toward the plain across which Manilo must come. She waits. Elisa waits with her, trying to calculate how long it will take eight hundred men to cover a dozen kilometres at a trot.

They arrive, a black line moving into position in the southwest. Elisa grips the butt of her rifle as she tries, without much success, to quieten her thumping heart. What is a pitched battle like? A real one? She remembers seeing films on the screens as a little girl. Surely Manilo isn't going to gallop forward head down, yelling, "Charge!" His horses must be too tired. Anyway, his men have no lances, and despite their swords and sabres the two armies must rely on firearms, at least in the early stages. No, Manilo must certainly have some plan of attack, some strategy.

Then Elisa sees the galloping horse, the white scrap floating in the wind. For a second she fears a shot will ring out, toppling rider or horse to the grass, but the signal of truce is respected. Elisa senses Judith stiffen at her side and tries to identify the approaching rider. Lia? On an impulse she urges her horse to a trot and goes out to meet the emissary.

Halter. He stops his horse as he hears Elisa.

"Manilo wants to parley with Judith."

"Is Lia with you?"

"Yes."

"And Abram?"

"With Corrio. I found an air duct leading to the surface. Manilo has sent for them."

They ride up to Judith. She looks steadily at Elisa, who bites her lips to stifle the impulse to justify herself. But Judith says nothing, listening instead to Halter's brief message and nodding her head.

"We shall parley, since he wishes it. Go and tell him. But only he and Lia are to come, no one else. There will be *her*," she adds, lifting her chin toward Elisa, "Kerri and myself. In fifteen minutes, near the tree down there." She points to a solitary, gnarled apple tree.

"You come too, Halter."

Judith shrugs. "Why not? Go." She watches Halter gallop away.

Elisa studies the hard, clean profile beneath the white hair. Judith is going to stall for time, since Manilo has given her the chance, but the end result will be the same.

Judith turns her head.

"What happened to your hair?" Elisa asks quickly—anything to put off the inevitable accusations.

A brief look of surprise flickers in Judith's stony stare. "I was burned at Vietelli fifteen years ago. It grew back like this."

"Burned?" says Elisa stupidly. She contemplates the clear skin, marked only by the fine lines of time.

"My skin heals easily. Lia's even more easily." Judith is strangely free from anger, as though detached. "You too, right? She's your daughter, despite everything."

Judith. Who came from the North. Like Hanse, the first Hanse, the white-haired barbarian. "Because you may have impregnated her," Paul had said, "I want to see the result." And Desprats, of course. Desprats helped Judith, protected Judith, preserved Judith. And Lia.

Elisa suddenly finds her voice. "Judith, Manilo really wants to parley. He's acting in good faith, I know it, I'm sure of it. He wants peace. I can also sense people's emotions. He is sincere. War is not inevitable, Judith."

Judith gives another shrug, but there is no violence in the gesture. "He's trying to gain time as well."

"There's still time to negotiate!" Elisa feels inane as she says the words, and Judith actually smiles a little.

"You really haven't the slightest idea what's going on here, have you?" she says indulgently. "This is war, Elisa, and it has been for a long time, even if we haven't fought an actual battle in fifteen years."

Elisa can only stare silently at Judith, baffled and horrified at this calm, this certainty, this—gentleness!

"But you didn't want to know anything about it," Judith goes on. "You knew nothing of what was happening in Vietelli, as you so truly said. You didn't even come here to stop us, my women and me. I bet you didn't even tell your ommach to warn Manilo. It was that girl, the new one. That boy you're looking for, he can change like you, can't he?"

Elisa bows her head. Very gently. A word, a sudden gesture could burst the bubble of unreal calm surrounding her and Judith, who is studying her with a sort of dreamy tenderness tinged with regret.

"We could have done great things together. You should have stayed with me and not gone back to your City. You didn't really kill that man, you see. He still has you in his grip."

⚡ 14 ⚡

THEY REACH THE TREE WHERE THE THREE others are waiting. Armed, of course, as are Judith and Kerri. As they are about to dismount, the drum of hoofbeats comes from the Vietelli lines. Judith frowns, her hand on her revolver. Two horses arrive at a gallop, covered in lather and kicking up clumps of earth as they come to a standstill.

Corrio. And Abram-Gavra.

"What a charming family reunion," smiles Judith as she gets off her horse.

Corrio dismounts and runs toward Manilo, who makes a move toward him then checks himself. The other halts two steps away, drops his head, and goes back to his horse, looping the reins around a low branch. Abram-Gavra gets down more coolly; she doesn't look at Elisa but goes over to stand by her.

"Well, since we're all here, Manilo, even your *buggeri*," says Judith, "what's this all about?"

Manilo turns pale and Corrio leans back against the tree trunk, folding his arms and scowling, a hard knot of fury and hate.

"Oh, no, Judith," replies Manilo at last, in a low voice. "No. I know you don't care whether or not Corrio is my lover." He breathes deeply. "You won't make me lose my temper. This is no time for that sort of game."

Judith curls her lip slightly. "All right, let's play at something else. I'm listening."

"I'll do the listening, Judith. Why are you here with your women?"

Judith is a little taken aback, but she shrugs. "I didn't ask for a parley."

"Why are you here?" Manilo repeats patiently. "Did we attack you? Have we done anything that would justify sending an army of women to Vietelli? We've lived in peace for fifteen years, Judith. Why now?" He gestures in Elisa's direction. "Is she the reason?"

Judith lifts a scornful eyebrow. "Lived in peace? What peace is that? We left for Libera despite you, and you stayed in your strongholds when you realized you couldn't force us out of Libera."

"I offered you peace, Judith. I've always wanted peace since the beginning, and you know it. We didn't fire the first shot fifteen years ago."

Judith pretends to stifle a yawn. "Have you got us here simply to go over the same old ground?"

With a sigh, Manilo struggles to control his temper. "No. I just wanted to remind you that we weren't and aren't the aggressors."

"Really."

"You won't raise my hackles on that subject, either, Judith. This isn't a question of the history of men and women since the dawn of time. It's a question of us, here and now. Listen to me. I have nearly eight hundred men. You have less than six hundred women. Troops from other chiefdoms will begin arriving tomorrow. I don't want to destroy you, Judith. It won't change the fact that more women than men are born. I'm proposing a deal: you return to Libera, and we'll return to our chiefdoms. I'll tell the other chieftains that there was a misunderstanding. I won't say anything about the underground passages. You'll go back to Libera, but you won't shut people out. We should know what's going on there, and you should be more involved in the life of the region. We could surely accomplish things together, even if it's just trade. You should be seen, our people should get used to you. It's the only way. Give up the war, Judith, because—."

"Because you're certain to lose it in the long run."

"Judith!" Manilo forces himself to keep calm. "If we crush you today, how long do you think it will take for a new movement of free women to get organized? What if we nip every rebellion in the bud, squash every women's protest before it gets going? What if each man becomes a guard, a censor, a jailer of women?"

"They already are."

"Not here. In the North and East, yes, but not here! All you'll do is escalate repression until, in the end, we'll be like the rest—the men butchers, and the women slaves, treated like cattle. Is that what you want? I don't! I didn't fifteen years ago and I don't now. We can get along. You can achieve a fairer deal for women. But it takes time, good will, and patience. We'll have to give pledges."

"Disarm," says Judith gravely. But she's playing with Manilo, needling him, keeping him talking while she counts the minutes. "Agreed," she continues. "We disarm and we'll even come back to live near you, with you. We'll disarm, come back, and you'll give us a representative voice in the Council of Chiefdoms. And in the army, naturally. The Council is all very well, but it doesn't *enforce* the law. What do you say?"

Manilo considers her and appears to hesitate. "You know very well that proportional representation is out of the question. But that's the one thing we can't agree on. Perhaps there could be equal representation, but not right away. Let there be sufficient time to establish confidence." He spreads his arms in a gesture of distress. "Haven't you learned anything in fifteen years? You can't treat human beings as pawns."

"You're the one who hasn't learned anything," says Judith scornfully. "We can't live with you on an equal footing. We're *not* equal, Manilo. There are fifty women born for every man, that's the reality. You can't win if you give us a chance. That's the truth."

Manilo shakes his head incredulously. "What do you want? Men's submission? That won't work either. You revolted; so will we, minority or not. That's no solution, as you must be well aware!"

"Men's slavery," comes Lia's hoarse voice. "Men's

slavery: that's the solution, isn't it, Judith? And a few studs for reproduction."

"That's what *you* need, no doubt," snaps Judith. "A stud."

Lia hurls herself at Judith, but Manilo restrains her.

"She might just as well be your daughter," sneers Judith. Her temper is beginning to fray.

"I *am* his daughter. Enough of this lie. You've lied for years, and these poor idiots believed you! Judith, the Chosen of God, Mother of the Divine Child! But look at her, your Elisa: is she divine? Is she a *man?*"

Judith turns ashen. "It *is* true. Manilo knows it. You never wanted to believe it because you never could metamorphose, but it's true!"

"Ah, so that's it? I was never able to change myself! You've never forgiven me, have you? How disappointed you must be! You've ended up believing your own lies, but I was always there to remind you. There's a name for that, Judith. You're mad, *mad!*"

Manilo shakes Lia. "Enough of this!" He turns to Judith, almost pleading. "Don't let's talk of this anymore, Judith. That's not what we're here for. Think about my proposal: you go back to Libera and I'll speak to the other leaders."

"I am not mad," says Judith through clenched teeth.

"I know, Judith," replies Manilo. "I fully realize that it was Hanse who fathered Lia. But that's not the question. We have to make peace. Now. Now, Judith! I still have enough authority to make the others agree to a peace. It will be too late afterward. I've been reassuring them for years. No peace will be possible if we do battle now. They'll be too afraid. It'll be all-out war between every man and woman, leading to what in the end? What? Slavery for one or the other, slavery for *both.* There will be no winners, Judith. If you go home now, if you allow observers into Libera—. I could use certain things, dazzle the other chieftains with what you've discovered in Libera and the benefits they'll reap from honest co-operation. Let's make peace, Judith. Now."

Judith stares at him in silence. A glimmer of uncertainty softens her features for an instant—a very brief instant—before she turns and looks to the south. Elisa can sense her sudden jubilation: a moving line. Doris.

"Peace," says Judith, keeping her back to Manilo. "You can't afford peace, I told you. Nor war. But I can."

She swings around. The switch in sentiment and the sudden gesture are too quick for Elisa, who is still moving when Judith fires at Manilo. He falls like a stone. Lia throws herself at him and the second bullet misses her. The third bullet bites the dust at Corrio's feet as Elisa grabs Judith's arm. Kerri and Halter are rolling on the ground, and Corrio falls to his knees beside Manilo. Abram is heading for Elisa as a fourth shot rings out. Judith gives a little cry and stops struggling. Elisa looks right into her face, into the wild grey eyes, as Judith collapses on her. How heavy she is for someone so little! Elisa lays her on the ground and opens the padded jacket. Blood is already oozing through the brown tunic just beneath the belt. She stretches a trembling hand toward the wound.

Judith's hand grasps her wrist. "We can fight. Do you remember? I asked you to let us fight. I knew it was the only way. Freedom isn't given away. You have to take it. He never understood." She coughs and grimaces with pain. "Do you understand? Do you?"

Elisa shakes her head, and the hand jerks her wrist. "Yes, Yes. He understood. You understood, Hanse. Listen, listen."

The earth trembles as riders gallop a hundred meters from the tree. The hand grips Elisa's arm; Judith smiles and moves her lips. Elisa bends over to hear above the dull thud of retreating hoofs.

"Hanse, I wasn't mad, was I? You came. Do you know . . . what I want? To see Hanse."

A long burst of gun-fire to the south, and the rumble of cavalry again with more gunfire, coming closer now. Abram-Gavra leans over. "Elisa! We've got to get out of here!"

Judith's grey eyes plead. "You *are* Hanse, aren't you? Show me."

Elisa closes her eyes, tearing herself from her surroundings, from the approaching thunder of hoofs, the gunshots, and the riders' yells. Brutally she forces her breathing and heartbeat under control, trying to achieve a state of trance. It's no use, it won't come. "I can't, I can't!"

She opens her eyes on Judith, who stares at her with enormous, absolute certainty. "Yes, you are Hanse. I know you are. I saw you change. We made love together. I bore your child. Remember." She still holds Elisa's wrist, and now she lifts it and rests Elisa's hand on her breast.

"You haven't forgotten?"

No, oh no. The first, the last time. The last time. There was no one after you. Oh no, I haven't forgotten.

"Kiss me, Hanse," whispers Judith. Elisa leans over and places her lips on Judith's, warm, soft, alive. . . .

She's going to die, *she's going to die!* The thought is like a silent, searing explosion tearing at Elisa's throat. She hears herself scream, a hoarse, strangled scream. She wraps Judith in her arms. *Yes, I am Hanse I am myself Elisa-Hanse no matter what body I bear I can be any body and you're going to die and they are all dead and it isn't my fault if I'm alive IT ISN'T MY FAULT!*

Elisa opens her eyes, her head echoing with silence. Judith, Judith's pain, hope, madness. Gone. She looks at the pale face near her own, at the closed eyes. Abruptly, as if someone had pressed a button, sound returns: a deafening jumble of yelling, shouting, and whinnying, accompanied by images, a swirl of horses, arms, legs, swords, rifles. Within the magic circle around the apple tree, Corrio kneels with Manilo in his arms, Halter and Kerri still struggle wordlessly. Lia and Abram-Gavra stand together, holding the reins of the terrified horses and staring at her. Across the space separating them she senses Lia's stupefaction, vast, seismic. A horse gallops up, masking Lia, and someone leaps down. Fedra, rifle in hand, Fedra looking at Judith on the ground as Elisa rises, Fedra, her face contorted with rage, hate and despair, lifting her rifle with one hand and firing.

(A shock, that's all. No pain. Crawling on all fours. A great silence. Everything in slow motion. Hands touching her. Too far. *Wait. Give me time. To get my breath. Breathe. Difficult. Going to get up. Just a minute. Wait. Don't shake me. Going to get up.*)

Sounds. A distant voice. *No, it's Hanse, Fedra, it's Hanse.* And above that, another voice. *Elisa, Elisa!*

Who?

⤚ 15 ⤜

ELISA IS IN THE CITY. SHE'S WALKING, RUN-ning, flying? The movement of her body is hard to discern, and the body itself, with its myriad familiar signals, is strangely blurred and distant. But she is moving at any rate, for the backdrop is changing. She's going somewhere. Where? She doesn't know. It's strange, this mingled certainty and ignorance. If she had more body she would surely be filled with anxiety; but she has no body.

It must be a dream. She's dreaming and she knows it. And it's not unpleasant, as a matter of fact, this impression of being a passenger, a spectator. She looks about, intrigued. After all these years, she's dreaming of the City? Dear old City, she thinks, with amused affection. Everything is familiar. The moving sidewalks, the staircases, the balconies hanging above the great, silent halls, the honeycomb pattern of the residential section, the park. She sees it all at the same time, as though floating through the City's different levels, as though her mind's eye—her dream's eye—effortlessly penetrated the layers of cement, metal, and plastic. She perceives the whole City, like a gigantic, multicellular organism stretching its pseudopods in all directions, numberless ducts wherein the breath and blood of the City circulates, the infinitely ramified network of electronic circuits, the eyes and ears of the City.

The City is alive, of course! A clean, clear life that knows neither rust nor rot. Elisa's absent heart swells with love in her absent body. The City, infinitely wise, infinitely powerful, the City with its ever-welcoming womb, the City that has survived all its humans, all its masters. How good it is to be back! Elisa would like to spread her immaterial self until it is diffused throughout the City, to match it exactly to each immortal cell of the City.

But she's moving *through* the City. Despite her magical vision, she is *somewhere* in the City, going *somewhere* in the City, even if she doesn't know where. She drifts along on her dream, still serenely amused. She's in the City. She's safe. Even when she recognizes the scene of the old dream. Even when she sees the street with its trees encased in their green squares, its sidewalks, cars, houses, and the tiny, manicured lawns that look so unlike grass, the tiny flowerbeds and tiny flowers carefully arranged in coloured clumps.

Oh, so it's the old dream? She's visiting an old dream. How funny! She remembers her fear as a little girl. But now she's a grown-up, just a visitor who knows exactly what's going to happen.

And with that, as though an invisible master of ceremonies had given the signal, the houses and street flatten out into what seems to be a rather bad drawing. She's got to see what's behind it now. Here's the painted door, and the painted handle on the door, and she's pretending to turn the handle in the old way.

Well! There really *is* a handle. The door opens on the red corridor with its other doors, but she had to push very hard, and Elisa is a little sulky now, a little exasperated because the dream isn't exactly the same as it used to be.

And look at this: her body is back. A body. She's not too sure what kind of body. Male? Female? A body. Surely female. Yes, there, she touches her chest and she has breasts, rather distended breasts, a little sore, and her dissatisfaction mounts. She steps quickly up to the first door and turns the handle.

Lots of colored lights, rows of dials, keys, switches, but it's as though someone had thrown the scenery together with whatever came to hand. Nothing moves, despite the overly loud humming and clicking, clearly a tape designed to substitute noise for the reality of movement.

The pink blob isn't there. Elisa is furious, and goes over to one of the false control panels that control nothing—bits of hardware, wood, and painted cardboard—and begins tearing the scenery from the wall. Underneath it's pink. Wet, shiny, with red and purple veins. Elisa is horrified now, but her hands keep on tearing off bits of the scenery. Soon nothing is left but four throbbing pink walls. And the floor and ceiling, pink and throbbing.

She's inside. Inside the pink blob.

But that's not how it was! There should be voices, Grandpa and Papa and the old familiar horror of going toward them to be eaten. Elisa is filled with rage beyond measure. The dream has cheated, the pink blob has cheated, the *City* has cheated! She stamps her foot and the pink walls quiver like jelly. She rushes at them, fists flying, determined to puncture the wall and return to the City. Further and further she penetrates, but it's like scummy, stagnant water now, sticky and revolting. What if it suddenly turns solid?

No, no, I didn't think that, I didn't!

She feels the pink blob solidify, begin to set, to entrap her as she flails her limbs in horrified anger. Now she understands. The pink blob has devoured the City. The pink blob *is* the City!

But it can't eat me! I've been Outside. Papa, Grandpa, tell it! I'm just visiting, it's got to let me go!

"You came back once too often," says a voice that she's not sure she recognizes.

"But I want to get out!"

"Then you must cut."

All at once Elisa realizes there is something in her right hand. A reverolver. She can see the word written as she thinks it, and it's not at all strange. How stupid, though: she can't *cut* with a reverolver. Anyway, she'd hurt them, because they're all in there, Papa, Grandpa, Judith. But she feels herself making a cutting motion anyway and sees a red slit appear and widen into glistening, purplish-pink lips, and she slips between them trying not to think.

The lips are closing around her waist. No, no! She hugs her arms against her body, consciously wanting to compress herself, to be quick, slippery and, and—

She is Outside!

⚡ 16 ⚡

PAIN, PAIN! THIRST. HUNGER. PAIN! BUT IT'S MY body, it's me, I am Outside, I am. . . .

Awake. She hears, smells, touches, sees. A multisensorial continuum that is reality. Crackling sounds, vague food smells, a hard surface beneath her shoulders, her buttocks, her legs. Prickly. The blanket is prickly beneath her fingers, the air cold on her cheeks, the night sky dotted with stars and framed by two black walls.

The pain is gone, leaving hunger, thirst, and a feeling of utter weakness and disorientation. She turns her head toward the sleeping, exhausted presences that she perceives around her, tries to savour their identities, and recognizes them. Abram, Lia, Fedra, and a motionless form that doesn't respond to her empathic touch. Halter? Outside a horse snuffles and shifts position. Farther off another does the same. She senses other presences, less definite, somnolent.

"Halter?"

The dark form stirs and moves toward her.

"I'm hungry," Elisa hears herself say. The ommach leaves the tent without a word.

A match is struck and suddenly Lia's face appears, a sharp sculpture of light and shadow beside the newly lit lamp. Abram mumbles a question, then wakes with a jerk.

"I'm hungry," Elisa repeats apologetically, feeling awash in Lia's incomprehensible amazement. The girl says nothing. The emotion subsides. All at once Elisa is reminded of something seen on a screen, long ago, a softly rolling stretch of grey and black where the wind had not yet blown away the cinders. The inner landscape of Lia's emotions resembles it, a frozen and imponderable sea beneath which the earth sleeps.

Outside, voices ask whispered questions. Abram is crouching beside Elisa, facing Lia. It really is Abram, he's come back, he's himself.

Himself? Oh no, Elisa, you can't think that anymore. Not now.

Abram looks at Elisa, fearful and uncertain. And on the other side is Lia, mute and opaque. But there is nothing to say, not now. Or too much. And what words could say it? What is done cannot be undone. They must do something else. Later.

Elisa examines her body. She can sense that the wound is healed. Right in the stomach, just beneath the solar plexus. No wonder she feels so weak.

"What time is it? What happened?"

"It's three o'clock in the morning," says Fedra, who has also wakened. Elisa senses the same grey despair as Lia's, but darker, heavier, more defined. "Judith is dead. Manilo is dead. The Vietellis have had heavy losses. So have we. They have retreated to Vietelli, but they'll come back. The others will be here soon."

Halter comes back with a steaming bowl of rice and nuts steeped in broth. No one says a word as Elisa gulps it down. She hands the bowl to Halter. "More. How many of us are left?" she asks as the ommach goes out.

"We haven't really had time to count heads. Over three hundred, I'd say. A lot of wounded," says Fedra's listless voice.

Halter comes back with another bowl of food and Elisa begins to eat, more slowly this time. She feels very lucid, very calm—a gift from her exhausted body, no doubt. Even the horror and heartbreak of her memories float in the distance. She sets down the half-empty bowl.

"What do you intend to do, Fedra?"

The woman shrugs. "Break camp, now that the horses and women are somewhat rested. Try to reach the Badlands. Perhaps they won't follow us there."

Elisa nods. "Halter, how far is it from here to our community?"

"About a hundred and eighty kilometres," replies Abram before the ommach can speak. "It will take time, considering their present condition and the fact that the horses haven't rested properly."

"But we'll be into the Badlands very soon. They don't usually venture there, do they?"

"Corrio will follow us," murmurs Lia.

"Maybe not," says Fedra.

"Manilo is dead." (Still that quiescent, grey expanse in Lia.)

"But so is Judith," says Abram, "and many of the Vietelli men. Perhaps Corrio won't want to weaken the chiefdom more than it already is."

How quickly Abram has learned to think in terms of strength and power! Yes, Corrio will certainly think of Vietelli's welfare. It's *his* chiefdom now. But he might not want to take a different line from Manilo.

Elisa turns to Fedra. "How long before the first troops arrive from the other chiefdoms?"

"The Callogris must be the nearest. Half a day. They should be here by noon."

"That gives us half a day's start. The women who aren't wounded could be left to carry out a rear-guard action."

"What makes you think we want to go with you?" asks Lia suddenly.

"We're going in the same direction, in any case," replies Elisa, maintaining her composure. She doesn't look at Lia (but she watches the slow movement over the inner plain, the hesitant breath of wind).

"We could care for the wounded properly in the community," says Abram.

"We don't need the people from the City," says Lia stubbornly (the movement comes nearer and nearer, the cinders ripple and rise, fluid as water, uncovering here and there the naked, solid earth).

"The community is not the City," says Elisa. The words echo through her body, and she stops to listen, surprised by the sudden clarity that fills her being.

The community is not the City. The community is *against* the City. The Project, the community, the children. A long message that she's taken twenty years to compose, to decipher: *Desprats is dead. Paul is dead. The City is dead. And I . . . I am alive.*

She'd been afraid to know. The City, the shadow of the City, was too close, a welcome alibi to protect her from a terrifying freedom. But she *had* known. One hand had tirelessly unravelled what the other had tirelessly woven.

For twenty years, with each child, I have unceasingly given birth to myself, opened the womb, cut the cord, torn myself from the City. It was an act carried out in a dream, the kind of dream that is so difficult to escape, the dream that imitates reality. The multi-faceted rationale of the Project, the children's faces, all different, all masks of the dream. *But at the same time the persistent little voice, suppressed but horrifying, the little voice that kept me awake: "Not real children, these children, not real lives, their lives, not real love, their love." Reality. Reality is Lia. And she has my face and she's* not *me.*

Voices and footsteps outside. The survivors are waking up and preparing for the road. Elisa looks at Lia, who turns her eyes toward Gavra—Abram—then away. In her way Lia, too, has discovered a reality. *But she's luckier than I am. She can't go back. She can't run away anymore.*

"You can at least come to the community to get your strength back," says Abram. "Afterward you can do what you like."

"We haven't much choice," says Fedra, rising with an effort.

Sometimes it's better that way, Fedra.

⚡ 17 ⚡

SLOW DEPARTURE IN THE NIGHT, HORSES plodding beneath the lingering stars. Fedra remains with the rear guard. Abram goes with the outriders on the southern flank, keeping watch over the plain toward Vietelli. Elisa finds herself at the head of the line with Lia and Halter. The darkness hides the battlefield and the tangled corpses of men and women. Manilo and Judith. There was no time to give them a decent burial, just a hole in the ground, a single tomb where they rest together.

Judith has indeed won. The men of Vietelli have fled the battlefield and all hope of reconciliation is as dead as Manilo. The free women have lost over a third of their forces, and several of the wounded won't make it on this march toward the Badlands. Strange victory. But Judith probably never imagined winning in any other way. She wanted blood, the baptism of blood, the single slash creating a breach between men and women, the birth of an implacable antagonism. She wanted the worst, the irremediable, the pact sealed by death.

But has Judith won completely? Elisa feels Lia's stubborn revolt beside her. Not so violent as before, not a fire, not even a burning ember. Beneath the blown cinders and blackened earth, seeds still sleep despite everything. But who knows what they will bring?

Day breaks slowly on this inner earth, too. "What's this community of yours got?" asks Lia suddenly, her aggressive tone covering a hint of curiosity.

"Children," says Elisa. "My children."

"And who else's?"

"Hanse's."

Elisa waits for the violent reaction that doesn't come. Hanse's name seems to have paralyzed Lia, and when at last she reacts, it's not anger, but disbelief. "But *you* are Hanse, I saw you—."

Saw?

"When she died, you changed, you were—that wasn't Hanse?"

I changed? But I wasn't even in a trance!

Elisa nudges her horse forward at a walk, incapable of thought. But she still perceives Lia's hope, a hope that grows.

"It wasn't Hanse?"

Oh no, Lia, don't hope to escape that way.

"Yes, it was Hanse. But I didn't know that I had changed. When—" *Did I become myself again? No.* "—did I change again?"

Lia doesn't answer right away, occupied with burying her last hope of denying the truth.

"While you were asleep, I suppose," she finally replies, her voice very low. "When you woke up you were Elisa."

The dream. To cut. Not to die. (But to kill, if necessary?) Metamorphosis wasn't linked to Paul, after all. It was linked to death. A defense mechanism. Determined to survive, the body changes. That's why she still feels so weak. Two successive metamorphoses even though the first must have been only superficial. Two metamorphoses on top of a serious wound, a mortal wound. Fedra saw a blood-spattered man beside a blood-spattered Judith and of course she fired. And Lia—Lia saw Hanse. Gavra's transformation into a man and Hanse's back to Elisa were probably the merest sparks added to the devastating blaze. All her certainties, all her shields turned to dust. Lia can't help being naked now. Ravaged. An immense compassion fills Elisa, and she senses Lia's violent, clumsy reaction, the reaction of someone who has never been trained to control her emotions, someone whose body betrays her.

Light diffuses through the sky, driving away the night as they ride forward. Elisa looks behind her. Silhouettes slumped in the saddle, makeshift stretchers swinging between pairs of horses, a pervasive despondency. She sighs and glances at Lia—Lia, who is staring straight ahead, her teeth clenched. This face that is hers, this unknown, this being yet to be discovered. The light spreads quickly. Perhaps the day will be fine. There isn't a cloud to be seen to the west and north. Once more Elisa looks at Lia's profile, sharp against the golden sky.

Suddenly she is startled. "Lia!"

The stubborn face turns to her. It's hard to see against the light, but beneath the thick wool cap pulled low are wisps of hair that—. Elisa leans over and tugs at the cap.

That are white.

Lia stares at Elisa, mystified, and instinctively passes a hand over her hair. "What's wrong?"

Elisa is speechless. So that's it. Judith. Lia. A distant relic of the reproduction program set up by Paul. The polygene must be incomplete, just enough genes for self-regeneration, Lia, just *not* enough for metamorphosis. But she has the mark. The trademark.

Lia frowns, takes out her knife, and slices off a bit of hair. One hand drops to the saddle, clinging to the wisp. A moment later the hand with the knife drops too, fumbling as it tries twice to replace the knife in its sheath.

The girl's horse comes to a halt, feeling the reins lying slack on its neck, but Lia digs her knees into its flanks to set it in motion again. Elisa leans over and lightly touches the hand holding the white hair. Lia doesn't react.

There is a pause, and finally Lia murmurs, "I never believed it. I thought she was lying. But it was true. She wasn't mad. I hated her for it. But everything was true."

Elisa strokes her hand. "Not everything, Lia. She lied about a lot of things. Not about this, that's all." She hesitates. Is it too soon to explain the subtleties of truth? Lia is not looking at her, but she's listening. "And, in a way, she really was mad. Not completely," *no, not like Paul,* "but mad with revolt, perhaps. She came from the North, you know. She wanted to be free."

Free, Judith, free! And like me you failed to recognize your freedom when it came. You chose flight, lies. As I did.

But who knows how Judith was affected by the confrontation between Paul and Elisa, by Paul's death, by the discovery of what was really behind Malverde? Perhaps she came to believe the lies that she told the men of Vietelli, perhaps later on she became caught in the mire of her own lies. And who can tell what happened with Manilo and Corrio and herself in the five years that she remained in Vietelli?

No. No more stories. There will be no more light shed on that past, no answers to these questions. Judith is dead. Judith no longer exists but in the treacherous memory of those who knew her (and perhaps in the equally false memory of the City, the images on the screens, the manifold illusion of being able to comprehend appearances).

"But you can't really be free that way," protests Lia. "By lying, by killing!"

Her dejection is beginning to fade as revolt flares. *Oh, you're her daughter all right!*

"Perhaps there are several ways of looking at freedom," hazards Elisa.

"But there aren't several kinds of freedom!"

Oh yes there are, Lia! But it's too soon. Lia has scarcely begun to free herself, has just embarked on the long struggle that only ends when one realizes that it is purposeless. *(Hopeless? No.)* How Lia must hate herself. Because she couldn't change, couldn't satisfy Judith. Because she didn't agree with Judith. Because she was the daughter of Judith. And, yes, it's very long, this self-liberation, this struggle to see oneself, to accept oneself, while fighting all the other incessant battles.

Halter stops his horse abruptly and points to the sky. A gleam of light reflecting the rising sun moves rapidly toward them. A moddex.

⚡ 18 ⚡

THE MODDEX LANDS FIFTY METERS IN FRONT of the column. Elisa reins in her prancing, frightened horse and watches the door open. Stairs emerge from the machine's belly, shapes jump to the ground and run toward her, stopping in front of her horse. Ari. Anders. And two female ommachs, Lussi and Clari.

She slides from her horse. Ari hugs her tightly as Anders tries to do the same, both talking at once and then bursting into laughter. Elisa senses their joy and cannot find it in her heart to be angry. "We were so worried!" says one. "We asked the City," says the other. "We wanted to know what was happening. Francis and Florie told us—. We saw them, the Vietellis and Halter, talking about you, Judith, a battle. We were so frightened you might—. So I decided—."

She pushes them away firmly with one hand, and they stop speaking, guilty and hesitant now.

"I entrusted the leadership of the community to you, Anders. You have done what you judged necessary."

A sense of great relief. Anders hugs her tightly again.

"You have some badly wounded people," says Ari. "We can take them right away; everything's ready back home. We could get more moddexes and take everyone all at once."

Suddenly Lia is beside her. Elisa hears her decided voice say, "Take the worst cases first—I'll show you which—and then come back."

The two boys look at Lia, then at Elisa, their eyes widening.

"She's right," says Elisa.

Anders goes off with Lia and the two ommachs as a rider gallops up from the rear of the column. Fedra must be anxious. Elisa sends Halter to meet her while

Ari explains that he and Anders spotted Abram and his outriders and told them to rejoin the column.

Deus ex machina. Or almost. But why not? She's not going to sacrifice human lives for her principles, after all. She's done it enough. But this isn't the moment to settle accounts with herself. Later. Now they must return to the community, care for the wounded, and get this crowd lodged and fed.

Everything's ready back home, Anders had said. They'd prepared it all. The children. Without her. She isn't *returning* to the community, she's going to a community transformed by Abram's departure, by her own, and by what the children did afterward. They consulted the City, got a moddex, and decided to intervene. They chose to come looking for her and these unknown women, chose to welcome them into their home.

They have chosen just as she has, in fact. But without her. By disobeying the one inflexible rule she'd ever laid down. Not that she'd ever actually *forbidden* them to use the City. But they have broken the taboo.

And she's no avenging angel. Elisa smiles wryly: they have found the Tree of Knowledge, but it's God who will be judged. *(God, Elisa?)* She realizes that she is only half joking, and her smile fades. Will the children judge *her*? No doubt they already have, years ago. They've never really been taken in by her highflown rationalizing. They know what she is, what she wants, what she fears, and they've accepted her for what she is. Do they love her for what she is? But *she* will judge herself, is already judging herself. Nothing will ever be the same again. The community, the snug dream, the blind Eden, that's over.

And who was the serpent, if not myself? She always did have a soft spot for Lucifer. And she always thought it unfair that snakes have such a bad reputation—after all, aren't they able to renew themselves, to change their skins? God and the Devil. It would be so much easier if they were clearly distinguishable. Black and white, good and evil. And, come to think of it, Hanse and Elisa. Manilo and Judith could believe in their antagonism: they inhabited separate bodies. But Elisa has no such loophole. She is Hanse, and she is Elisa. For all her body's capacity to change, she is neither God nor Devil, she is a human being, neither as fallible nor as infallible as she would like to think.

Not a very awesome revelation. Nor very original. But perhaps necessary from time to time. Perhaps *that* is the revelation: to learn that you have to keep tearing yourself away from your illusions, that you never stop discovering the lies you tell yourself; to learn how you manipulate yourself. Never stop giving birth to yourself?

⚡ 19 ⚡

WITHOUT OPENING HER EYES, ELISA CAN TELL she's not the first to wake. She listens to the quiet voices wafting up from the common room. Abram and Lia, Francis and Florie. She can't distinguish the words, but the younger pair are asking questions and Abram is answering, with Lia commenting or correcting. The peaceful noise of kitchen activity rises with the smell of roast meat. Elisa stretches and opens her eyes. It's morning and the sun is shining. The two other beds that have been put in her room are empty, and the door is open. She gets clean clothes from the cupboard, sniffing the familiar odor of dried plants, feeling the soft yet pliant texture of her wool tunic and leather pants. *I have come home.* Everything is the same. Everything has changed. How is it possible?

I have changed.

The voices stop as she starts down the stairs, then two of the little ones aged three or four break off from the group and rush up to her. She recalls their names after a brief effort: Naomi and Nestra. She takes one in each arm, kisses their fresh cheeks, and goes down to the others. Lia is holding another youngster in her arms.

"Sleep well?" asks Abram.

"I slept in, it seems. Is everyone else up?"

"Nearly."

"How are the wounded?"

"Pretty well, for the time being," says Lia. She uncurls the child's fingers from her bone and pearl necklace. As her eyes meet Elisa's there is something of an inner smile, although her lips don't move.

"Give her to me," Abram offers.

"She isn't heavy." Lia removes the stubborn little fingers again and imprisons them in her hand. "At first she thought I was you," she says to Elisa.

"Can she tell the difference now?"

Lia perceives Elisa's amusement but doesn't understand it. She can't tell that the sudden irony is not for her, and hesitates. "Yes, I think so."

A group of women come in, their arms full of pots and sacks. They greet Elisa with a nod and go into the kitchen.

It's going to be a problem to feed and lodge three hundred extra people. But they probably won't all stay. Anyway, the problems will iron themselves out. Elisa feels curiously calm. The children and the community. The Project. It will all work out. How? She has no idea, but she's not worried. The children will decide, and the Sestis, and the new arrivals.

And I won't say a thing? Not the way she used to. As far as she's concerned the Project no longer exists. *I am free. Free.*

She sets the two little girls down on the stairs and moves away from the little group to get an apple from the wooden bowl on the big table. Twenty years of her life—twenty years of the oldest children's lives—gone? No. It's the Project such as she imagined it that is gone. The dream, the illusion, the lie, the refuge. The children, the community still exist. Some of the children will no doubt go to live in the Exterior. Others will live with the Sestis, and perhaps others will move in with the women who stay. And she will certainly find out how the children manage to change themselves the way they do. She has plenty of time to mull it over, now. Change faster than she does—that's easy enough. But into animals? Fascinating. Only a superficial change, or do they go all the way? But then how do they manage to change back? She forces herself to stop asking, to stop trying to answer.

As for the community's future, there's no lack of possible scenarios! The essence of the Project will be achieved, of that she is sure. The children will have children. The genes of change will spread fairly quickly to the Exterior.

And yet everything is different.

Elisa contemplates her teeth marks in the polished apple peel: two symmetrical curves. She turns the apple and bites gently. Now the circle is complete. With the third bite a hole will appear. And so it goes, the apple changing its appearance with each bite. But it will still be an apple. *The meaning will change, the meaning I give it.* This fine object, round, red, and gleaming, will turn into food, bit by bit, then core, then garbage. *But the apple will continue to exist in me, to change in me, to become me.*

And so we feed ourselves incessantly on dreams, illusions, lies that are forever renewed, forever becoming acts, beings, an entire memory, an entire life that changes itself and ourselves with each bite? *Have I changed so much?* Just a brief journey, just a step to one side. The whole scenery has changed, and yet it is the same scenery. And one must always move forward one step at a time.

With a little smile, Elisa bites into the apple and moves toward the others, who are watching her silently. She perceives their mixed emotions—affection, curiosity, uncertainty—and yet somehow, at the same time, Abram is tranquil, the children are tranquil. Even Lia, with her devastated inner landscape, seems to have found a kind of peace. Where does this serenity come from? *From me, because I've come back? Because they sense that I've changed? Because life goes on? No. Or not only for these reasons. They, too, have changed.*

"Would you like us to get everyone together this afternoon?" asks Abram.

"It's a bit soon, don't you think? Let's wait until things calm down a bit and everyone has had time to think."

"Are we going to tell all the women what we are?" asks Francis.

Elisa bites into the apple. "Don't try to hide it, that's all. Just as we did with the Sestis. If they ask questions, answer them. But don't force things. In any case, they're prepared for it."

Out of the corner of her eye she sees Lia bow her head, and senses a slight drifting.

Abram asks suddenly, "What are you going to do now?"

In the young face that is Paul—but not quite Paul, as she can now see—the grey eyes are serious and intense. Elisa looks at Abram with a slightly sad tenderness, a little amused. Does he know what he's done? Did he want to, did he really understand it? Or was he like a stone on a slope: once set in motion, he kept on rolling from act to act, his course altered by each new event? She'll ask him. One day.

"I'm going to the City."

Abram blinks, but doesn't avert his eyes.

"Now?"

Elisa finishes the apple and contemplates the neatly shaped core. Two bites, and the core is gone.

"Now."

⚡ 20 ⚡

ELISA SITS IN THE CHAIR, PLACING HER HANDS on the armrests, and looks at the empty screens. For the last time. But she feels neither sad nor hesitant. Nor really curious, which surprises her.

But she is not surprised when a screen lights up after she has typed Desprats' code. The familiar face looks at her: the yellowed mustache, the white hair, the observant eyes. An image. The dream of survival of a man dead these forty years.

She no longer feels anger. The dead are dead. All the dead: Paul, Desprats, Judith. *And I don't have to answer for their acts. My own are enough.*

The image says nothing, and Elisa is silent as well. What is there to say, really? There's no one there, only millions of electronic impulses in a program that imitates life. But she has summoned him. In a way he does exist. She remembers her anger, her desire to call him to account. To call a machine to account? No, there is no one who can be blamed for the smallest detail of her life. There is no one to call to account but herself. It's her responsibility, the final act before closing the book . . . and opening another.

Is she being theatrical? After all, why not leave it all dormant, turn out the lights, and go?

She smiles somewhat sadly. Theatrical? Or simply the irrational but irresistible feeling that she owes it to Desprats' memory to have this last meeting.

"Why Judith?" she asks finally.

The program takes the question in its stride. Naturally. "First of all because she carried a gene quite similar to yours and she was expecting your child. Then because she set in motion events that I felt would considerably change the Exterior. I was always very interested in the Exterior, as you know."

Elisa wants to say that the Exterior always interested *Desprats*, but she keeps quiet. Why argue with a machine? What light can this machine really throw on the motives of a man who has been dead for forty years? Nothing certain. Educated guesses. But what's the point? To find out whether the program kept her and the children under surveillance? Or lied to her? What does it matter?

Free will. Choice. Well, it means behaving as though one were free, choosing consciously and accepting the consequences of one's choices. And who is certain of truth, anyway? From what pinnacle can freedom be seen as illusory or real? Perhaps it doesn't exist. Everyone watches everyone else, and no one sees everything. Manipulated and manipulators, all together, with everyday life to be lived whatever happens—a stronger force than all the great projects, the truth that perpetually speaks through lies, perhaps needs lies.

Elisa looks at Desprats' image one last time, then stretches out a hand and obliterates it.

"Are you going to stop everything?"

She pivots her chair. Abram. Of course, Abram.

"You think we shouldn't?"

Hesitation. "I don't know." Abram comes over and sits on the arm of the chair beside her. "It's the last City."

"You'd like to keep it as a monument? Or use it? You and the children?"

Abram stares at the empty screens, frowning. "Use it? I don't think so. But keep the ommachs. We can't if we stop the City?"

"No, they have to recharge themselves from time to time." Elisa throws herself back in the chair and folds her arms. "And you, what do you want to do, Abram? Not for the City, for yourself."

He looks away. "I thought I'd go away again, with the ommachs and others who want to come with me. To gather information in the Exterior. More or less everywhere. Come back here. I don't know."

"And afterward?"

He watches her doubtfully. "I don't know. To leave. But I'm not in a position to decide now. So many things could happen. The community, the others—everything's changed."

"But you wanted to keep the ommachs."

"I'm not the only one. They're very useful. And we're accustomed to them. It would be strange if they weren't there. Do you understand?"

Yes, she understands. Their whole life is bound up with ommachs. They are part of the familiar scenery, part of the family. Unlike her, the children don't see them as sad or painful memories linked to the City. Does she think she can destroy these memories forever by stopping the City? That's not the way to make them disappear. The memories aren't in the City, but in her. The City is merely the City. It cannot die; it was never alive. Elisa's image of the City, the life she attributed to it, *that's* what is dead, worn out, stopped. There's nothing to do; it's already done.

I have no need to stop the City. But I don't want the children to be tempted to use it too much.

It's very simple.

⚡ 21 ⚡

MUCH LATER, WHEN SHE HAS FINISHED GIVING all her instructions to the City, Elisa gets up and Abram does the same. Together they walk through the corridors and along the galleries, the lights going out behind them. They reach the end, and for the last time the airlocks open and close. The last door slides silently shut. It will open only for ommachs, as long as there are ommachs. No organic life can enter now. A small, faceless robot is installing a metal plaque on the wall beside the door. It has an indentation in the form of a hand, and in the palm a small, retractable blade is hidden to take samples of skin and blood. Above the door is a tiny red light, the only sign that the City sleeps with one eye open.

Elisa and Abram walk on, their steps in unison as they thread their way through the underground labyrinth that leads to the caves and up to the daylight.

"Do you think five hundred years is enough?" asks Abram suddenly.

"I don't know."

In five hundred years the children's descendants will surely have forgotten the City, or will remember it only as a legend. If they come then. But will they be men or women? Maybe the problem of the distribution of sexes will have resolved itself by that time. If *someone* comes whose cells carry Elisa's whole genetic heritage, the door will open. Other keys will be needed to enter the City. And those keys may take more than five hundred years to be forged anew.

Have I thought of everything? Where is the inevitable error, the gap, the oversight?

She smiles, knowing full well she hasn't thought of everything, and that even if she has, she won't be here in five hundred years to find out, to discover the results of her wager with fate. She can neither predict no control how the City will be used by those who find enough keys to wake it.

She hasn't tried, hasn't left any thread to guide them through the thick wood surrounding Sleeping Beauty's palace. No simulated electronic being to greet her hypothetical descendants. For a moment, a very brief moment, she thought of organizing a series of screen images for whomever makes contact with the City for the first time, to explain. . . . And immediately she felt like laughing. How easily she forgets, how often she's obliged to begin again! *Explain what? My life, my work? But they're not finished, not complete. Why should I have a privileged point of view about my life? How can I tell whether the people of the future will understand these images as I want them to be understood, these images that I would arrange in a story but which are merely the reflection of reality?*

And who knows—in twenty years she herself may comprehend today quite differently. All the more reason, then, to doubt her vision of yesterday.

No, let all these images lie stored in the City's memory. Let those who find them draw their own conclusions, make up their own stories. There will always be some truth in them.

And perhaps no one will ever come.

About The Author

ELISABETH VONARBURG lives in Chicoutimi, Quebec. She has published numerous SF stories and has worked tirelessly to encourge the genre in Canada. She has attended many SF conventions in the U.S., Canada, and Europe, and several international conventions of SF writers held in Chicoutimi. She has received various awards for her work in both France and Canada. She recently completed her third novel for Bantam Books, and is currently working on a novel for young adults.

JANE BRIERLEY lives in Montreal and has translated works of fiction, biography, history, and philosophy. She won the 1990 Governor General's Award for her translation, *Yellow-Wolf & Other Tales of the Saint Lawrence* by the 19th-century Canadian writer, Philippe-Joseph Aubert de Gaspé. Her translations of two further Vonarburg SF novels will appear with Bantam Books. She is currently president of the Literary Translators' Association of Canada.

A Special Preview of
IN THE MOTHERS' LAND
by
Elisabeth Vonarburg

It is the far future, a post-holocaust world so far removed from our time that the end of our civilization is referred to as the Decline. Between the Decline and the time of Lisbeï of Betheley, hundreds of years have passed, a whole history upon which Lisbeï's world has been built. Her world is one where males are scarce due to a genetic plague, where women have lived through a savage history, and where—finally—due to the work of one woman named Garde, who suffered for her pacifist belief in the goddess Elli and whose six followers were walled up alive— women have made their peace through structure, tradition and careful genetic planning. But all that is about to change.

When Lisbeï discovers ancient passages hidden beneath the grounds of Betheley, she must tread carefully, for what she discovers in those passages challenges everything she has been taught about the history of her people and will shake the very foundations of her world. . . .

The light from the setting sun blinded Lisbeï as she climbed out of the pit. She pushed back the earth-smudged curls that kept slipping out of the kerchief knotted around her forehead. Meï's figure stood silhouetted against the apricot sky. Of course they'd sent Meï. Why not Meralda while they were at it? Lisbeï didn't need to see Meï's face to guess at her worried yet disapproving expression.

"Tell her I'm coming. I'm going to wash up a bit first."

The young Red pursed her lips, deprived of the scolding she'd no doubt been primed to administer. "The Mother said *right away.*"

Lisbeï gave her a quizzical smile. "My mother probably wouldn't appreciate dirt in her rooms, would she?"

Without waiting for a reply, she began carefully replacing the boards over the excavation. As she straightened up she glanced at the Red with studied amazement—what, still here? "Run along and tell Selva. Go on!"

She turned her back on the messenger and stalked off toward the calm expanse of the Douve, catching up her satchel near a pile of earth and rubble as she went.

Meï was determined to have the last word, as usual. "The Mother won't be pleased!" she shouted before scurrying off. Lisbeï kept going as though she'd heard nothing. It wouldn't make much difference anyhow. The Mother was never pleased with her.

All the same, she was rather annoyed with herself for letting the time slip by. The afternoon was nearly over and the shadow of the Towers stretched beyond the grazing areas on the Esplanade to the Douve and the ball field. The three Towers stood tall against the western sky—flat, black rectangles edged with the lace of outside staircases spiralling with mathematical precision on a gold background. The sunset wouldn't be much, though: no clouds building cliffs and seas in the heavens. An ordinary sunset in an ordinary sprinna sky at the end of a day that was . . . not entirely ordinary, thank Elli! As she had hoped when she began clearing, the conduit uncovered by the cave-in led somewhere. She was positive she'd vindicate her theories by discovering one of Bethely's ancient subterranean passages. Legends weren't just legends!

Energy flowed back. She peeled off work clothes that were stiff with sweat and soil, and crouched down beside

the water. The surface was smooth, motionless: the locks
upstream were closed. She washed quickly. A little dirt remained under her fingernails and bits of earth clung to
her tangled hair. But you couldn't keep *the Mother* waiting
any longer, could you? Mustn't overdo it. She had surely
stayed longer than the allotted two hours. Lisbeï dried
herself off with the towel brought for just this purpose,
and slipped into a clean tunic and slacks. They were
rather wrinkled from sitting in a ball in her satchel.
Loathsome green clothes! If she had any choice in the
matter she'd have torn them to shreds. Anger overwhelmed her once more and she threw her satchel
roughly over her shoulder. Two hours late? So what! The
world wouldn't stop turning. After all, you could take your
time when training to be a Memory, couldn't you? The
past wasn't going to run away overnight. The Library and
its Archives would be there in the morning. If only it were
just the past! But there was also the present, those interminable figures for Farm production and inventories and
accounts! You could certainly be two hours late for the
chore of toting up those rows of digits yet one more time.

(But the Library and Archives hadn't always been
there, observed the part of Lisbeï that couldn't resist arguing, even against herself. The past *could* disappear, or
at least be blurred in legend—like the underground passages of Bethely.)

And be rediscovered! If only she could keep on digging . . . No, tomorrow—if she weren't punished for the
rest of the week.

Tomorrow, no matter what!

She could have retraced her steps toward the main entrance, crossing the Esplanade directly to the West Tower,
but instead she followed the curve of the Douve, making a
wide circle by the South Tower. This only added five or six
minutes, but she did it on principle. Six o'clock really had
come and gone, and the workas returning from the gardens
and the paper mill straggled in little groups along the road.
Among them were two or three Reds crossing the little
bridge. They greeted Lisbeï by name. She muttered an answer and walked faster. Of course she had no idea who they
were. But who did not know Lisbeï these days in Bethely?

Rather than follow them on the road to the Esplanade, she continued along the path beside the river until

she reached the South Garderie. She stood there a while, fists jammed into her pockets, looking at the high, ivy-covered wall behind which the little mostas laughed and played in another world. Was she now nostalgic for her days in the garderie? Days when she'd been no one, an almost-person? She knew nothing then and could dream of everything. . . .

She began running as hard as she could, and it must have been the wind in her eyes that brought the tears. She rounded the circular garderie wall, left the path halfway up the hill, and cut across the wide terreplein. She scrambled down the other side and headed for the Towers, zig-zagging between piles of straw and bales of hay, past the warm, strong odors of the South Tower barns, faster and faster now, running as though she were late, as though it mattered, for the benefit of any Reds, Greens, or Blues who might be watching. *See? I'm hurrying, the Mother is waiting, am I not an obedient daughter?* In reality she ran for the mere sake of running, for the ambiguous pleasure of arriving out of breath and being able to say to Selva, who wouldn't be taken in for a moment, "I ran the whole way."

Selva didn't answer. Her red head, hair screwed back, remained bowed over the thick ledger, and the pen continued scratching across the page. Lisbeï kept up her act, gulping air, wiping her forehead, shifting from one foot to the other. She was used to Selva's tactics. It was all a question of who would tire of the silence first. It wouldn't be Lisbeï.

"You'd have to run pretty fast to make up for those three and a half hours," said Mooreï, rising from the hidden depths of a large armchair.

Selva was cheating! She'd got Mooreï to give the lecture!

"I lost track of time," said Lisbeï with false joviality. But because it was Mooreï she added, "There really is an underground passage and it's heading for the South Tower!"

A flash of interest shot through Mooreï's calm aura, but Lisbeï realized she was wasting her time. She wasn't dealing with Mooreï now but with the Memory of Bethely, speaking for the Mother.

"Your digging mustn't impinge on your work, Lisbeï. It's the second time this week."

But this was part of her work! She was going to be the Memory of Bethely, wasn't she? Bethely's history was her field. Something had to be added to the Archives once in a while, didn't it?

So Mooreï had argued when trying to convince Selva to allow digging after a subsidence had revealed the tip of the underground passage. But not any longer.

"It's only part of a Memory's work. And you'd have to know everything already in the Archives before thinking of adding more."

Lisbeï kept dancing from one foot to another. It wasn't fair having to answer to Mooreï. She refused to get into a fight with *Mooreï*!

"After all, two hours . . ."

"Three and a half," said Selva. Lisbeï turned to the Mother, almost relieved, but the red head was bowed over the ledger still.

"It's a matter of principle, Lisbeï," continued Mooreï. "Do you think you can have your way all the time?"

"I found a replacement for . . ."

"You had no business finding a replacement. For the last two weeks you've spent every free minute in that hole and . . ."

Well, free time was free time wasn't it?

Mooreï came over and took her by the chin. Lisbeï could sense the compassion that hung about her like a desolate fog. She stiffened, and Mooreï let go of her chin. "Lisbeï, we've discussed this a dozen times."

So why begin again?

"Enough!" snapped Selva. This time she meant it. She rose and came round the desk to confront Lisbeï. "You're not a law unto yourself, Lisbeï. This so-called archaeological dig is finished and done with. You will spend your free time doing everything you've let slide, beginning with taking your turn in the gardens and kitchens. No more replacements. Tomorrow morning you will report directly to the captas, who will keep me informed. Is that clear? And you will go back to the chorale and resume your other training."

Lisbeï couldn't contain herself. "I won't go the Games!"

"You're registered."

"You can't make me."

"You'll make yourself! Have you no sense of decency, for Elli's sake?"

"There's no rule saying I have to take part just because I'm registered!"

The two fell silent for a moment, hackles raised as they confronted each other. Suddenly Lisbeï could sense Selva's pained anger, sharp as the smell of burnt bread, but she was too furious herself to take any pleasure in it.

As usual it was Mooreï who tried to mend things. "You're the best archa in your age group, Lisbeï, the third best in Litale. And you sing so well. Surely you're not going to give it all up?"

"She knows her duty perfectly well," said Selva, returning to her seat. "She's the first-living and the Mother-designate." The cold mirror-wall was distinctly there again.

"A Blue!" Lisbeï exploded at last. "A Blue, Blue, Blue! I'm a Blue and I have no duties!"

"You'll be a Blue officially next Juna. Meanwhile, until Tula has been named, you are still the Mother-designate of Bethely and you will conduct yourself accordingly. You may go now."

Selva's vioce had the merciless cutting edge that Lisbeï had come to recognize. It had always made her yield. Until now.

"Everyone knows," she cried hoarsely, her voice really shaking now (but it didn't matter, she wasn't listening to herself, wasn't playing games any more). "You can't force me, you have no right. Everyone knows I'm sterile!"

There. The word was out. She'd said it at last. She turned on her heel, shrugging off Mooreï's hands outstretched to touch, to calm her. Lisbeï grabbed the door handle, feeling as though she could have wrenched it from its socket rather than turn it, ripped the door from its frame, the wall from . . . and she rushed out into the corridor and on toward the spiralling outside staircase.

There were people in the corridor when Lisbeï burst out of Selva's office. She paid no attention. There were always people in the corridors of Bethely, always somebody going somewhere doing something. Sometimes she imagined the Towers being transparent like Antonë's ant terrarium. It was just the same, all these blue dots, or red, or green, forever moving in all directions. There had been a time when this incessant activity had fascinated her, when the adult world and its certainties had been a desired goal. One day she would have all the answers to all the questions and be as powerful as the Reds and Blues. But answers were like fireflies: when you caught them, their lights went out, and there was always another lighting up just a bit farther on. Power . . . who really had power in Bethely? Not Selva, not the Mother. Not Mooreï, who would have been more worthy of it. Nor Antonë nor Kelys nor any of the captas. The Family Assembly, then, the delegates of the Reds and Blues? No. Everybody. Nobody. Tradition with its stupid rules was the true mistress of Bethely, this invisible shell that everyone always carried around, preventing them from really seeing their surroundings.

Just as she was about to push open the glass door to the outside stairs, Lisbeï halted. The sky was already darkening but the gleam of the setting sun still caught one façade of the East Tower, lighting up row upon row of molten orange mirrors, broken here and there by the black gap of an open window. She began to descend the staircase into the dark well of the court. In childehood days, she used to see crossword patterns on the Bethely façades, used to imagine them as messages to be deciphered. Night used to bring different messages: "I am awake despite the late hour," or "someone is with me tonight," "I'm sleeping." But she used to find messages in everything when she was little.

Do we invent the messages the world sends us? Or are they there always for us merely to decipher? "Elli's design in the pattern of the Tapestry," Mooreï had said in answer to these childeish questions. But Elli hadn't built Bethely. Elli was too distant, Elli's time was not really human time. No, another message was hidden in the giant crossword of Bethely's windows. When had Lisbeï really noticed it? She doesn't remember, although she recalls the instant of comprehension, the moment when everything had clicked into place, much as the illusion of perspective, the illusion of the hollow cube had suddenly become clear.

All at once she was Bethely in perspective *in time*. She was gazing at the East Tower façade from her bedroom, staring unthinkingly at the rows of identical windows, wider than they were high, and the red brick set in the gray walls where all the windows had been made smaller. Suddenly a flash of illumination linked the familiar sight with the pictures in the Book of Bethely. The Towers were ancient!

Older than the Mothers, older than the Hives or even the Harems. All these societies had occupied them, transformed and adapted them, but the Towers themselves came from much further back, from a time when people could construct perfectly rectilinear buildings of thirty stories or more, with all those wide (too wide) windows so incredibly wasteful of energy—but that was normal in the Decline, for the Towers must date at least from the Decline . . .

Not much was left of the original buildings, apart from the skeleton. The inside and outside had been renovated several times, but the general aspect had always been preserved for the very reason that the frame placed uncompromising restraints on change. Even the Hives, so anxious to wipe out the past, had not razed the Towers in order to start from scratch as they had so often done elsewhere. The task would have been too daunting, it was customarily said.

Lisbeï had another explanation: the women of the Bethely Hive who had risen up against their Queene had been born in the Towers, as had their mothers, grandmothers and great-grandmothers before them. Probably they'd forgotten how old the Towers really were, blinded by familiarity just as women were today. Isn't it strange to think we forget the thing that has shaped us most deeply, perhaps just because we have taken on its shape ourselves?

Lisbeï had felt comfortable in Bethely once, like a hand in a well-fitting glove. But that time was long gone. What called to her now was the other Bethely, the subterranean Bethely. Each time she emerged from her excavation, the Towers and their occupants seemed farther away. The present inhabitants seemed no more sensitive to the past than the Hive women who had tried to destroy it. For them, what existed now had existed always. But what did their present matter? What did Selva's narrow view of a Memory's task matter? Or Mooreï's, even hers! A Memory's true task was to bring the past to light, not embalm it in interminable copies, lists, and inventories. The real memory of Bethely wasn't on the Archives shelves or in the great Book. It lay somewhere beneath the basement where only maintenance teams and gardianas went. It lay in the darkness of underground passages, walled tunnels that ran beneath the Capterie, forgotten in legend—another, obscure Bethely running deep like a root, far from the sun, burrowing into the real past, the past of question, not answers.

• • •

The pungent smell of damp earth filled the gloom at the foot of the ladder as she gropingly lit the gasole. She climbed back up and pulled the boards over the excavation from inside. If by chance anyone was looking for her, there'd be no tell-tale light. She put the pickaxe into the wheelbarrow with the spade and gasole, and trundled along, slightly hunched as she descended the steeply angled conduit leading to the underground passage.

It may have been an air vent. Beneath the deep layer of soil surrounding Bethely, patiently accumulated and fertilized by generations of people, lay a strata of stones, bits of irrecuperable metal, and chunks of various ancient materials that time had not yet destroyed—the residue of the nameless city on which the Towers, the only visible relics, had once stood. Lisbeï had immediately recognized the nature of the rubble mixed with the soil and had soon cleared the conduit's circular opening. All that had barred her way was a huge half-disintegrated grating through which the soil had sifted to form a compact earth wall at the lower end. The conduit must open into one of the underground passages that supposedly ran beneath Bethely (and even between Bethely and neighboring Capteries, if tradition were to be believed). She'd had a tough time convincing Selva to let her keep digging.

When at last the wall of earth had been breached late that afternoon, a strange, indescribable odor had assailed Lisbeï's nostrils—the dank smell of stagnant air, sealed off for . . . how long? She had attacked the wall of earth with renewed energy. When she'd finally been able to pass the gasole through the opening, there hadn't been much to see: walls rising to a vaulted ceiling, covered with something discolored by time—tiles perhaps—with the occasional damp spot that glinted silver in the lamplight. Instinctively she'd thought, "I've got to tell them!" Then she'd remembered she wasn't really supposed to be there and wondered about the time.

But time wasn't a problem now. She cleared away enough earth to make the opening passable, checked her pocket for her compass, and weighed the lamp in her hand, trying to estimate how long the fuel would last. Three hours at least. She gathered up spade and pickaxe and climbed through the hole.

The passage was at least ten meters wide, but the ceiling was fairly low. A checkerboard of tiny tiles, greenish white and dirty brown, covered the floor. Large rectangular cavities in the ceiling must have contained some form of lighting. The passage ran straight forward into the darkness. South-southeast. Lisbeï started walking, counting her steps in an attempt to keep track of the distance. She must be . . . under the Esplanade now . . . under the courtyard . . . under the dairy. Nothing much to see, no corridors branching off, no doors, not even a rusty pipe. The occasional little pile flattened by time: leaves, earth, the bones of a few small rodents. Somewhere there must be another surface opening.

Was that a wall ahead? In the weak light of the gasole it was hard to tell, but the passage did seem to come to an abrupt halt farther on. Lisbeï slowed down, disappointed. Had she taken all this trouble just to come up against another wall? But as she got nearer, hope returned: bricks, crude masonry much more recent than the passage itself. And when she knocked hard she could feel the wall vibrate. She put the lamp and spade down and raised the pickaxe, braced her feet well apart, and struck the wall with all her might. A shower of masonry fell away, leaving a gap about a meter wide. Lisbeï smiled in triumph as she picked up the gasole again. When the dust settled, she leaned through the opening. The vault seemed to continue from the other side of the opening as did the floor, but new walls had been built, making the corridor narrower. Storerooms? These walls seemed more carefully constructed than the masonry partition, with stones set in cement, and much thicker, judging by the dull echo when she knocked on one. But there were no doors! Storage bays without doors? Walled up?

Suddenly, in a dazzling focus of comprehension, she knew: not storerooms. Cells!

She backed into the middle of the passage, heart pounding, throat constricted. The last stone in these walls had been laid four hundred and eighty-nine years ago. By smoking torches, workas had pushed wheelbarrows while wielded trowels while the stern-faced Chief looked on, surrounded by his female soldiers. Women, *women* had cemented the final stone and women had watched then do it—and darkness had closed forever on the six Compagnas. It was the day after the great march organized by the Juddites following Garde's first execution and first resurrection.

So it was true, *true*! The Compagnas had really been walled up alive in Bethely, in subterranean passages. That was why their cells had never been found. The basements of present-day Bethely weren't the same thing as these deeper levels! There must have been entrances to the real subterranean passages at one time, but the Harems had walled them up, sealed off their crime and their shame. Oh, to think of Selva's face when Lisbeï proved she'd been right in believing the underground passages existed!

A sobering thought occurred to her. What if the cells were empty? If the legend were only half true? But in that case why would the cells be sealed?

For others, maybe, not the Compagnas? After all, Harem justice had been indiscriminately merciless.

Lisbeï's rather awed respect for this wall, this tomb, began to fade. She knocked on it again at intervals covering several meters. It did seem very thick. Perhaps she could open a cell from the side, from the wall she'd breached first. It had crumbed at one blow. She checked and found she'd been lucky that first time. On either side of the breach, the masonry was backed by a much stronger stone wall.

With a sigh Lisbeï rolled up her sleeves, spat on her hands, and began to hack at the wall.

Two hours later (judging by the weight of the gasole) Lisbeï at last heard a different sort of thud. A few more blows—and the pickaxe hit air. Lisbeï staggered, awkwardly retrieving her balance. Her legs shook, her back ached, and her ears rang.

She stood still, catching her breath. Then she attacked the hole with her hands, tearing her nails as she enlarged it. But what did a few scratches matter? She was a hair's breadth from her goal. When the gap was big enough to tilt the gasole through, she crouched in the niche she'd hacked out and pushed her face up against the opening.

The air hung dry and odorless. The bare floor was decorated by the same dingy checkerboard mosaic, the same ceramic tiles covered the vaulted walls.

But in the corner of the ceramic wall and the stone masonry . . .

Lisbeï closed her eyes and opened them again. Beside the stone wall lay a dark pile. Fabric, thick-looking, soft.

On the near side the lamplight caught a yellowish-white object, something spherical . . . a skull?

Lisbeï set to work once more with redoubled energy. She hadn't much time. A space large enough to wriggle through, that was all she needed. She scraped her arms and knees as she squirmed past the rough opening.

She knelt by the dark pile. It was some kind of robe or cloak made of felt, stretched out full length. The skull lay half-hidden beneath the hood and the sleeves were folded across the cloak. She lifted one sleeve gently. Something rolled against her knee and tinkled to the floor. A tarnished metal ring, gold-colored. She rubbed it against her tunic. A crudely engraved double spiral, the double helix of Elli. Lisbeï felt a lump in her throat. She folded back the other sleeve. A bone fell away with a brittle click as the whole arm came apart and the knuckles, invisible until now, slid out of the sleeve.

Lisbeï felt sick with helpless compassion. She opened the cape to reveal the symmetrical curve of the rib cage. Nestled in the pelvis lay the rectangular object—the bulge she had noticed beneath the felt. It was some sort of large purse made of brown leather, attached to a belt that must have been worn next to the skin.

The leather thongs, stiff with age, broke as she tried to undo them. She lifted the purse flap. Inside was something that looked like a book, perhaps a thick notebook. Hands trembling, she nudged it gently out of the purse, fearful it would dissolve into dust.

It was a fat notebook with the pages held together by a metal coil! Clearly from the Decline. Even in the Harem period metal hadn't been used this way—they wouldn't have known how, apart from anything else. The thick blue plastic cover was still fresh despite a few small cracks. The paper inside was very worn, even dog-eared in places, like a well-thumbed book. The first page yielded nothing. The second contained crowded lines of figures grouped in a seemingly random way. The numbers were painstakingly formed, like a childe's. And there was a lot of blocking out—entire sections blackened line by line. It went on like this for eight pages, then changed to handwriting, a finer, more slanting hand, less deliberately careful, occasionally illegible—but words, clearly words. Not Litali, though.

Lisbeï summoned up her taïtche training. Breathe in,

breathe out, fill your mind and spirit with the rhythm of breathing. Her hands stopped shaking. She reached for the pendant magnifying glass she always wore around her neck, and quickly scanned the pages as Mooreï had taught her to do with the most ancient Archive documents, not trying to comprehend, but merely to pick out familiar constructions in the words and sentences. It looked like some kind of Old Frangleï.

Lisbeï glanced anxiously at the gasole. Time had run out. She opened the notebook again, at the end this time, just to get an idea. The writing had changed completely. This wasn't really very legible, either, since the ink was rather faded. But there was no mistaking it this time: Old Litali, unusual spelling but fairly recognizable. When the lines stopped dancing before her eyes, she began to decipher the first one: 3 . . . 145 . . . of the Harems.

The meaning suddenly leapt out at her: 3 *January* (the old name for the month now called Ellième), 145 *of the Harems.*

The gasole began to flicker, and Lisbeï, startled out of her reverie, scrambled from the cell with the notebook. For the last half of the underground passage she had to feel her way in the dark.

I, Halde of Melorney, bear witness before dying that I have seen the Voice of Elli dead and that I have seen her living. The Voice of Elli called to me in the night and I saw her before me. I touched her breast and the wounds were gone. Glory be to Elli who will make us as the Voice of Elli, Glory be to Elli, Life Everlasting, Glory be to Elli

Lisbeï had slipped like a thief into her room, and was feverishly deciphering the first words of what was to become the Testament of Halde. She remembers how wildly her heart pounded, how her whole body shivered with nervous excitement, and how she had to grit her teeth to prevent them chattering. Excitement soon turned to unbounded stupefaction. Halde was indeed one of the martyred Compagnas, as Lisbeï knew from the Appendices of Hallera. But what she had written in her notebook differed in every way from what Lisbeï, like all Maerlande dottas, had learned since childehood.

The official History was this: toward the end of the Harems, Garde and her Compagnas had brought the

Word of Elli to the slave-women. The Word had given them succor, restoring their courage and dignity. Gradually they had organized themselves around the nucleus of Juddites—so-called after a Discipla who had paid for her courage with her life during one of the first peaceful demonstrations in the Bethely Harem. The movement had spread from Harem to Harem, rising like a tide with the journeys of Garde and her Compagnas. The Harem Chiefs had suppressed all demonstrations with ferocious cruelty until the day Leandro, Chief of Bethely, had captured Garde. He'd had her shot. But three days later, Garde had reappeared to lead the huge demonstration organized by the Bethely Juddites. In the course of the demonstration, six of the Compagnas had been captured and Garde had been killed again. She had risen once more, this time after five days, reappearing to lead the second demonstration, the one that had toppled the Bethely Harem.

Garde had never been seen again. She had left her Disciplas with the enigmatic legacy of the Promise transmitted by the sole surviving Compagna, Hallera. One day, said the Promise, all human beings would be like Garde: no longer would they fear death, for it was part of their Creator's plan, Elli's plan, that they all become like Elli. But the victorious women of the Hives, still infected with the poisonous violence of the Harems, had rejected Garde's message and had persecuted the Disciplas until peace and tolerance triumphed at last.

Halde's account drew a quite different picture, at least for part of the story. Garde had indeed brought the Word of Elli. She had been executed by a firing squad in Bethely and had been resurrected afterward. However, she had not returned to lead the great demonstration but to *prevent* it, to stop the Juddites from inciting a massacre—for the Juddites had not been Garde's first Disciplas, but her enemies! Not only did they disbelieve the Word of Elli, they had delivered Garde and her Compagnas into the hands of the Bethely Chief!

The Juddites had long been in a state of rebellion. They wanted to seize power from the Harem Chiefs and wreak vengeance for their years of oppression. They hadn't the patience to wait for a pacifist victory—in fact they didn't believe in non-violence. The Word of Elli had lived on in secret among the Harem women since the régime began.

Juddites were forever persecuting Believras in the despicable little *wars* that the Harem women waged among themselves under the indifferent or amused eyes of the Chiefs. The Juddites had actually been part of the Harem armies! There had been Juddites among the drugged, fanatic killers used by the Chiefs to fight other Chiefs.

Garde had converted a few of them, however, and they had converted others. They had tried to influence those Juddites who wanted to wage war against the Harems. They didn't succeed. The first great protest had ended in a bloodbath in which most of the Disciplas of Bethely had been massacred. And according to Halde, the Compagna Hallera was among those walled up in the underground cells! The Compagna *Fedra* was the only one whom Hallera had seen escaping with Garde.

The Harems had never really persecuted Elli's followers. A pacifist religion suited the Harem leaders perfectly—something for which the Juddites had always reproached the Disciplas. But the triumphant Hive women had brutally suppressed Believras. As a result the Word had gone underground. It took another century—eighty-seven years, to be exact—before the Word regained its influence and the Hives one by one abandoned their harsh rule to become the Capteries of Maerlande. But this transition was sometimes violent, and once again the bloodiest changeover took place in Bethely. Markali, the last Queene of the Hive, was brought to justice. During the great trial, the daughter of Hallera produced documents left her by her mother (Hallera's Appendices as they came to be known) and glowingly affirmed the divinity of Garde, a Garde who had twice died and risen.

Of course all this wasn't in the notebook—the Notebook, as Lisbeï now thought of it—especially not the second dying and rising of Garde after Halde's capture. As the Compagna waited for death, she had only sketched briefly the events leading to her present plight. But Lisbeï didn't think of this that night as she blinked with fatigue beside her reading lamp. She was still in a state of shock. Garde was part of her daily life, as for so many: the sort of fabled figure that, once discovered in childhood, one never questions—something that later becomes too much a part of one's inner and outer landscape to elicit wonder in adolescence or adulthood. From her earliest days,

Lisbeï had loved the story of Garde because it blended History and legend rather than setting them against one another, as happened all too often. But what fascinated her most was how Garde's history and legend bore out Lisbeï's private intuition. Despite Hallera's Appendices and the formal recognition of Garde's divinity, Garde must be mortal *and* divine because she had died *and* risen. Garde was on both sides of the line, so to speak—she provided a threshold, one of those magical places of passage where you could make the leap from the everyday reality of pro and con to alight on the thread between the two, the vantage point from which you could see the unity of the world. When you balanced on the thread, some apparent contradictions ceased to exist: you had the power to rise above them, to resolve them. It was an experience dear to Lisbeï, this resolution of contradictions. It filled her with joy—a joy always too brief, for it was only in performing the taïtche that she could sustain it.

Now, as Lisbeï looked at Halde's Notebook, what she saw wasn't so much the familiar story of Garde, despite Halde's variants, as the confirmation of her intuition: legend could be true, story could be History. And she, Lisbeï of Bethely, was the first to know this truth. On the morrow it would spread, radiate outward from her. She probably had in mind the image of light pushing back the darkness rather than the ripple from a stone disturbing quiet waters. Not for an instant did she dream anyone could question her truth. . . .

But they do question her truth, at length. And for the rest of her life, Lisbeï will be driven to find the powerful truth behind the story of Garde and her Compagnas, and the legacy of a people caught in the midst of a subtle and yet dramatic evolutionary change.

IN THE MOTHERS' LAND
Elisabeth Vonarburg

Coming this winter
wherever Bantam Spectra Special Editions
are sold.